CINDY R. ESCOBAR

A Gift of Grace

Cindy ☙ Escobar
2021

First published by KDP Select 2021

First edition

ISBN: 9798573413921

This book was professionally typeset on Reedsy.
Find out more at reedsy.com

To my husband, Miguel Escobar, and my parents, Mark and Janelle Buschman. Thank you for believing in me and encouraging me to pursue my dream.

Acknowledgements

I have enjoyed the adventure of writing this book, and I am grateful for the help I received from my friend, Nicole Huddleston. Thank you for the many hours you spent proofreading and editing my book, and I'll always be grateful that you helped me get to this point in the publishing process.

I also find my parents, Mark and Janelle Buschman, to be a blessing to me. Both of my parents encouraged me to continue writing, even when I did not think I would be able to publish a story. They saw my talent and passion to create stories, and I will always be grateful for their positivity towards my abilities.

Of course, I also want to include my loving husband, Miguel Escobar. He spent several hours helping me research the best way to publish A Gift of Grace, and he has encouraged me not only as a writer, but as a wife and woman in Christ. I am always grateful for our marriage and his partnership.

None of this would even be possible without my Lord and Savior. I do honestly believe that He gave me this talent for a reason, and I am excited to share my faith through a fictional story. God has never abandoned me, and that is very evident by the things He has done in my life.

~Cindy R. Escobar

Matthew 7:1-2 (NIV)

"Do not judge, or you too will be judged. For in the same way you judge others, you will be judged, and with the measure you use, it will be measured to you."

~ONE~

Smoke billowed out of the swinging double doors as the odor from the cigars mixed in with the stench of liquor, perspiration, and vomit. Visiting cowboys and depressed gentlemen lined themselves up along the bar as several fancily dressed card sharks outwitted the locals of their money. Crude women pranced from table to table as they delivered drinks and flirted with the men close by, and the sight of the dresses they wore turned my stomach. Overhaul's Bull's Head Saloon was the largest business in town, and the sight of it disgusted most of the ladies and churchgoers. It disgusted me as well.

Standing on my toes, my eyes found a brunette in the hubbub of the evening crowd. She wore an outrageous red gown with a neckline that dipped almost too low, and straps that kept falling off her shoulders. The corset she wore cinched her waist so small it almost looked unhealthy, but it pronounced her still-forming curves that caused the drunks to pay her extra attention. Fishnet pantyhose decorated her shins, and the tall black heels that she wore made walking seem painful. Her lips were painted a vibrant red, which exaggerated their fullness, and her eyelashes were heavily darkened and sprinkled with some sort of glitter. Rouge lined her cheekbones in a delicate manner, and make-up tried to hide the youthful freckles that dotted her nose. Her hair was piled high on top of her head, and a silly-looking black feather bounced with each step she took. A smile appeared to be glued on her face, but well-hidden sorrow held its dim glow in her blue-gray eyes. She was a gorgeous young woman, and she had mastered the horrible art of hiding her pain well, for on her shoulder blade, halfway hidden under her dress, was a dark purple bruise that had formed from some sort of despicable lesson dealt to her the night before.

She was brave, braver than I knew I'd ever be. At the tender age of eleven, she had been hired on at the Bull's Head to wash glasses and clean up after sickly drunks. It was a nasty job, but one she deemed necessary to take care of her then six-year-old little sister. Her mother had died a few weeks before her eleventh birthday, leaving her to fend for herself without a father, and with a small child to feed and clothe. By age thirteen, she began entertaining in one of Overhaul's improper gowns, and by fourteen, she knew she could never fare outside of a saloon. I used to watch her cry herself to sleep when she'd come home from a nightshift. She had never wanted to shed a tear in my presence, but I saw her pain. In her mind, she was trapped. She had lost her innocence and would never be good enough to work anywhere else but a brothel.

Although I had grown up to be very independent and mischievous, my respect for my sister never died, and I always made sure she was as protected as she could be in a saloon. Men used her for their entertainment, but even if that fact burned heavily on my mind, Ryleigh was still my sister, and I wanted the best for her.

As she sashayed from one table to the other, I could tell her mind was only half-listening to the flirts and conversation pointed her way. Her smile never faded as she leaned forward to set a drink in front of a man, but her eyes were directed at something in the far corner of the saloon. Curiosity drove me to follow her gaze. A man sat alone at the farthest table, and an untouched stack of cards sat inches away from his fingertips. No cigar hung out of his mouth. His black hat was pulled low on his brow, and though one could barely see his eyes, it was obvious he was watching Ryleigh.

Instantly, I didn't like the way he reclined in his chair, or the way he crossed his ankle over his knee. Giant spurs decorated the heels of his boots, which glowed silver against the orange of the lanterns. A thick layer

4

of black whiskers covered his jawline and upper lip, and the smoothness of his skin showed his youth. I grabbed the tops of the swinging doors as I rose on my toes to get a better look at the man. He was large, big enough to harm my sister without much trouble. Ryleigh stood at five feet even and weighed not much more than a hummingbird. As I studied his profile, I wondered what help I'd be. I was barely an inch taller than my sister, and my small appearance didn't offer much of a threat.

Suddenly, the doors moved as an impatient cowboy bulled his way inside. I hadn't seen anyone behind me, and I was unable to catch myself as I stumbled over the threshold. I managed to stay on my feet without directing too much attention, but when I glanced at the stranger, his eyes were leveled on me. A chill raced down my backbone the longer I looked in his icy gaze. No wonder Ryleigh acted so uncomfortable. I'd panic if he had been staring at me. Several seconds seemed to drag by before he lazily turned his eyes back onto my sister. I swallowed hard and straightened my dusty, worn shirt. Maybe if I acted casual, I could keep an eye on him and prevent him from harming Ryleigh.

Clearing my throat, I puffed out my chest and swaggered toward the bar at the back of the room. The bartender, Wil, had been wiping down glasses when his eyes found me. I ducked my head, hoping he wouldn't recognize me, but by his groan, I knew I had been too late. Running my tongue over my teeth, I leaned against the bar and rubbed my chin.

"Give me a beer, Wil," I ordered in as low a voice as I could muster.

Wil didn't look at me as he picked up another glass to wipe. "You know you ain't supposed to be in here. Get on home before Clyde sees you."

I frowned and looked at him from under my eyebrows. "You know I'm harmless, Wil. Do your job and serve me! I promise, if you don't tell Overhaul, I'll behave myself this time. You just wait and see."

With a sigh, Wil set his glass down a little too hard and leaned forward. "You're too young for a beer." He motioned toward the exit with his finger. "Now get outta here!"

"I can judge what I can or can't handle." I shook my head as I waved a hand in the air. "Never mind, I ain't in the mood to argue. Just give me something to drink!"

"Sarsaparilla," he growled, popping the cork off a bottle before pouring its contents in a small glass.

I accepted the drink begrudgingly and snarled, "I'll be back later to pay for it."

Walking as manly as I dared, I set myself down at the nearest table in a position where I could keep an eye on the stranger, who had gone back to studying my sister with an oddly uncomfortable gaze. Ice blue eyes shockingly stood out against his tan skin and black hair. They were hard to read, and I didn't like that. Curiosity built a wall of dread in my chest, and I began to wish I had enough guts to march over to him and demand he leave. If I had my way, no man would ever look at my sister rudely again. How badly I wanted her out of that place, but I had no control over her actions.

Suddenly, I had the feeling that someone was standing over me. I swallowed hard and felt my shoulders slump in defeat as I slowly raised my head to see who had invaded my space. Clyde Overhaul had his arms crossed over his pot belly, his eyes burning with irritation, and his lips pursed into a thin white line. Attempting to smile, I motioned to the dirty glass in front of me.

"I was thirsty," I answered lamely.

Clyde's face flooded with red as he knit his brows together. "I told you that you're not welcome here, kid. Get out before I lose my temper!"

I extended my bottom lip in a mock pout as I raised big, sad eyes into his gaze. "Oh, I wasn't hurtin' nothin'," I drawled. "Honest, I wasn't. All I wanted was a drink and a place to rest my bones."

Clyde wrapped his fingers around the front of my collar as he jerked me to my feet. "You cost me every time you step into my place. Now get out!" he bellowed, causing the laughter and conversation to stop abruptly.

I wrenched out of his grasp and stumbled a few feet away before I caught my balance. "You're a selfish pig of a man!" I shouted as anger began to boil in the pit of my stomach. "I had never wanted to come in this place, except you stole my sister from me. But I can guarantee I'll be back, just you wait!"

The fat man lunged toward me, but I jumped backward to elude his claw-like grasp, and accidentally bumped into a slender girl holding an empty tray. She squealed, and we both crashed into a table. Our weight was too much for the poorly built piece of wood, and the top flew off as we tumbled to the floor. I watched in horror as the tabletop smashed into Clyde, and I knew my life would end if I didn't get out of that saloon quickly.

Wrestling out of the skirts of the tart beneath me, I staggered to my feet and whirled for the door, but someone's hand gripped my arm painfully. Determined to disappear, I sank my teeth into his flesh until he screamed and flung me away like an empty sack of feed. I fell in a heap on the floor, but Clyde was onto me before I could squirm out of the saloon. Holding his bleeding hand next to his chest, he twisted my ear in between his index finger and thumb and dragged me toward the door.

"Ow!" I exclaimed when his grip tightened. "Let go, you selfish pig! Let go of me, or I'll burn down your saloon!"

He barged through the double doors and threw me in the street. "You busted up my table, and I'll make sure your sister pays me for the damages. If I catch you in my saloon one more time, I'll fix you so you can't come in again!"

My eyes widened at his undescriptive threat and nodded my head as if to say I understood. Wiping the blood from his hand, he muttered a curse and marched back inside.

Brushing the dust from my filthy shirt, I pushed myself to my feet and aimed my tongue toward the doors. "I didn't mean no harm in the first place," I growled, rubbing my throbbing ear.

Just by instinct, I looked through the filmy window and saw the stranger staring at me again. Through all the excitement of trying to get away from Overhaul, I had forgotten why I had entered the saloon in the beginning. My heart began to race the more I stared into his icy gaze, and at last I couldn't take it any longer. Whirling on my heel, I raced down the street in hopes of forgetting the situation. My heart pounded at the thought of leaving Ryleigh alone, but she could fend for herself until I could collect my thoughts and calm down. I wasn't going near that saloon in the meantime.

I finally slowed my pace when I reached the west side of town, near the little shack my sister and I called home. I entered the dilapidated building and rushed to the kitchen. My stomach was eating away at my spine, and the thought of food made me half-crazed, but all the cupboards were empty except for a mouse and some cobwebs. Ryleigh must not have had enough time to run to the mercantile earlier.

Slamming a door closed, I crossed my arms over my chest and curled my lip in disgust. I had barely eaten, and my stomach was rolling with hunger. Frustrated at the lack of food, I marched out of the house and stomped my way down the street. The evening air was filled with the greasy smells of supper and sweet scents of desserts, which were unkind to the claws scraping away at my insides. I clutched my belly and found myself wandering toward the nearest store, which was still opened.

Mayor Wilkes owned the mercantile, but the Reverend Atkins' wife would sometimes bake dozens of delicious rolls, tarts, and breads that she would sell a few days a week. I paused outside of the door to smell the aroma of Mrs. Atkins' sweets, and licked my lips as my stomach rolled over again. Perhaps she wouldn't notice a few morsels of bread disappear, and even if she did, she wouldn't mind if a needy child took them. Prompted on that notion, I entered the mercantile and sneaked toward the back where she kept her baked goods.

Cinnamon and frosting met my nostrils, and fresh yeast boasted of the bread she had taken from the oven earlier that afternoon. I glanced over both shoulders to make sure nobody was around before sneaking to the counter on my right and bending over the various breads to choose my supper. My mouth watered the more I studied the sticky rolls. Maybe one wouldn't be missed.

Like a snake striking its prey, my hand shot out to grab a delicious delicacy. Hiding it behind my back, I began strolling casually toward the door. The store was empty, and I couldn't help noticing the jars of licorice and peppermint sticks at the end of the counter. I glanced over my shoulder to make sure no one was watching, then tip-toed to the licorice jar. I quietly lifted the lid from the jar and set it on the counter before I reached in to grab a few sticks of the licorice.

"What are you doing?"

I gasped when I heard the low baritone and dropped the candy as I spun around to see who had caught me in the devious scheme. The stranger in the saloon, appearing much taller than I imagined now that he was standing in front of me, had just stepped into the soft lantern light and was staring at me with his thumbs hooked through his belt loops. I felt the blood drain from my face, and I couldn't come up with the words to explain my sudden predicament. Pivoting on my heel, I raced for the door and tripped on the threshold in my haste to disappear in the street.

I fell onto the boardwalk and felt the wind exit my lungs in a rush before the stranger grabbed my arm to pull me to my feet. I attempted to wrench from his grasp, but he held on tighter than I expected. I stomped on his toe, but even that didn't budge him. I raised my gaze to meet his and shook with fear for what he might have in mind.

He held out his other hand, palm up, and raised an eyebrow. "Give me the roll, unless you can come up with the money to pay for it."

I found his voice unbelievably scary, and my heart began to beat hard against my ribcage. Swallowing past my fear, I quickly raised the roll to my mouth and took as big a bite as I could. "I already paid for it. Now be kind enough to let me go."

He shook his head and raised a second brow to meet the first. "Don't lie. I saw you."

My jaw dropped to reveal the half-chewed food in my mouth. "You what? But that's impossible! I made sure nobody was watching!"

"You didn't look in the shadows. Being so concerned for what's behind, you don't see what's around you. Get inside, you're gonna have to tell them what happened."

I swallowed the lump in my mouth and choked. "No! I was hungry and didn't have any money. I didn't think they cared if I borrowed a roll for my supper."

"Borrowed means you asked first. You didn't ask, you stole. I'm not letting you go until you march inside that store and apologize."

My lip curled in disgust, and I hung my head. "You ain't gonna have it any other way, huh?"

"No. Now get."

Defeated, I shuffled my feet as I allowed him to lead me toward the door. My insides quivered at the thought of admitting what I had done, and in one last desperate attempt, I lowered my head to sink my teeth in his hand. He cried out in surprise and let go as if I were a potato fresh from the boiling pot. The instant I felt his grip loosen, I bolted down the boardwalk in hopes of losing him forever.

Something snagged on my shirttail, and my feet slipped on the boards as I fell partially to the ground. The stranger helped me plant my feet firmly on the floor, then gave me a scowl that raised the hair on the back of my neck.

"You sure don't have manners, do you?" he mumbled as he wrapped my shoulder seam around his hand. "You may get out of trouble a lot, but you ain't gonna get out of it with me around. C'mon, the sooner you get this over, the sooner you can relax."

I stomped my foot on the boardwalk and crossed my arms over my chest. "I ain't goin' nowhere, and you ain't gonna make me! I don't gotta listen to you! Let me go!"

"Not 'til you go in and apologize. C'mon."

I pulled against his force, but he won and successfully dragged me back into the store. Mrs. Atkins was standing behind the counter once we crossed the threshold, and she greeted us with a cheerful grin. "Good evening," she greeted in a pleasant tone.

The stranger nodded his head and pushed me in front of him as he yanked the cinnamon roll out of my grip. "I'm afraid I caught this disrespectful runt trying to snitch a free roll. I do believe she's got something to say to you."

I swallowed hard and looked between the two before hanging my head and biting my lip. "I-I'm sorry, ma'am," I mumbled. "I was just hungry, and I didn't have any money. I meant to pay you back, honest I did. I... I just didn't know what to do. I haven't eaten in two or three days, and I thought a roll wouldn't be missed by you until I could give you the money to pay for it."

I chanced a peek to see how my story was working. Mrs. Atkins' eyes were soft and sympathetic, and at last she sighed. "You should have asked," she reprimanded softly. "I understand you're hungry, but we could work out a deal. I'll trade you one roll for a promise that you'll be in church come Sunday."

A grin broke out across my mouth as I snatched the roll off the counter. "I will! Thank you, ma'am!"

"Now wait a minute!" the stranger interrupted. He leaned toward Mrs. Atkins and motioned to me. "She doesn't owe you anything? I was willing to pay for it."

Mrs. Atkins showed us the palm of her hand while she shook her head. "Money isn't as important as the well-being of that child. If she keeps her promise, I'll let her have the roll just this once."

The stranger glanced at me and frowned at my victorious grin. "You sure?"

"Of course," she assured with a sweet smile on her lips.

Backing away from the counter, the stranger nodded his head and turned to Mrs. Atkins. "Many thanks, ma'am. Have a good evening."

She nodded farewell and smiled at me as I followed the stranger outside. Once on the boardwalk, I tossed one last triumphant look his way and turned to disappear from his side. Before I could vanish, he grabbed my arm and pulled me back.

Anger coursed through my veins at his persistence, and I whirled to growl at him. "Let go of me!"

He shook his head as he headed toward a diner that sat underneath the boardinghouse on the opposite side of the street. "I'd be ignoring my manners if I didn't give you a good, nourishing meal. Besides that, I'd like to talk to you."

I stiffened when I heard what I thought was a threat in his voice, but curiosity outweighed my fear as I stuffed the roll in my pocket and allowed him to lead me across the street. The single room of the diner was empty, except for dirty tables and chairs that had been scattered in haste. The stranger pushed me gently into a seat at a clean table and sat in the chair next to me. I curled my lip as I scooted to the far edge of my seat and stared out the window to estimate my chances of a run. Out of the corner of my eye, I studied the man dressed in black and judged that he was in incredibly good condition. Besides, if I ran, he might go back to Ryleigh, and I wanted to spare my sister as much as I could.

The stranger flagged down the waitress and ordered coffee and beef stew. Hiding my disappointment at being captured, I told the young lady that I'd have the same. She nodded without the least hint of a smile and scurried back into the kitchen. Once alone, I found myself staring the man beside me. He looked vaguely familiar, but I didn't know where I would've seen him. His strong jaw and masculine cheekbones were covered with a thick layer of whiskers with two or three specks of gray, and his dark curly locks resembled my own. His hands, though large and rough from years of work, appeared to be gentle. He was a handsome man, but his appearance unnerved me. My sister was enslaved by men with an appealing presence.

The stranger caught me staring, and I quickly averted my gaze. "You must be Cheyenne," he spoke, breaking the ice that surrounded us.

My head bounced up at full attention as I studied him with narrowed eyes.

"That is your name, isn't it?" he continued, meeting my gaze with a harmless one of his own.

I nodded slowly. "Yeah, but I ain't too fond of you knowing it. I'm known as many things in this town, but you gotta earn the right to speak my name."

He leaned back in his chair as he took off his hat and set it on the table. "What do you want me to call you, then?"

"Most of the names I'd give you would earn me a lecture for repeating, but I don't like you using Cheyenne. Call me kid or something."

"Just me, but I like Cheyenne better."

I curled my lip in disgust. "I don't like anyone but my sister to call me by my real name. Everyone else calls me 'that street brat'. How do you know about me?"

He scratched the back of his neck as ran his tongue over his teeth. "I came out here because I gave my word, but after seeing the situation, I'm beginning to wonder if I finally bit off more than I can chew."

His explanation confused me more than his presence, and I found my brows being drawn together in frustration. "Would you at least tell me your name?" I demanded, my temper rising. "I saw you watching my sister in the Bull's Head, and you ain't left me alone since you caught me in that mercantile. I don't like you, and if you ever get close to my sister again, I'll—"

"You'll act like a fool, just like you have been all evening. I'm not here to harm either of you. We've never met, so you probably don't know who I am, but I know your sister does. My name is Jethro Douglas, but I'm more known to y'all as Uncle Jet."

The name was familiar, but I refused to let him think he had any impact on me. "So what? I've heard of you. You're Pa's kid brother who disappeared from the face of the earth. Chasing some fantasy that you made up in your head. I see you came up empty handed." I folded my arms over my chest and set my jaw. "If you came here for money, I'm sorry. We ain't got none to spare."

He shook his head. "I didn't come here for money. I want to take care of you and your sister. I swore I would the day we buried my brother."

I jumped at that piece of news. "Pa's dead?"

Jet studied me before he nodded solemnly. "We ran into each other about three months ago. I was passing through Texas when I heard he took sick. Consumption, they said. I found him drinking whiskey in a saloon and tried to visit with him. He wouldn't tell me much, except that his wife was dead, and his girls were in Sunset, Arizona. The next morning, he was found dead in an alley. We buried him on a beautiful day, and I swore to his grave I would find y'all and make sure you girls had someone to take care of you. Kids shouldn't be left to fend for themselves. I packed my belongings and set about coming here."

I turned my head so he wouldn't see that the news of Pa's death bothered me and scoffed with sarcasm. "Pa left us before Mama took sick. I was still a baby, and Mama died when I was six. If Pa wanted us took care of, he'd have come himself. He abandoned us, and I really don't care for the man. I'm glad the devil's dead. Now I don't have to worry about him showing up on our doorstep." I leveled fiery eyes on my uncle and curled my lip. "And we don't need you. We're getting along fine, and we don't need your charity."

The waitress came with a tray full of two bowls and two mugs of coffee before Jet could answer. She set a bowl in front of me, and I leaned forward to stare at the gray liquid. Something inside of it hopped around as if it were still alive, and a stench like that of death wafted up my nostrils. I wrinkled my nose and pushed the stew away.

"You call this a nourishing meal?" I snapped, fixing my eyes on the waitress. "What do you call this slop? It smells awful, and I would never pay good money to eat such grime!"

The waitress fumbled with a mug of coffee as she set it in front of Jet and tried not to let her anger show. "If you're gonna act like a brat, we do have a steak on the stove if you would rather have that."

"What's it made of? Someone's dog that annoyed you? I wouldn't bring my worst enemy into your doors, and I won't eat any of the poison you place in front of me! How is this supposed to go down my gullet, huh?"

Jet slammed his napkin on the table as he leveled piercing eyes on me. "That's enough!" he muttered under his breath. Turning to the waitress, he handed her some bills and nodded my direction. "I apologize for my niece's behavior. I promise she'll be more in line the next time we come here."

The waitress took the money, glanced at me, and fled back into the kitchen. I turned lazy eyes on my uncle and shrugged when I noticed his stern gaze. "Don't look at me that way," I argued. "I didn't want this supper, anyway. A few words won't hurt a soul."

"I may have signed myself up for a chore, but I ain't gonna tolerate that kind of behavior from anybody, much less my niece."

I scoffed. "What are you gonna do? Take your belt off and whip me? I don't think so. You wouldn't have the guts!"

Jet let out a slow breath as he glared at me from under his eyebrows. "I am not afraid to discipline you. I promised my brother that I would help you girls, and I'll do what I see fit to get through that tough layer of yours."

I leaned back in my chair as I folded my arms over my chest. "I still don't believe you. Why didn't you just stay in that saloon so that you didn't have to see me get my own supper? I would be glad to get rid of you, and I would have a full stomach. Now, because of you, neither has happened. And I ain't gonna stay here and get yelled at by some relative I don't even know. I ain't gonna ask to be excused, 'cause I know I good and well can do whatever I please, and you can't stop me!"

Giving my head a firm nod, I stood abruptly from the table and turned to march toward the door, but he grabbed my arm to stop me. Setting his hat back on his head, he rose to his feet and led me back outside, his grip firm around my bicep. Once the night air blew in my face, I dug my heel into his instep and bit his hand as hard as I could until he shouted and let go. Like a loosed wild mustang, I bounded from the boardwalk and raced down the street where I hoped to disappear. Before I ducked in an alley, I glanced over my shoulder to see if Jet was chasing me, but he was nowhere to be found. Curling my lip, I continued running until I had reached our pathetic shack.

I reached into my pocket and brought out the roll as I threw a glare over my shoulder. That man would regret the day he came to us, forcing me to do his bidding and threatening us with his presence. I didn't want that man around my sister, and I didn't want him around me. The way he carried himself and boasted about being my uncle made me uneasy, and I would kick him as hard as I could and bite him until I tasted blood to make him leave. He'd soon figure out that Ryleigh and I were not the kind of people he wanted to be around.

Locking the door just for comfort's sake, I ambled to the kitchen where I lit the lantern that was hanging from a rusted nail stuck by the doorway. Warm light washed over the sad construction, and I turned around in time to see a rat scurry through a hole by the cabinet.

"Don't worry, little scuzzer," I drawled, slouching my shoulders as I shuffled to my room. "I ain't gonna hurt you. Could use the company."

My bedroom sat near the entrance to the hallway. It was the smallest room of the shack, and the only window was filled with broken glass. The wind whistled through the shards, but if I put enough blankets on my bed, it didn't bother me much. I flopped on the lumpy mattress and stared at the dusty picture sitting on my nightstand. Ryleigh had insisted we pay most of her savings to get our picture taken a few years after Mama died. I was about nine years old, making her around fourteen. I remembered that day.

She had come home after her usual morning shift and told me she had gotten a promotion with a raise. Clyde Overhaul had heard her humming Mama's favorite hymn and had hired her for his newest night entertainment. Neither of us knew exactly what that meant, but when Ryleigh was happy, I was happy. She fixed us the best noon meal she could muster, and then she took me shopping. She was so excited that she was willing to buy me new clothes, and then she declared we should get our picture taken. I had never done that before, and the experience excited me.

We spent all afternoon together, laughing and having a good time as two kid sisters. When evening came, she gave me the instructions to be in bed by eight-thirty as she would most likely be late. I had gone to bed happy and excited for what we could do with the extra money she'd be earning. I had nothing but good dreams all night, but when I got up the next morning, I found Ryleigh crying in the kitchen. I didn't fully understand what had happened, but then I saw the claw marks on her arms from the man who had stolen her innocence.

I blinked back sudden tears that spilled onto my cheeks without my permission. We hardly laughed together since. She spent most of her time alone, almost as though she was ashamed to bring herself in my presence. Whenever we were together, she was pleasant, but she was so distant it hurt. It hurt to think about what she endured every night, and the shame she must carry. And it was that Clyde Overhaul's fault. All of it. He had promised Ryleigh when she first went to work for him that we could stay in his rent house for a small sum of money if she worked hard and didn't complain. Ryleigh, being so young and so ignorant, didn't see his scheme and didn't think she had another choice.

If I had my way, I would've killed myself so that she didn't have to care for me. I still would, except I thought I was the only thing my sister had left to stabilize her sanity. I rolled over so my back was to the picture and rubbed the tears off my nose.

"Many a night you've cried yourself to sleep," I muttered softly, "but not tonight. You ain't gonna show your weakness tonight."

~TWO~

T he bell above the church rang in the near distance to let the pupils know that class was about to begin, and I knew as I slung my fishing pole over my shoulder that I should attend school at least once that week. I really didn't welcome the idea of sitting on a wooden bench and listening to some dull lecture about dead people. It was Wednesday, and the third time that I had skipped school that week. I smiled to myself as I realized that I had only attended school for ten minutes on Monday. If I did go to school, I'd just end up standing in the corner or getting licks or cleaning the chalk boards.

With a spring in my step and a whistle on my lips, I strode in the opposite direction of the school. I was gonna have a good morning, and after I caught myself a snooze and a passel of fish down by the creek, I'd skin my lunch and feast. It would taste better than whatever Jet threw in front of me the night before, since I would provide it for myself. The thought of the man slowed my step, and I quickly scanned the area in case he was in sight. He was nowhere to be found. I smiled again and continued whistling the happy tune until I passed the Bull's Head.

Ryleigh sat on the steps of the boardwalk, her face in her hands, and I couldn't tell if she was crying. I glanced down the street at the people who passed by her with their noses in the air, then shook my head. No, she wouldn't cry in front of the people who thought her to be weak. I noticed a new bruise on her shoulder and felt my heart break in two. I was about to go to her when Jet appeared around the corner. My lip curled as I saw him stop in front of her, and my fingers balled into fists when his voice made

18

her jump to full attention.

Fishing momentarily forgotten, I began to cross the street, but stopped when I noticed Ryleigh's back stiffen. Not wanting to reveal myself just yet, I hunkered down behind a parked wagon in front of the post office to hear what was being said.

"I figured it was you," Ryleigh drawled in her pretty Southern accent. "But I don't understand why you're here."

Jet lowered himself on the boardwalk beside my sister and took off his hat. "I promised your pa I'd come, that's why. How come you never told Cheyenne that Rod was dead? I sent a telegram."

Ryleigh stiffened her back and turned a glare on the man. "Cheyenne is just a child. I was trying to protect her from the pain of his death. You don't understand Cheyenne like I do. Don't tell me how to raise her."

"Well, that's another thing. It ain't right for a child to be raising another child."

I bristled at his words. If he said one more thing like that to my sister, I was going to jump out and strangle him with my bare hands!

"I'm not a child," Ryleigh defended. "And I'm doing the best I can with Cheyenne."

"Maybe you're not a child now, but you were when you first took over the job. And you need some help, Ryleigh. You ain't got time to be raising a willful girl like Cheyenne. She needs a firm hand, and you're too busy working here to apply that firm hand. Let me help. I don't want you to work in the saloon, either. I'll look for a job so I can provide for you and Cheyenne."

Ryleigh stood to her feet and glared at our uncle as he rose to his full height. "Mr. Douglas, we do not need your help, and I cannot quit my job. I'll thank you kindly to leave us be. We're getting along fine without you. If you'll excuse me, I need to go home. It's been a long night, and I'd like to rest before I have to go back to work!"

Tightening the shawl around her shoulders, she tossed him one last glare as she whirled on her heel and barged down the street. I grinned to myself as I watched Jet, hat still in hand, with a defeated expression on his brow.

"Hey, kid."

I glanced over my shoulder and saw a man towering above me.

"You're gonna get run over if you stay there, now scoot."

"Well, learn to have a little patience," I snapped as I stood to my feet. "I ain't done a thing to you, so next time you best not be so snappy."

"Snappy, huh?" The man planted his fists on his hips as he sized me up with narrowed eyes. "You ought to have your mouth washed out for talking so disrespectful toward your elders. You're just lucky I'm in a good mood today, young'un."

"Well, I ain't in such a good mood, and I'd prefer if you didn't sound so harsh. Next time I might as well belt you with a fist than to take the manure flowin' from your mouth!"

A large hand landed on my shoulder, and I glanced up to see Jet giving me a disapproving look. I ducked my head and bit my lip to keep from shouting what was on my mind. "I overheard what was said, and I apologize, sir," Jet addressed to the man in front of us.

The man thumbed back his hat as he studied my uncle. "Ain't your fault she's got a mouth."

"Maybe not, sir, but I feel responsible. She's my niece."

I cringed at that last word and wished I could run, but Jet tightened his hold on my shoulder as if he read my mind. The other man glanced down at me, then turned his head to spit a stream of tobacco juice. "If she was my kid," he growled in a gravelly voice, "I'd scrub her tongue with lye."

"That ain't a bad idea, sir," Jet muttered as he glared down at me. "I'll discipline her as she rightly deserves."

The man nodded and stepped onto his wagon. I watched him drive away before turning a menacing glare on Jet. "Let go of me!"

Jet sent me a warning look that should have made my knees quake. "Now look here, young lady, you are not going to run around like a wild animal without a halter on your tongue. You've got to learn to take hold of that temper of yours, and if the only way to learn is through me, I'll teach you. That makes twice in twenty-four hours that I've caught you disrespecting your elders, and I'm not going to stand for that." He glanced at the fishing rod still in my hand and crossed his arms. "And where do you think you're going on a school day?"

I shifted all my weight on my right leg as I rolled my eyes. "I don't have to answer to you. I don't even know you. I just know your name. I can talk however I want to, and I can go fishing any time of the day. Like I said last night, I don't have to obey you. And I won't!"

"You are going to school, but not until I talk to you somewhere other than the street where people can watch us argue. Whether you want to or not, you'll do as I say. I am your uncle, and your only living relative besides your sister. You're too young to be on your own, and obviously too young to determine what's right and wrong. C'mon."

I pulled against him and couldn't seem to stop my jaw from dropping. "I-I'm not going anywhere with you. I don't trust you, and I'm not gonna—"

Jet grabbed my forearm firmly as he marched toward the boardinghouse across the street. I fought against him, but his grip was unrelenting. He burst through the door, marched up the stairs, and pulled me inside his room before closing the door shut. Swallowing hard, I whirled around and tried to think of a way to skirt around him. Jet turned around with his thumbs hooked in his pockets, and I found myself cowering in his presence.

I swallowed hard and straightened my backbone. "Whatever you aim to do, you'll never get away with it!"

Jet studied me with a stoic expression before he finally spoke. "I don't plan to hurt you, Cheyenne. You got out of trouble last night, but I won't let you get away today. You need to learn to control your temper, and I aim to teach you."

"What makes you think I'll learn from you? Several other people have tried, and some would say they failed. I ain't gonna do anything you say!"

"I don't care what other people have done in the past," Jet answered calmly. "I'm here now, and I expect you to answer to me. You'll listen to what I have to say sooner or later, so I suggest you calm down."

I curled my lip into a snarl as I crossed my arms over my chest. "I don't have to listen to anything you say. I never asked you to come to Sunset!"

Jet took a step toward me, but I jumped behind the bed before he could grab me. "I came along because you girls need help, and I want to guide you before you do something stupid."

"I was doing fine before you interrupted!" I shouted. I saw a chance to escape and raced toward the door.

Jet blocked my path suddenly, and I couldn't dodge around him. He wrapped his fingers around my arm and pulled me away from the door. "I have a different opinion. Stop fighting me."

"I will not!" I bellowed, waving my captured arm wildly in hopes I would somehow be let loose. "Let me go!"

Jet took hold of both of my shoulders and knelt so that he was eye level with me. "You are safe with me. Calm down so I can talk to you."

Gritting my teeth, I kicked his leg as hard as I could. He grunted, and his grip loosened just enough for me to wiggle loose. Once my arms popped free, I grabbed my fishing pole and opened the door. Before I ran into the hallway, I turned a fiery gaze on him.

"You will never help me! You can't barge in our lives and demand on 'fixing' everything in a few hours. You have no idea what you're doing or who you're dealing with. Now leave us plumb alone!"

I slammed the door before I could hear his reply, and ran down the stairs in fright, hoping to flee far from him before he emerged from his room. Once in the street, I dodged wagons and citizens as I fled town and aimed east toward the creek. Anger flowed through my veins, and I kicked a rock, causing it to skip down the path in front of me. Clenching my jaw, I ran up to dead tree and smashed my foot into its trunk. Crying out in pain, I suddenly realized it was past time for a new pair of shoes, and my toes had flung through one of many holes.

"You know it's stupid to kick trees," I muttered to myself, staring at the blood dripping from a toenail that had chipped in half. "Now you got a sore toe on top of your other problems."

I hit my rod against the trunk, but my anger only intensified when it broke in half. A roar erupted from my throat, and I flung the rest of the rod as far as I could.

"The tree didn't do anything to you. Don't take your anger out on it," a low voice rang out.

I whirled on my heel, and felt my insides fall to the ground. Jet was striding down the path with his hat hiding half of his face. I bit my lip and turned my back to him. "I don't want you here. Leave me alone!"

Jet stopped a few feet away and stuffed his hands in his pockets. "I'm not going to leave you alone. You better get used to having me around."

"Why are you so stubborn?" I shouted. "We don't want you here. Why can't you just do as we ask and leave us alone? We don't want your help!"

"I can't leave, Cheyenne."

"Stop it!" I bellowed, and my voice seemed to echo in my ears. "Stop lying! Why can't you leave us?"

Jet leaned against the tree trunk and shrugged. "I'm not sure. The easy thing to do would be to give y'all some money and leave."

"Why don't you?" I snarled. "I hate you, and I heard you talking with Ryleigh. We don't want you here!"

He nodded slowly. "I know. But I can't stand the thought of leaving when you need me the most."

"*Need* you?" I grumped, refusing to look at him. "I'm tired of you here. Can't I fish alone with the peace and quiet?"

"There's two reasons why you can't. You need to go to school, and you just broke your fishing rod."

I narrowed my eyes as anger threatened to choke me. "I'll break you if I have to! I'm not going to school to sit around and get my ears talked off, and I am not going to obey *you*, of all people. I can do pretty much anything I have a mind to, and I'm going fishing, with or without a pole. I had nothing to eat this morning, and I ain't gonna let foolish education get in the way of what my body needs!"

"I tried to feed you last night, but you insulted the help and ran before you could get any food in your belly." Jet leaned forward as he lowered his voice. "And you will obey me because you'll find you can't avoid me. You are going to school."

"I am not, and you can't make me!"

He raised both eyebrows as he cocked his head to the side. "You're going.

23

Even if I have to throw you over my shoulder and carry you."

I leaned forward as my lip curled into a snarl. "You. Wouldn't. Dare."

With a shrug and a sigh, Jet wrapped his hands around my middle and draped me over his broad shoulder as if I were nothing more than a deer he had just shot for supper. My jaw dropped in shock as he turned and walked the path back to town, but it didn't take long for my shock to turn to rage. Balling my hands into fists, I pummeled his back as hard as I could.

"Set me down!" I screamed at the top of my lungs. "Set me down *now!*"

"If I did that, I'm afraid I'll never get you back in that classroom."

I slammed a fist into his shoulder blade, but Jet hardly noticed. "You can't make me go to school!"

He didn't reply as we entered town, and I felt my cheeks flush with embarrassment as I began to hear snickers from curious people who had ventured out of stores to see what was going on. Jet tipped his hat respectfully toward a group of women, but as we passed, I sent them a chiller glare in hopes that would dim their amusement. It just seemed to make them laugh more. Grumbling my discontent, I finally forced myself to remain calm and allowed him to carry me to the church where most kids regularly attended school. The closer we came, the more irritated I grew, until at last Jet stopped and pulled me off his shoulder.

Before I could yell at him, he aimed a finger toward my nose as he raised an eyebrow. "Now you go to school, and you behave yourself. Don't try to pull any tricks because I'll be keeping an eye on you. I'll ask the teacher how you behaved at the end of the day, so if you create a ruckus, I'll know. Have a good day. I'll see you when school lets out."

Turning his back to me, he ignored my glare and walked across the street to the feed mill. Fierce hatred seemed to increase my anger. Reluctantly, I spun to face the wooden door, filled my lungs with air, and marched up the steps to the door. For either too much use or lack of use, the hinges squealed their protest as I opened the door wide enough for me to slither through. Almost instantly, every head swiveled around to see who had interrupted their lesson, but it was the eyes of the teacher that filled me with dread. Swallowing my discomfort, I arrogantly walked down the aisle until I came to the first empty seat, which was beside a carrot topped boy around my same age. I nodded a greeting to Chad as I lowered myself beside him, then leveled lazy eyes on Mr. Hyndman.

Our teacher, when he wasn't grading assignments or preparing for the next day's lesson, worked hard as a farm hand, and his shoulders were broad with pure muscle. Though he was shorter than most of his male students, he held a certain confident authority that made most pupils obey his orders. If a student were well-behaved, Mr. Hyndman would treat that pupil with respect, but if one happened to have a reputation of ignoring his frivolous rules, his attitude became a little hostile. Although he wasn't overly strict, I had received several punishments from him for interrupting his lecture one too many times, or for fighting during lunch recess. Chad and I were often found guilty in our young teacher's eyes, but even if we never got away with any of our minor crimes, we would always conjure up some plan to anger the poor gent.

"Nice of you to join us, Cheyenne," Mr. Hyndman greeted at last, crossing his arms in front of him. "You're more than an hour late."

I leaned my elbows on the desk in front of me, shrugged, and grinned cockily. "I guess I overslept."

"If that were the case, I'd think you were hibernating," he answered wittily before sitting on the corner of the teacher's desk. A few students snickered at his comment, and I shot them a glare over my shoulder. "Perhaps you had forgotten that today we would have a recitation test over history. You got here right on time."

My upper lip curled as a groan rose in my throat. My most disliked subject, and Jet had thrown me into the schoolhouse. My opinion of the newly found uncle dropped even lower, and I began thinking of a way to get revenge as Mr. Hyndman turned to write a few questions on the chalkboard. After reading the first question, I glanced at Chad, but he shrugged as if to say he knew as much about history as me.

Moaning my misery, I brought my knee to my chest as I pulled a rock out of one of the holes of my boot. After a few seconds, a grin spread across my face as I caught Chad's eye and I pulled back my arm to fling the small rock towards Mr. Hyndman. It bounced off the back of his head, but by the time he turned around to see who had thrown the stone, I was studying the back of the bench in front of me.

Mr. Hyndman cleared his throat until every student looked up, and his eyes were less than amused. "Education is a treasured tool to help us proceed in life. Now, I realize schooling isn't as easy or come as naturally to some as it does others, and some don't really care. But what I won't tolerate is someone who prefers to distract others by throwing objects during a test. It's selfish to do so, and I want to know who the culprit is."

Mr. Hyndman's eyes scanned the crowd of students, but no one raised their hand. And I wasn't going to expose myself. The silence dragged on for a solid minute before an eleven-year-old girl sitting in a pew across from me cautiously raised her hand.

"I know who it was," she whispered, seeming almost scared to speak.

Mr. Hyndman tilted his head back. "You can tell me, Rebekah."

She leaned back in her seat, glanced at me, and lowered her head. I sneaked a peek at our teacher and found his eyes drilling into me. Getting turned in without words hurt worse than being thrown into Mr. Hyndman's wrath in the first place. Biting my lip to keep from muttering a curse, I concentrated on keeping my head down to fake my innocence.

"Cheyenne."

Raising my eyebrows, I placed a smile on my lips and met his gaze. "Yes?"

"Did you throw a rock at me?"

I leaned back and let my grin widen. "I thought I saw a bee and tried to kill it with the rock. Don't be mad. Your tests are kinda boring, and a little bit of excitement is just what this class needs on this fine day." I flashed an arrogant smile when his brows knit together. "Sides that, it's fun to see how far I can push you before you lose it."

Mr. Hyndman lowered his head and shook it as he sighed. When he looked up, he crooked his finger for me to come to him. I raised my eyebrows and stuffed my tongue in my cheek as I stood to swagger down the aisle toward our teacher. Without saying a word, Mr. Hyndman pointed to the corner of the room and raised his eyebrows.

26

"I don't read sign language," I joked, "but I'll stand where you point, anyway. You don't scare me, and your corny punishment of standing in the corner ain't gonna change my behavior, or my opinion of you."

Mr. Hyndman jabbed his finger toward the corner. "Stand in the corner, Cheyenne, and stay after class to clean the chalkboards."

I smiled cheekily. "Yes sir. We'll see."

* * *

Jet stepped out of the feed mill office with a spring in his step. He'd gotten the job. With the steady income, he would be able to take care of Cheyenne's needs, and once Ryleigh found that he could provide for her little sister, maybe she'd be more open to his advice. Things were beginning to look positive, and that encouraged him to pursue his promise. Although it would be a hard challenge, Jet was more than willing to step into his brother's place. The girls may say they didn't want him around, but maybe he could convince them he only wanted the best for them. Jet didn't bother adding up the years that they had been left alone in an adult's world. It had been too long. Ryleigh had recently entered the marrying age, and she had been raising her sister when she should have been enjoying childhood adventures. The thought of the fear she must have felt, or the pressure piled on her to be the adult she wasn't, tied a knot in the pit of his stomach and made him want to punch some sense into his dead brother. He didn't understand why Rod had abandoned his family for so long, especially since his two girls desperately needed his help, but the past was gone.

As he crossed the street, Jet glanced to his left and saw the petite girl on his mind. She wore a shawl wrapped tightly around her shoulders to cover any skin that might be exposed, but the shortness of the dress was hard to hide. He didn't fail to notice how people obviously avoided her to keep from being dragged into the snare they thought she had, but even if she didn't gain much respect from the fellow townsfolk, she kept her head high. She carried herself with confidence, not shame or cockiness. Several women held on tighter to their husbands as she went on her way, but she ignored their silent judgments as she disappeared into the mercantile.

Without a second thought, Jet darted across the street and entered the same store, scanning the aisles for his abused niece. He finally found her fingering a beautiful blue checkered dress, her eyes downcast as she studied the price. To keep from being seen, he turned his back to her, but kept a close eye. For several minutes, she gazed at the material. It would look beautiful on her. Her skin was flawless except for the accent of freckles on her face, and her eyes were the same shade as the clear summer sky. She would look like the beauty God had created her to be in a dress made from the material that matched her perfectly.

With a sigh and dip of her shoulders, she reluctantly turned away from the dress and moved to a roll of gingham material more in her price range. She took the bolt off the shelf and lifted her chin as she strode to the counter in a tomboyish manner like her sister.

"I'd like three yards, please."

The lady behind the desk curled her lip when she realized who had called for her help. "What's this for?" she asked suspiciously, and the way she held her nose in the air made Jet want to defend his niece.

"It is past due for my sister to have a new shirt," Ryleigh answered coldly.

The woman harrumphed as she counted out the yards. "That sister of yours is despicable! Why, on a windy day that child's clothes will blow right off, and I swear she'd run around raw! And she doesn't have the respect and manners most children her age should have." She leaned in close and wrinkled her nose. "She takes after her sister."

Ryleigh's back stiffened, but she attempted not to let the woman's words get to her. "How much do I owe you, Mrs. Wilkes?"

The woman pursed her lips as she turned an icy glare on Ryleigh. "Nine cents."

Ryleigh reached into her small purse and pulled out the right amount. "No need to package it," she replied without emotion. "I'll just take it home and get to work."

Without so much as a farewell, Ryleigh picked up the material and spun on her heel. She caught movement out of the corner of her eye and turned her head to meet Jet's gaze. She paused momentarily, then lifted her head higher and strode confidently out the door. Ignoring the curious glances from the Mrs. Wilkes behind the counter, Jet jumped onto the boardwalk and had to trot to catch up to the young woman.

"What are you still doing here?" she snapped, staring straight ahead. "I told you we don't need your help."

He shrugged and stuffed his hands into his pockets. "I know, but I kinda like this town. I got me a job at the feed mill."

"I am not stupid, Mr. Douglas," she replied, stopping as she turned to face him. "You are as stubborn as a mule, and you won't leave until you feel your promise to Pa has been filled. You can say what you want, but we've been doing fine without you or Pa for years, and we can get along fine when you leave. There's a stage leaving town three days from now. Please be on it. Now if you'll excuse me, I have a lot of work to do today before my shift starts. Good day to you, sir."

She turned to leave, but Jet grabbed her elbow before she could run. "Wait!" he pleaded. She reluctantly turned back to face him and crossed her arms over her chest. "I understand your hesitation," he answered slowly, "but please hear me out. I'd like to talk to you in private. Would you be kind enough to join me for the noon meal?"

Ryleigh sighed and lifted her shoulders in a shrug. "You won't relent. I'll do my best, but I've got a lot to do."

Jet let out a breath of relief and let go of her arm. "Then can I pick you up at eleven thirty?"

She shook her head. "I'll meet you at the diner at noon if I'm not busy. Don't go out of your way to help us. I meant what I said this morning."

Afraid to disagree in case she changed her mind, Jet nodded his head. She stared at him for a few seconds longer before she continued to hurry down the street. It almost appeared to him that she was fleeing from him. Scratching the back of his neck, Jet started to turn to head back to the boardinghouse when he caught sight of a familiar pair of trousers sneaking around the back of the school. His shoulders slumped as he recognized Cheyenne's black curls.

Shaking his head, Jet closed the distance between him and his youngest niece. "What do you think you're doing?" he demanded when he strode

29

into her hearing range.

She yelped and jumped high in the air before she spun on her heel to see who had snuck up on her. Almost instantly, her gaze turned hard. "You. Where did you come from? I made sure you weren't around!"

"Next time look in the crowds, not around them. But hopefully there won't be a next time." He crossed his arms and shifted all his weight to his left leg. "Now, are you gonna tell me how you sneaked around your teacher?"

She mimicked his stance but stuffed her vicious tongue in her cheek. "His name's Mr. Hyndman. And Chad helped me."

"Who's Chad?"

Cheyenne shifted to the other leg and nodded at the schoolhouse. "Chad Dillon. He's the red headed boy 'bout my age. We run together."

"What happened?"

The teen turned so she faced a path of escape, but Jet braced himself to grab her if she decided to bolt. "There was just a ruckus that broke out, and I found it suddenly necessary to visit the outhouse."

Jet raised his eyebrows as he nodded unbelievingly. "Uh-huh. I didn't know a trip to the outhouse involved such a sneaky attitude."

He noticed the glare she threw him out of the corner of her eye. "I'm hungry. My growling belly is a distraction, and I can't think. I'll just be gone for a few minutes, just long enough to grab something to settle my stomach."

"No." The answer was simple, but it appeared she didn't understand the definition of the word. Jet pointed at the door and placed his other hand on his hip. "You're gonna go back inside and finish today's worth of school."

Cheyenne bounced on her leg, her jaw tightening in anger. Jet raised an eyebrow in mild surprise. She seemed to be a close friend to anger, and that was a trait he would have to help her to lose. "I told you before, I ain't gonna listen. I'm old enough to make my own decisions, so leave me be!" She swiveled her head around so her eyes could burn holes into Jet's skull. "I thought Overhaul was a pig, but you're worse than a snake."

His tolerance had just worn itself out. Without a word, he wrapped his hand around her arm and pulled her behind the school so that they could have some privacy from any curious onlooker. Spinning her around, he raised a finger to keep her silent as he spoke.

"I have been trying to get through your head that you need to respect your elders, but you don't seem to want to listen to me. You think you can dodge around me because I won't do anything to you, but that's gonna change right now. I've told you that I ain't afraid to discipline you, and if a stern hand is what it takes to make you listen, I'll gladly oblige."

Cheyenne's eyes grew large, but quickly narrowed as if she thought he couldn't see her fear. "And I've been trying to get through your head that I don't need you. I don't know why you're so stubborn, but I ain't gonna do what you want. I ain't gonna apologize for what I said to you, and I ain't gonna go back inside that dull room. Just leave already! We don't need another animal in this town!"

Jet studied his niece for a few seconds, but when she refused to back down, he gripped both of her shoulders in a tight squeeze. She squirmed slightly under his hold, but he ignored her harsh scowl as he tried to keep his anger at bay. "That's enough, Cheyenne. You don't want to listen to me, so I guess what I have to do is feed you soap for calling me a snake. I will not tolerate your disrespectful behavior to your elders. Someone should have given you five or six good licks when you were younger to stop this kind of attitude."

Cheyenne's jaw dropped momentarily before she narrowed her eyes once more. "I hate you!"

"Don't act like you haven't asked for this, Cheyenne. You know you're pushing your limits, and now you'll know that I'll discipline you when you cross your boundaries."

Tightening his hold on the wild young girl, Jet marched across the street to the boardinghouse. He ignored Cheyenne's cries of protest and pretended he could not see the disapproving glances the attendant cast his way when they entered the building. Once he scaled the stairs and closed the door of the rented room, Jet quickly grabbed the bar of soap by the wash basin and broke off a corner.

"Open your mouth," he demanded, but Cheyenne only clenched her jaw. "I said open your mouth. You need to know that you will be punished if you test me again."

Cheyenne's glare darkened, but she finally loosened her jaw enough to let Jet place the soap on her tongue. He removed his fingers quickly for fear that she might bite him, but she only looked at him with disgust as the bitter flavor of the soap began to infiltrate her mouth. Jet studied her dark eyes as she mulled the piece of soap around with her tongue, and he finally let go of her shirt as he folded his arms over his chest.

"When I tell you to do something, I expect you to obey me," Jet scolded in a softer tone. "Is that clear?"

Cheyenne's lip curled as her face turned a bright shade of red. She mumbled something around the soap suds, and Jet handed her the wash basin to spit the bubbles out of her mouth. "Clear as the mud you roll in," she muttered now that most of the soap was gone.

Jet raised an eyebrow. "I beg your pardon?"

"Clear as the mud you roll in!" she shouted. "You can punish me again, I ain't takin' it back! I don't know you, and I'm tired of you telling me how to live my life! I don't gotta go to school if I don't want to, and I can say whatever I please. You ain't gonna make no difference in how I live my life. And I hate you more than dark hates light," she finished, sending a spit-wad flying toward his boots.

Jet stared at the saliva as it stretched from the toe of his boot to the wood floor below. Just like the past times he had confronted Cheyenne, he wondered if he was sane jumping into the middle of a family who was too stubborn for their own good. If only they could see what he saw. Two girls, on the better half of being grown up, who ignored their need for help. Maybe he was going about helping them in the wrong way. After all, he had just met Cheyenne for the first time twenty-four hours ago. Raising his eyes, he looked in Cheyenne's fiery gaze and wished he could make her see he was not her enemy. Before he could try to explain anything to her, she spun on her heel and raced from the room.

"You got a little too carried away, Jethro boy," Jet muttered to himself as he stared at the door she had just slammed. "Again."

~THREE~

Dark wavy hair and thick beard. Ice blue eyes and stubbornly strong arms.

Just the thought of Jet's appearance sent a ripple of rage coursing through my veins. Cocking my head to the side in anger, I clenched my jaw and began muttering to myself. "If that lowly man lays a hand on me again, I'll tear him a new one! I shoulda lit into him this afternoon. After all, he treated me like a child when I know I ain't!"

A voice in the street stood out among the others, and the sound of my uncle sent shivers of hate down my backbone. Cowering in the alley, I peeked around the corner to see Jet stride down the street in that annoying, manly gait of his. He was headed toward the livery stables. An evil thought passed through my mind to get back at him for my injustice, and I found it suddenly necessary to follow him. He waved a greeting toward the stable boy, Levi Hendershot, who had started the job about two months prior. I scoffed at Jet's appearance. He carried himself with an arrogance that boasted of his authority, and I wanted to hurt him.

I ran on tiptoes so as not to make a sound. The silent attempt was useless, since my footsteps would have been covered up by the wagons and townsfolk, but the motion seemed to set my devious mood. Once inside the stables, I could hear the men's words, and began to plot my actions.

"Your horse has been in good hands," Levi stated as he followed Jet around the stable.

"I appreciate it," Jet replied, walking into the tack room to retrieve a bridle. "I had no doubt he would be well fed and groomed."

The young man leaned against the doorjamb as he combed his fingers through his hair. "I appreciate your trust, sir. Most people don't seem to want me to handle their horses."

Jet scooted around Levi. "Give them time, son. Most times it takes a while for one to build trust between another," he said as he set his saddle on the stall door.

I resisted the urge to scoff. If such wise words escaped his lips to advise a young man who meant nothing to him, why couldn't he live by them? Surely, he didn't expect me to trust and obey him after barely meeting him. I made a solemn swear to myself that, no matter how persistent he became, I would never give Jet my trust. The longer the two talked about such hypocritical things, the hotter my temper boiled. Just when I had worked up enough courage to run into the aisle and confront my uncle, a slim, petite shadow flowed over the uneven dirt floor like a calm stream on a sunny day.

I glanced over my shoulder, afraid that I had been seen though I hid behind a stack of hay. A beautiful young lady stood in the doorway, a shawl covering her otherwise bare shoulders and chest. Her chin held high, she attempted to ignore the shortness of her skirt as she strode into the barn with a boldness in her step. Seeing my sister was such a shock to me that all thoughts of revenge were momentarily forgotten.

A deep red blush crept up Levi's neck as he watched my sister approach, but his expression didn't hold the normal disapproval or embarrassment to be in her same company as the other church-going men. Jet seemed just as shocked to see Ryleigh as I felt, and my heart hardened when she closed the distance between her and our last living relative.

"I've thought about what you've said," she said in a bold voice, all hints of a greeting hidden beneath her invisible fear. "And I'm sorry I didn't speak to you over the noon meal like we planned, but I'd like to talk to you now." She leveled her large blue eyes on the stable boy, who only seemed to squirm under her gaze. "Excuse us. I'd like to speak in private." Turning back to our uncle, she hooked her hand in his elbow and led him toward the door.

The sight sickened me.

I watched the two disappear through the door and resisted the urge to slam my fist into the closest bale of hay. Levi stared after my sister with a strange look in his eyes. "You're a fool, Levi," he muttered to himself, cupping a hand around his neck as he wandered into a back room.

I glanced over my shoulder at the door again and ground my teeth in anger. Why had she asked to talk to such a lowly character? And why had she appeared to be in need? She never bowed to anybody, not even that pig of a man who employed her. Grunting with anger, I leaped over the bale of hay and raced to the saddle Jet had forgotten. Reaching into my pocket, I brought out my favored tool and weapon, grabbed a cinch, and ripped the blade of my pocketknife through the leather. It felt good to tear something up, so I reached for another cinch.

"You think you can help us?" I muttered as I continued my rant. "I'll show you how much you're welcome here!"

Letting out a soft growl, I stabbed the saddle as hard as I could, intent on ruining the item. A word gurgled in my throat, one that I had learned in the saloon when Overhaul was frustrated at my presence, but for once, the vileness of the insult didn't shame me. Anger that I had let build up inside of me rushed out in a blast, the danger of my mind matching the danger of my blade.

"What in tarnation... you stop that!"

I spun on my heel, my blade pointed at the intruder, and I made a lunge. The intruder grabbed my wrist just as I attempted to plunge the knife into his body, and within a few seconds the weapon had been twisted out of my hand and now lay on the ground. I stared at the wooden handle, surprised at what I had just done. Never had I aimed a weapon at any sacred soul, and the thought of what I might've done if this man hadn't taken my knife sickened me more than the knowledge of my sister alone with Jet.

Levi held me at arm's length away, his eyes filled with shock. "You're the girl who's got the reputation in this town like Billy the Kid! What are you doing to Mr. Douglas' saddle?"

I refused to answer as I lowered my head.

After picking up my knife, Levi led me toward the door in a rush. Jet and Ryleigh were standing by the corral, but when we exited the barn, they both stiffened and hurried to stand in front of me.

"Cheyenne," Jet spoke in surprise. "I didn't know where you'd gone. It's been nearly five hours since I last saw you. Where have you been?"

"I found her cutting up your saddle, Mr. Douglas," Levi answered for me. "I tried to stop her, and she turned her knife on me."

Ryleigh's eyes grew wide as she glanced between Levi and me. "Cheyenne, are you okay? You've never done anything... what's gotten into you?"

I narrowed my eyes to slits. "You traitor," I growled. Regret told me to keep my anger intact, but the temper burning a hole in my skull insisted otherwise. "You turned your back to me, and then you go to this animal," I continued, motioning toward Jet. "How could you betray me?"

Ryleigh stared at me in shock before she lowered her head, a motion she hadn't done in my presence since the night after her promotion. She covered her mouth with her hand and turned her back, but I noticed the tears shimmering in her eyes. Jet grabbed my arm and pulled me away from Levi.

"You have no right to talk to your sister that way," Jet scolded in a low voice. "And what do you think you're doing, turning a knife on this young man? What do you have to say for yourself?"

I tried to shrug away from him, but he wouldn't relinquish his hold. Jet waited impatiently for an answer I wasn't willing to give, and I noticed that Levi stood awkwardly beside Ryleigh as he kept his eyes on the toes of his boots. Ryleigh tried to compose herself, though my words had cut a deeper wound in her soul than the abuse she had endured for eight long years.

"Your anger is your worst attribute, and because of it you almost hurt this young man," Jet continued. "Not to mention you now owe me for a new saddle."

"I owe you for nothing," I muttered, barely loud enough for him to hear.

With a sigh of frustration, Jet turned to Levi. "Thank you for catching this temperamental niece of mine. Don't feel responsible for her actions, it was mostly my fault for leaving my saddle in the open unattended. I'm sorry if she scared you." Jet took the knife from Levi and slipped it into his pocket.

Levi shrugged and ducked his head slightly. "I appreciate it, sir."

Jet reached back to grab my sister's elbow as he nudged us in the direction of our house. I combed my mind to try to figure out how he knew where we lived as we walked in silence, but I finally settled on the fact that nothing Jet did surprised me. The walk from one end of town to the other only took a few minutes, but it felt like an eternity before Jet marched up the rickety steps to our falling down front porch and allowed Ryleigh and me to enter before him.

"Let me get one thing straight," he said sternly after he closed the door and approached us. "Both of you don't like my being around here, I get that, but I'm not leaving. Ryleigh, you can't be mother, provider, and sister at the same time. I aim to help you in more ways than one. And Cheyenne…"

I chanced a peek at my uncle and crossed my eyes at him when I found his gaze.

"Cheyenne, you need to behave, and your sister is too busy to teach you how to do that," Jet finished, not at all pleased with the look I had just given him.

Ryleigh stiffened and pulled her shawl tighter around her shoulders. "I can take care of my own sister. I only met you once in my life, how do you propose I team up with you when I barely know you're my father's brother! I accepted you staying in town, and I even accepted that we would have to put up with your presence for a few years, but I will not have you telling me how to interact with my sister! We've survived quite a number of years without you, or Pa, or any other holy citizen of this town. We don't need your help!"

Jet crossed his arms over his chest and nodded my direction. "What about the episode this afternoon? She could've hurt a man in anger if that he hadn't been so quick on his toes. She tore up my saddle, skipped school, and has been creating havoc ever since I met her last night. Do you really think you're raising her right?"

Ryleigh glanced at me and hung her head a second time. "I'm doing the best I can," she whispered, hugging her arms as tight as she could.

"I don't think so. I think you're too selfish thinking about yourself that you have no idea what your kid sister is doing. You can hate me for those words as much as you like, but I ain't leaving you two alone, especially now."

I watched Ryleigh cringe as if she had just been landed a blow, and the hatred I held toward our uncle built up in my chest once again. Gritting my teeth, I sank a fist into Jet's arm as hard as I could. "You leave her alone!" I screamed, rearing back to hit him again.

Jet caught my wrist before I could punch him and held on tightly so that I couldn't run. "I'll have a discussion with you about your hostile behavior once I'm done talking with your sister."

"I don't want to hear what you have to say," Ryleigh answered, tears finding a way to restrain her voice. "I don't want you around me, and I don't want Cheyenne to see me like this!"

Ryleigh spun on her high heel and disappeared through the back door, ducking her head as she ran so no one would notice the tears running down her face. We both cringed when the door slammed behind her, and I turned fiery eyes on the man who caused my sister's sadness.

"You're a good-for-nothin', irritatin' man!" I snarled. If I had been a dog, I was sure I'd have a strip of hair standing along my backbone as I growled at the intruder who still captured my wrist.

Jet scowled at me, then forced me to sit in a rickety chair at the dining table as he blocked any path to escape. "Your words are like that knife you just had, and those words you said to Ryleigh earlier were the sharpest of them all. The temper you have is extremely harsh, and you have to learn to control it."

I crossed my arms over my chest and rolled my eyes. "If you punish me again, I'll only hate you more."

Jet crouched so that he became eye level with me. "I'm not going to hurt you, but I do have something in mind. You tore up my saddle, which cost the better half of my savings. I want you to pay me back."

My jaw dropped to my chest. "But how? I'm flat broke!"

Jet shrugged unsympathetically. "You should've thought of that before you destroyed someone else's property. You have to get an honest job to earn honest money, that's how you'll pay me back."

"Don't you think I've tried to get a job?" I growled. "Nobody wants to hire me, and I won't allow myself to leave town without Ryleigh."

Jet sighed as he raised a palm to silence me. "Just keep in mind what I gotta say. This house needs sprucing up, and I'm gonna make enough at my job at the feed mill to purchase lumber. I'm willing to make a proposition with you."

I studied him from the corner of my eye. "I'm not sure I trust you."

Jet continued his speech as if I hadn't spoken. "You work for me. You help me rebuild your house, since you seem to favor boyish things. While I'm working in the mill, you go to school and get an education."

"Go to school?" I shouted. "I am *not* going to school, and you can't make me!"

"Now, just hear me out," Jet warned before I could argue any further. "If you don't agree, I will have you put in a jail cell for destroying my property."

My eyes widened, and my heart skipped a beat. "You can't do that!"

"Yes, I can. I told you that I'm not afraid to discipline you. I gave you two options. What's your choice?"

My tongue balled inside my cheek, and if he wasn't so close in front of me, I would've darted out the door following my sister. "I ain't gonna choose any of them!"

Jet pursed his lips and cocked his head to the side. "Then what do you propose to do?"

I narrowed my eyes as I leaned forward so our noses almost touched. "I'm gonna make you wish you never came here!"

"You don't believe I'll send you to jail?" Jet asked bluntly.

My mouth remained closed. All the responses I came up with appeared childish, and I refused to let him think I was a child. Several seconds dragged by, and when I didn't answer, Jet stood to his feet and hooked his thumbs in his pockets.

"Alright. Your job starts tomorrow, along with your education. I'm gonna get the lumber to start on the porch. I'll pay you seventy-five cents a day and let me get one thing straight. Every time I hear of you getting in trouble, I'll dock your pay by five cents. Do I make myself clear?"

I slid lower in my chair and curled my lip in disgust. "Clear as mud, you—"

"That's another thing," he interrupted. "Every time I hear a vile word slip from your lips all work will come to a standstill as I wash your mouth out with soap. And you know I will, Cheyenne."

A groan of displeasure rumbled in my throat. "I don't want to be around you, and I especially don't wanna go to school. I got no use for that kinda stuff."

"Life's unfair. Sometimes we gotta do what we don't want to do."

My eyes came up with fire blazing in their irises. "Don't tell me about life. You ain't got a clue what you're saying when you're talking about life. My sister went to work in the Bull's Head when she was eleven years old, and she was a broken woman when she was my age. You said life ain't fair. Try telling that to Ryleigh, she already knows."

"And yet Ryleigh does stuff she doesn't want to do, while you parade around town looking for trouble, and finding it all too often. If you don't change your behavior any time soon, you may find it hard to get out of trouble in the future. I don't want a niece of mine ruining her life because she was too stubborn to admit that she was wrong. You're going to start school again in the morning, and I'll make sure you get there. I expect you back here to help me work on the porch when you're done."

I rolled my eyes and rose from the chair. "Fine."

Jet crossed his arms over his chest and raised an eyebrow. "I'm your uncle, and I expect a 'yes, sir' when I ask you something."

My lip curled involuntarily, and I felt the desire to tear out his eyeballs with my fingernails. "Yes, *sir!*" I snarled with as much disrespect in that one phrase as I could muster.

Jet sighed and lifted a shoulder in a shrug. "That's a start, I suppose." He turned and walked to the table where I noticed a package for the first time. "Here," he said as he tossed the package to me. "If you're going to work for me, might as well have the proper clothing."

41

I frowned as I opened the package. A brand-new pair of boots stared up at me from their box, and I glanced at him suspiciously. "I have nothing to give you in return. Does this get added to that debt I owe with the saddle?"

Jet shook his head. "Consider it a gift. I don't want you to be stepping on any nails while we're rebuilding the house."

I carefully held a boot close to my face for a better inspection. I couldn't remember owning a nicer pair of boots in my life, and a large unease settled in my chest. I couldn't tell what my uncle wanted, and the fact that he was giving me something as expensive as new boots unnerved me. Still, they were a nice pair.

"Fine. I'll accept," I spoke at last, "but this changes nothing between us."

* * *

Five o'clock rolled around all too soon. Her chores were mostly finished, and she had even started sewing the new shirt for Cheyenne. Fidgeting in her chair, Ryleigh glanced at the clock again. Why did the daylight fade so quickly? She had long since began to fill with dread when her shift lined up with the clock on the wall. She felt dirty and ashamed as she smeared the bright red on her lips and darkened her eyelashes with the face paint she abhorred. In just thirty minutes, she would walk down the stairs, wearing scarcely a thing, and sing a few songs before serving alcoholic drinks. She wanted to quit, and had voiced so several times to Clyde, but his reaction was always the same.

Her eyes found the bruise on her neck from the last such confrontation with her boss. Tears blurred her eyes as she remembered her failure. Failure to succeed, failure to quit, failure to guide her sister down the right path. Ryleigh held the heels of her hands to her eyes to keep the tears from spilling over, but they still created black runs down her cheeks. Where had she gone wrong? She had always known Cheyenne was high-spirited, but she had never seen the side of her sister she was beginning to show.

If only our long-lost uncle Jethro hadn't arrived, then things would have remained the same.

"No, quit that," she scolded herself in a whisper. "He said he came to guide her. He said… he said he wanted to help."

But the words that kept ringing in her mind refused to shut off the valve of tears. *You traitor. You turn your back to me, and then go to this animal.* Those words hurt as much as if she had stabbed Ryleigh in the heart. Had all the years of providing for Cheyenne been in vain? All she had ever wanted to do was make sure Cheyenne had a full belly, roof over her head, and clothes on her back. Living in a small town, Ryleigh had struggled to find work, and when Clyde had offered her a job, she had thought it was a gift from God. She was trapped. Buried underneath the sin in her life, and she couldn't find a way back to the surface. Failure stung. More than she cared to admit to anyone.

She wished Mr. Douglas would jump on the stage that would leave town, but his offer to help was one she couldn't turn down. She had worn herself sick with her routine of waking up feeling dirty in the morning to pay a debt that seemed to keep building and taking care of chores at the house. Then she would dress up and endure another tortuous night. When she was a little girl, she had wanted to get married and live a respectable life, but those childish dreams were dead. All true happiness had been drained out of her that night so many years ago, and along with it she had taken her sister's joy.

Lifting her head to look at her reflection, Ryleigh wiped the blackness from her eyes and reached for the bottle of mascara on the desk. Her hair was piled high on her head to expose her shoulders, and she felt like a hypocrite by ignoring her mother's Sunday school teachings during the night and begging for the Lord's forgiveness in the morning. Tears threatened to spill over her lashes again, and she slapped herself to gain control.

"Put on your dumb smile," she whispered hoarsely to herself. "The more drinks you serve, the more you get paid. The more you..." A sigh slipped through her lips as she closed her eyes. "The more you flirt, the higher your paycheck. Now smile." Mentally pushing her struggles to the back of her mind, she widened her eyes and pasted on a smile that looked as fake and miserable as she felt.

A knock on her door jarred Ryleigh from her thoughts of self-pity, and she quickly wiped her wet face with her hands. "Come in."

A young woman with long blond hair poked her head inside the room, but her friendly smile faded when she saw Ryleigh. "Honey, what's wrong?"

Ryleigh felt a moment of relief as she sniffed her nose. "Thank goodness it's you, Violet. I don't think I could ignore my stupid emotions if Clyde came in."

Violet entered the room and closed the door soundlessly behind her. "It is your monthly? I know how uncomfortable it can be during your time."

Ryleigh blushed and shook her head as she reached up to clean the smudges off her cheekbones. "It's Mr. Douglas. I don't know what to do. I tried to talk to him today, but I don't know what I was expecting. I want him to go away, but he says he can help Cheyenne."

Violet moved behind Ryleigh and began to pin some of the loose hairs back into her bun. Violet was a young woman in her mid-twenties, and she was the only one who had taken Ryleigh under her wing all those years ago. Violet had worked in a saloon in Colorado when Clyde met her. He instantly found her to be attractive and lent her money to leave Colorado and work in the Bull's Head in Arizona. She started working shortly after Ryleigh's fourteenth birthday, and she instantly took to the young teen. Violet was as close to a woman figure that Ryleigh ever experienced, and she trusted her advice.

"Do you think your uncle means to hurt you?" Violet asked as she moved to clean off the rest of the makeup on Ryleigh's face.

"Well, no," Ryleigh admitted, but the butterflies didn't stop fluttering in the pit of her stomach. "He's not like Pa. I saw Mr. Douglas angry this afternoon, but he didn't try to hit me or Cheyenne. He knows we don't have any money. He saw our house today."

"What do you suppose he wants?" Violet began to apply the mascara and rouge to Ryleigh's features again.

"He wants to help us. He says he can look after Cheyenne, and maybe I should let him. She cut his saddle and tried to hurt the stable boy today. I just don't know what to do with her." Ryleigh closed her eyes as tears began to well up in her throat. "I know she's hurt, but she gets angry like

Pa. I know what she hears from folks. I think she tries to act angry and tough to try to prove that she's not a weak orphan."

Violet laid a hand on Ryleigh's shoulder. "I know you try your best with her," Violet began slowly, "but do you think you're trying to do too much? Maybe consistency is what she needs."

Ryleigh offered a small smile as she rose to her feet. "I think so, too, but I'm scared of what she'll think. She saw me talking to Mr. Douglas in private, and it made her upset. I'm afraid that if I let Mr. Douglas take care of her, she'll resent me."

Violet enveloped her into a warm embrace. "I know, honey. It will be okay. Maybe Mr. Douglas is that godsend you've been praying for." A gasp emerged from Violet's lips when she heard the pianist hit a few notes in the bar below. "Oh, honey, that's your number." She pushed away from Ryleigh and cupped her head in her hands. "Just make it through tonight. We'll talk about this again tomorrow."

Ryleigh nodded her head and hurried from the room to stand at the top of the stairs. Off-key piano music burned her eardrums, and she cringed. Stiffening her back, she listened to her musical cue, then strode down the stairs in a flirtatious style, letting notes flow from her tongue like a peaceful river. Despite the clunky tunes from the yellowish keys and the lyrics she secretly hated, Ryleigh lost herself in the music as she danced from one table to the other. The only thing she genuinely loved doing was singing. If only she could get paid the amount she already did for such simple, innocent entertainment.

As the last note ended, the atmosphere erupted with vile laughter, whoops, and disturbing "darlings," "babies," and "why don't you come over here's." Ryleigh faked a smile and retreated to the counter where she reached for a few drinks. Already she could feel several eyes on her back as she accepted tips down her front to serve as flirtatious gratitude for the drinks she provided. The darker the outside became, the more crowded the saloon grew. The hand on the clock rapidly came upon the next hour, then the next, and soon Ryleigh's knees began to knock together, and her palms grew sweaty.

Leaning against the bar to catch her breath, she found several of her regulars, and she couldn't help but wonder which one it would be that night. The same sickening feeling rose in her throat, and she was afraid for a while that she would have to step outside for a few minutes. Swallowing the bile on the back of her tongue, she set her elbows on the counter and pressed her back against the edge so she could see the crowd. A young man she never met before swaggered up beside her and grinned toothily.

"Howdy," he greeted, his voice dripping with hunger.

Her insides turned upside down, but she hid her feelings with a playful smile. "Well, hello there."

A grin spread across his lips as he thumbed his hat back on his brow. "Can I buy you a drink?"

"I've been craving a drink the whole night," she lied, flashing the young man a winning smile as she turned to face the bartender.

A dirty glass was placed in front of her, filled to the brim with frothy beer. Her insides churned as she lifted the mug to her lips and took a sip. *The more you flirt, the more drinks he'll buy, the higher you get paid*, she kept telling herself. *Just get this night out of the way, and you'll be fine.*

"What are your plans for the night, honey bunches?" the stranger slurred. It was obvious that he had already enjoyed a few drinks.

Ryleigh forced her smile to grow to hide the dread she felt. "My plans are as unwritten as the law in the West, mister."

The smile he returned sent shivers down her backbone. "How 'bout you and me get outta here?"

"Maybe later. I would like to finish my drink."

"Sure. Take all the time you need, darlin'."

Just keep your head straight. Don't let your feelings show.

Above the hubbub of the crowd, Ryleigh heard the hinges squeal as the doors let in another individual, but she kept her mind on the beer in front of her since she was already dealing with a customer. While enduring the flirts from the young cowboy beside her, she glanced to a corner of the room where Clyde Overhaul always sat. His eyes were trained on her, and she didn't like the way they were narrowed to slits. After taking a sip of the liquor, she turned her back to Overhaul to give her full attention on the cowboy, who was talking about how beautiful she was. She'd heard that line before.

"Excuse me," a voice commanded from the other side of the room.

It was familiar, so familiar that her eyes grew large. Her knees buckling beneath her, she whirled to face the man who had just walked into the saloon. Jet glanced at her, but quickly looked away when a drunk stumbled in front of him. Turning to the cowboy, Ryleigh leaned against his side desperately and hooked an arm through his elbow.

"I think I'll take you up on that offer now," she replied, smiling lazily.

The cowboy grinned hungrily and wrapped an arm too tightly around her waist. "Yes, ma'am."

As they headed toward the stairs, she glanced at Overhaul and found an approving eye cast her way. With a sigh of both relief and dread, she placed her foot on the first step, the cowboy right beside her.

"Stop!"

Ryleigh gasped. Jet had caught up to her, and she really hadn't wanted him to see her at work. Turning slowly around, she faced her uncle, who looked red as he glared at the young man beside her.

"What are you doing? That's my woman!" Jet bellowed, reaching for the cowboy.

The young lad jerked away and tightened his grip on Ryleigh. "I already asked for a poke, mister, and I would suggest you find yourself another woman!"

"That's my suggestion to you, boy, before I lose my temper and land a fist in your jowls!"

Ryleigh's eyes widened, and she wanted to tell Mr. Douglas to let it drop, but she could tell he wouldn't have listened if she had beaten him over the head with a rotten fish. Out of the corner of her eye, she could see Clyde Overhaul pushing his overweight self to his feet and ambling toward the trio, who were beginning to draw an audience.

"What's going on here?" Overhaul demanded as he leaned against the railing.

The cowboy gathered Ryleigh to his chest. "This man is trying to take from me, that's what's goin' on! I had this wench first, and he demands this is *his* woman!"

Overhaul turned to Jet and sucked particles of food from his yellow-stained teeth. "There's plenty of other women if that's what you want, mister. I could offer you the best one I have, but of course, a small fee would be asked of you."

Jet crossed his arms over his chest and wagged his head back and forth. "No others will do besides this woman. How much is the kid paying you?"

"Enough to spend a few hours with her," the cowboy growled like a dog with an old bone.

Ignoring the cowboy, Jet continued to address Overhaul. "What if I said I had enough to spend the whole night with this pretty lady? I'd gladly pay for a full night."

Ryleigh could see the greed spread in Overhaul's ugly, rat like eyes. "Supposin' you're makin' this all up," the saloon owner mused. "How would I know, unless I have actual, physical proof that your word is right?"

Much to Ryleigh's horror, Jet pulled out his wallet and counted out a large sum of bills. Overhaul greedily snatched the money from her uncle's hand and grinned maliciously at Jet. "It's been a mighty good pleasure dealing business with you, sir. She's all yours."

"That ain't fair!" the cowboy exclaimed when Jet moved to take his spot.

"Settle down, boy, settle down," Overhaul comforted as he counted the cash in his fist. "You'll get your money back. Or you could spend it on another woman, or more drinks. C'mon, lad, the night's still young, and I guarantee you I've got prettier women than Ryleigh here."

The cowboy threw a glare at Jet as he stepped down from Ryleigh, but the snarl barely seemed to bother her uncle as he gently urged her up the stairs. Ignoring her trembling knees, she walked down the hall with short steps, dreading the lecture she was sure to hear the moment she closed the door to her bedroom. Swallowing hard, she twisted the doorknob of her room, and slipped inside without a word. Jet closed it behind him and watched her sink onto her mattress.

"Don't look so afraid," he said softly after studying her for several seconds. "I'm not here to hurt you."

"I realize you wouldn't be so twisted as to spend the night in bed with your niece, if that's what you're hinting at."

Jet cringed at her choice of words and dragged a chair in front of her door. "I would never abuse any woman, let that be clear. I only came tonight because the thought of you losing sleep again made me uneasy. I want you to be able to trust me, Ryleigh." He sat in the chair and crossed his arms over his chest. "I wanted to apologize to you for losing my temper this afternoon. I was wrong to have said those things to you, and I'm sorry."

Ryleigh stared at him silently, knowing she herself should apologize for running away from him, but she was unable to find the words to utter.

Jet cleared his throat when she didn't reply. "Another reason was to let you get a good night's sleep. You looked too worn, and I thought you should be able to get some rest. Besides, you do so much that you'll make yourself sick."

Ryleigh lowered her gaze. "Is that all you came to do? People will think you're disgusting when they find out you are related to me."

"I don't care what they think. I don't want you to be afraid of me."

Tears burned the back of her eyes as she stood abruptly to her feet, snatched a house coat from her dressing panel, and swung it around her shoulders. For a while, she couldn't find the words to speak as she hugged the material close to her body. Hanging her head, she swallowed the lump in her throat and took a deep breath.

"I don't want you around me," she whispered. "I don't want you to see me like this. That's why I'm never near Cheyenne. You want the truth?" she asked as she turned to face him. "I'll give you the truth. The truth is I'm a soiled dove because I was stupid enough to fall into a trap I can't get out of. Cheyenne hates me because I'm too ashamed to come home after my shift is over. I'm too ashamed for her to have a sister who is less than human, so I pretend she doesn't have a sister at all. I don't want her to see me in my dresses, I don't want her to see me at work, I don't want her to know the mistakes I've made. And now there's you. You come riding in on your steed with the news of help and of a new way of life. Your visions sound too good to be true, but it's too late for anyone to help me now."

Ryleigh paused as tears gathered in her throat again, but she stifled them and continued. "I've worked in this hellhole for eight years, and I'll die working in one just like it. There's no use for me outside of these doors. You said you wanted to help, and that you wouldn't leave until we were taken care of. Fine. Take care of Cheyenne, and make sure she's raised right. I have been fooling myself for all these years. She needs help, and I can't do any of it. She needs to forget about me. Help her, Mr. Douglas. She needs to live a better life than me. She needs to grow up to be the lady Mama wanted us to be, and she needs to find a man who will love her unconditionally and who will give her children of her own to raise. She needs guidance, and I've never been in any position to guide her. She needs an education, and she needs to learn her manners. I know she's almost out of her childhood and she's a handful, but please, Mr. Douglas, don't let her turn out to be like me."

Jet listened to her speech without any emotion on his face, and when she finished, he crossed his ankle over his knee as he replied. "I know Cheyenne needs help, but I need your permission to do as I see fit with her."

"Well, you've got it." Ryleigh sat on her bed with her head hanging low. "I'm afraid she's going to do something stupid. I'm scared she's going to work in a saloon someday, thinking there is no other way. Like I did." She smoothed her hand over the quilt and blinked until her vision cleared. "There's got to be a better way for her, Mr. Douglas. I've ruined myself in this bed. I don't want her to do the same."

"Ryleigh, you have my word. I'll do all I can to help her. And I'll do all I can to help you."

Ryleigh took a shaky breath as she shook her head vigorously. "Don't waste your time on me. Just see that Cheyenne gets raised right."

"You talk as if you're never going to see Cheyenne again," Jet pointed out gently.

"That's because I'm not. Overhaul wanted me to work double shifts a while back, but I had refused because I thought Cheyenne needed me. Now that you're here, I'm going to accept it. She needs to forget about me, and this will be as good a chance as any."

Jet's expression changed suddenly, and she could sense him stiffen. "I will not let you lose yourself in this dump of a job! You can't accept, your sister needs you as much as you need her. You're not a piece of dirt to get stomped on, Ryleigh. You're as beautiful a gem as any other woman walking the streets down below."

The lump in her throat grew until it hurt. Swallowing hard, she inhaled a shaky breath as she hooked a brown curl behind her ear. "Mr. Douglas, please. I'm tired, and I think I'll retire early." Lifting her face, she leveled empty eyes on the stubborn mule of a man sitting in front of her door. "Just make sure Cheyenne's taken care of. I don't care about anything else."

~FOUR~

The rusted hinges moaned their protests when a man's fist hit the front door three hard times. Curling my lip in a groan, I rolled on my belly and covered my head with the pillow. I had just crawled in bed an hour ago, and I was in no mood to deal with Jet and his nonsense. If he wanted to talk to me, he would just have to barge in. He did. The door squealed loudly when he pushed it open, and his boots thumped a rhythmic pattern on the old, wooden floor until he appeared in the doorway of my bedroom. I pretended to be in a deep sleep, wishing he would turn on his heel and march back outside.

"Rise and shine, Cheyenne. School starts in forty-five minutes, and you're gonna be standing by the front steps by the time they ring that bell. C'mon, get them feet on the floor and get a move on."

I growled my protest and inched deeper under the thin quilt covering my body.

Jet grabbed a corner of the blanket and tore it from my fists. "C'mon, you best get up."

"Go away," I snarled, pushing the pillow harder over my head. "I got home a few minutes ago. Let me sleep!"

Jet grabbed the pillow and jerked it out of my grasp as he tossed it to the floor. I rolled on my back to give him a harsh glare, but he was already giving me a warning look of his own.

"Yesterday you tore up a thirty-dollar saddle. We made a deal that you would do as I say to earn the money until you can pay back the damages. Part of the deal was that you would go to school. It ain't too late, I could send you to jail, and that way you won't owe me a dime."

"I hate school."

Jet sighed as he grabbed my arm to pull me into a sitting position. "I don't care. You're gonna do as I say, and you best keep in mind what I told you about misbehaving in school. I'll dock your pay by five cents for every disruption. And don't think I won't find out. I'll ask Mr. Hyndman myself." He wrinkled his nose and raised an eyebrow. "When was the last time you took a bath?"

I wrenched my arm out of his hand and curled my lip. "I don't care much for baths."

"Well, after work tonight, you should take one. Now get ready. School will start before you know it."

"I walked through that front door less than an hour ago, I'll bet," I snarled as I sank back down on the mattress. "I ain't goin' to no school, I can tell you that."

"What were you doing last night?" Jet asked as he folded his arms over his broad chest.

I scoffed as I plopped my head on the goose feathers. "I ain't tellin' you."

Jet raised an eyebrow. "Well, you're going to tell me, unless you really want to start the day on my bad side."

My eyes widened at his threat. After dealing with my uncle's persistence the day before, I knew that he wouldn't fail to punish me if I ignored him. Crossing my arms over my chest, I curled my lip and snorted.

"I hate you, and nothing's gonna change that, but I'll humor you." I rolled my eyes and shimmied deeper onto the mattress. "Chad and I had a little dare, that's all. It went longer than I thought, but I didn't think it'd be any big deal. I figured I could make you understand my point of view, and I wouldn't have to go to school. It's Thursday. It'd make more sense if I started on a Monday."

"What was the dare?"

"What?"

Jet shifted his weight to his right leg and cocked his head to the side. "You heard me. And you best answer me."

53

I pushed myself off the mattress and walked around him to the dresser where a hairbrush sat covered in dust. I flicked the bigger dust balls off and began to brush the tangles out of my hair. Jet watched me for a few seconds, then grabbed my wrist to keep me from finishing the job and forced me to face him.

"I asked you a question, Cheyenne."

"Yeah, I know, but it's a free country. I don't gotta answer you. I bet you did some dares when you were my age that you didn't tell your pa about."

"I did, but my pa would beat my backside with a switch whenever I was out all night. I asked you what kind of dare you were doing, and I want an answer now. Then you're gonna get to school before you're late."

"I ain't even had breakfast!"

"You'll get some after you answer my question."

I attempted to twist my wrist from his grasp, but his hold was unrelenting. "I don't want to tell you a single thing!"

"Fine, then I'll discipline you as I see fit."

"If you lay one hand on me, I'll—"

"Cheyenne!" he interrupted with his voice sharp. "Your arguing is wasting time. They are gonna ring that bell in thirty minutes, and you've got some explaining to do. It would be wise for you to tell me the truth. Do I make myself clear?"

"Let go of me!" I shouted, wrestling for my arm.

Jet resisted my attempts to break free as he spoke in an authoritative voice. "I really don't want to correct you this early in the morning. I need an answer, and you will be punished if you brush me off one more time."

I studied his gaze, then stopped fighting against him. "Fine! I'll tell you, but you ain't gonna like it. And neither will I, 'cause I know you are gonna force me to do something I really don't wanna do!"

"We'll have to see about that. I haven't heard anything yet."

I cleared my throat and lowered my head as well as my voice. "Al dared Chad and me to do something to Levi Hendershot, the kid who works at the livery. We had to wait until he was asleep, and it was after midnight before we did anything."

Jet's grip around my wrist tightened. "What did you do?"

"Do I gotta tell you?" I complained. "I done said where we were, who I was with, who dealt the dare, and who was the victim. Why do I gotta say anything more?"

"If it embarrasses you, then maybe you shouldn't have done it. But I need to know. I'm responsible for you, and if you did something horrible, I have to pay the damages."

Grumbling my discontent, I sighed and stared at my shuffling feet. "Nobody likes Levi. He ain't much older than us, and he's always worried about doing his job right. Well, Al especially don't like him. Levi caught him trying to steal a bridle and got onto him. But Al's pa warned him not to mess with Levi, so he couldn't get his revenge." I glanced up at Jet, then bit my lip and hung my head. "It was one or two in the morning when Chad and I made it to the livery. All the lights were off, and the town was dead asleep. We dug a hole under the door and slipped inside."

I bit my tongue and refused to look at my uncle as I waited for his response. Jet remained silent as he expected me to continue, but when I remained silent, he let go of my wrist and marched out of the door. I watched him until he vanished out my bedroom but felt the urge to follow him. Worried about what he would see and what he might do, I ran after him in hopes of persuading him to find something else to occupy his mind.

The town was already bustling with activity, but it only took a few seconds to spot Jet marching toward the livery in long strides. Jumping off the porch, I caught up to him in no time and grabbed his wrist in hopes he would stop.

"Jet, you don't want to go in there!"

He didn't slow his pace. "You wouldn't tell me, so I figured I'd find out for myself."

"We trashed the place," I rushed, hoping that would stop him. "We busted the hay bales and scattered them on the floor and busted all the windows in the tack room. I tore holes in the wooden floor of the loft with the pitchfork. But I won a whole dollar for doing it!"

Jet slid to a sudden halt, but I kept going until I tripped when his arm stopped moving. "You did *what?*"

I bit the inside of my lip as I stared into his gaze. I suddenly found it necessary to run.

Spinning on my heel, I jumped to a start, but his arms were like lightning as he caught me. "You're not going anywhere, Cheyenne," he muttered sternly.

"But… you said I had to be on time for school," I argued pathetically.

He raised an eyebrow but didn't reply as he dragged me into the livery. Levi and an older man stood in the middle of the stables with their backs to the door, but they both turned when we entered. Levi recognized us and glanced at his employer.

"I apologize for the mess," the old man said as he stepped over a clump of hay. "I'm not sure what happened last night."

"I could've sworn I locked the doors when I left, but someone came in," Levi added, rubbing his hands on his jeans. He appeared nervous.

I attempted to duck behind Jet, but he pulled me out in the open. Jet cast a stern look my way, then turned to the two men in front of us. "I'm the one who should be apologizing, Mr. Shepherd. My niece told me she and her friend are responsible for this. I don't know all the details, but I know enough to figure out I owe you both an apology and perhaps for damages."

Mr. Shepherd looked my way and shifted a ball of chewing tobacco into his left cheek. "I shoulda known it was that child." He turned to my uncle and hooked both thumbs in his pockets. "You're new to this town, and I'm not sure you know exactly what you're dealing with. That child you have captured in your fist has got the reputation of a snake in this town. She's always gettin' into somethin' she shouldn't. You can't say 'Cheyenne' without saying 'trouble' in the same sentence. You've bit off more than you can chew if you think you can help that wayward mind."

Jet stiffened. "Cheyenne is my niece, and I will discipline her as I see fit. How much do I owe you?"

Mr. Shepherd turned his head to send a stream of tobacco flying. "You don't owe me. She does, and her little carrot topped friend. That boy has got the sense of a mule, hangin' out with such riffraff like that curly headed snot in your hand."

56

"Sir, I'm responsible for Cheyenne *and* her mischief from now on. How much do I owe you?" Jet insisted.

Mr. Shepherd gnawed on his chaw, then wiped the corner of his mouth and shrugged. "Alright. Them windows cost a pretty penny, and they tore up three of my square bales. There's at least thirteen new floorboards to replace the torn ones." The older gent mulled his chaw to the other cheek as he cocked his head. "You speakin' for the boy, too?"

"He's not my responsibility," Jet replied in a calm voice.

"Alright. Alright," Mr. Shepherd said as he ran his hand over his mouth. "Then you'll pay half the damages. I'll go talk to the boy's pa when I find 'im." He told Jet an amount and sent another stream flying.

Jet let go of my wrist as he reached in his back pocket for his wallet. Counting out the bills, he slapped the estimated sum in Mr. Shepherd's wrinkled palm. The livery owner's eyes landed on me, and he snorted a humorless laugh.

"Nobody can tame that beast. She ain't fit for buzzard bait."

No word was spoken as the middle-aged man ambled back into his office, mumbling under his breath about kids these days. I watched his retreating back until he disappeared in an office, then slowly lifted my eyes to meet my uncle's gaze. I swallowed hard and found it extremely important to relocate in a hurry. Jet must have read my thoughts since his hand snaked out to capture my upper arm.

"Don't you have something to say to Mr. Hendershot?" Jet persisted. His voice was edged with a sternness I had come to abhor.

I curled my lip in disgust and growled, "I ain't gonna apologize. I've already stooped too low, and I ain't gonna fall in deeper."

"Cheyenne!"

"It's okay, Mr. Douglas," Levi interrupted. "She's a little hot tempered, that's all."

Jet turned to the young man and wagged his head back and forth. "It ain't okay, son. She could've gotten you in trouble and wouldn't have cared. Your boss might think otherwise, but I am going to tame my niece."

A growl rumbled deep in my throat as anger warmed my veins. "I am not some dog somebody cast aside, Douglas," I snarled. "I ain't gonna let you or Ryleigh or anybody else change me into some creature I ain't! You let go of me! I ain't gonna listen to a word you say or do a thing you tell me to do! I'm gonna remain the same as I've always been, and you can't stop me! Let me go!"

"Cheyenne—"

"I don't wanna hear it!" I shouted. Drawing my leg back, I smashed the toe of my boot into Jet's shin bone and was satisfied when I heard him groan. Twisting out of his grasp, I spun on my heel and ran for the door, glad to leave him behind me.

I dodged wagons and judgmental women as I raced down the street at a high rate of speed. I had almost made it to the Bull's Head when Jet wrapped an arm around my middle. Lifting me off the ground, he carried me behind the saloon and took hold of both my arms to keep me from running away. I glared into his eyes when I turned to face him, and there was nothing I wanted more than to hurt him.

"I said I don't wanna hear it," I uttered through clenched teeth. "I don't wanna see your ugly face again!"

"Cheyenne Loraine, that's enough!"

My jaw dropped when I heard my middle name. I hadn't known Jet knew my full name, and the knowledge that he did infuriated me more.

Jet seemed to ignore my shock as he leveled piercing eyes on me. "I have had enough of your harsh tongue this morning. You're not going to say another vile thing again, do you understand?"

I narrowed my eyes threateningly. "I don't gotta listen to you, you snake! And go ahead! Do what you been threatening all morning long. Hit me, punish me. Make me wish I had listened to you in the first place! What's gonna stop you? I already hate you, so what's another outlandish deed gonna do? Go ahead! Bend me over your knee, I dare you!"

Jet waited until I was done ranting before he spoke again. "Cheyenne, I am not going to hit you. I don't want you to hate me, but you're already determined to do that. I'm gonna—"

"Don't you say another word," I interrupted, my teeth clenched tight against each other.

Jet studied me for a few seconds, then continued. "You seem to enjoy getting in trouble too often, young lady. I won't stand for that. You need to do as I say, and it'd be a lot easier on the both of us if you stop trying to run away or insult me. You can't run from everything in life, and insults can get you into more trouble than you want to be."

"Let go of me," I growled. "I ain't no child! And besides, I ain't some creature you gotta tame. You *won't* tame me, as you put it back in the livery stable."

Jet's expression softened, as did his grip. "So, that's it. I insulted you, didn't I? Cheyenne, I'm sorry. I didn't intend to hurt you."

"Yeah, right," I muttered under my breath. "I don't believe you!"

Before he could say another ridiculous thing, I tore from his grasp and jumped through the back door of the Bull's Head. "Cheyenne!" he called, but I didn't listen to him.

Barging into the main room, I darted past Clyde Overhaul and found my sister standing by a table in the corner with her head hanging low as she picked up empty glasses. Ignoring the fat saloon owner as he groped for me, I took hold of Ryleigh's arm and turned her away from the table.

"Cheyenne, what's wrong?" she asked, concern filling her eyes when she saw me.

"You gotta come home," I demanded. "I can't deal with Jet. Tell him to leave, he'll listen to you. Please, Ryleigh, tell him to leave us alone!"

Clyde wrapped an arm around my middle to pull me away from her. "You can't be in here," he growled in my ear. "The next time I see you in here, I'm gonna get the sheriff to lock you in jail!"

I slammed my elbow in his gut and wrestled out of his grasp. The hinges on the double doors squeaked, and I turned to see Jet stride in to scan the empty room for me. I grabbed Ryleigh's hand and dragged her toward our uncle.

"Tell him!" I demanded. "Tell him to leave us alone! We don't need him. Tell him!"

Jet glanced at my sister, who was hanging her head. I looked at her, waiting for her to tell Jet what we both thought, but she remained quiet. I frowned and glanced at Jet, then back at her. "Go on, Ryleigh. What are you waiting for?"

Ryleigh took a ragged breath and lifted her head high enough to make eye contact with me. "I can't."

My frown deepened. "What do you mean, you can't?"

"I have my job, Cheyenne. I can't look after you when I have this job."

"That's okay, Ryleigh. You come home in the mornings, and I'll help you all I can. I promise, I could even help you darn socks. Just tell Jet to leave."

She shook her head and looked away as a hint of tears shimmered in her eyes. "I won't be coming home, Cheyenne. I'm working double shifts now. I can't take care of you."

Her news hit me like a hard rock. I let go of her hand and took a step back. "Then I'll find work and take care of myself! You were taking care of yourself at my age, I can do the same!"

"No!"

I stared at Ryleigh in shock. In all our days, she had never yelled at me, and the fact that she did now hurt more than if she had hit me.

Ryleigh shook her head slowly and refused to look at me. "I won't allow you to follow in my footsteps. I can't see you anymore, Cheyenne, and I demand that you listen to Mr. Douglas. You need his help."

"But Ryleigh—"

"Just do as I say, Cheyenne!" she shouted again, drowning out any of my complaints. "Don't argue. Just leave. And don't come back."

I gaped at her as my mind raced for a reason to protest. A reason that would persuade Ryleigh into coming home, and to apologize and say she needed me. A reason that would mend the relationship that had so abruptly been broken, but nothing entered my head. Biting my lip to keep it from quivering, I whirled on my heel and brushed past Jet as I disappeared outside. Ignoring the townspeople around me, I ran down the street to the isolated path that led to the creek. My vision blurred with tears that formed against my will, and I forced my legs to pump faster.

"Cheyenne, please stop!" Jet called from a few feet behind me.

Uttering a soft groan, I forced my legs to slow to a stop and turned to face him. "Can't you leave me well enough alone?" I cried in a strained voice.

"I wanted to talk to you," he responded, slowing his pace as he closed the distance between us.

I turned back to the path and folded my arms over my chest. "That's all you ever do. Can't you see I wanna be alone?"

"Ryleigh didn't mean what she said," he replied, coming to a stop a few feet behind me. "She told all of that to me last night, but I don't think she means it."

"She means it," I argued, sniffling as I cleared my throat of tears. "She never lies to me. But it don't matter. I've never needed her to begin with! She had a steady job for three years by the time she was my age. I don't need her. I can take care of my own self!"

Jet cleared his throat. "Cheyenne, you don't mean that."

"I don't care about her anymore," I argued, scuffing the ground with my toe. "I just don't care."

"Don't lie to yourself, or to me. Cheyenne, please look at me."

I rolled my eyes and swiveled on my hips so I could look in his gaze. Jet wet his lips with the tip of his tongue and hid his hands inside his pockets. "I know you're upset. I was too, but you can't just keep running when you're faced with something you don't like."

"No, you don't understand," I snarled. "You've made matters worse by coming here, and I hate you for it. You won't leave me alone, and you persuade Ryleigh into working twice as much so she can run from me. It's all your fault that she abandoned me. You made her feel worthless! She thinks you can do a better job than she can, but what she don't know is that I don't need you!"

"Cheyenne..."

I lifted my hands as a sign for him to remain quiet. "I don't want to hear you try to explain your reasoning. You've tried, and I still hate you for showing up. Ryleigh can't take care of me anymore, and I will never rely on you. I have a job, and unfortunately, it's been offered by you. I guess I owe you a saddle, and after I pay off that debt, I'll find work to provide for myself. I'll do what you say." I aimed a finger at his chest. "But I will *not* go to school. And no matter what you say, I determine what I do."

Jet exhaled slowly as he studied me. "Fine. That's a start for today. Well, then you best run to your house and get ready. I'll get some lumber at the mercantile and we can get started."

I wiped my nose with the back of my hand and swallowed hard as I looked away. "Don't think that you've won. You haven't. I'm just doing one last favor for Ryleigh."

Jet shrugged and turned to walk back to town. "Whatever you say. You best get a move on so we can get started."

I aimed my tongue between his shoulder blades, then stiffened my spine and followed him back to town at a distance. I was more than willing to take my time, hoping no other person would associate him with me. Once my feet planted themselves on the boardwalk again, I let Jet see where I was going and headed toward the house. The trip took longer than usual since I went around the Bull's Head to avoid any confrontation with Ryleigh. She didn't want me, and I most definitely didn't want her. Bounding up our rickety stairs, I entered the dinky living room and skirted around the mouse droppings and piles of dust until I appeared in my bedroom doorway.

Almost instantly when I entered the room my eyes found the old frame that surrounded the only picture I had of Ryleigh when we were both such little girls. Tears stung my eyes as I reminisced to a happier relationship with my sister, and her words of abandonment cut deeper wounds into my heart. Letting out a cry of desolation, I ran to my bed, snatched the photograph off the nightstand, and flung it across the room. The picture collided with the opposite wall, and the glass in the frame shattered. It fell to the floor in a heap, and I noticed a brand-new scratch under Ryleigh's chin.

Finally giving in to the tears that had long since threatened to spill over, I collapsed onto the goose feather mattress and buried my head in the greasy pillow. What I never wanted Jet to know was just how easily I was hurt. I had thought I couldn't be hurt again, not after Mama died and Pa left. I thought the tenderness of childhood had left me forever, but then Ryleigh had to reject me. Reject me in front of her fat boss and reject me in front of the man I deeply loathed. But what hurt most of all was to say she wouldn't be around to see me or hear me again. She wouldn't be around to listen to my stories, even if they were not always honest. She wouldn't be around to encourage me. She wouldn't be around to tell me that she loved me.

I balled a fist and buried it deep within the mattress. Why did she have to go and bury herself in the saloon? She didn't belong in that prison, and it bothered me too much to see her waste her life behind those invisible bars. To let unwanted hands touch her in places she shouldn't be touched, and to let her mind lose its senses with the drink of alcohol. To lose all sense of pride and respect by wearing something barely more than her under things. The thought of her never leaving that place tied a knot in my stomach as bile gathered in my throat.

"Why?" I shouted into the empty room, tears choking out my voice. "Why, Ryleigh? *Why?*"

No answer soothed the ache in my soul. No gentle words or pat of reassurance. Nothing but the still quiet air of a Thursday morning as birds chirped merrily to greet the happy people below. If a lightning bolt appeared and struck everything down, I wouldn't be gloomier.

The rusty hinges of the front door squealed an intruder, and I bolted from the mattress in hopes of hiding my sorrow from Jet.

"They'll have to cut the lumber, and it should be ready by tomorrow," Jet said as he made his way through the living room. "In the meantime, I figured we could start stripping the porch down to the support beams and see where to go from there."

He stopped in the doorway of my bedroom, and I brushed past him with my head hanging low. "I've been waiting for you," I growled. "Daylight's burning, don't you reckon?"

Jet watched me as I marched toward the door, and when he didn't answer, I spun around to glare at him. "Well? What are you waiting for?"

He shrugged and closed the distance between us. "Nothing, I guess. Have you ever done work like this before?"

I returned the shrug as I pulled the door open and stepped on the porch. "Not the proper way."

Jet chuckled and handed me a hammer. "Then let's get started."

I glanced at him, then took the tool without a word.

We crouched on our hands and knees, pulling out rusted nails and throwing the rotten boards over the broken-down railing to be hauled off later. The sun climbed higher and higher in the sky, and the temperature rose so that sweat dripped off my nose and plinked on the gray wood under my hands. For the first thirty minutes or so, not a word was spoken, and then Jet had to break the wonderful peace and quiet.

"Work is much more pleasurable when you make conversation," he pointed out pleasantly. "You ain't said two words since we started this."

"I don't like to talk."

Jet chuckled merrily at that. "For the past two days all you've ever done is chew my ear off about how much you hate me and want me to leave. I don't reckon I believe you."

I gave him a sideways glare and pulled a nail a little too vigorously.

"Well, if you ain't gonna talk," Jet continued, "I will. I used to be just as ornery as you when I was your age, believe it or not. I did lots of things I probably shouldn't have, and I guarantee I caused my pa a lot of headache." He chuckled to himself as he threw a board over the railing. "I reckon I'm getting my payback with you. Ain't felt so frustrated at one person this much in a long time."

I glared at him and was tempted to throw a handful of nails his direction. "I don't wanna hear 'bout your dumb stories."

He shrugged and continued his work. "Just thought I'd make conversation."

I sat back on my knees and studied him as he freed another piece of wood. He kept silent as he

continued his work, and the longer I watched him, the higher a question in the form of a knot rose in

my throat. Shaking my head, I wet my lips with the tip of my tongue as I turned a frustrated glare toward the sky.

"What are you doing?" I snapped at last.

Jet raised his eyebrows as he swiveled on his hips to look at me. "Tearing down a porch."

"That's not what I mean, and you know it," I snarled back, turning my gaze to the board between my knees. "What are you doing here?"

He pulled another nail and placed the rusted piece of metal in the palm of his hand. "You should know the answer by now. I've told you the same thing for the last two days. I came to help you and your sister."

"Yeah, but why? You said you made a promise to Pa, but why?"

Jet blew air between his lips as he set his hammer aside and turned to face me. "It's hard to explain, Cheyenne. I'm not sure I fully understand why, and I know I can't explain it to you. If I tried, you would just get more confused."

I twirled the hammer in my hand as my jaw muscles began to work. "I don't trust your intentions, Jet. You won't tell me why you're here, and I hate you. You swore a promise to a..." My voice faded as my lip quivered against my will. "To a man who abandoned his family and refused to come home no matter what. A man who was worse than scum, and who never came to the funeral of the only woman who could stand him." A tear tumbled down my cheek, and I brushed it away roughly with the heel of my palm. "A man who let himself die before he could say goodbye to the rest of his pathetic family."

I glanced at Jet, who stared at me from under the brim of his hat. Clenching my jaw as tight as I could, I threw the hammer aside and struggled to my feet to run.

"Cheyenne," Jet commanded as he stood to chase me.

I turned to race down the street, but Jet grabbed my arm to stop me. "Go ahead," I spoke before he had a chance. "Scold me on how I acted wrong. Tell me I said the wrong things. Make me eat soap like you did the other day. You think I'm spoiled and crazy and wild."

"I think you deal with more than you're willing to show. The death of your father bothers you more than I thought."

I gripped my elbows when he let go of my arm and bit my lip in a poor attempt to hide the tears. "That man you call your brother means as much to me as the dirt I walk on. I've hated his guts for years, and I'm… I'm glad he's dead. Don't ever mention his name again, Jet. Every time you do I want to vomit."

Jet laid a hand on my shoulder as he urged me to turn around. I ran my gaze up to meet his, then bowed my head as more tears began to fall. "Cheyenne."

I shook my head and backed away as far as he would let me. "Don't. Just don't."

"Look at me," he muttered as he hooked a finger under my chin. I gradually obeyed, though I wanted to hide the salty drops of water from his sight. "Why do you always run? Please don't run from me. I want to help you."

"I run because I don't like being confused," I told him bluntly. "I don't want you to see me in my weakest moments." I ducked my head again. "Pa didn't give a penny for us, so I don't care for him. If he wanted to die, that was his business. I'm glad he ain't around to see us. Let me go, Jet. Please."

Jet let out a soft sigh as he backed away. "I don't want you to try to hide. You can talk if you want to, or cry, I wouldn't care which you do."

I stiffened my backbone and lifted my head high. "I ain't gonna talk, and I ain't gonna cry. Mama's dead, Pa's dead, Ryleigh hates me, and you ain't gonna leave me alone." I bent to pick up the hammer and turned my back to him. "I'm gonna work as hard as I can and pretend you ain't around. Maybe these next few weeks won't be as slow as I fear."

* * *

The sun disappeared into its bed on the horizon as the sliver of a half-moon rose from its sheets. Most of the town had closed shop and gone home to enjoy a relaxing evening with their families. Jet had put away our tools and invited me to join him in the diner nearly half an hour ago, but I sat perched on the porch railing instead. The usual hubbub of the townspeople as they hustled to finish their errands had stilled to a gentle lull except for the drunken hollers and horrid singing that bellowed from the Bull's Head. Though the saloon was a ways away, I imagined my sister as she flirted, waited on the sleazy men, and endured inappropriate touches, unwanted kisses, and painful arms that would hold her during the night.

Her words cut through my mind for the umpteenth time that day, and I curled into a tight ball on the porch railing as I bowed my head and let a few tears drip onto my sleeve. All my childhood dreams of having Ryleigh come home to stay came crashing down around me, and all I could think about was that I was lost in a giant world. In the near distance, a coyote howled its lonely song, and I knew how the mangy critter felt. After several minutes of staring at the material of my sleeve, I slammed a fist into my thigh and let out a low growl.

"Enough!" I snarled to myself, wiping the last of the tears from my face. "You've cried enough, you street rat! You need to find something more productive to do."

I raised my head from my arm and turned a glare down the street where the saloon stood. The temptation to bust all the windows and set the place on fire rose high in my chest, but with a grunt of dissatisfaction, I slid from the rail and scuffed the dirt with the toe of my boot. Anger burned through the lining in my blood vessels, and for once in my life I couldn't find a way to release it. Though I ached with the desire to destroy the Bull's Head, I couldn't stand the thought of accidentally harming Ryleigh in the process. There was no one to argue with, nothing to break, too many listening ears to yell, and too many invisible eyes to melt in tears. I felt completely alone for the first time in my life.

An instant longing to find my uncle entered my mind, but I pushed the thought aside as I scanned the porch. There was absolutely nothing that ignorant man could do to calm the confusion I felt hovering over my head like an anvil. He could do nothing but make matters worse. The idea of going to him disturbed me almost as much as Ryleigh falling deeper into the snare at the Bull's Head. I picked up a nail from a small metal tin and played with the flat head as I attempted to ignore the discomforting emotions bombarding my chest.

The porch had been stripped down to the support beams that afternoon, but my mind was too full of thoughts to let my sore muscles relax from the physical labor done that day. Groaning my discomfort, my eyes landed on a piece of board piled in the corner of our property. Without a second thought, I picked up the chunk of wood and began to dig into the wood grains with the sharp tip of the nail.

"Here's what I think of you, Overhaul," I growled under my breath as I pushed the tip of the nail into the wood as hard as I could. "And this is for you, Pa," I continued, creating another scratch. I began to mutter all the reasons for my anger as I pressed harder and harder on the nail.

I scarred the wood until my thumb slipped and was pierced by the nail. My vision blurred again, but I quickly swallowed the lump in my throat when I noticed a dark shadow stretch across the land that had turned silver-blue in the moonlight. Glancing over my shoulder, I saw a familiar form of a man as he blocked the light coming from the saloon. I lowered my gaze to my thumb and pulled out the nail without making a sound. I watched as blood oozed around the cuticles of my thumb and down my finger toward my wrist.

"What are you doing here?" I asked with a small shudder in my voice.

Jet ran a hand over his mouth and sighed. "I got nervous when you never showed up for supper. Thought you might have tried something foolish."

I continued to watch the blood and didn't answer.

Jet closed the distance between us and reached for my hand. "You're hurt."

"No kidding," I snarled as I watched him take my fist in his hand.

"No, this ain't what I mean. You've been hurt all day. That's why you haven't fought me or argued about work. I don't like that you're upset, and I wish you could trust me."

I shook my head and wiped the tip of my nose with the cuff of my sleeve. "That's where you're wrong. If I wasn't working, I'd be going to school, and I didn't want to sit on a bench all day. I ain't hurt at all, except I set about stabbing my thumb. There's nothing to get excited about."

Jet grabbed a bandanna from his back pocket and wiped the red liquid off my skin. "Well, maybe, but you've worked hard today and need to get some sort of fuel in that belly. I've seen how much you eat, and I ain't about to have a stick for a niece."

I glared mildly at his silhouette and huffed. "I'm not a stick, and I'm not your niece. I hate the thought of being kin to you. And I can't eat even if I tried. I don't feel I could hold it down," I finished, leveling my eyes toward the Bull's Head.

Jet followed my gaze and sighed almost inaudibly. Turning back to me, he tore a piece from the bandanna and wrapped it around my thumb. "But you're still gonna get fed. You didn't get breakfast, and you barely ate a thing at noon. Being my employee, I feel responsible for you to be healthy and in good working condition. If you won't eat for me, do it for your job."

I heard a woman shout a laugh from the saloon and cringed as bile rose in the back of my throat. "There are no guarantees that I'll be able to swallow, but I'll go with you," I added with a snarl.

Jet rose to his feet and extended a hand to help me up. I ignored his gesture of support and pushed myself to my feet. Keeping a five-foot distance between us, we walked side by side to the diner where an orange light still glowed. Jet held the door open for me, and I stepped through the threshold without an argument. Claws of a tiger teared at the lining of my belly when I walked into the warm atmosphere. The aroma of grease, bread, and dessert entangled itself in my nostrils, which created a pain in my stomach I hadn't realized was there.

Jet skirted around me and headed toward a table in the middle of the room. Holding a hand over my midriff, I followed my uncle and cautiously sat in a chair opposite him. I remembered the first time Jet had taken me into this diner, and I felt a new surge of anger burn in my chest. Ignoring the hunger that crept up my throat, I leveled two fiery eyes on my uncle and folded my arms over my chest.

"I hope you understand that I ain't hungry," I snarled quietly. "I'm just gonna sit with you and that's it."

Jet didn't seem to hear my protests as he crossed an ankle over his knee and reclined in his chair. The same flour coated young waitress scampered to our table as she wiped her hands on her apron.

"Good evening," she greeted, ignoring me as she addressed my uncle. "What can I get you?"

"A cup of coffee for me to start off with," Jet answered, leveling kind eyes my direction. "What about you?"

I lowered my head as I stared at the bandanna that had formed a small blood stain where the cut had been. "I'll have the same," I mumbled, deciding that a cup of coffee sounded good.

She nodded, flashed Jet a friendly smile, and trotted back to the kitchen. I could feel Jet's eyes on me, but I refused to look at him as I began to toy with an end of the bandanna. A few minutes later, the waitress set two steaming cups in front of us and asked if we were ready to order. I glanced up at her and noticed she was purposely overlooking me. I couldn't help but smile softly to myself.

Jet rattled off what he thought sounded good, then turned to me as if waiting for me to order. I looked at him from under my eyebrows and shook my head. "Coffee's all I want," I drawled when he didn't seem to take a hint.

The waitress turned to leave, but Jet cleared his throat to stop her. "Just get her a warm ham and cheese," he said quickly.

She nodded, scowled at me, and disappeared into the kitchen again.

Jet let out a sigh and studied at me with those disturbing eyes of his. "You've got to be hungry after all that work you did today."

I knit my brows together as the corners of my mouth drooped downward. "I told you I wasn't. You made her create a sandwich for no good reason, Jet."

He shrugged. "Okay, so maybe you ain't hungry. At least answer one question. How much have you eaten in the last two days since I've been here?"

I stared at him expressionlessly, then shrugged.

"Cheyenne, use your words, not your shoulders."

My lip curled at his ridicule, and I slumped lower in my chair. "I don't know. I honestly can't remember taking time to eat. I was too busy dodging you and your foolishness to even give food a second thought. But it don't matter how much I've eaten in two days. I ain't hungry now, and I ain't gonna eat that sandwich you ordered."

"It *doesn't* matter," he corrected. "And I'm not about to let you starve yourself. Either you eat that sandwich, or I'll conjure up some concoction to spoon down your throat that a Crow woman taught me to make. Her soup has just enough nutrients to put meat back on your bones, but the taste isn't as good as a ham and cheese sandwich."

My lip rose higher as I shook my head defiantly. "Save your breath, old man. I couldn't possibly eat tonight, and I ain't gonna."

He nodded to the mug of coffee in front of me. "If you were sick, you wouldn't be drinking a cup of coffee."

"I never said I was sick," I argued, my voice rising slightly. "I just said I couldn't hold food. I was thirsty, that's why I got coffee." I narrowed my eyes to slits and slouched in the chair. "And don't you dare argue with me. I'm tired of hearing your worthless words that are full of so much manure it stinks! Just shut up, drink your coffee, and eat your food, then leave me well enough alone!"

His eyes narrowed a little as his jaw tightened. "Cheyenne, you were my concern to begin with, and if you didn't think so before, you certainly are now that you are working for me. If you won't believe me when I say I'm concerned for your health, then consider that I want you to work your hardest and have the strength to do so."

"I think you'd rather see me dead than alive," I argued with my voice lower. "That's what most folks in this town wish would happen. You'd be free from your responsibility."

Jet cocked his head to the side as he leaned back suddenly in his chair. "Why must you turn every conversation I have with you into an argument?"

My eyes filled with a venom like that from a snake. "Why must you always have your way?"

He opened his mouth to respond, but thankfully the waitress came with two plates of food. I glanced at the sandwich in front of me and shoved the plate aside. "I'm not going to eat that," I snarled, leveling the same venomous eyes on her, "so you can just take it right back in that kitchen and feed it to the strays."

She narrowed her eyes as she leaned toward me. "I was right. You'll never change."

I leapt to my feet, but Jet's hand flew across the table and grabbed my shirt tail to keep me from lunging at the waitress. "Let me go," I snapped at my uncle.

"Sit down!" Jet ordered in a sharp voice.

Biting my bottom lip reluctantly, I watched her stalk away arrogantly, then turned to Jet. "Let go of my shirt! I ain't staying here, you can't make me!"

"Yes, you are. And yes, I can. Sit down before I lose my temper."

Folding my arms over my chest, I plopped sideways in my chair and stared at the wall. "I really hate you, and I hope you know that. I'd hate for you to misunderstand my feelings," I grumbled under my breath. "I wanna go home."

Jet leaned his forearms on the table as he let out a slow breath. "You are staying here until I finish my supper, and hopefully you'll have the manners enough to eat with me. Now sit in your chair properly before you break it."

I slowly turned my head until I met his frustrated gaze. Raising an eyebrow, I lifted my leg over the back of the chair and leaned on the table as I reclined comfortably. Jet stared at me with his unblinking blue eyes, then rose suddenly from the table as his shoulders settled into a threatening stance. He sent me a warning look that sent shivers down my spine, and my mind raced back to the other day when Jet had caught me sneaking out of the schoolhouse. Knowing that he wouldn't fail to punish me, I dropped my leg and quickly positioned myself to sit the right way in the wooden chair, but that didn't stop my uncle from striding around the table to take hold of my shoulder seam.

"Don't you dare touch me!" I shouted when he pulled me to my feet.

"I'm not gonna hurt you," he assured as he led me to his side of the table. "I'm just making you sit by me so I can keep a better eye on you."

He placed me in a chair much too close to my side for my liking, then lowered himself into his own seat. Uttering a soft sigh, he bowed his head and cleared his throat. "Lord, thank You for letting us survive another day, and thank You for the food You've provided. Bless it to our bodies. In Your Son's name I pray, amen." He raised his head and shoveled a forkful of mashed potatoes in his mouth.

I stared at him in disgust. "How dare you."

Jet glanced at me and swallowed the mouthful. "What now?"

My jaw tightened until it hurt, but I forced myself to speak. "How dare you pray to a god who don't care? You can pray to him all you want to, but how dare you do it in front of me. And how dare you pray for me! I gave up on that god a long time ago, how dare you use his name in my presence!"

Jet's eyes widened with surprise, then softened. "Cheyenne, I—"

"Don't you defend him, neither!" I snarled. "He abandoned my family a long time ago."

I jumped to my feet, but Jet grabbed my sleeve. "Cheyenne."

Shaking my head, I fought his grasp until the cuff tore. "I don't wanna hear what you have to say, Jet!"

The waitress poked her head out from the kitchen with an amused look on her face. Jet caught her gaze and stood. "Don't take our food away, we'll be right back," he told her as he attempted to usher me toward the door.

"I'm not going anywhere with you!" I shouted, tearing my cuff more.

"She ain't gonna change, mister. You're just wasting your time," the waitress called behind us.

Jet stiffened but didn't say a word as he wrapped an arm around my shoulders and guided me out of the front door. Stepping off the boardwalk, Jet knelt to look me in the eye, but I didn't give him the chance to speak.

"You're not going to change my mind about what I said! You might as well let go of me, jump on the next stage, and forget you ever saw us! Thanks to you Ryleigh is working double shifts, my life's miserable, and I've lost my freedom! I *hate* you bad, Jet!"

Jet wrapped his fingers around my arms gently and sighed. "I know you blame me, Cheyenne, and I realize I should've approached you two differently, but there's no turning back. I care a lot for you two girls, and I hope you can understand that I don't want to hurt you."

73

Curling my lip in disgust, I gathered a spit wad in my mouth and set it flying toward his knee. "That's what I think about your dumb apology. You can't just come waltzing in here expecting our lives to be flawless, and us willing to accept you. Your brother abandoned us before Mama drew her last breath, and even Mama abandoned us when she lost her will to live." I narrowed my eyes as my voice hardened to a cold, heartless tone. "And now you've convinced Ryleigh to abandon me. I hate you for what you've done."

Twisting out of his grasp, I ran down the street as fast as I could and blinked back sudden tears as I disappeared into a dark alley. I ran through the dark until I came to the livery, where I slipped under the door and climbed the ladder to the loft. Curling into a tight ball on a bale of hay, I covered my face when the tears began to fall. For several hours, I let myself dwell in my sorrows until at last sleep claimed my restless mind.

~FIVE~

"Wake up, miss," a voice called from the other side of the haze in my mind. "The sun's up, and Mr. Douglas has been looking for you."

I groaned a complaint and rolled on my back to find Levi Hendershot bending over me with a hand on my shoulder. I rubbed my eyes with the tips of my fingers and stretched. "What time is it?"

"A quarter 'til noon. You must've had a rough night, you're all covered in hay," he observed as he pulled a piece of straw from my hair.

I rubbed my eyes as I sat up. "It was fine enough. Did you say Jet was looking for me?"

Levi nodded as he knelt to my eye level. "Yes, ma'am. Told me several hours ago he didn't find you in your house and was afraid something happened to you. I told him I'd help him find you. He's awfully worried."

I scoffed to myself and shook my head. "It ain't that. He just wants me to get to work. He can wait."

Levi scratched his jaw and draped his hands on his knees. "Did you have a bad argument?"

I studied him out of the corner of my eye and didn't say a word for a long time. "No," I replied sharply. "We didn't have any type of argument. He should know where I stand, and I know where he stands. He knows he can't be in my life, but he refuses to leave. I wish he'd buy a ticket and jump on the next stage."

A chuckle rumbled softly in Levi's throat. "Sometimes it takes a while for people to take hints. Other times they understand them but know you

75

can do better than what you think you want."

I wrinkled my nose at his explanation as I rose to my feet. "I think I'm beginning to dislike your choice of sides, Hendershot."

Suddenly, the ground shifted underneath my feet, and I felt myself pitch backwards toward a pile of hay. Levi reached out a hand to catch me, but his attempt failed as I fell against the floorboards. I blinked my eyes rapidly, but my head didn't stop spinning.

"Kid?" Levi questioned as he rushed to my side. "Are you alright?"

I shoved his hands away and struggled to a sitting position, though my body felt diseased and weak. "I'm fine," I whispered as my hand gripped my belly, which suddenly burned with a pain that was unfamiliar to me. "I just… got up too soon."

Levi bit his lip as he studied my gaze. "You're looking awful pale. Are you sure you feel alright?"

My eyebrows knit together as if someone had laced a threaded needle through them and pulled tight. "I said I was fine," I growled, but it sounded more like a whimper. Shaking my head, I shoved him away and crawled toward the ladder, fighting the dizziness that numbed my mind.

For some reason, my legs refused to move, and I collapsed to the wooden floor of the loft. Stifling a moan, I rolled on my back in time to see worried wrinkles on Levi's brow before the blackness in the corners of my eyes claimed me.

* * *

Jet exited the sheriff's office, frustrated at the town's cooperation. Sheriff Hodgkinson hadn't even been in his office all that morning. His excuse was that he had a checker game in an upper room of the saloon. And when Jet had mentioned his niece was missing, the sheriff acted as though a grasshopper had just been crushed. He had let Jet know in the politest, most ridiculous way that he couldn't be chasing all the street rats all the time, especially a girl who already had a guardian. It took all Jet had not to belt the lazy man in the mouth, even though he wore a silver star on his chest.

"Mr. Douglas! Mr. Douglas!"

Jet turned his head to the left, where Levi was hurrying down the boardwalk with a familiar bundle of rags in his arms. Forgetting his frustration at the town's excuse for a sheriff, Jet's brow wrinkled with worry as he closed the distance between him and the loyal stable boy holding his ghastly pale niece.

"What happened? Where did you find her?" Jet rattled as he took Cheyenne's limp body into his own arms.

"She was asleep in Mr. Shepherd's loft," Levi explained, struggling to keep up with Jet as they marched around townsfolk toward the doctor's office. "She woke up in a foul mood, but she sort of crumpled when she tried to get up. I thought she might be really sick."

"It's alright, Levi," Jet assured. "I'm just glad you found her."

The young lad nodded solemnly but remained silent at his side.

Slowing to a stop in front of the doctor's office, Jet used his boot to force the door open and barged in without permission. A middle-aged man with thick red hair glanced up from his desk when the two men entered his office, and when his eyes flicked to the limp bundle in Jet's arms, he snatched the spectacles off his nose and stood.

"Bring her to the back," the doctor instructed as he led the way behind a black curtain.

Jet followed obediently, laying Cheyenne on the awaiting table in the center of the second room. Rolling up his sleeves, the doctor stuck the two buds of the stethoscope in his ears and listened to her heartbeat and breath. Jet watched protectively as the doctor examined his niece, and after a few long minutes, the doctor straightened his back and let out a gentle sigh.

"She's fine," he told Jet, his light green eyes piercingly searing Jet's gaze. "That is, if she gets some soft food in her belly. She's half starved, man. Her body collapsed because it didn't have the energy to function."

Jet exhaled loudly, snatched his hat off his head, and ran his fingers through his curly hair. "I'm a fool," he muttered as he stared into Cheyenne's pale face. "I can fix her some broth and spoon it to her," he assured the doctor absentmindedly.

"I've heard about you," the doctor said as he leaned his shoulder against the wall. "They say you're determined to tame this one and her sister."

Jet leveled his eyes on the stringy doctor, suspicion creeping into his expression. "That's right."

The doctor shook his head as he glanced at the sick girl beside him. "You either have to be determined or stupid. Nobody's lent a helping hand toward these two for as long as I've been a doctor in this town." He raised his eyes on Jet again. "I helped bury their mother."

"That's what I don't understand about this town," Jet snapped. "Couldn't they see that Ryleigh and Cheyenne were just children? They weren't some sort of creature you find scrounging in the garbage. This town is willing to help a neighbor during a bad time, but when it comes to two innocent girls, they shuck their hands of them."

"I wasn't arguing with you," the doctor replied softly. "I respect you for stepping up to guide them. It may not look like it, but there are a few people in this town that have a heart toward the widows and orphans."

"Then why didn't they help them?"

The doctor sighed and lifted a shoulder in a shrug as he shook his head. "Ryleigh was a proud young lady when her mother passed on. She refused to accept charity, and she scrimped for some time on the meager portions they had left. A few months passed by, and over time their already worn clothes turned to rags, and the healthy glow in their cheeks turned gray. They only ate the necessities to live, that was all they could afford. People tried to help Ryleigh, but she loathed their sympathy. Every cent that was given to her was put into the church offering, and every piece of clothing was given away. She would've tossed the food given to her to the dogs if Cheyenne wasn't near to starving. Shortly Clyde Overhaul made a move toward her and said he was looking for young women who were willing to work. Ryleigh didn't like the idea of working in a saloon, but I suppose her options were slim, so she accepted. The rest is history."

Jet let his eyes wander back to his youngest niece. "What about Cheyenne? Why did she turn so vile?"

"She was a child without parental supervision," the doctor answered. "If she wanted to skip school she would, and if she wanted a piece of candy, she just took it. Because she didn't have a steady woman figure in her life, she turned tomboy and was inseparable from the other ornery boys. The older she became, the more hateful she grew. I can't explain it more than that."

Jet's shoulders slumped with weariness. "I think I've bitten off more than I can chew."

"Maybe, but I've always admired a man who insisted on doing what's right." The doctor raised his brows in contemplation. "Maybe you'll have better luck with those girls than the rest of us did."

"Maybe." *Yet you let her starve herself while in your care*, he thought to himself. Shaking his head, he extended his hand toward the doctor. "Thanks, doc. I'll be back later to pay you what I owe."

The doctor accepted the proffered hand with a firm grip. "Let's just say seeing those girls in better hands is payment enough. And the name's Amos Harding."

Jet nodded his appreciation, then gathered Cheyenne in his arms. Staring into her pale face, which accentuated the purple coloring on her eyelids that declared her fatigue, his protective instincts grew more intense. The muscle in his jaw twitched as he felt a determination to show his nieces that they were not alone.

* * *

Something warm landed on my tongue, and I instinctively swallowed the liquid, enjoying the warm path it left as it slid down to my stomach. My eyebrows drew together in confusion. Where was I? What was going down my throat? I tried to open my eyes, but the light on the other side of my lids was almost too bright. A groan rose in my throat as I pushed someone's hands away, succeeding then to open my eyes. Jet's face slowly came into view, and my eyes flicked to the bowl of broth he cradled in his hand. My frown deepened.

"What in tarnation are you doing?" I demanded in a weak voice.

Jet dipped the spoon into the broth again. "When I was a sick boy my ma would feed me chicken broth. I figured I'd do the same to you."

"I ain't sick," I argued as I massaged the side of my forehead.

79

"Yes, you are," Jet replied softly as he lifted the spoon to my lips. "Just relax and let me take care of you."

My eyes narrowed, and I shook my head, ignoring the spoon in his hands. "No. I can take care of myself. I don't need you." I attempted to sit up, but my head spun as my stomach clenched, and I collapsed in the pillow.

Jet smoothed my forehead with the back of his fingers and brushed the hair from my eyes. "You're weak, Cheyenne. Just you rest and regain your strength. Trust me and let me take care of you."

"I don't need you," I repeated before reluctantly accepting the spoon he offered. I swallowed hard and closed my eyes. "What happened?"

"Your body was just telling you it was overworked, and it needed a rest."

I scoffed and peeked at him from under my lashes. "Just say it, Jet. Don't tip toe around it."

Jet frowned. "Say what?"

"You were right, and I was wrong. I'm a fool and you knew it!"

A strange light flashed in my uncle's eyes before he shook his head. "I'm not going to say that. Mainly because I don't think you're a fool."

"Then you're a liar," I mumbled.

Jet studied me with those unreadable eyes of his, then spooned the rest of the broth into my mouth. With my belly warm and full, my eye lids began to droop, and I found myself drifting off to sleep.

Several hours passed, and when I opened my eyes again, the sun had set an orange glow in the room. Rubbing my eyes, I threw the quilt aside and rose to a sitting position on the edge of the bed. I felt weak, and my stomach ached for more sustenance. The aroma of eggs drifted into my room, and the corners of my mouth turned downward in confusion.

"Ryleigh?" I muttered to myself.

I pushed myself to my feet and staggered into the main room that was connected to the kitchen. Jet stood in front of the stove, spatula in hand, watching the yellow concoction of scrambled eggs cook in the skillet. A loaf of bread sat on the counter with four pieces having been cut from its end. Two cucumbers, freshly picked and still coated thinly with mud, waited by the wash basin to be cleaned. Scratching my temple, I hooked a curl behind my ear and meandered into the kitchen.

"You look ridiculous just watching those eggs," I stated in a flat tone.

Jet glanced over his shoulder and offered a soft smile. "Glad to see you up. Feel any better?"

I pulled a chair out from under the shaky table and sank onto its seat. "I feel like I've been run over by a pack of wild horses. What are you doing?"

"Fixing supper. I thought you'd be hungry after you woke up from your nap."

Shaking my head, I let my hand flop on the table. "Why are you doing this?"

Jet set the spatula on the counter and turned to face me. "Because I promised you that I'd look after you. Besides, you're too weak to find yourself something to eat."

I stared at him with hollow eyes. The man confused me, and I didn't want to spend the time to listen to his confounded words and deal with his pathetic gestures. "When is it gonna be ready?"

"Oh, a little while yet," Jet answered as he turned back to the skillet. "I just started the eggs, and I wanted to toast the bread."

I ran a hand down my face and rose to my feet. "I think I'll go for a walk."

Jet's head swiveled around until his eyes forked me. "I don't think that's such a good idea,

Cheyenne."

I scoffed and placed a hand on my hip. "I'll be careful. I'll go slow and won't go far. I'll be back in

time to eat, don't get your trousers in a wad. I'm tired of lazing about."

Jet chewed on the inside of his cheek as he narrowed one eye in contemplation. "Well... I guess. If

you're not back in twenty minutes, I'm gonna look for you."

I rolled my eyes but nodded slowly. "Fine. It's a deal."

Turning slowly around, I marched to the door and stepped on the porch. The evening air still held the heat of summer, and the gentle breeze ran its fingers through my curly mess of hair as I entered the dusty street. My eyes pin-pointed one building, and I cringed at the off-key tunes that played

A GIFT OF GRACE

inside. Stuffing my hands in my pockets, I directed my feet toward the Bull's Head, but my steps faltered when I heard a beautiful voice join in with the piano music. A face came to mind, one that still boasted of its childhood freckles. Beautiful, young eyes stared into my soul, and curly hair almost identical to mine blew across the girl's features. Ryleigh was far too beautiful to waste her life inside Overhaul's doors. Kicking a rock across the road, I continued my walk until I found myself standing in front of the double doors.

Ryleigh stood on the stairs, making a slow descent as she grinned toward the men below. Her face was painted brightly, and glitter sparkled in her hair. Her dress fit too snuggly around her waist, and her perfect little shoulders were laid bare. Her voice rose above the piano as she sang a song that was unfamiliar to me. As she stepped onto the main floor, several men grinned, hooted, and whistled. The scene dug a hole deeper inside my heart as I watched her prance around each table, leaning on men and playing with their hats as she sang.

Standing in a corner, halfway hidden in cigar smoke, Overhaul watched my sister's performance with a greedy smirk on his lips. His pot belly hung over his belt, a sign of just how much he indulged on his own inventory. His beady eyes held a certain light in them that made me shudder, and I wanted to sink my fist into his soft gut. Turning my gaze back to my sister, I tried to remember the last time I had seen her smile, truly smile. Her flirtatious attempts on a tip didn't count. It had been years since I heard a sincere laugh erupt from her lungs. Her smile used to remind me of spring. Fresh, new, and beautiful. Now it reminded me of the dryness of winter. The light in her eyes had changed to a dim glow, and the sincerity in her smile was as cold as a blizzard.

Ryleigh flung herself onto the bar as she continued her song, crossing a leg over her knee. Her grin grew as she ran her gaze among the crowd, but when her eyes passed by the doors, her smile vanished, and her words ceased. For several drawn-out seconds, we stared into each other's eyes. Hers grew with surprise and guilt, and mine dimmed with the hurt and disappointment of seeing her in the place she stood. The piano player continued to bang on the keys, eyeing my sister in confusion as to why she had stopped singing. Ryleigh's mouth opened as if she was fixing to say something, but she remained silent.

Shaking my head, I finally broke my gaze and backed away from the doors. The piano continued to play by itself until I disappeared from the entrance. Ryleigh's voice rang out once again, but this time her notes took on a mournful sound. When she finished, applause sounded from the drunks and gamblers, and I felt my stomach clench at the thought of her job.

If my legs didn't feel like a pile of raw dough, I would've run down the boardwalk until the saloon's noise became a distant memory. Instead of racing away, I strolled past the storefronts with my head hanging low and my heart sinking to my toes. If only she hadn't felt the need to support me those many years ago. Maybe if she had used her head instead of her heart, she wouldn't be in a dress so revealing, and she wouldn't have to sell her body to earn a dollar. If only she had been older when Mama died, maybe she could've gotten a job as a waitress, or storekeeper, or even a seamstress.

"If only I hadn't been around," I voiced aloud.

I was the reason she took the job in the first place. If she had been an only child, or if I had died as an infant, she would only have herself to look after, and maybe she could walk down the street without being judged for the lifestyle she was forced to live. I shook my head again. We were both foolish girls.

"Good evening."

I turned my head to the right, and saw Levi Hendershot leaning on the corral fence. I had been so consumed by my thoughts that I hadn't realized which direction I was walking. "Evening," I replied, forcing my feet to stop.

"I see you're doing better," he observed. "You sure did give me a scare."

"I'm sorry." I wandered to the corral and leaned on a rail as I watched some of the horses laze about in the grass trap.

Levi stood next to me and followed my gaze. "Those animals aren't the best things to take care of. They leave messes in their stalls that are unpleasant to clean up, and their overall smell might turn other's noses, but

I enjoy working in this livery. I've learned to ignore people's assumptions about me based off what I do. I love the smell of horses and cattle, and I honestly don't care what the uppity types think of me. God planted my feet on this earth, and maybe my only purpose is to clean up after horses and smell like manure for the rest of the day. If that's the case, I don't mind all the judgments. I choose to be happy every day I rise from my pillow, and I thank God for the day He permitted me to live."

I glanced at the young man out of the corner of my eye, then rested my chin on my wrists.

Levi glanced down at me. "I suppose you know a lot about judgments and what people think about you."

I lifted a shoulder in a shrug. "I guess."

"You know, there will always be people who think less of you than you really are. It took me a while to learn that lesson myself. But occasionally you find people who think the world of you and want to help you. For you, it's Mr. Douglas. Don't categorize him in the same place as you do the rest of this town."

I scoffed and turned my back on the horses. "I didn't ask for your advice."

"I know you didn't." Levi scuffed the ground with the toe of his boot. "C'mon, I'll walk you home."

I pushed away from the wooden corral as I followed him back to my house. As much as I resented the words he spoke, they kept lingering in my head, and I found it hard to forget them. What did Levi know about Jet? And how was I to know Jet was being honest when he said he wasn't going to hurt us? My uncle was waiting on the porch when Levi and I came into view. I looked into his eyes and wondered what it would be like to have a father. Shaking my head, I mumbled my gratitude to Levi and ascended the steps into the house.

~SIX~

Ryleigh stared at the ceiling of her bedroom, unable to catch up on some much-needed sleep. Her eyelids felt heavy, her muscles ached, her body cried for rest, but the look on her sister's face kept her from slumber. The disappointment she saw written on Cheyenne's features bugged her more than the fact that her wages dipped for lack of a partner that night. Tears blurred her vision, but she refused to let them fall.

When the clock hanging on her wall pointed to the five o'clock hour, she threw the covers back, confident that she wouldn't be able to gain any more minutes of sleep that night. Snatching her shawl from the peg on the wall, she wrapped the thin material around her shoulders, straightened the dress she had on the night before, and opened the door. It was two hours before her shift started over again, and she decided on taking a walk to help ease her mind. The saloon was quiet, except for Wil, who was sweeping up the mess from the previous night, and he hardly said a word. Smoothing her hair with the palm of her hand, Ryleigh descended the stairs in a more modest manner than Cheyenne had seen her do just a few hours ago.

Shaking her head as if the motion would clear her memory of her sister's hurt, Ryleigh lifted her chin several inches higher than she felt it needed to be, then marched out of the door in bold steps. The tears that had been threatening to spill over all night were pushed to the back of her throat, where she concentrated on swallowing them. Forgetting her struggles for just an hour or two would be good to lift her mood and lighten her spirits.

The stores were closed. The only lights illuminated in the street were that coming from the saloon, and from the kitchen area of the diner. There was a mild bite in the air, which served as a reminder that fall would soon arrive in just a few short months. Pulling the shawl tighter across her shoulders, she shuddered from the breeze and continued down the empty street with her mind fighting to forget Cheyenne.

She was better with Jet. Jet could provide for her the way Ryleigh never could. He could give her protection against the drunks Ryleigh worked with, and he could also give Cheyenne the home she so desperately needed. Ryleigh was stuck in the past and couldn't climb out of the hole to catch a breath of fresh air. Cheyenne thought she needed Ryleigh, but she was wrong. What could she give the teen? Despite her attempts to feed and clothe the girl, Cheyenne had been surrounded by vile accusations and disgusting rumors. *What good have I done for her?*

Ryleigh found herself standing in front of the livery's corrals, watching the horses graze as they rested from whatever journey that brought them to Sunset, Arizona. Ryleigh wished she could jump in a saddle and ride until she reached the end of the earth. If there even was an end. If there wasn't, she would drive the horse over the cliff and rid the world of a worthless saloon tart that wasn't even the price of two pennies. Two tiny tears gathered in the outer corners of her eyes, and she pushed them away with the knuckle of her finger. Cheyenne would be better without her.

Grain pelleted against the metal of a trough, and the horses raised their heads to see who had interrupted their peaceful morning. Ryleigh turned her head as well, surprised that she hadn't heard the stable boy approach from the doors. The young man spotted her when he emptied his bucket of feed, and his jaw dropped when recognition flashed in his eyes.

"I-I… well… I-I'm sorry, ma'am, I didn't see you there."

Ryleigh snorted softly at his awkward greeting and pulled the ends of her shawl tighter across her chest. "You needn't apologize. I was just leaving."

"Oh, no, I didn't mean for you to leave. I-I mean, well, you can stay here as long as you like." He set the bucket on the ground and rubbed his palms on his soiled trousers. "I mean, I'm sorry to have interrupted whatever it was you were doing. Ma'am."

This time she couldn't hold back a gentle chuckle. "You fumble with your words like I fumble with a pitchfork."

He let out a rushed sigh and joined in a nervous laugh of his own. "Yes, ma'am. I ain't never been good at speaking."

Ryleigh's smile disappeared as she turned back to the horses, who had crowded themselves around the feed the stable boy had just given them. "I was just out for a walk, and I didn't mean to hold you back from your chores. I don't even need anything here."

"Oh, you're fine. We don't open for another hour. I just found myself awake in bed and thought I'd best fill my time since I couldn't sleep." He hid his hands in his pockets and leaned a shoulder against a post. "I was thinking 'bout Cheyenne. Did you know she took sick?"

Ryleigh's head jerked around as her eyes grew. "Took sick? Is she okay? I just saw her last night. She couldn't have been gravely ill. Did she have a high fever? How long has she been sick?"

"Now, I didn't mean to get you to worrying," he responded gently. "She's fine last I seen. Mr. Douglas took care of her, and she's gonna be her normal self in a day or two. She slept all day yesterday and went for a walk last night. I guess that's when you must've seen her. She just feels weak, but with your uncle looking after her, I bet she'll be hopping before you know it."

Ryleigh's shoulders slumped with relief as she smoothed a hand over her hair. "I'm sorry. Of course, Mr. Douglas is taking care of her." She scoffed at her own foolishness and turned to face him fully. "I'm obliged that you told me, but she's not in my care anymore. Please give my regards to Mr. Douglas and tell him my thanks for looking after her."

The young man peeked at Ryleigh from under his brows, seeming almost cautious. "I wish you'd tell him that yourself. Cheyenne might like a visit from you, too. She ain't been herself since you started working more, no offense, ma'am. She came here last night, that's how come I know how she's holding up. I think she needs to see you."

Shaking her head, Ryleigh tightened her jaw and glared into his kind gaze. "Cheyenne will get over my not being around, you'll see. And when she does, she'll thank me for separating us. In the meantime, I would appreciate it if you kept your skinny nose out of our business and occupy your overly active mind with shoveling horse dung!"

Before he could say another word on the matter, Ryleigh spun on her heel and marched toward the Bull's Head. What right did the stable boy have, telling her what her sister needed? Didn't she know Cheyenne better than anyone? She had protected Cheyenne when they were children and cared for her after they were alone. How could anyone claim that she did not know what was best for the girl?

Ryleigh burst through the saloon doors and ignored Wil's inquisitive gaze as she hurried up the stairs. Ryleigh could see the hurt in Cheyenne's eyes the previous night. Cheyenne did not need to be around to see her sister waste away in a saloon. Distance was the only sure way to protect her. The longer Cheyenne would watch Ryleigh, the more she would start to imitate what she saw. She feared that the fate of the youngest Douglas sister would be no different than the precedent set before they were born. Douglas' were known to be trash, but maybe there was still hope for the last one.

Ryleigh gasped softly when she rounded the corner and came face to face with her old friend. "Violet! What are you doing up so early?"

Violet crossed her arms over the corset she was wearing and leaned a shoulder against the wall. "I couldn't sleep, same as you. Honey, are you sure you're alright? Overhaul was kinda grumpy last night when you retired early. I don't know how many times he'll let you do that."

"Oh, he'll get over it," Ryleigh answered quickly, then cringed and glanced over her shoulder half expecting for her boss to be standing behind her. Ryleigh turned back to her friend and waved a hand in the air. "Never mind what I said. I guess I have a lot on my mind."

"Want to talk about it?"

Ryleigh studied Violet's expression before shaking her head. "I'd just be repeating myself. It's the same thing that's bothered me in the past. People say I'm doing the wrong thing."

Violet's eyes turned compassionate as she wrapped an arm around her friend and led her down the hallway. "I don't think you have much choice.

Overhaul would have forced this new change on you sooner or later. I think the arrival of your uncle couldn't have happened at a better time."

"But what if I'm wrong, Violet? What if I should quit and spend actual time with Cheyenne?"

Violet looked downcast as she closed the door to her room behind them. "Quitting this job is unlikely, and you know that. At least Cheyenne has a place to live, and you both are getting fed."

"That doesn't clear my conscience, Vi." Ryleigh lowered herself on the bed and covered her face in her hands. "I feel so helpless. And I just yelled at a poor young man who didn't mean to upset me."

"I'm sure things aren't as bad as they seem, honey," Violet encouraged as she stepped into a satin dress and pulled the straps over her shoulders. "You've wound yourself up too tight. You need to relax and go with the flow."

Ryleigh nodded as she ran her fingers through her tangled hair. "How do you do it, Vi? It doesn't seem to bother you. Y'know, going to work every night and dealing with Overhaul."

Violet sighed as she leaned her forearms on the bedpost. "You've got to learn to be like a duck in water. You have to let the comments roll off your back and not soak into your skin. You'd be much happier if you can forget what you're doing for a moment. Just pretend that you're going to work like any normal person and that Overhaul is just an annoying gnat in your ear."

"But you don't have a debt like I do," Ryleigh defended. "You can afford not to listen to Overhaul. If I mistreat him in any way, I pay for it."

"You don't think that I pay his price?" Violet asked as she lifted her skirt to show a scar on her thigh. "He gave me this scar a few months after I started working here. You know how he gets when he's drunk. You're not alone, Ryleigh."

Ryleigh nodded her head and remained quiet as she watched Violet get ready for the day. She wished she could believe her friend and know she was in good company, but she could not escape the isolation in her mind. She had felt the same ensnarement since she could remember. When she was younger, she used to believe that the solitude would leave once she was an adult, but she knew now that it was a trap that would never go away. She glanced out the window and hoped that Cheyenne would no longer feel the curse that seemed to be passed down on their family. Perhaps Cheyenne would feel loved and cared for now that Ryleigh was out of her way.

* * *

My stomach rolled violently, alerting the rest of my body that it was morning and well past time for breakfast. Stifling a groan, I rolled on my side and opened one eye. Warm daylight spilled through my window, announcing the lateness of the hour. Shoving the blankets aside, I rose from the mattress and ignored any urge to brush the rat's nest I knew had formed in my hair sometime during the night. I shuffled into the hallway and glanced at the same oversized shirt and torn trousers I wore as I entered the living room.

Jet was nowhere in sight, and I rubbed my throbbing head with the heel of my palm. My belly gurgled again. Placing a hand over my stomach, I meandered onto the porch, which had been rebuilt sometime without my realizing it. Grumbling my discontent with Jet, I stepped into the street and heard scuffling noises above me. Squinting against the sun, I noticed my uncle squatting on the roof, shucking off the shingles one by one. I crossed my arms over my chest and frowned at his back.

"How long you been up there?"

Jet glanced over his shoulder. "Not long. How are you feeling this morning?"

"Good as new," I lied. "I thought I was hired to do that for you."

"You were hired to work under my supervision," he corrected as he backed toward a ladder. "You hungry?"

"No. I need to get to work."

Jet set his feet on the ground and came over to me, his eyes judging if I had been honest or not. "Work can wait. You're still weak, and you need breakfast." A shy grin peeked out from the thick shadow of whiskers on his upper lip and jaw. "Besides, your hair's a mess."

I harrumphed my displeasure at his worthless attempt at a tease and

90

shuffled back in the house without a word. Jet passed me to rummage through the cabinets to find something to fill the hole in my belly, and I lowered myself into a chair to watch him.

"I don't like this," I grunted softly.

Jet set a pot on the stove and kept his back to me. "What don't you like?"

I rubbed my eyelids with my thumb and first finger. "This situation. I don't understand why you're still here."

"Well, it's not all that confusing. I've told you that I want to take care of you."

"That's what I don't understand." I rose from the table and pushed him away from the stove with my hip. "Everybody else in this dumb town wouldn't care if I slept in an alley during a blizzard, and I've given you enough guff for you to feel the same way, yet you refuse to leave me alone. I don't understand it." I grabbed a wooden spoon to stir the grits. "See? I can take care of myself. I don't need you."

Jet curled his fingers around the spoon and gently tugged it out of my grip. "Cheyenne, listen to me," he gently argued in a gravelly voice. "I want to help you because you're my niece, and I care about you. Trust me. That's all I'm doing."

My lip curled involuntarily. "You don't care about me, or Ryleigh. I don't trust you. You want something from us, but you ain't gettin' nothing! And I ain't gonna sit here and let you brainwash me!"

I turned to run, but he grabbed my arm and pulled me back. "Cheyenne, please don't run away until I know you've had breakfast. Go sit at the table while I warm up the grits."

"No! I won't obey you, Jet!"

"Calm down, Cheyenne. There's no reason for you to get upset this morning."

I tried to pull my arm out of his grasp, but he held on tighter. "No reason? I'll give you one good reason. You are tearing my family apart! I saw Ryleigh last night. Because of you, she hid even more in that sinful place. I don't understand how driving her away is helping me!"

Jet grabbed my other arm. I pulled against him with all my might, but he wouldn't let me break free. "That was Ryleigh's own doing, Cheyenne. If I had my way, both you girls would be sitting at that table this morning. I realize my being here is scaring you, but I'm not leaving you alone."

"I'm not scared," I defended.

"Yes, you are. You're scared because I'm not treating you like the other people in this prideful town. I'm telling you, there's no reason to be afraid of me. All I want to do today is make sure you take it easy and are fed. What harm is there in that? Tell me, Cheyenne, what is there to be afraid of?"

I leveled two large eyes on my uncle and kept my expression blank. "Let go of me."

Jet searched my gaze, then let out an exasperated sigh and dropped his hands. "Fine. Have it your way. But you are gonna eat breakfast before you leave this house."

"No, I ain't," I snarled. "I'm not hungry, and I wouldn't do anything that a liar asks of me."

"The next time you say something like that to me," Jet replied with his eyes narrowed, "I'll wash your mouth out with lye."

I chuckled heartlessly at his threat and folded my arms over my chest. "That would be appropriate. Getting fed lye from the liar."

Jet's frown deepened as he slowly shook his head. "Cheyenne, I'm not in the mood for this."

"You know, you say I have nothing to be afraid of." I narrowed my eyes to a squint. "Every person I know tries to come out ahead every time they talk to me. Yeah, I'm not scared of you, but you lie out your teeth every time you talk to me." I pivoted on my heel and marched toward the door.

"Where are you going?" Jet asked sternly.

I glanced over my shoulder. "Somewhere you'll finally leave me alone. I ain't coming back, not if you're here. I aim to disappear and never see you again."

Jet laid the wooden spoon on the counter and marched toward me in determined strides. I whirled to race outside, but he grabbed my wrist and led me back into the kitchen. He pulled one of the two broken chairs out from under the table and forced me to sit in it. Before I could respond, he pointed a finger at my chest and bent over the table so that he was eye level with me.

"I do not want to fight with you, but if you want to be stubborn, I'll be stubborn," he scolded in a low, calm voice. "You made yourself sick from not eating, and I am just making sure that you regain your strength and don't get malnourished again."

I sighed loudly as I tried to push myself to my feet, but he placed a hand on my shoulder and pushed me back in the chair. "Jet—"

"Stop arguing. There's no reason for you to fight with me." Jet walked back to the stove and began to stir the grits again. "If you fight me, there will be consequences."

I folded my arms over my chest. "Do you think threatening me will make me obey you?"

"I'm not threatening you. I'm just telling you how it is." Jet spooned a bowl full of the grits and walked back to the table. "I hope you like grits. I figured they would be good for you in case your stomach may still feel a little upset."

I glared at the bowl, then at my uncle. "What if I don't eat them?" I questioned with an air of defiance in my voice.

Jet glanced at me as he slowly set the bowl on the table in front of me but did not let go of it. "If you don't eat them, I will only pay you seventy cents today."

I rolled my eyes. "Oh, please, Jet. You haven't even paid me a penny for that debt you say I owe you. That threat means nothing to me. Maybe I won't eat the grits and risk getting paid seventy cents instead of the seventy-five."

"Alright, if that doesn't convince you then I'll have you write lines for me."

I frowned as I leaned back in the chair. "Write lines? What do you mean, write lines?"

"If you do not eat your grits, I'll have you write, 'I need to eat my breakfast' on your slate fifty times."

My frown deepened as I cocked my head to the side. "But that sounds like homework."

Jet nodded as he headed toward the front door. "That's exactly right. You love school so much I think I'll give you practice in case your teacher makes you write an essay on your first day back." He motioned to the bowl of grits in front of me again. "I'll check on you in half an hour. That bowl better be empty when I come back."

I watched him leave, then slid down the back of the chair as I picked up the spoon. I had never been fond of grits and didn't particularly know why people served them. I pushed the bowl away and glanced around the dingy house as I listened to the activities of a beautiful Saturday morning. I could hear some kids whooping as they enjoyed their day free of school. I glanced toward the front door again. Perhaps Jet wouldn't even notice my leaving. Smirking to myself, I pushed away from the table and hurried to my bedroom where I raised the window and stepped into the street.

Sunset was busy, just like any other Saturday morning, and I ducked behind a wagon to keep out of sight of Jet. Once I was several blocks away from the house, I straightened my back and curled my arms by my head. It sure felt nice to be out from Jet's sight for once, and to be in the street like old times. It was a beautiful morning, with birds singing, the sun shining, and the locals greeting each other with friendly smiles and warm handshakes. Hiding my fingers in my back pockets, I swaggered down the boardwalk, enjoying the warmth on the bottom of my bare feet.

My eye caught the glint of a shiny red apple, and my mouth began to water. I refused to eat the grits, but that didn't stop my belly from rumbling. I strolled by the fruit stands just outside the mercantile front door, and casually glanced over my shoulder to make sure nobody had noticed the greed in my eyes. Nobody paid me a second thought, so I moved my gaze toward the glass window and people inside the store. All backs were turned. Grinning to myself, I snatched the largest, reddest apple from the pile and sank my teeth into its crisp flesh.

"Hey there, young lady."

My eyes widened as I stopped mid chew when I heard the familiar voice of a man I had learned to dodge since I was a small child. Twisting at my waist, I glanced over my shoulder to see him approaching me. He wore a silver badge on the left side of his chest that read SHERIFF in bold letters. Curling my lip with disappointment, I swallowed hard and hid my treasure between my shoulder blades.

"Good mornin', Sheriff Hodgkinson," I greeted to hide my guilt.

The middle-aged man closed the distance between us and thumbed back his hat to reveal his forehead. "I'm not sure if it's a good 'un yet." He jutted his chin toward me. "What's that you have behind your back?"

I frowned and cocked my head to the side. "Behind my back? Why, just my empty hand, I swear that's all."

He raised his brows and rocked back and forth on his toes as he extended his palm. "Well, just for the sake of conversation, let's just see that hand."

"Um…" I dropped my gaze as my mind raced for a believable explanation. When five seconds passed and I still didn't have any ideas, I glanced at Sheriff Hodgkinson from under my eyebrows, flashed a toothy grin, spun on my heel, and took off as fast as I could on the normal cat-and-mouse chase I enjoyed.

Sliding around a woman's skirts, I ran around the back of the Bull's Head in hopes of losing the sheriff in the crowd of passersby. Once back on the boardwalk, I hurried across the street and jumped in front of the gunsmith store. After glancing over my shoulder to make sure the sheriff wasn't in sight, I disappeared inside and hid behind a shelf of firearms. Rapid footprints gradually grew louder, and I peeked around the stalk of a rifle in time to see Sheriff Hodgkinson hobble past. Grinning to myself, I took another bite of the apple and rose to my feet. Not wanting to announce my presence too soon, I glanced around the store at the shelves on the walls.

There was not much to the store, except a few rifles and ammunition, but my eyes quickly landed on a beautifully carved pocketknife displayed near the window. Jet had confiscated my old knife after the confrontation with the saddle, and I yearned to feel the coldness of a steel blade in my pocket for safety. One could never be sure when a knife could come in handy. I glanced around the store to see if anybody was watching, then bent over the display with envy in my eyes.

After taking a bite of the apple, I reached out a hand to caress the shiny object, and my eyes found the bone handle appealing. Very carefully, I picked up the knife from its velvet pillow and felt the blade with the pad of my thumb. I sliced off a chunk of the apple and slipped it in my mouth. It sure was sharp and would make quite the accessory to show my comrades. I glanced toward the counter and noticed the man for the first time. He looked old, too old to catch a spry youngster like myself. If he saw me carrying his precious cargo out of his store, I could lose him without too much trouble. Stifling a cocky grin, I slipped the knife into my pocket as I casually wandered to the door.

I glanced at the old man, who looked up from the papers he was working on when I set my hand on the doorknob. Smiling around the apple, I mumbled a hello and twisted my wrist to open my escape route.

"That'll be a dollar twenty-five," he growled in a gruff voice.

I took the apple from my mouth so I could speak. "Do what, sir?"

He motioned to my trousers and glared at me with a piercing stare. "That knife. If you want it, you pay me a dollar twenty-five."

I pressed my back to the door and contorted my face into a thoughtful frown as I pretended to weigh my options. "Well, I don't have a dollar and a quarter on me at the moment," I told him. "I'm afraid this beautiful knife will be sold by the time I can come up with the money, so you'll just have to take my word that I'll pay you back. Good day to you, sir."

Biting my lip to keep from smiling, I darted out the door and down the street as fast as my legs could carry me.

"Hey! Stop that kid!" the man shouted from his doorway, limping after me.

Several by-standers were alerted at the old man's voice, and men left their positions to chase me as well. A near-by cowboy was the first to reach me, his hands shaped like claws and a frown set deep on his mouth. I dodged his fingers as he leapt for me and slithered between the legs of the second man. A third man grabbed the sleeve of my shirt, but I tugged it out of his fist and heard a rip in the material. I glanced at my arm and noticed a new hole in the sleeve. As I slipped around a fourth man, I felt a fist latch onto my upper arm, and I came to an abrupt stop. The apple fell from my hand and rolled in the dirt, and anger of losing my breakfast burned through my chest as I lifted my eyes to see who had been quick enough to catch me.

Levi Hendershot met my gaze, the corners of his mouth drooping downward as his eyes seemed to ask why I had taken something that wasn't mine. I bit my tongue, but the words that ran through my mind poured out of my eyes as I glared up at my captor.

The old man came up behind Levi, panting for air as he dug the knife out of my pocket. "If I ever get my hands on you…" he snarled, shaking a fist in my face.

"There's no need for violence," Levi defended, tugging me out of the man's reach. "I'll make sure she understands her actions."

The old man's eyes flicked up to Levi before he sent a stream of tobacco juice flying to the ground. "I'm obliged for you catchin' the little thief for me, son, but that girl needs to be taught manners!"

"Yes, sir. I'm sure she'll be dealt as she deserves."

The man curled his lip, shot me a glare, and ambled back to his store.

Levi's shoulders slumped as he glanced down at me. "Where's your uncle?"

"How should I know? I don't get along with that man. Am I supposed to keep track of him?"

"Well, then I'll take you to the sheriff. You're not getting away with this, Cheyenne."

I scoffed and rolled my eyes. "Do you really think the sheriff's gonna scare me? I've spent a night in a jail cell before. Nothing that man can do will frighten me."

Levi didn't reply as he strode toward Sheriff Hodgkinson's office on the north side of town. I grumbled to myself at his ignorance. The sheriff never scared me, even when he would whip me in front of Ryleigh when I was younger. In fact, I found it to be entertaining to upset the sheriff.

The hinges on the sheriff's door squealed when we entered his office, and I sighed as Levi pushed me toward the desk. Sheriff Hodgkinson, who had since given up on catching me, was cleaning one of his rifles when Levi brought me to him.

The sheriff leveled nonchalant eyes on me as he set the barrel of his gun on his desk. "What did you do now?"

I crossed my eyes and stuck out my tongue, which rewarded me with a painful squeeze from Levi.

"She was caught trying to steal a pocketknife, sir," the stable boy explained as he glanced down at me.

The sheriff leaned a hip on the corner of his desk and folded his arms over his chest. "Two in less than thirty minutes. That's a record." Shaking his head, he took hold of my other arm and pulled me away from Levi. "Thank you for bringing her in. I'm getting too old to be chasing these street rats around anymore."

Levi hesitated before he glanced at me and stepped out the door without a word. The sheriff took the keys off the peg in the wall and dragged me to the back, where two cells stood empty. He pushed me in one and locked the barred door before leveling his brown eyes on me.

"I'm keeping you in here until someone comes to get you. Where's that uncle of yours? I heard he was trying to keep you in line."

"It don't matter to me where he is. I'll be happy to carry out my sentence in this cell."

"Don't tempt me." Sheriff Hodgkinson turned to the front and hooked his thumbs in his gun belt. "He'll be here shortly. News of your being in jail should travel fast, especially when these folks know you're his."

"I am not his!" I corrected when he turned to leave. "And I never will be," I finished under my breath as I settled down on the rickety old cot. *Yet he's gonna be here in two shakes of a dog's tail, and there's nothing I can do about it.*

Hanging my head, I covered my eyes with my fingers and let out an irritated sigh. I had spent several hours in a jail cell, and many times I had been let out, but this time was different. Times before, Ryleigh would pick me up when she got off work, apologize to the sheriff, and never say another word about it. Guilt was out of the question back then, but I felt a bit of it creep into my chest now. The thought of looking into Jet's gaze once he found out what I'd done shamed me, and that disturbed me more than getting caught. What difference was there between Jet and Ryleigh? Ryleigh had been the only parent I knew for most of my life, and Jet's not so subtle attempts to fill the place of Pa was greatly unwanted.

As far as I was concerned, a father wasn't a good person, anyway. Ryleigh had tried to tell me the good things about Pa, but after a few years, I found those stories were not true. He'd abandoned his family. It was as simple as tying two pieces of rope together. And Jet was worse. He'd left his ma when he wasn't much older than me, and he thrived to get whatever he wanted before he magically showed up on my and Ryleigh's doorstep.

The noises from the sheriff's office drifted through the bars, and I peeked through my fingers as I listened to the footprints and low voices. They were both familiar; one voice was the sheriff's, and the other belonged to Jet. Curling my lip, I wagged my head back and forth slowly, then reclined on the cot and cocked my head to the right as I waited for the men to come into the back.

The doorknob twisted, and the sheriff's head peeked in first, followed by Jet. I let a grin spread across my mouth, though what I wanted to do was curl into a ball and avoid Jet's gaze. "That hardly gave me enough time to catch up on some shut-eye."

Sheriff Hodgkinson opened my door and let it swing wide. "Your uncle's here. It's time for you to go."

I scoffed. "He's not my uncle. There's no proof."

"Cheyenne, let's go," Jet mumbled, glancing at the sheriff out of the corner of his eye.

"I ain't going nowhere, least not with the likes of you."

The sheriff wrapped a hand around my arm and pulled me out of the cell. "You ain't my responsibility anymore, young lady. I want you out of my jail."

Jerking my arm free, I smoothed the front of my shirt and marched ahead of the men. Just like Ryleigh, Jet mumbled an apology to the sheriff, exchanged a few words I ignored, and ushered me out the door. The instant our feet hit the boardwalk, Jet pinched my ear lobe between his thumb and index finger. Without speaking a single word, he marched toward the little shack my sister and I called our home.

I groaned my pain as his grip tightened. "Take it easy, Jet. It's not as bad as it looks," I whimpered, but he ignored my complaints until he dragged me through the front door.

Jet pulled me in front of him and finally let go of my ear. "What do you think you were doing?" he demanded in a voice that awoke the beehive in the pit of my stomach.

I rubbed my ear and glared up at him. "I was hungry, and I wanted to get breakfast."

"You had a bowl of grits this morning that I cooked for you!" he snapped, motioning an arm toward the dining room. "I'm disappointed in you. Why did you disobey me?"

"You think being disappointed in me is supposed to shame me?" I scoffed. "I've disappointed more people than you realize."

Jet straightened to his full height and inhaled deeply. "I asked you to eat your breakfast," he answered in an even voice. It was obvious he was trying not to let his anger show.

"I don't care what you asked," I argued. "I hate grits. I wanted something different for breakfast."

"You have no excuse for what you did this morning. If you had just done what I told you, you would have had a filling breakfast and be out there helping me with the house. Instead, you try to steal an apple and a pocketknife. Just what were you planning to do with that knife?"

"It's not that big of a deal, Jet," I defended as I crossed my arms over my chest. "I don't have the knife, do I? And an apple doesn't cost much. I'm sure they didn't feel the loss."

"That's not the point, Cheyenne. I don't want you to steal, and I've had it with your defiance." He glanced out the window, then back down at me. "Which hand took the knife and the apple?"

I frowned at him. "What?"

"Cheyenne, which hand took the knife and the apple?" he repeated with impatience.

I lowered my gaze before I mumbled, "My right hand."

"Hold it out."

I glanced up at my uncle to see if I could convince him to forget a punishment, but his steel eyes were unwavering. Deciding against an argument, I slowly extended my hand in front of me. Jet firmly took hold of my fingers and slapped the back of my hand twice. I cringed at the little sting, but I felt more shame than pain. When he let go of my hand, I rubbed my knuckles as I refused to raise my gaze from the floor. Jet stood in front of me for several long seconds before he spoke in a quiet voice.

"I don't want to hear that you've stolen something else. Now, I want you to finish your breakfast and then we'll get to work on the roof."

"Yes, sir," I muttered as I turned to obey him.

I quietly walked back to the dining table, and this time Jet lowered himself in the second chair beside me. He waited until the bowl was mostly empty before he washed it and motioned for me to go outside. We began the tedious task of taking off the old shingles, and I decided to keep my thoughts to myself for most of the day. The day dragged on and felt like an eternity to me, but I only complained in my mind as I listened to Jet's instruction. At long last, the sun had drifted lower to the horizon, which cast an orange glow over the land and its occupants. I sat back on my knees and watched the town of Sunset as the stores began to close.

Jet glanced over his shoulder to see why I had stopped pulling nails. I met his gaze after watching the sun set for a few seconds, then turned back to the shingles by my knees.

"I figure we'll call it a day here shortly," he stated, breaking the thick silence. "It's Saturday, so I'll clean up while you heat up some water."

I frowned. "Heat water? Whatever for?"

Jet stared at me like I had lost my mind. "Tomorrow's Sunday. We're going to church, and I thought it'd be respectful for you to get rid of that protective layer of dust you've accumulated. I saw a wash basin hanging on a nail by the back door. If you would heat up enough water to fill that up, you can take the first bath."

I brought my eyebrows together as I scoffed a sarcastic laugh. "Are you kidding me? I ain't been in church in years, and I ain't about to start. I ain't

101

even gonna take a bath. Smelling like flowers and pretty things has never appealed to me."

"Well, I'm going to church, and I'd like for you to join me." He frowned as he scratched his jaw. "Besides, it's about time you met with a bar of soap."

"I don't like baths," I argued halfheartedly. "Ryleigh forced me to take one several days ago, but I don't fancy smelling like a rose."

Jet raised his eyebrows and wiggled the tip of his nose. "Well, you'll take one tonight because I'm tired of smelling you. Now head on down that ladder and heat up some water."

I sighed exasperatedly as I stood. "Alright, fine. I'll heat some water. But it ain't me who's gonna take a bath. It's a free country. If you wanna get fancied up to go to church, by all means, drown yourself in soapy water."

Jet brushed off his jeans and popped his back as he stood. "As long as I've got a say in it, you are taking a bath."

My eyes narrowed, but I didn't bother to utter a retort as I knew Jet wouldn't listen to any more arguments. Turning my back on him, I climbed down the ladder and moseyed to the back door to retrieve the basin. Glancing up toward the roof, I curled my lip and shook my head in disgust. I begrudgingly ripped the basin off its nail and trudged inside after thinking a few rude phrases that fit my uncle perfectly. After rummaging in Ryleigh's cupboards, I finally found a pot that wasn't too rusted and full of holes and began the slow process of filling the tub with warm water.

Half the basin was filled by the time Jet walked through the front door, and I turned to stare at him with an icy gaze. He tossed his hat on the dining room table and set the tools on the floor before looking into my eyes.

"Don't you reckon you'd want that tub in a more private corner than in the middle of the kitchen?" he pointed out bluntly.

"No," I snarled, "because it ain't me takin' no bath, and while you wash your toes I'll be elsewhere!"

"Now, I already told you that you were going to take a bath this evening, and I don't want to hear any more argument from you. I'll be more than happy to move that before it gets too heavy."

I crossed my arms over my chest and cocked my head to the side arrogantly. "You can't force me to take a bath. If you did, people might think that you're worse than Ryleigh and me put together."

Jet cocked his head to the side as he narrowed his eyes slightly. "I told your sister that I would never abuse a woman, and that statement holds true to you. Don't insinuate that I'm a worse man than I am."

I shrugged and repositioned my weight to one leg. "What's it to you? I'm sure these people will come up with some kind of rumor about you since your last name is Douglas. You still can't make me take a bath."

Jet hooked his thumbs in his belt loops as he leaned his weight to the side. "There's nothing I can do to convince you to take a bath?"

"Absolutely nothing," I growled under my breath as I narrowed my eyes. "I dodged around you at breakfast this morning, didn't I? I'm pretty sure I can dodge around you now."

Jet frowned at me as he placed his hands on his hips. "I told you that I can be stubborn. We're going to church tomorrow, and I don't want you to smell like perspiration and sand."

I snorted a humorless laugh as I turned to walk to my room, but Jet grabbed my arm to stop me. He didn't bother to give me an explanation as he scooped me in his arms and carried me toward the basin in the middle of the room. My eyes widened when I realized his intention and I kicked against him.

"Jet, set me down now!" I demanded, clawing at his neck as he attempted to lower me into the water. "Jet!"

With a soft grunt, Jet suddenly dropped his arms, and I fell with a big splash into the water I had just warmed up. Choking on a droplet that flew down my airways, I rubbed the water from my eyes and looked up to glare at him, but he tossed a bar of soap toward me before I could argue with him.

"You can do me a favor and wash your clothes as you wash yourself," he explained as he strode toward the living room. "I'll be outside when you're finished."

I narrowed my eyes in anger as I threw the soap in between his shoulder blades. "I hate you! What am I supposed to do with my wet clothes? I'll catch a cold if I wait for them to dry!"

Jet picked up the soap from the floor and tossed it back in the water as he headed toward the hallway. "I'll let you borrow my night shirt until your clothes are dry," he stated as he disappeared from my sight.

I slapped the water in anger and growled my discontent when a few droplets of water flew up my nose and into my face. When I wiped the water from my eyes, I noticed Jet was standing in front of me with a grin plastered on his face. When a small chuckle gurgled in his throat, I frowned and gave him a glare that I hoped would silence him. Instead, it made him laugh a little louder.

"What is so funny?" I growled.

Jet bit his lip to quit laughing, but that annoying smile poked out again as his chest heaved with amusement. "I'm sorry, Cheyenne," he apologized, but his laughter still thickly coated his voice. "You look like a sulking cat in a stock tank!"

I stared at him like he had completely lost his mind, but the more I glared at him, the harder he laughed. I felt my anger dissipate the longer he chuckled, and I soon found myself smiling at his ridiculousness. I wiped some of my hair out of my face when I realized I probably looked strange, and a chuckle escaped my lips as I listened to Jet's booming guffaws.

Jet wiped the moisture from the corner of his eyes when his laughter died, then he glanced at me. "You know, I believe that's the first time I've heard you laugh."

My smile vanished as I glanced at the soap in my hands. "Yeah, well, don't get used to it. I don't find many things to laugh at nowadays."

"Ah, don't say that. Laughter is good for a person," Jet replied as he tossed his shirt toward me. "Here, you can change into this while your clothes dry."

I watched him exit the room before I lathered up the soap and massaged my scalp. I thought I should have felt angry at him for throwing me into the water, but I found it hard to hold a grudge when I remembered the sound of his laughter. Jet was supposed to be upset that I was testing him, but instead he didn't become angry with me. My uncle was a puzzle, and I wondered if I would ever figure out his intentions.

* * *

The room was dark, and my bed was warm and comfortable, but my mind refused to unwind to allow me to sleep. Cradling my head in the crook of my elbow, I watched the shadow of the tree limbs dance across the ceiling. My mind replayed the sound of Jet's laughter until it echoed through my brain. I shouldn't have been surprised at his amusement. In fact, several people had their fair share of cackles over me, but it was the way it made me feel that bothered me. His laughter had been contagious and being able to laugh had felt good. It reminded me of that day when Ryleigh had our picture taken. I glanced at the photograph standing on my nightstand and narrowed my eyes. Why had it felt so natural?

A pebble thumped against the side of the house, jarring me out of deep thought and bringing me back to reality. When a second rock flew through the broken window onto the floor, I threw back the quilt and jumped to my feet. I crouched by the glass and squinted against the darkness to see Chad grinning back at me. I folded my arms over my chest and frowned at his excited expression.

"What are you doing here, Chad? Don't you know what time it is?"

"Yeah, time you and I got caught up." He leaned in closer and wiggled his pale eyebrows. "You wanna chance to see Ryleigh, don't you?"

I glanced over my shoulder, then pressed a finger over my lips. "Shh! Keep it down, that uncle of mine is staying here now."

Chad wrinkled his nose and backed away from the window. "That's gross. Doesn't he know he ain't welcome?"

"Yeah, well, he can't take a hint," I explained as I lifted the window open so I could slip to the ground. "Back to business. What about Ryleigh?"

Chad's mischievous grin spread from one ear to the other. "Follow me."

Without another word, Chad spun on his heel and disappeared down the dark alley. Curiosity and the desire to see Ryleigh urged me to follow him, no matter what kind of trouble he had stirring in his mind. It didn't take me long to catch up to my lifelong friend, especially since his footprints led directly to the back of the Bull's Head Saloon.

"What are you aiming to do?" I whispered, peeking through the nearest window.

"I'm lookin' for some fun. It's been ages since we had any, and you never hang out with me anymore."

I rolled my eyes and groaned. "Oh, please, Chad. If you live two hours with Jet, you'll understand why I've been busy lately. What did you have in mind?"

Chad's grin returned, and this time an evil glint appeared in his gaze. "Whiskey. You go in there and distract 'em, maybe talk to Ryleigh, while I sneak in the back and grab us a bottle or two. Dumb ol' Overhaul will never miss a thing. You've always wanted to hurt him, right?"

I shrugged and studied my bare feet. "Right, but how do we know we won't get caught?"

Chad wrinkled his nose and waved a hand in the air. "Ah, you worry too much, Cheyenne. They won't blame you. You'll be in their plain sight. And they won't associate me with you 'cause I don't get in trouble as much as you do."

"Well, that's because you always leave me with the cargo to get caught," I argued back. "I just want to know there'll be no chance in us getting put behind bars. Or worse."

"Hey, I've got it all under control. Now I want you to go around to the front and cause some big ruckus, just so they don't get some wise idea to check the storage room. When I hear things breaking or shouts or something loud, I'll dodge in there and dodge out. Three minutes, tops."

"And what if it doesn't work?"

Chad gave me a malicious glare. "I got you outta school, didn't I?"

I frowned. "Long enough for my uncle to catch me and make me regret that decision."

He sighed, shook his head, and finally met my gaze again. "Okay. If it doesn't work, I'll say it was all my fault and you won't be blamed."

Pursing my lips, I pondered his proposition, then gave my head a firm nod and extended my hand. "Shake on it."

Chad accepted my hand and grinned. "Great. Now go break a leg, Cheyenne."

Nodding slightly, I crept around the corner toward the front door, wondering if I had lost my sanity to trust Chad. *Forget Chad. Do your work and have fun, just like old times.* Pasting a friendly smile on my lips, I pushed through the double doors and let my eyes adjust to the smoky atmosphere of the saloon. Business was alive at that hour, with the poker tables involved in constant games, and the saloon girls bouncing from one customer to the next as they delivered drinks with a flirt. I swallowed hard and glanced around the room. Ryleigh wasn't in sight, but more importantly, neither was Clyde Overhaul.

Puffing out my chest, I sauntered to the bar and leaned against its edge as I flagged down a new bartender. I ignored the unease that settled in my throat when he glanced up at me and narrowed his eyes. He never looked away as he continued to wipe down the dirty shot glasses in front of him.

Clearing my throat, I motioned for him to come closer, and he reluctantly left the glasses to stand in front of me. "Give me a beer," I demanded, already knowing his answer.

"How old are you, kid?" he snarled in a voice that should've belonged to a grizzly bear.

I shuddered and squared my shoulders. "Old enough to decide whether I want a beer or not."

"Scram before your ma has to change your diapers for you." He sent me a glare as he moved to another man who had just swaggered up to the bar.

I bit my lip and studied the liquor on the other side of the counter. Chad was waiting for my move, and the longer I hesitated, the angrier he would become. Swallowing hard, I glanced over my shoulder to make sure Ryleigh wasn't watching, then rasped my knuckles against the hard wood.

"Hey!" I called.

The bartender glanced my direction and ambled back. I didn't miss the fact that he rolled his eyes as he came closer. "You're still here? Ain't it past your bedtime, kid?"

"I told you I want a beer." I leaned in close and lowered my voice. "So, get me... a beer."

"Look kid," the bartender replied coolly, "why don't you just leave before I lose my temper and throw you out?"

I reached over the side of the bar and grabbed the bottle of whiskey he had left uncorked. Using just about every ounce of strength I had, I smashed the bottle over the gent's head and hoped I could handle his reaction. The bronze glass shattered, and whiskey dripped into the bartender's face. The atmosphere grew deathly silent as every eye turned to see what had happened.

Something that resembled fire lit the man's otherwise calm eyes, and my knees began to shake

violently. "Why you little..."

I cringed at the word he chose. "I don't think you should call me that. It ain't good customer service."

His hand shot out to grab my collar, but I saw it coming and was able to dodge him.

"Stop that brat!" the bartender shouted, and I suddenly found it necessary to exit the building. The only thing that kept me back was Chad and his stupid idea of snitching a couple of bottles of free whiskey.

I whirled to run, but instead of finding a place to hide, my eyes landed on the man who enslaved my sister in the worst kind of business possible. Clyde Overhaul's menacing stare sent shivers down my spine, and a new brand of hatred boiled in my chest. Forgetting about Chad and the mischief we planned to do, I grabbed a glass and threw it with all my might at the disgusting pig of a man who employed my sister.

He raised an arm to block the blow, but the cup shattered when it collided with his forearm and tiny pieces of glass pierced his skin. The fire in his eyes grew, and I found my eyes narrowing with anger. "You brat, just you wait until I get my hands on you!" Overhaul snarled, reminding me of an aggravated badger.

"Funny you should say that," I answered. "I'll be moving so fast you won't be able to lay a finger on me!"

I threw another glass his direction before darting under a table in hopes to make it out the front door without physical harm to my body. *The next time Chad comes up with a brilliant idea like this one...* I shook my head violently, took a deep breath, and darted out from the table in giant leaps. I could almost feel the breath of Overhaul on the back of my neck like a charging buffalo when I hit the swinging double doors. Because of my haste to get out of the saloon, I tripped over the threshold. The sounds of the overweight saloon owner urged me to run down the street as if a whole herd of wild horses were on my tail.

When I realized nobody was chasing me, I turned into an alley and met up with Chad, who was still hiding behind the Bull's Head. "What took you so long?" Chad complained when I slowed to a stop beside him.

"The next time... you get such a... big idea," I said, shaking a finger in his face as I tried to catch my breath, "get someone else... to be your sucker. You get the stuff?"

Chad lifted two whiskey bottles with a grin set wide on his mouth. "Let's go get drunk, Cheyenne!"

~SEVEN~

The sun shone brightly on my face and split my pounding head with unbearable pain. I groaned and rolled onto my side with my back facing the sun and rubbed my eye lids with the pads of my fingers. A whiskey bottle was still clenched in my fist, but it felt more empty than full. The next time Chad came up with some great idea of stealing whiskey, I would just laugh at him for wasting my time. The church bell chimed in the near distance, and I moaned when my head pounded harder, almost as if someone sat inside it with a hammer and a Chinese gong.

"Oh, please leave me alone," I moaned to no one in particular. Holding my stomach, I hiccupped and tasted the vileness of the liquor. "The next time, Chad... oooh!"

The streets were quiet that morning, which I counted as a blessing.

"Cheyenne..."

The call was soft but held a sense of sternness that sent chills down my spine. Lifting my eyelids, I caught a sight of Jet marching from one alley to the other, and I remembered his promise of bringing me to church. Cringing at the thought of what he'd think, I covered my eyes with the palm of my hand. If Clyde Overhaul had caught me the night before and twisted my head off, I'd be in better health than if Jet found me.

The sound of boots pounding a rhythmic pattern on the dirt met my ears, and I curled into a tight ball, hoping that would make me invisible. The footsteps grew louder but came to a sudden stop as a shadow passed over my body. I pretended I was passed out in hopes that if it were Jet, he'd leave me well enough alone. I was in no mood to do anything but lie there in a pool of my own destruction.

"Cheyenne!"

The voice was loud, too loud. It awoke that Chinese gong again, and I groaned as I covered my ears. Rough fingers curled around my upper arm and jerked me to my feet. An invisible rope seemed to pull tightly around my middle, and a small moan escaped my lips. "Please don't…" I moped as I fell against Jet's chest.

"Cheyenne, what do you think you are doing?" he demanded in a voice that thrived on banging that gong inside my head. His eyes forked the bottle still clenched in my grasp and ripped it from my fingers with too strong of force. "Where were you last night, and what did you do? Didn't you remember today was Sunday and we were going to church?"

I cringed and held onto my stomach with a death grip. "Please don't yell, Jet. Just let me die."

"You ain't gonna die, and I won't quit yelling at you. Not until I get a straight answer. Are you sober enough to answer my questions, or do I have to throw you in the creek to wake you up?"

"Jet, I'm not a drunk. Of course I'm s-s… so…" The knot in my stomach tightened, and I turned away from my uncle as the whiskey in the pit of my belly bubbled into my mouth and spilled on the ground. "Oooh, please leave me alone, Jet!" I groaned, holding my belly as I slid to the dirt.

Jet grabbed my arm and pulled me back up beside him. "I'm not about to leave you to wallow in liquor and your own vomit. Are you sober, or do I need to sober you up?"

"I'm not drunk," I replied weakly. "Please, Jet, leave me alone. I need to be alone!"

"If you're not drunk, then how come your words are slurred?"

I squinted my eyes up at him with my mouth hanging open. "I-I… I don't drink."

Jet sized me up under the brim of a freshly brushed hat, his expression unreadable. Without another word, he dragged me out of the alley with long strides. My legs didn't quite work, and I fell more than I walked. My stomach tightened again, but all I could do was groan. Jet was obviously not in any mood to hear me repeat myself. The town was empty as most of the people were in church or resting on the otherwise fine day, and that made me feel less embarrassed about the situation.

Jet dragged me down to the creek just on the outskirts of town, picked me up, and walked into the water without taking off his boots. I felt too horrible to fight him, so I allowed him to dunk me into the cold water. I came up sputtering, but Jet placed a hand on the back of my head and pushed me under before I could catch my breath. Fear settled in my chest when I realized he may not let me out of the water. With panic operating my brain, I tried to fight against him, but he didn't let me up until my lungs were about to burst with the lack of air. When my head barely poked out of the water, I gasped for sweet oxygen, choking on the rivulets that were sucked down my airways, but then I was back under.

When I thought my funeral would be in the middle of the week, Jet pulled me back on the air side of the creek and held me at arm's length away as I gasped to find my breath. "Did that sober you up, or do you need some more?"

"You aim to kill me!"

"No, I aim to teach you a lesson." Jet pulled me to my feet and dragged me to the sandy bank. "Sit down," he ordered, shoving me toward the ground. I plopped into the sand and held my head in my hands. "What did you do last night?" Jet demanded, jamming his hands on his hips as he shifted all weight to his left leg.

"I don't know. It wasn't my idea," I moaned.

"I don't care if it was your idea or not, you participated in whatever this was, and I demand to know what you did. I'm very disappointed, Cheyenne. I got up this morning thinking you were still in bed. I got ready for church, and when you still didn't show up, I went into your room only to find your bed empty and the window wide open. An hour and a half later I find my niece passed out in the street after a night drinking this," he shouted, shaking the almost-empty whiskey bottle in the air. "What did you do, Cheyenne? Answer me!"

I opened my mouth to speak, but my stomach clenched, and I pitched forward. The whiskey burned a hole in my esophagus, and my throat tingled. Wishing Jet wasn't there to see me, I turned my back to him again and spat the bitter taste on the ground. I belched, cringed, and melted into the sand.

"Can't you see I feel the worst I've ever been?"

"You should've thought of the aftereffects last night. Now answer the question."

I groaned and leaned my head against the log. "We wanted to have some fun," I began, determined to make the story sound as innocent as possible. "There was a little scuffle in Overhaul's smelly saloon, and we just sorta found two bottles. They landed right in our laps, and we thought, why let them go to waste?" I cringed as my stomach tightened again. "I don't remember much after that."

"Who's we?" Jet demanded.

I sobbed softly as I held my head in my hands. "Me and a friend. Please help me, my belly's got a hole in it and I'm gonna die!"

Jet rolled his eyes and shook his head. "Quit being dramatic and sit up."

"I can't sit up," I argued back, feeling desperation rise in my chest. "My belly hurts so bad! I'll just hurl if I sit up."

"You'll hurl no matter what you do. Who's this *friend?*"

"I ain't tellin' you. Friends stick with friends, and nobody's gonna drag his name out of me."

Jet raised an eyebrow and rocked on his toes. "*His* name? You mean to tell me your friend Chad was involved in this?"

I cringed and rolled on my side. "For the record books, I didn't say anything."

Jet let out a sigh that sounded harsh to my ears. "Well, you stink and are soaking wet, but c'mon, let's go."

I glanced up at him and curled my lip with dread. "Go? Go where?"

"Church. Get up, I ain't carrying you all the way to the church."

"But I can't go," I argued. "I'm sick to my stomach, my head feels like it was run over by an elephant, and besides all that, I don't care for church. I ain't goin'!"

Jet pulled me to my feet again and gave me a frown. "You can't get drunk on Saturday night and sleep in on Sunday. I would prefer that you never get drunk, but apparently I'm too late on the first warning."

I slouched as I hugged myself around my midsection. "Please spare me from your lecture just this once," I begged, panting for air. "I don't feel good. Please let me stay home!"

"Stand straight," Jet scolded. "Well, I'm going to church, and since all you got is a hangover, I'm afraid you'll get in more trouble before I come home. You're still going to church, but believe me, this lecture ain't over yet."

I looked up at him and blinked past the sandy feeling in my eyes. "But—"

"Cheyenne, I won't stand for any arguments from you."

Slumping against his side, I rolled my eyes and forced my feet to work. All too soon, Jet helped me up the steps of the church and stopped just outside the door. He turned to me and attempted to tame the tangles in my wet hair before looking into my eyes.

"Listen to me, Cheyenne," he said over the hymn being sung on the other side of the wall. "I won't stand for any disruptions. Do you understand?"

"I think I have to hurl."

Jet blinked his eyes and turned me toward the stairs. "That would be a disruption."

I glanced at the scenery in front of me and decided that the open street of Sunset was more inviting than the suffocating atmosphere inside the church. Glancing at Jet over my shoulder, I forced my feet to work as I attempted to run down the steps that I had just so carefully climbed, but Jet latched onto my arm and pulled me back.

"Nice try, Cheyenne," he said in an irritated tone. "Enough foolishness, we're late enough as it is."

Jet dragged me back inside and pushed me toward the aisle in the center of the room. I swallowed hard when a few women on the back row turned to see who the late comers were, and as Jet pushed me down the center of the aisle, I noticed several of the churchgoers wrinkle their noses. The Reverend, who stood behind the pulpit in front of his congregation, noticed us walking and staggering between the benches to find a place to sit. I couldn't help but wonder what he thought of a large man dragging a dirty, drunk girl beside him.

Jet finally found a mostly empty bench near the front of the church and ushered me in it as he took his hat off his head. I sat next to a girl named Penelope Wilkes and noticed that she wore a weird bird nest on her head. I stared at her hat until she glanced at me out of the corner of her eye. Smiling rather pathetically, I hoped to pass an apology for being caught staring, but then I hiccupped and tasted that vile whiskey all over again. She wrinkled her nose and turned back to the front. Exhaling loudly, I lowered myself on the bench and concentrated on stopping the hiccups.

The hymn went on for far too long, and then people sat down all around me. As Reverend Atkins brought out his Bible, I couldn't help but squirm in my seat. My head ached, my stomach wasn't feeling much better, and I was concentrating too hard on holding my breath. Jet glanced at me from the corner of his eye and cleared his throat softly. I rolled my eyes and took a deep breath. He could clear his throat all he wanted to, but I found it hard to get comfortable on that hard bench. Mrs. Wilkes, who sat on the other side of Penelope, glanced my way, then turned a full glare on Jet.

My uncle glanced at her, then bumped me with his elbow. Swallowing hard, I aimed my gaze toward the pulpit where the Reverend began his sermon. I took a deep breath and slumped lower in my seat as I listened to the Godly man's monotone. I couldn't make sense of his words as I was too distracted by my rebellious body. The minutes dragged by, and the longer the seconds ticked, the more beads of sweat popped out along my upper lip and forehead. The knot in my belly, which I had hoped would untie itself, instead started tightening with a painful tug every few moments. Stifling a groan, I laid an arm across my middle and stared straight ahead.

Jet watched me closely, then bent slightly to whisper in my ear. "Sit up, Cheyenne."

I turned a glare on him and shifted my body in hopes of relaxing the muscles in my digestive system. "I can't," I snarled back.

He watched me for a few seconds, then nodded toward the door. "Get a breath of fresh air. You look pale." He pointed to my right, where Penelope sat stiffly. "Go out that way, it's shorter."

I nodded and rose to my feet. My stomach tightened as more sweat poured down my temple. "Excuse me," I whispered toward Penelope, but she pretended to ignore me. My throat began to open, and my eyes widened. "Excuse me!" I said a little louder.

Penelope turned lazy eyes on me and snarled, "Sit down."

I opened my mouth to explain my situation, but instead of words, the last of the whiskey spilled out, landing directly on the yoke of her dress. She squealed, Jet just about fell out of his seat, and every eye turned on me. The Reverend stopped mid-sentence and stared agape at the scene unfolding before his eyes. At last, Jet gathered his feet under him, grabbed me around the waist, and rushed outside as fast as he could scurry. Penelope and Mrs. Wilkes left just as quickly, but not as quietly.

Jet stopped on the porch and ripped his hat off his head when the women stumbled out the door. Penelope curled her lip at me but turned to my uncle. "Look at what that little heathen did to my dress!" she exclaimed. "It's absolutely ruined!" Squaring her shoulders, she raised her nose in the air and sized me up with a frown. Huffing in disgust, she stormed down the steps and marched through the dusty street before disappearing in the yard leading to a large white house just behind the church.

Mrs. Wilkes folded her arms over her chest and narrowed her eyes at Jet. "I've heard of you, sir," she snapped in a shrill voice. "You came to Sunset for your two nieces. Well, you won't tame them! Especially that one you have captured in your fist. She's drunk! How dare you bring a drunken brat into the doors of the Lord's House! That child lives in the streets! It's hopeless for you to try to take the reins of that girl."

Jet's back stiffened, and I noticed his jaw clenching as his face turned red. "Ma'am, I believe the Good Lord came for all. I doubt He would mind if my niece and I attended church in His House."

She narrowed her eyes, glared at me, and followed her daughter down the street.

I swallowed hard and glanced up at Jet. "I'm sorry," I mumbled softly.

Jet looked down at me, and his gaze softened. "Don't apologize, Cheyenne.

116

There was nothing you could do about it."

I hung my head and shrugged. "But she was right. I am a brat."

"Cheyenne, look at me." When I didn't move to obey him, he curled a finger under my chin and lifted my head until he could look into my eyes. "Don't you ever hang your head, not to that woman, not to me, and especially not to yourself. Don't listen to what other people have to say."

"Whatever," I huffed. "She's still right. You don't know what I've done."

"Okay, so I don't know all that you've done," Jet agreed. "But all I care about is what you do now."

I frowned. "I don't understand you."

Jet chuckled and lifted a shoulder in a shrug. "Well, I don't either, so we're even. What do you say we join the congregation for the conclusion of the sermon?"

I shook my head. "Uh-uh, I ain't welcomed in that place."

"Don't be foolish. You're as welcomed in this place as I am, c'mon."

I groaned but allowed him to lead me into the church. The Reverend glanced at us as we entered the building again and stumbled over his words as he tried to make a point in his message. Jet remained standing in the back, holding me next to him as the Reverend ended the service with a quick prayer and a final hymn. I stood still as a statue, feeling out of place as I listened to the hymn's words. As the congregation finished the last verse, the Reverend made his way down the aisle to greet his people as they left for their Sunday dinner, but he hesitated when he passed by Jet and me. Flashing a weak smile, he hurried out the door and waited patiently for his parishioners.

Jet nodded at a few people who passed us by, but I felt more than one hateful look cast my direction. When the church was mostly empty, Jet patted my shoulder and guided me toward the door. Once outside, Jet stopped in front of the Reverend and extended his hand.

"Fine sermon, parson," he complimented. "I, uh, apologize for the interruption this morning."

Relief registered on the elderly man's face, and he accepted Jet's hand with a warm smile. "The interruption, as you put it, was completely on accident. I was nervous both you and Cheyenne were run out of my fine sermon."

Jet chuckled and planted his hands on his hips. "Well, I'm glad there are no hard feelings."

"None at all!" the Reverend replied cheerfully. "Say, there is a picnic down by the creek. There will be fried chicken, a monstrous amount of dessert, and there's always a game or two to be played. You can clean up and join us if you wish."

I curled my lip and held onto my stomach. "Fried chicken? Ughh...."

Jet grinned and set a hand on my shoulder. "Thank you for the invitation, but I believe we'll have to decline. Maybe next time."

The Reverend offered a friendly smile and nodded his head. "Yes of course. Will I see you next Sunday?"

"Wouldn't miss it. Thanks again, Reverend."

Exchanging final greetings, Jet guided me down the steps toward our little shack hidden behind the rest of the town. Once inside, he told me to sit at the dining room table and poured a glass of buttermilk before he pinched some corn starch and sprinkled it in the liquid. I slumped against the chair and stared at his back.

"What are you doing?" I asked at last, my voice groggy.

"Making a concoction called a Highland Fling. It helps with the hangover."

I grunted and laid my forehead on the table. "I don't think I could keep it down."

"You'd be surprised." He seasoned the drink with salt and pepper before he placed it on the stove and sat beside me as he waited for it to come to a boil. "You think you can tell me about last night now?"

"I already told you what happened," I answered, shaking my head slowly. "There's nothing more to it."

"The story you gave me left out a lot of details, and I believe something happened more than just you two stealing a couple bottles of whiskey. Are you ready to tell me yet?"

"No. Leave me alone, Jet. Please."

Jet leaned against the back of his chair and folded his arms over his chest. "You ever been drunk before?"

I shook my head again but refused to look at him. "No, and I don't want to be again. I've tried beer before, but whiskey…" I burped and groaned at the after taste in my mouth. "Never again."

My uncle chuckled humorlessly, and I could feel his eyes on me. "Before church I wondered how I would punish you for doing such a stupid stunt, but I think you're being punished enough. What I wanna know is, have you learned your lesson?"

I turned my head ever so slightly so I could meet his gaze and curled my lip. "Don't talk to me like that. You sound as if I'm too stupid to do anything right."

"That was not my intention. I just want to make sure you don't pull that stunt again. A father wants to see his children raised right."

I sat up straight in my chair and looked at him through narrowed eyes. "You're not my father. You're an uncle who ran away from his family, and you've given me no reason why I should trust you."

Jet studied me with his unreadable eyes before he spoke in an even voice. "Do you think I'm here to hurt you, Cheyenne?"

My mouth opened to speak, but no words came to mind. I examined his gaze, then stared at the wall as I clenched my jaw.

"You're right, I'm not your father," he continued. "I'd be ashamed of myself if I were, leaving two young girls to fend for themselves. But I'm your uncle, and the only guardian you have left in this world. I may have come late, perhaps too late, but I'm here now and that's all that matters. And whether you believe me or not, I do care what happens to you and Ryleigh."

I snorted a somber laugh and stared into the living room. "We're already not worth much. Most people don't seem to care what happens to us."

Jet laid his hand on my arm and waited until I looked at him. "Don't think that about yourself. I know you think that a lot of people have given up on you, but I'm staying here. There's nothing you can do that will drive me away."

119

"Stop lying, Jet," I argued in a defeated voice. "Everyone in this town knows it's true. Most of them believe I'll sell my body like my sister has, and if something horrible happens to either of us it would be a relief to the rest of the world. It's no use. I was born worthless, and that's what I'll be until I die."

Jet studied me for several long seconds, then stood to take the brew off the stove. He poured some into a mug and set it in front of me. "Drink all of that. It'll help you feel better."

I avoided his gaze and fingered the mug's handle. "I shouldn't have said anything. You'll never understand."

Jet lowered himself in the chair again and stared at his hands as he spoke. "I'm trying to understand, Cheyenne."

I took a sip of the hot liquid and cringed at the taste. "You'll be here a week come Tuesday. Why have you stayed so long?"

"I've already told you why many times." Jet raised his eyes so that he could look at me again. "I want to help you. I can see now that you've been hurt in the past, and I'm upset that your father let you girls go through this alone. I'm not going to leave you like he did."

"Yes, you will," I argued as I drank more of the buttermilk brew. "Everyone leaves us." I exhaled slowly and began to toy with the mug. "You asked what else we did last night. Chad came to my window and wanted to steal some whiskey. I went along because I was angry with Overhaul and wanted him to suffer even just a little, and I thought I might see Ryleigh. Chad's plan was that I cause a distraction in the bar and he would grab the whiskey. I didn't know what to do, so I tried ordering a beer. The bartender refused, so I pretended to get mad and smashed a bottle over his head."

I glanced at my uncle to see if he would say anything, but he just watched me with his stoic eyes. I brought the mug to my lips and breathed in the steam that rose from the yellowish liquid. "Overhaul came out, and I got angry when I saw him. I threw some glasses at him. I didn't stick around long after that, but I know the glass broke skin."

Jet remained silent after I finished my explanation, and I wished I could melt through the chair and disappear through the floorboards. I drank more of the concoction in hopes that would settle the unease in my mind, but I still jumped when he spoke at last.

"Thank you for telling me, Cheyenne. I appreciate your honesty. When you finish your drink, I'm going to the saloon to pay for the glasses you broke and for the whiskey you stole. I want you to come with me and apologize to Mr. Overhaul for what you did."

My jaw dropped as I set the mug a little too hard on the table. "Jet, I am *not* going to apologize to Clyde Overhaul! I hate that man more than anything! And why do you have to pay the damages? He's rich enough to buy a ten thousand bottles of whiskey!"

"Cheyenne," he said more sternly than before. "I have to pay for the damages because it's the right thing to do, same as your apology. I told you before that I want you to respect your elders. What happened last night is in the past, but you can apologize for what you did."

"But Jet, you don't know what he's done to us. He's sleezy and—"

Jet sent me a look that made my stomach tie in knots again. "Cheyenne, enough. I know you're mad at Mr. Overhaul because Ryleigh works for him, but that's no cause for you to disrespect him like you have."

"It's not fair, Jet! You said you're trying to understand, but you're not even listening to me!"

"Cheyenne, that's enough. Finish your drink so we can go."

I glared at him and folded my arms over my chest. "Maybe I won't finish it. You can go pay for the damages if it's what you feel you need to do, but please don't make me go."

"Enough arguing. If you're not going to finish your drink, we'll just go now and get it over with. It's your choice."

I slid down the back of the chair. "Why are you making me do this?"

"Because you know you were wrong, and you need to own up to your mistakes. Are you going to finish it?" He motioned to the mug in front of me.

"No," I answered. I could tell in Jet's voice that he wouldn't listen to what I had to say.

Jet shrugged as he rose from the table. "Alright, then let's go."

I didn't make a move to get out of my chair. Jet tapped my shoulder with his finger and motioned toward the door. Biting my tongue to keep from saying a retort, I let out a sigh and followed him outside. It was a short walk over to the saloon, too short for my liking. He pushed the double doors open and kept them from swinging in my face as I entered behind him. The new bartender and Wil were wiping down the countertop when we walked in, and the new bartender frowned and rubbed his scalp when his eyes landed on me.

"Howdy," Wil greeted when Jet walked up to the bar. "What can I get you?"

"Well, I'm here to talk about what happened last night. I came to pay the damages."

The other bartender snarled and aimed a bony finger at my nose. "You keep that brat away from me! She liked to have split my head open. If I ever get my hands on her—"

"She came along to apologize," Jet interrupted.

Wil cleared his throat and rocked on his toes. "Calm down, Bob." He lifted his chin a few notches and nodded at Jet. "You'll have to talk to Clyde if you wanna know the damages. I just sell drinks."

"Well, where is he?"

Wil nodded toward the back of the building and picked up a glass as he wiped it off with his apron. "In his office, but he's in a sour mood. I'd be careful if I was you, mister."

"I intend to." Jet waved his arm at me. "Don't you have some business here, Cheyenne?"

I shot him a mild glare, then walked up to the bar. "I, uh, I'm sorry that I broke a bottle on your head," I said quickly as I glanced at Bob.

Bob scoffed and shook his head. "I don't think you're the least bit sorry. I'll be on the lookout for you and will make sure you don't hit me again."

I narrowed my eyes at Bob and felt the bitterness of a retort on the tip of my tongue, but Jet placed a hand on my shoulder and guided me away from the bar before I could lash out. We headed to a door just behind the bar, and the sign at the top read Clyde Overhaul's name. I had never been in

Overhaul's office before, and I really didn't want to explore that corner of the saloon. Jet tapped on the wood with his knuckle, and after a gruff *come in*, he turned the doorknob and moved to the side to let me enter ahead of him. Overhaul's eyes narrowed when he saw me, and I knew that the feeling crawling inside his chest was mutual.

"What do you want?" Overhaul demanded in a voice like an aggravated rattler.

"I came to pay the damages from last night," Jet explained again. "How much would that be?"

Overhaul glanced at me, then leaned back in his chair. "Just for last night, or the other times she's busted something of mine this past week?"

Jet studied the swine as he shifted his weight to one leg. "Well, I reckon if I'm here to pay damages, I should pay them all."

"She broke a thirty-dollar table of mine last week. I was gonna take it out of her sister's wages over time, but I'd rather get my money in full. And with them two bottles missing from my inventory, that bottle she smashed over Bob's head, plus those glasses she chunked at me—"

"How much do I owe you," Jet interrupted, finally sensing how conniving the sneak could be.

Overhaul offered a slimy grin and folded his hands over his ample belly. "I'd say forty dollars, or forty-five, should cover it all."

I rolled my eyes, hoping Jet wouldn't take him up on that offer.

Jet slipped his hands into his pockets as he answered. "I've seen your tables, and I watched her break the one you mentioned. I'd say your tables are worth five dollars at the most, and I should know. I used to make tables in a lumber yard. And at a dollar a whiskey bottle, that makes three more dollars. Those glasses can't be worth more than fifty cents apiece, and she said she threw two of them. That adds up to nine dollars even."

Overhaul's smile dipped a little, but a chuckle bubbled in the tobacco juice in his throat. "Well, that sounds more reasonable. I never was one for numbers. Alright, nine dollars." He motioned to me. "What's she doing here? She breaks something every time she comes through my doors!"

"I do not, and you know it," I snarled.

"Cheyenne," Jet muttered under his breath. He turned back to Overhaul. "She came here to apologize, Mr. Overhaul." He reached into his shirt pocket and brought out his wallet. Counting out the correct number of bills, he placed the money in Overhaul's sweaty palm and glanced at me.

"I'll believe that when I hear it," Overhaul growled, leveling his rat-like eyes on me.

My upper lip twitched as it attempted to curl in disgust. I knew Jet was waiting for an apology, but I couldn't stop the anger when I saw the saloon owner's yellow-stained grin. "You don't deserve anything from me," I growled in a low voice. "You are an evil man, and you'll never have my respect!"

"Cheyenne!"

I ignored my uncle as I continued to glare at Overhaul. "I won't apologize to you. You took everything from me, and I'll make you pay for what you're doing to Ryleigh!"

Overhaul's grin vanished, and he placed his elbows on his desk as he leaned forward. "Get out!" he bellowed, his voice piercing my eardrums.

Jet reached a hand to grab my arm, but I dodged out of his range. "I'm glad I broke your stupid table!" I shouted at the top of my lungs. "And if I had to bust a thousand bottles to hurt you I would!"

Jet grabbed my arm quite painfully and pulled me toward the door. "That's enough, Cheyenne!"

"Let me go, Jet!" I snarled, but Jet resisted my attempts to pull away.

Without saying another word, Jet dragged me out of the door, through the bar and onto the boardwalk. Once outside, I tried to yank my arm out of Jet's grasp, but his fingers tightened their hold. Jet barely seemed to notice the struggle I was giving him as he marched down the street to our shack. Within a few minutes, he marched up the porch steps and pushed me inside the house before closing the door soundly behind him.

"Why on earth did you say all those disrespectful things?" he demanded in a stern voice that was oddly quiet.

"Why?" My voice was echoing off the dingy walls as it scraped out of my throat. "I would tell you why, but you won't listen! You'll never listen to me! Didn't you see how that man tried to swindle more money out of you than you owed? He is a dirty crook, Jet!"

Jet aimed a finger toward my nose and raised his voice slightly. "Don't yell at me, Cheyenne. I told you to respect your elders, and Mr. Overhaul deserves your respect just as much as I do. I asked you to apologize to him, and you disobeyed me."

"You don't know what he's done!"

"Enough, Cheyenne!"

I stared at my uncle and shook my head in disbelief. "You lied to me. You're not even trying to understand."

Jet placed a hand on his hip as he slid his fingers through his hair. "Then explain it to me."

I lowered my gaze and shook my head. "You just won't listen. I don't care what you do to me."

Jet studied me and sighed softly. "You can trust me, Cheyenne. Believe it or not, I'm on your side. Please let me help you."

I shook my head and backed away from him. "You're a Douglas, and Douglas' have the urge to abandon people when things get too tough. It's just a matter of time before you leave. It'd be best that you don't know much about me."

Jet's eyes softened as his shoulders relaxed. "Cheyenne, I'm sorry. You don't have to be afraid of me."

I avoided his gaze as I cleared my throat. "Can we just forget this whole thing happened? I can work on the house this afternoon."

Jet shook his head as he headed toward the kitchen. "Today is Sunday. I won't make you work on Sundays. I'll make some lunch and then you can rest. If you sleep it could help with the headache."

I watched him retreat into the kitchen and breathed a sigh of relief. I was tired of Jet's constant interrogations, and it was comforting to know he would drop the subject. I sat in a chair at the dining table and placed my head on top of my forearm. Somewhere below my relief I felt a sense of longing. I wanted Jet to understand why we were in such trouble, but I was afraid of how he would react. I didn't want to get used to his presence in case he realized we were in too much trouble and leave. I knew I couldn't stand to go through the challenge of losing someone else, so it was best that I didn't get attached to my uncle.

I glanced up to watch Jet fry some bacon in a skillet. His presence confused me. I couldn't understand why he would stick around. I couldn't make myself believe that he was there because he wanted to help us. I barely knew he existed, so perhaps he wanted something else from us. We had no money, but maybe there was something else he thought we had that he desired. A slight frown pulled on the corners of my mouth as I watched him cook. If he was using us, why did he act so different from the other people?

~EIGHT~

I stared at the ceiling as I laid on my bed. Jet had left me alone for most of the afternoon as I slept through the migraine. He had ventured to the livery to check on his horse a few minutes ago, which left me completely alone in our tiny shack. I found the isolation comforting as it reminded me of how I had lived my life for the last several years. There was a sense of peace without the company of another person, and I enjoyed the opportunity to avoid conversation. I still felt a twinge of bitterness in my chest at Jet's persistence of an apology to Overhaul. He had no right in forcing me to be polite to a man I loathed, but he did have the right to punish me for disobeying him.

A frown tugged at my lips, and I pushed myself into a sitting position on the bed. I couldn't understand the compassion I had sensed from my uncle, and I wasn't sure how to handle it. Since I was a child, I could recall several times when the townspeople would sneer at my sister and I, but I could barely remember if anyone ever showed us compassion. Perhaps Jet did speak the truth about wanting to help us, but even if he wasn't trying to hide something from us, I wanted him to leave.

Slowly, an idea began to form in the back of my mind. Jet had insisted time and again that we needed help, and he wanted to offer that help. If he continued to view us as vulnerable, he would stay in Sunset forever, but if I showed him that I could fend for myself as Ryleigh worked, maybe he would see he wasn't needed and leave. I grinned to myself as I slid to the floor and hurried to the kitchen. The first thing to do would be to make supper by myself. Once he saw that he wouldn't have to cook any meals, he would start to feel less needed.

I bit my lip as I opened the cabinet doors to find something to cook. Although I hadn't had much practice in the kitchen, I did watch Ryleigh create a few meals from time to time. I finally found four potatoes that I could mash and set about finding the main dish. After rummaging for a moment or two, I found a package of salt pork that Jet had cut into for a previous meal. Surely it wouldn't take long for me to cook a meal of mashed potatoes and roasted pork.

I glanced at the stove and frowned as I scratched the side of my head. Where had I seen firewood? I raced through the kitchen and stepped on the back porch, but there was no kindling to start a fire. I wandered back inside and glanced down the hallway toward the room where our parents had stayed. The door was closed, and I rarely saw it open except for when Ryleigh would come home for some sleep. I bit my lip and slowly walked down the hallway until my hand circled around the doorknob. I closed my eyes as I exhaled softly, then pushed against the door until it opened wide enough for me to slip through.

The room was dark as curtains covered the only window, but when my eyes adjusted to the dim light, I could see that Jet had already made himself at home in the room. A worn black Bible sat on top of the nightstand next to the bed, and I glowered at the book for a moment. Jet had made known his faith in the short time I had known him, but I doubted the sincerity of the religion. Ryleigh had sworn that there was a God and that he was looking out for us, but I never saw the signs.

Shaking my head to clear my thoughts, I tore my gaze away from the book and rummaged through a chest at the foot of the bed until I found one of Pa's old shirts that I could use for kindling. I backed out of the room hurriedly, then retraced my steps to the kitchen. Within a few minutes, I had placed a pot full of water and potatoes onto a burning stove and was also frying a few slabs of salt pork in a skillet.

"There," I murmured to myself as I watched the water begin to boil. "This ain't so bad."

I left the food on the stove as I tiptoed to the living room and looked outside. Jet was not in sight, and a thrill of excitement pounded in my chest. Maybe the food would be done cooking by the time he came back. The surprise on his face would be well worth the time it took to conjure a plan. Jet could be on the road out of our lives by the end of the week if all went well.

A loud sizzling sound sent a jolt of fright down my spine, and I raced into the kitchen to see that the boiling water had spilled over the pot of potatoes and onto the stove. Without thinking, I grabbed the pot to remove it from the heat but shouted in pain when I felt the hot metal burn my palms.

"Daggum you!" I growled as I rubbed my hands on my trousers. My palms had turned a shade of red. I grabbed the remaining material from the kindling and wrapped it around the pot as I placed it on the counter. "Why can't you just behave?"

As soon as I had set the potatoes on the counter, I smelled something burnt as I noticed that the room was beginning to fill with smoke. I whirled around and realized that I hadn't flipped the salt pork, and the side against the skillet was turning black. Grunting my misery, I grabbed a fork and tried to flip the piece of meat, but it was stuck to the cast iron. After struggling for a moment to loosen the meat, I finally succeeded in flipping it over and turned back to the potatoes.

They still felt crisp when I tapped them with my finger, so I placed the pot back on the stove and stared angrily at the water to make sure it did not bubble over this time. The smoke in the kitchen stung my eyes, and I had to blink fast to keep the tears from blurring my vision. At last, I pulled the skillet with the salt pork off the stove and transferred the meat onto a tin plate. The meat resembled charcoal. Curling my lip in determination, I wiped my forehead with the back of my wrist and ignored how my black curls clung to the perspiration on my skin.

I grabbed a knife and began to slice the salt pork into manageable bite-sized pieces when I heard the familiar sizzle from the potato pot. I glanced over my shoulder to see the water spill onto the stove again and felt a sharp pain in my left thumb.

"Ouch!" I cried as I returned my gaze to the salt pork in front of me. In my haste to see the potato pot I had sliced my thumb instead of the meat. I groaned a curse word I had heard in the saloon and held my bleeding thumb with my other hand. The red liquid dripped down my wrist and onto the counter. "I am fed up with you!" I snarled as I ripped the pot off the stove once again. "Why can't you work with me?"

I heard the front door open and felt my insides fall to the ground. Wagging my wounded hand in the air, I brushed my hair back and sneaked around the corner to come face-to-face with Jet, who had a worried expression on his features.

"What's wrong? I smell smoke."

I pursed my lips and shifted my weight on one leg. "It's nothing. I have it all under control."

Jet glanced over my shoulder at the mess in the kitchen and hurried to extinguish the fire in the stove. Once everything was turned off, he leveled his piercing eyes on me. I expected him to begin another long lecture, but after looking into my eyes for a moment, he glanced down at my hands.

"Is that blood?" he asked as he nodded toward my injury.

I quickly hid my hands behind my back. "I don't see anything. I'm not sure what you mean." I broke my gaze with him as I hurried to tend to the potatoes. "This was supposed to be ready before you got back."

Jet grabbed my wrist and pulled my hand up to expose my bleeding thumb. "What did you do?"

"It's nothing," I defended, trying to tug my hand away. "It's just a little scratch."

Jet frowned as he shook his head. "No, it's not. That's deep." He reached into his back pocket and brought out a handkerchief. I stopped resisting him as I watched him wiped some of the blood from my hand with the bandanna. "I ought to take you to the doc to see if you need stitches," he commented as he walked to the sink to pump some water into a bowl.

I bristled at the thought of going to the doctor and shook my head firmly. "I don't need a doctor. I told you, it's nothing. It was just an accident, and I'm sure it'll heal fine."

Jet brought the bowl of water to the dining table and motioned for me to wash the blood off my hands. "I would feel better knowing it heals right. We'll go to the doc and then see what to do about supper."

"No!" I argued. I cringed when my voice quivered with fear. "I-I mean… the doc is probably busy anyway. Let me just wash the blood off and you'll see that it ain't so bad."

I turned my back to Jet as I began to wash my hands, but I could feel his eyes on me. At last, he lowered himself into the chair closest to me and studied my profile. The smoke in the kitchen was thinning as the minutes ticked by, which made it slightly easier to breathe. I glanced at my uncle out of the corner of my eye, then focused on my thumb. I wondered why he was so quiet when I expected him to tell me I was wrong in some way or another, but I refused to ask him.

"See?" I finally spoke as I showed him my thumb. "It just looked worse with all the blood on it."

Jet glanced at the cut, then returned his gaze to my eyes. I studied him for a moment before I ducked my head. "What were you doing?" he asked gently.

I snorted as I motioned to the mess behind me. "I think that's quite obvious, Jet."

"Yes, but why were you doing it?"

A thought crossed my mind that I should be honest with him, but I was afraid of what he would think if I opened even a little to him. "I… I was just tired of your cooking, is all. I've seen Ryleigh cook a meal before and I thought it wouldn't be that hard."

Jet glanced toward the mess again. "I'll help you clean up. I can teach you how to cook if you'd like."

"You'd do what?" I asked as I studied him.

"I can teach you how to cook. I know it may not look like it, but I know how to fix a few things," he finished with a chuckle. "C'mon, I'll show you how to make scrambled eggs."

I watched him as he rose and entered the kitchen, then cautiously followed him. As he had promised, he helped me clean up the blackened salt pork and potatoes. He grabbed some kindling that was hidden beside the stove and started a fresh fire.

"Cooking really is simple," he explained as he turned to face me. "It's a lot like building something. The ingredients are like the nails and boards. All you got to do is know how to put it all together." He pulled out an egg basket and motioned for me to stand beside him. "Come here and I'll walk you through it."

I hesitated and bit my lip as I contemplated what to do.

Jet smiled kindly. "I don't bite, Cheyenne."

I squared my shoulders as I inched closer to him. "I'm not afraid of you. I just…" My voice faded whenever I couldn't think of a retort, and I shook my head. "Never mind."

Jet turned back to the basket in front of us. "Go ahead and grab five eggs. I think that should be enough for the both of us." He watched as I grabbed the eggs, then motioned toward the cabinet. "Grab a bowl and crack the eggs inside it. Be sure you don't leave any eggshell. I don't know about you, but I'm not a big fan of eating something crunchy in my soft eggs."

I silently obeyed Jet's instruction as he explained how to season the eggs and whisk them together so that the yolk blended in with the whites. When I poured the eggs into the skillet, he handed me a metal spatula.

"Make sure you gently push them around occasionally so that they don't burn," he continued as he watched me work. "There you go. When they are mostly solid, take them off the fire. The eggs will cook a little bit longer since the skillet is still hot. You don't want to over cook them, or they will be rubbery."

I glanced over my shoulder at him. "Where did you learn how to cook?"

Jet leaned against the counter as he slid his fingers into his pockets. "My ma made sure us boys could cook a few meals by ourselves." He chuckled to himself as he recalled the memory. "Looking back, I guess she was scared we wouldn't find wives to cook for us. I suppose she was right with half of her boys."

"How come you never married?" I asked as I turned back to the finished eggs.

"Never got around to it, I suppose. When I was younger, I was more interested in an adventure than settling down somewhere. Rod was a little different."

My back stiffened at the sound of my father's name. "What was he like?"

Silence settled over us momentarily. "You don't remember him, do you?" Jet asked at last, but his voice was compassionate again.

I glanced up at him, then shrugged. "Not really. Ryleigh said he left us when I was just a baby. She told me some stories about him, but I don't know if they were true."

Jet lowered his gaze to his boots as he cleared his throat. "Your pa had his faults, but I do believe he had some good in him. He liked to gamble, even when we were kids. I remember he always made bets with me on who could run the fastest or who could fight the hardest, but he had a nasty habit of letting his anger control him. As we got older, I would let him win so that he wouldn't take his anger out on me, but he did save my neck a time or two as kids."

I grabbed some plates and began to dish up the eggs. "What did he look like?"

"He looked a lot like you. He had black hair and the same shade of brown eyes. He was a little bit shorter than I am, and a little thinner, too. Your pa didn't like to work much, so he gambled for a living."

Jet grabbed one of the plates and walked to the dining table with me. I sat in the chair opposite from him and stared at the eggs as he said a short prayer. When he was done praying, I raised my eyes to study him.

"Did you ever meet Mama?" I asked cautiously.

Jet glanced at me, then nodded. "A few times."

I grabbed a fork as I pushed the eggs from one side of the plate to the other. "I remember her. She looked like Ryleigh. She died when I was just a child."

"I didn't know she had died until I met with Rod before coming here. I'm sorry."

I frowned. "Why do people say that when someone dies? It's not like you killed her. Pa's the one who did that."

Jet lowered his fork and swallowed the mouthful of eggs, but he thankfully

133

didn't continue the conversation. At last, he motioned to my plate. "You should eat your supper. You're going back to school tomorrow, and I'd like you to go to bed early."

"I hate school," I growled as I continued to push the eggs around.

"I know, but that's part of our deal," Jet argued mildly. "You go to school in the mornings and then help me with the house in the afternoons."

"I'm not going to school."

"Yes, you are. If you don't, I'll dock your pay for tomorrow."

I rolled my eyes but didn't respond as I slowly lifted a forkful of eggs to my mouth. I wasn't in the mood to argue with him in that moment. Come the morrow I would have the energy to argue with Jet and convince him to skip school. Perhaps I would even escape from him for a few moments of solitude. I would show Jet that he was as unwelcomed in my life as my parents had been, then he would have no choice but to leave Sunset forever.

* * *

A group of boys threw a homemade ball around a circle, and three nearby girls played jump rope in the schoolyard. A few of the younger kids sat on the see-saw and swing someone had tied to a branch on a dying oak tree. Pursing my lips tightly, I adjusted the lunch pail I had slung over my shoulder and sauntered into the hubbub of before-school activity. My argument with Jet that morning had consisted of many reasons why I shouldn't be in the classroom, but my attempts to persuade him were futile. Jet had made sure I was on time before he left for his job at the feed mill.

As I came closer to the schoolhouse steps, one of the older girls, Penelope Wilkes, stopped talking with her friends to turn an annoyed glare in my direction. "Oh, look, girls. Guess who decided to join us for school this morning."

I let the pail drop from my shoulder as I turned a glare of my own on her. "Don't you all faint at once. I'll be around to autograph your books later."

She set her hands on her rounded hips and narrowed her eyes to slits. "If you get cocky, you'll pull a stupid trick. And if you pull a stupid trick, you'll cause a distraction. If you cause a distraction, I'll lose my concentration and my grades will fall. Does that make any sense to that pea-sized brain of yours?"

The corners of my mouth turned upward in an amused smile. "There are too many five-dollar words in this two-bit conversation, and I would rather not share them five-dollar words with a dumb person like yourself. Try to keep up, Penelope."

Before she could utter another word, I hurried up the steps to enter the school. A few of the more mature, serious students milled around by the chalkboards, discussing the latest problems of certain subjects I chose to ignore. Mr. Hyndman was looking over some books on his desk when I stepped into the aisle. He hadn't seen me yet, so I found it suddenly necessary to duck my head and see what interesting things I could find in the yard. Or down the path toward the creek.

I had just wrapped my hand around the doorknob when I heard a man's voice behind me. "Good to see you this morning, Cheyenne."

My lip curled as I cringed, but I pasted on a fake smile as I whirled around to face Mr. Hyndman's gaze. "I just-a swung in to say howdy. I ain't gonna be a-wastin' yer time no more," I drawled, trying my best to use the worst grammar I could.

Mr. Hyndman studied me before he motioned his hand toward the classroom. "Why don't you find a seat? I was just fixing to call the children in for the morning's lessons."

I forced a return smile. "Of course." I watched him step out to ring the bell and stuck my tongue at his back. Jet may have forced me to go to school, but he couldn't force me to sit still and listen to what Hyndman had to say.

One by one, the children begrudgingly entered the building, few faces aglow with excitement for the things they would learn on this beautiful Monday morning. I stood with my back in the corner of the room, ignoring mild glares from a few of the pupils as they passed me to find their seats. Chad wasn't among the crowd, and I felt my hopes die. Without my best friend, a morning of classes would be long and uneventful.

When everyone had filed into the claustrophobic room, I lowered myself in a seat toward the back where the other students my age sat. Mr.

Hyndman picked up a large black Bible and flipped toward the middle of the book as he read a few verses in Proverbs as part of his morning routine. When he finished reading, he glanced up from the Bible and offered a smile toward his pupils.

"Good morning, children," he greeted as he lowered himself behind his desk.

"Good morning."

I scoffed at the flat answer from the fellow students and sank lower in my seat. Mr. Hyndman pulled out a book from his desk drawer and opened it flat in front of him.

"We're going to start today with spelling words." A chorus of groans rumbled through the classroom as books slammed on their desks. I folded my arms over my chest and stared straight ahead. "You have ten minutes to study the words on your assigned pages, and then I'll quiz you on how good you've learned them."

Jet had purchased the supplies I would need a few days ago, and my spell book sat on the desk in front of me unopened. Sitting in the back of the room gave me the advantage of hiding my rebellious moves from our teacher, and since I had the pew to myself, I had time to think up a plan to leave the school. I rolled my eyes around to the clock hanging above my head and counted the seconds. Steven, a fifteen-year-old country boy, glanced my way, frowned, and turned back to his book. I couldn't resist the urge to snarl in his direction.

Finally, Mr. Hyndman glanced at his pocket watch and cleared his throat. "Alright, students, close your books. I'm going to call some names, and if I call your name, I want you to stand up and spell the word I give you. Penelope, spell chrysanthemum."

The arrogant blond bounced to her feet and flashed a warm smile toward Mr. Hyndman. "Chrysanthemum. C-H-R-Y-S-A-N-T-H-E-M-U-M. Chrysanthemum."

Mr. Hyndman nodded and scanned his gaze among the crowd of children. "Sammie, spell triumph."

A nine-year-old girl rose to her feet cautiously and clasped her hands behind her back as she rocked on her toes. "Triumph. Uh, T-R-Y...." She licked her lips as she glanced at the ceiling. "No, T-R-I... U-M-P-H?"

Mr. Hyndman smiled at her attempt and nodded. "That's correct, Sammie. Your spelling has improved."

She beamed a proud smile and slipped back in her chair.

Mr. Hyndman continued calling out names until almost every student had a turn to stand up. I listened to their oral recitations and found my lips turning downward in a frown. Hardly any student spelled a word incorrectly, and I couldn't help but think they were arrogant as they followed the teacher's instruction.

"Steven, I want you to spell despondency."

The country boy rose to his feet and seemed to tower over every student in the room, including the teacher, and cleared his throat as he ran his fingers through the thick mass of dark hair. "Despondency," he began in the deepest voice I had heard for a boy. "D-E-S-P-O-N-D-E-N-C-Y. Despondency."

"That's right, Steven. Could you tell us what that word means?"

"Um... desperation?"

Mr. Hyndman nodded. "Right. It's a state of hopelessness or desperation. Good job, Steven." The boy sat, and I suddenly felt Mr. Hyndman's stare on me. Rolling my eyes, I turned my head to find him looking at me with a soft gaze. I exhaled annoyingly and crossed my arms over my chest. "Cheyenne," he called out, "please spell guarantee."

I rolled my eyes and slowly pushed myself out of my seat. Every eye turned on me, and I found myself returning a glare toward Penelope. Clearing my throat, I leveled my gaze on our teacher. "Guarantee. S-T-U-P-I-D. Guarantee."

A few snickers scattered across the room, but Mr. Hyndman looked less than amused. "That's incorrect, Cheyenne. Did you study your spelling words like I asked you to?"

A grin exposed my teeth as I leaned forward. "Nope."

Mr. Hyndman let out a low breath and set the spell book down on his desk. "Cheyenne, at least try to spell guarantee."

"I did try, but you didn't like my attempt. Shouldn't someone else go now?"

"Try it again," Mr. Hyndman argued as he raised his eyebrows.

My grin grew until it almost reached my ears. "Fine. Guarantee. D-U-M-B."

Mr. Hyndman gave me a disapproving look as he pointed rigidly to the west. "Stand in the corner, Cheyenne. While the other kids are at recess, you will write your list of words on the chalkboard twenty times."

I smiled smugly and obeyed. I listened to the rest of the morning session, and at last Mr. Hyndman called for lunch break and recess. Glancing over my shoulder, I watched the children race outside and slowly turned around. Mr. Hyndman handed me a piece of chalk and pointed to the chalkboard without saying a word. I took the chalk and positioned myself in front of the board. I reached up to begin writing in my poor penmanship, but before I started on the first word, I glanced over my shoulder to see if Mr. Hyndman was watching. He was bent over his desk as he wrote something on a paper tablet.

I turned back to the board and began writing *Mr. Hyndman smells like horse dung.* I had written the sentence at least five times when I heard something thud behind me. I whirled around to see Mr. Hyndman jump to his feet and charge around his desk. Dropping the chalk, I found it suddenly necessary to find what the kids were doing outside. I darted out the front door and ran around to the back of the school in hopes he would give up the chase and leave me alone.

"What are you doing?"

I glanced over my shoulder to see Penelope glaring at me with both hands planted firmly on her hips. "Will you shut up?" I hissed. "What does it look like I'm doing?"

"You're supposed to be inside writing on the chalkboard," she growled. "How dare you disobey Mr. Hyndman? I'll tell on you where you are, and then you'll see if you can get away free of charge."

I waved a hand in the air and glanced around the corner to see if Mr. Hyndman was in sight. "There's those five-dollar words again. You really ought to get an education so I can carry on a decent conversation with you."

She huffed a protest and advanced on me. "You shut up! I'll tell Mr. Hyndman what you said, and you just see how funny you think you are after he's done with you!"

"You don't scare me," I snarled, turning my back to the front of the school so that I could face her. "Neither does Mr. Hyndman. I've survived his licks before, and I can certainly handle any other kind of measly punishment he will throw my way. I ain't taking them words back, and I ain't gonna let Mr. Hyndman hold me inside on such a beautiful day."

Penelope glanced behind me, then poked her finger in my chest. "That's not funny, Cheyenne. How dare you accuse me of such a thing? I can't believe you!"

I frowned. "What? I never accused you of anything, you pipsqueak. What's your problem?"

"What's going on here?"

I jumped when I heard the baritone voice and turned around to find Mr. Hyndman standing behind me with his arms crossed over his chest. "Nothing," I answered quickly, but it was apparent he didn't believe that answer.

"Cheyenne accused me of using wiles on you to get a good grade!" Penelope whined. "I've never been so insulted in my life!"

My jaw dropped as I stared at her. "I never said that!" I turned back to our teacher. "I swear, I never did!"

Mr. Hyndman placed his hands on his hips and frowned. "You're in enough trouble as it is. I don't think it'd be smart for you to add lying on top of it."

"I'm not scared of you," I protested. "You barely hit hard enough to tickle!"

"Well, if I don't scare you, maybe we'll make a trip to the feed mill and talk to your uncle."

I stiffened as my eyes widened. "There's no need for that. I mean, Jet's awfully busy, and if you interrupted his work, he'll be plenty mad."

"Then behave yourself. I believe you have some writing to do inside,

Cheyenne. You best get to it."

He motioned to the front of the building, and I curled my lip in disgust as I stuffed my hands in my pockets. "Yes, sir," I snarled as I trudged back inside the building.

The rest of the day dragged on slowly, but at last mid-afternoon came, and Mr. Hyndman dismissed us. I gathered the books on my desk and grabbed my lunch pail before hurrying outside with the rest of the crowd. One day of school was over, and I hoped I would never go back again. Jet had no say in what I did with myself, whether he thought he did or not.

As I descended the stairs of the building, I couldn't help noticing Steven and a few other boys milling around at the base of the steps, all of them glaring at me. I lifted my chin in the air and stopped in front of them.

"Afternoon," I greeted flatly. "What's got your trousers in a bunch?"

Ben, a pencil of a boy with glasses, crossed his arms and frowned. "It ain't proper for a girl to mention a man's trousers."

I rolled my eyes. "I don't care. Did I do something to offend y'all or what? I know I ain't wanted 'round these here parts, but today seems like I'm cold-shouldered more than usual."

"It's just you," Steven answered, his lips firming. "You know, some of us go to school so we can learn to read and write. Arithmetic helps when you want to farm for a living. When you join class, you act as if it's a game to see how many buttons you can push before the day's over. It makes it hard for the rest of us to concentrate."

I raised an eyebrow and scoffed. "Well, gee whiz, I didn't realize boys who loved to fish and play games were as concerned over learning as that snobby Penelope Wilkes. I guess I'll just leave your Highnesses alone and let you grow arrogant like the rest of these people."

Steven's jaw tightened. "You have it backwards. We ain't arrogant and snobby like Penelope. You are."

His simple insult sent a jolt of anger flying through my veins, and I balled my fingers into a fist. Dropping my books and pail, I leapt on him and sank my knuckles into his nose. The pounce surprised him, but he retaliated quickly and landed a blow to my left eye. His fist only angered me more,

140

and we began rolling in the dirt as we both tried to hurt each other. A crowd of students circled around us as they began shouting their encouragements to who they wanted to win. I ignored all distractions and was instead focused on harming Steven as badly as I could.

"Hold it, hold it!"

A man grabbed my arm, but I wrestled out of his grasp and dove on top of Steven again. Wrapping an arm around my middle, the same gent pulled me off the boy as another man pulled Steven in the opposite direction.

"Let go of me!" I growled as I lunged for my fellow school mate.

The man tightened his hold on me and growled in my ear. "Stop it, Cheyenne!"

I froze when I recognized Jet's voice and watched as Steven's father consoled his son. When we both calmed down enough to think straight, I felt a strange surge of guilt settle in my chest that I despised more than being caught fighting.

"Haven't I taught you better than to hit a girl?" Steven's father snarled at his son.

Steven spat blood that oozed from his bottom lip and frowned. "That ain't no girl, Pa. That's just Cheyenne Douglas."

His father frowned. "We'll talk about this at home." He straightened to his full height and eyed Jet from under the brim of his hat. "You must be Cheyenne's uncle. We've never met, and I would've wished to introduce myself under better circumstances. I'm Andy Butte," he said as he extended his hand.

Jet accepted his hand and gave it a firm shake. "Jet Douglas."

Mr. Butte glanced down at his son and frowned under a full beard. "I apologize for my son's behavior. I promise it won't happen again."

"I didn't start it, Pa," Steven protested.

"That's enough, son," Mr. Butte hushed. "We'll discuss this on the way home."

I narrowed my eyes and curled my lip at the thought of what I was fixing to do. Letting out a breath of air, I scuffed the toe of my boot in the dirt and stuffed my hands in my pockets. "He ain't wrong," I muttered loud enough for the two men to hear. "I swung the first fist."

Mr. Butte hooked his thumbs in his pockets and looked down at me. "Well, I appreciate your honesty, young lady, but it takes two to fight." He touched the brim of his hat before he laid a hand on Steven's shoulder. "We'll be seeing y'all around. Let's go, son."

Steven glanced at me, then followed his father to a wagon parked nearby. Jet wrapped a hand around my arm and led me toward the house. When we were a few yards from the porch, I pulled out of his grasp and ran the rest of the way to the shack. I closed the front door firmly behind me and disappeared into my bedroom, hoping Jet wouldn't stick his nose in my face. I heard the front door open when I jumped on my bed, and soon Jet appeared in my doorway.

"Don't say a thing," I said before he could open his mouth. "I don't want to hear what you have to say."

Jet folded his arms over his chest and leaned against the doorjamb. "That eye's gonna be a real shiner in a couple of hours. You should put some ice on that."

I sighed and fell on top of my pillow. "You're not going to lecture me?"

Jet pushed himself away from the doorway and ambled over to my bed where he sat down. I scooted my feet away from him in disgust. "A lecture right now in your condition and state of mind would be a waste of time. I told you before you started helping me on the house that I would dock your pay by five cents. That fight cost you that much."

I covered my face with my palm and groaned. "You think that bothers me? I'll never pay for that dumb saddle of yours. I got nothing to lose."

"Is that so?" Jet took his hat off and let it hang on the bedpost. "Seems to me that the more you misbehave, the longer it'll take you to raise the money to pay for my saddle. The longer it takes for you to pay for my saddle, the more you'll go to school and work hard for me. You won't have time to play and cause mischief."

I moved my fingers to glare at him. "I won't work my backside off for you or listen to you. How many times have I told you that and you still ain't learned?"

"Maybe I'm stubborn." He slapped my shoulder playfully as he rose to his feet. "C'mon, let's get something on that eye before it swells shut."

I watched him leave the room and moaned my discontent. I pushed myself from the mattress and wandered into the living room where I plopped down on the bench. Jet rummaged around in the other room, and finally came into view with a cool piece of meat that he pressed against my eye. I flinched and flashed him a mild glare as I held the steak in place.

"Don't look at me that way," he said as he lowered himself beside me. "I didn't tell you to fight that young man."

"I don't care," I muttered.

Jet cleared his throat and crossed an ankle over his knee. "Cheyenne, I'm not trying to anger you. I just want to make sure we stop the swelling in that eye."

"I don't care what you're trying to do. You have a way of irritating me, and you'll never leave me alone until rain floods in the desert." I mumbled a curse word under my breath, halfway hoping Jet wouldn't hear it.

He stiffened suddenly and let his foot drop to the floor. "Cheyenne, I don't want to ever hear you say that again," he said in a low, stern voice that sent shivers down my spine. I curled my lip at my discomfort and stared straight ahead as I waited for him to continue. "You keep pushing your limits. Do you want me to punish you?"

I cringed and slipped lower in my seat.

"What has gotten into you? After that argument this morning, the fight at school, and that vulgar language, I've about had it." He shook his head as he sighed. "Stand up."

I dropped the steak as my eyes widened. "What for?"

Jet rose to his feet and motioned with his hand for me to do the same. "Because I said so. C'mon, we ain't got all day."

I shook my head and laid my chin on my chest. "No. I think I can defend myself better from down here."

Jet grabbed my wrist and pulled me to my feet as he marched to the kitchen. I swallowed my fear and tugged away from him, but he pulled me back.

143

"What are you gonna do?" I asked cautiously.

He turned me around so he could look in my eye and raised an eyebrow. "I don't want you to use that kind of language again. I'm tempted to wash your mouth out with soap."

I cringed when I remembered the bitter taste of lye. "Can we just forget that I said it?"

Jet seemed to ignore my question. "You never learn. I'm trying to help you, but none of you girls seem to welcome my presence. Maybe I shouldn't have come here. You've both said you don't need me anyway."

For some reason I couldn't explain, his words created a sense of dread inside my chest. Old, forgotten feelings of neglect crept into my throat, and I felt a sense of fear like I had as a child when we were suddenly left on our own. My eyebrows twitched and my lower lip trembled. I didn't want to cave into the fear I had felt as a child again.

I cleared my throat and lowered my head. "Well, maybe you should leave. I don't care what you do, and it would sure be... sure be..." I couldn't make myself lie, not then. I straightened my spine and swallowed hard. "I just don't care."

Jet studied me in silence for several seconds. "If that's the way you feel, you'll never listen to me for the rest of the time I'm here. Fine, I give up. If I'm not getting anywhere with you two, I might as well leave."

The back of my eyes stung with unwanted tears. I tore from his grip as I marched into the kitchen and snatched the bar of soap from the counter. Grabbing his hand, I plopped the lye in his palm and crossed my arms over my chest as I met his bewildered gaze. "Well? What are you waiting for?" I growled. "It's too hot for a trip, anyway."

Jet stared at the soap in his hand and raised an eyebrow when he met my gaze. "You don't want me to leave?" he asked quietly.

"I never said that. Just quit being so dramatic and blowing things out of proportion. Go ahead and get it over with. Like you say, we got work to do."

Jet tried to hide the smile that spread underneath his thick whiskers. He set the bar of soap on the counter and laid a hand on my shoulder as he led me toward the door. "Well, like you say, we have work to do."

~NINE~

I sat on the last step of the school as I watched the children wander nearby with their groups of friends to eat their lunches together. I glanced at the untouched sandwich in my lap that Jet had fixed just that morning and felt my hunger fade away. Jet had worked me until the natural light was no more for the last two days, and my muscles ached more than they ever had in all my life. I lowered my head to stretch my sore neck muscles and rubbed my shoulder with my fingers.

Penelope glanced my way, and I felt my insides curdle. Smiling cheekily, she swaggered toward me, and my spine stiffened with each sauntering step she took. "I made an 'A' on my math test," she bragged when she was in range. "What did *you* make?"

I ran my tongue over my teeth and unwrapped Jet's sandwich. "I failed."

She scoffed and crossed her arms over her chest. "I knew it. I just knew it. You come from a family of failures. You fail to do the right thing, your mother failed to pay her bills, and your father failed to be the man of the house." She leaned her snotty nose in close and shook her head in an annoying way. "Your sister failed to measure up to be a real woman. Now she lives like a cow in a herd full of bulls. She's no better than an animal, letting men paw her in such a way."

My head slowly raised up until my eyes met with hers. "Ryleigh ain't no animal," I muttered slowly in a low voice. "You take that back."

"She works in a saloon, doesn't she? Hopefully, you're not so stupid that you don't know what kind of foolishness happens in a saloon. I won't take it back unless you can tell me she doesn't entertain men in an improper

146

way." She narrowed her eyes. "You and I both know she does. She's an animal. Nothing more than a cow fit for breeding."

My lip twitched angrily as I jumped to my full height, knocking the unwrapped sandwich to the ground at my feet. The sudden movement startled Penelope, and she backed up a few steps.

"But I see the apple doesn't fall far from the tree," Penelope continued with firm lips. "Your sister is a cow, while you're a badger. You can do nothing right, and your temper sure turns ferocious. And you're as ugly as a badger, too. Why, that black eye even makes you look like one!"

I made a move to throw a fist square in her nose, but someone grabbed my arm to keep me from hurting her. I glanced up to see Steven Butte beside me, a disgusted frown on his lips.

"Penelope, that ain't no way to speak to a person," he scolded sternly. "You're a fool to purposefully hurt someone."

"Why are you sticking up for her?" Penelope snarled. "She busted your lip a few days ago! You hated her as much as me once. She's no good, and you know it!"

I lunged toward the uppity girl, but Steven blocked me. "You open your mouth again and I'll stuff a cactus in there!" I shouted.

Her eyes widened as she backed up some more. "She's crazy! Low-down and crazy!" Whirling on her heel, she raced across the school yard to join her friends a safe distance away.

Steven turned to me and studied my fiery gaze. "Are you alright?"

"Why do you care?" I snarled as I bent to snatch the sandwich off the ground. "You were in her shoes not that long ago."

He shrugged and shoved his hands into his pockets. "I guess I was. Pa and me, we had us a good long talk that day of the fight. I realized where I was wrong, and I'm sorry. I shouldn't have judged you like I did."

I brushed the dirt off the bread and peeked up at him, squinting my eyes against the sun. "Don't get all mushy. I didn't ask you to butt in. I can handle my own fights."

"I know that," he agreed with a smirk, rubbing his jaw. "I just didn't want Mr. Hyndman to jump down your throat." He glanced at my sandwich.

"My ma always packs enough lunch for me to get fat on. I got an extra sandwich if you want it."

"There's no need for—"

"It's too much for me to eat, anyway. I'd sure hate for Ma's good sandwich to go to waste."

I sighed and narrowed my eyes nonthreateningly. "I'm not one to accept charity."

"It's not charity. Your sandwich fell on the ground and is now all gritty with dirt. My ma always packs more than I can eat, so you can have my last sandwich." I continued to eye him, and he threw his hands in the air in exasperation. "C'mon! Lunch recess is almost over, and your uncle wouldn't want you to eat that."

I straightened my shirt and shook my head to knock the hair out of my face. "Fine. I just don't understand how you hate me at the beginning of the week and try to be nice to me halfway through it."

He shrugged. "I guess you'd say I had a change of mind."

I followed him to a group of boys sitting in the shade of a nearby tree and took the peanut butter and jelly sandwich Steven handed to me. I noticed none of the other boys seemed to be as cheerful as Steven, and I felt my spine stiffen again. When no one moved their lips to say a word, I forced a smile to stretch lamely across my mouth and turned to leave.

"Thanks for the sandwich," I muttered as I retreated from the circle as casually as I could.

Glancing across the street, I could see Jet working alongside several other men, sweat dripping from his nose due to the warm sun beating on his back. I raised an eyebrow and shifted my weight to my right leg. He was a stubborn man. He knew I'd rather work dawn to dusk doing something I hated than sit in a boring schoolroom and let the day go to waste, yet he persisted I learned my lousy numbers and be able to read words that were meaningless. And endure Penelope's insults.

Penelope was the daughter of Sunset's mayor, a man who had more money than sense, but who was nice enough to lift his hat to most of the town's citizens. His wife and daughter, on the other hand, wouldn't give the time of day to a respectable person, much less acknowledge the less fortunate. Mrs. Wilkes had given Jet the most severe talking to after I had emptied my stomach on Penelope's dress, and I was almost certain that wouldn't be the only lecture he heard from her. She was quick to wag her tongue in somebody's face and slow to accept the blame for starting a riot.

Mr. Hyndman stepped onto the porch and rang the bell, a signal for the children to clean up their lunches and file inside for the rest of school. Curling my lip, I took a bite of the sandwich and ambled toward the school steps begrudgingly. When I reached the top of the stairs, Mr. Hyndman held out his hand to stop me.

"I'll have the rest of that sandwich, Cheyenne," he muttered in a low voice. "I'd hate to have something happen while I'm teaching."

I narrowed my eyes and filled my mouth with another bite. Without saying a word, I skirted around his hand and entered the school, but Mr. Hyndman snatched my arm and held me back until the rest of the students had found their own seats.

Mr. Hyndman lowered his voice so the rest of the pupils couldn't hear him. "Cheyenne, I need you to listen when I tell you something. If you don't, I'm going to have to talk to your uncle."

"That don't scare me." I waved the sandwich in the air. "You ain't taking this from me. I'm gonna eat it."

Air gushed from his lungs in a frustrated sigh. "Give the sandwich to me, young lady. I won't have you making a mess while I'm giving a lecture."

A grin stretched from one ear to the other. "Alright, I'll give it to you." Without giving thought to the consequences, I smeared the last half of the peanut butter sandwich on his white shirt and noticed that the jelly created a stain on his front pocket.

Slowly, he raised flaming eyes to meet mine and clenched his jaw tightly. "Go home," he growled in a voice barely audible. "You're suspended."

The grin spread further across my features. "That's probably the nicest thing you've ever said to me. Good day, fine teacher," I finished sarcastically.

I darted out of the door before he could reply and glanced at the feed mill as I hurried down the steps. Jet wasn't in sight. Stuffing my hands in my pockets, I began whistling a bar tune I once heard Ryleigh sing and filled my lungs with the fresh air. It was going to be a good day after all. With a spring in my step, I started down the street in hopes of meandering to the creek for a few hours before Jet got suspicious and came looking for me.

As I made my way down the boardwalk, I happened to notice a familiar bird of a woman. When she turned to glance over her shoulder, I saw Ryleigh for the first time in nearly a week. She looked to have changed a lot in just a few short days. She was thinner than usual, with her face pale and eyes surrounded by purple circles of fatigue. She was in a hurry, and her legs pumped as fast as they could go as she bustled down the street. She hadn't seen me yet, and she was alone.

Quickening my step, I ran up to meet my sister, hoping I could exchange a few words before we were pulled apart again. "Ryleigh!" I called out.

My sister came to an abrupt stop and spun around when she heard her name. "Cheyenne," she exclaimed, her face seeming to grow even grayer. "What are you doing out of school?"

I came to a stop in front of her and shrugged. "Mr. Hyndman said there was some sort of emergency, so he let us out early. You running errands?"

She nodded cautiously. "Yes, I... I needed material to make new curtains for Mr. Overhaul's quarters. Where's Mr. Douglas?"

I wrinkled my nose. "I was in his office just the other day. He needs new curtains like I need a satin dress. He's just using you for labor."

"Cheyenne, I asked where Mr. Douglas was."

The sternness in her voice surprised me, and I found myself staring at her strangely. "Oh, Jet? He's... around. He's got a job at the feed mill, you know."

"Go to him."

My frown deepened. "I'll see him in a bit, Ryleigh. I'm helping him rebuild our house. He moved into Mama and Pa's room, but I can tell him to move out so that you'll feel more comfortable to live there again. There's room at the boardinghouse, I could just tell him to—"

"I said go to him!" Ryleigh held firm eyes on me that kept my tongue from moving correctly. "I don't want to see you, Cheyenne. You're not my responsibility anymore, and I'm not moving back in that house." She straightened her backbone and folded her arms over her chest. "I live in the saloon now. I had Mr. Douglas take over raising you because I don't want to be around you. I don't want to talk to you, and I don't even want to see you."

Her words hurt worse than if someone had stabbed my heart with a knife. "But... Ryleigh, I only wanted to say hi."

"Well, you did. Now, please, leave me alone, Cheyenne." She pulled the shawl tighter around her shoulders and set a firm frown on her mouth. "It's better this way. Go to Mr. Douglas, and don't come back."

I opened my mouth to tell her she didn't have to push me away, but I could tell by the expression on her face that any word I said wouldn't be acknowledged. Biting my lip, I spun on my heel and ran as fast as I could down the old familiar path to the creek. The trail began to blur as I ran, and when I couldn't breathe, I slowed my pace and fell to my knees at the bank of the creek. My greatest fear had become true. Ryleigh had said she didn't want me. That was what Pa said when he left, and what Mama said on her deathbed.

Fingering a rock, I sucked on my lip to keep from sobbing aloud. If she didn't want me, then I didn't want her either. My shoulders shook from the tears. I couldn't convince myself of the lie, no matter how much I tried to tell myself I'd feel better if I learned to forget Ryleigh. Ripping my boots off my feet, I decided to soak my feet in the cool water in hopes of distracting my mind from the neglect I felt.

My mind flashed back to my tenth birthday. Ryleigh had already worked in her new promotion for over a year and her smile had started to dim, but she baked me the best cake I had ever eaten. She couldn't afford a gift, but I didn't want one at the time. I blew out the candles she had stuck in the icing, and we laughed until the sun went down. She had gotten the day off, and after supper was cleaned up, we both crawled into her bed and talked about the future until we fell asleep. I had been tired after all the day's happenings and fell asleep before Ryleigh had, but before I began to dream, I remembered her promise to be there for the rest of my birthdays.

She had said that she loved me. Had she forgotten that day?

She's an animal. Nothing more than a cow fit for breeding.

Penelope's words rang crystal clear in my mind, and I found myself wondering if she was right. The words cut deeper than I ever believed words could.

I don't want to see you, Cheyenne. You're not my responsibility anymore.

What did I do to make her hate me? If it was bad grades, why didn't she tell me? If it was misbehavior, why hadn't she set me down and told me?

"There you are! I've been looking everywhere for you!"

I glanced up from the water and realized the sun was stretching long shadows toward the east. I looked over my shoulder to find Jet marching down the trail toward me.

"I had a good long talk with your teacher," he continued sternly. "Suspended, Cheyenne? Mr. Hyndman filled me in on the other things you've been doing in class. Snide remarks, making fun of this girl named Penelope, cheating on a test? Would you mind explaining all of that to me?"

I swallowed hard and turned back to the water.

"Aren't you going to answer me?" Jet stopped beside me, and his voice was softer when he spoke again. "Cheyenne?"

I wiped the tip of my nose on my sleeve and turned my head to hide my face from him. "What's wrong?"

"I saw Ryleigh this afternoon," I answered coldly, shifting on the rock as I bit my lip and rubbed my hands on my arms. "I didn't mean any harm. Honest I didn't. I wanted to tell her she could come back. She was running errands for that pig, that selfish man… and she told me she didn't want me." I caught a drip from my nose with the back of my hand.

Jet shifted his weight to his left leg and stuffed his hands in his pockets. "Cheyenne, I—"

"Penelope was right," I interrupted. "She told me today that Ryleigh was like a breeding cow. Like a cow and a calf, Ryleigh must've gotten tired of me tagging along and kicked me away. Maybe Penelope was on the right track. Maybe all we are is animals. Ryleigh didn't want me. She pushed me away like Mama and Pa did."

Jet squatted next to me and looked at the side of my face, but I refused to meet his gaze. "Your sister made some poor choices, and she's lost and confused. She doesn't realize you still want her. I bet she didn't mean those things that she said."

I angrily threw a rock across the water, and it sank with a splash. "You don't understand. It's in her blood to abandon things, like it is in mine. Mama and Pa, they had a big fight before he left. I was too young to remember, but I know the story of that night. Mama was crying, and Ryleigh was holding me in hopes to keep me quiet. Pa abandoned us because he couldn't stand Mama's bickering anymore. It wasn't long after he left that Mama took sick. I know she could've got better, but she gave in to the sickness. One day, when Mama couldn't get out of bed, I went into her room and told her I loved her. She told me to stop lying. She was never fond of me, and she wanted to leave so she could be rid of us. She died the next day."

I turned to meet his gaze and ignored the tears that were still drying on my cheekbones. "I had no use for anyone else. Ryleigh was the only one who I trusted. Now Ryleigh's acting all strange, but I guess it was her time to leave. I don't suppose you'll believe that. Nobody else seems to."

"I'm not like everybody else, Cheyenne. I'm your uncle."

"Yeah, and Pa's kid brother. You got the same blood in you that's in us. Eventually it will be your turn to leave, just you wait."

"I'm not going to abandon you," Jet assured, but I curled my lip at his insistence.

"Yeah, you're not. I totally believe you." I lifted my feet out of the water and rose to my full height. "I've talked too much as it is. I'm sorry for not getting work done today, and that apology ain't because I care what you think."

I turned to leave, but Jet grabbed my upper arm as he rose to his feet. "Cheyenne..." He met my gaze and sighed when I glared back. "You don't have to push me away every time."

"I like to keep my emotions hidden. Especially if you happen to be the kind of man that I think you are."

Jet's eyes dimmed as he let go of my arm. "I wish you could see that I'm not going to hurt you. What can I do to make you believe me?"

Shaking my head, I grabbed my boots and began walking down the trail. "Nothing will make me believe you. I already know what you are because you disappeared so many years ago. Nobody knew where you went, and then suddenly, several years later, you show up on our doorstep. You're not a trustworthy source, Jet."

Jet fell into step beside me and hid his fingertips into his pockets again. "You said that leaving is in our blood as Douglas's. My brother, his wife, you, and your sister. You say you all had your turn to leave. I've already abandoned my family, but I realized that running was worse than staying. There's nothing lonelier than running, and I wish you girls would understand that."

A whimper slipped through my lips as I wiped the corners of my eyes on my sleeve. "Loneliness is a black hole that grows no matter what you do."

"See, that's where you're wrong." Jet grabbed my shoulders and turned me to face him. "That hole only grows when you shove people away. I learned that the hard way, and I would rather you girls don't go through all that I did. You're not doing a good job of hiding how you feel about Ryleigh. She's your sister, and you love her. Don't try to fool me or yourself."

I felt my lip begin to tremble and quickened my step. "I-I'm not trying to fool anyone. I don't care. I don't care if she would rather stay with Overhaul in the saloon than with me. I don't care if our parents would rather please their own selves than raise two girls. I don't care if people think I'm an animal. I don't even care that I'm worthless."

"You care. Look at you, you're trying to run away from me so that I won't see your tears."

"That's 'cause tears are a sign of weakness!"

"You only say that because nobody taught you to trust."

"There's nobody on earth that can be trusted!"

"I disagree."

I ground my teeth in frustration and balled my hands into tight fists. "Leave me alone, Jet. I don't want your sympathy. I have no more family, and I'm beginning to like that. There's no one that can hurt you when you're all alone, and there's no one around that puts their problems on your shoulders. I prefer to be alone."

Jet took hold of my arms firmly, this time intent on holding on. He knelt on his knee and looked through my stringy hair into my eyes. "The problem of being alone is that you never have anyone to love. You never have a shoulder to cry on or a friend to listen to you. Cheyenne, please don't run. I don't want you to seclude yourself. I'm not leaving, and you don't have to be afraid of me. You can trust me."

A tear tumbled down my face, and I longed to collapse into his embrace and let my frustration leave a wet stain on his shirt, but I couldn't make myself trust him. "No," I muttered in a shaky voice. "You lie."

Twisting out of his grasp, I spun on my heel and retreated toward the western horizon, where a lone coyote raced for cover. In a lot of ways, I found several qualities in that coyote that matched some of my own. We were both hated vermin in the eyes of the people in Sunset, and we were both running from whatever spooked us, searching for a place where we could recuperate. But we would always be running.

* * *

The moon cast long shadows on the ground when I opened the door of our little shack wide enough for me to squeeze through, and I squinted my eyes against the soft glow of a lantern. Jet looked up from a book he was reading when I walked through the threshold and closed the door behind me.

"It's late," he said in a calm voice.

I avoided his gaze and headed toward my bedroom, but he stopped me with his voice.

"I don't like you staying out this late."

My feet stopped suddenly and my back stiffened, but I refused to meet his gaze. "I don't think it's so late. I've come in later."

"I understand that, Cheyenne, but some things need to change, and I don't like you being out alone after dark. Especially when I don't know where you've gone."

155

I clenched my jaw and spun on my heel to face him. "I wasn't alone, and you ain't the boss of me, Jet. I don't care what you like or don't like. I can come home whenever I want."

"Don't raise your voice to me," he rebuked gently as he rose to his feet and set the book on the bench behind him. "Now, unless you have an explanation as to where you were, I suggest you get to bed. Since you got yourself suspended, I have some things in mind for you to be doing in the morning."

I groaned and waved a hand in the air. "Like what?"

"Well, just to make sure you ain't getting into any trouble, I talked to Levi some this afternoon, and he agreed to let you work alongside him until I get off at the feed mill."

The air exploded out of my lungs as I rolled my eyes in exasperation. "I won't be shoveling horse dung all day, and then work for you, Jet."

"Yes, you will. Mr. Hyndman said you were suspended until Monday, and until then you will work with Levi and me. Maybe then you'll be too tired to fight in class." He sighed softly as he hid his fingertips in his jean pockets. "Now I suggest you get to bed so you'll have enough energy for tomorrow."

I wanted to argue with him, but I could tell by the authoritative look in his eye that he wouldn't listen. I hung my head as I marched to my room and slammed the door loudly to drown out any further explanation from Jet. I folded my arms over my chest once I was alone in the darkness. *It's not even that late,* I thought to myself as I heard a clock chime the eleven o'clock hour. The more I thought about Jet's reaction, the more I resented his authority. Shaking my head, I figured there was nothing better for me to do than to obey his request and go to bed, but before I could climb onto the mattress, I heard a gentle knocking on my broken windowpane.

Growling my discontent, I strode to the window and parted the curtain to see the blue eyes of Chad. I sighed and cupped my chin in my hand as I addressed him. "What do you want? The last time I went with you I got into worse trouble than I've ever been in."

Chad placed a hand over his gut and nodded with a curl in his lip. "I know what you mean. My pa gave me the tanning of my life when I came home drunk. Sobered me up quicker than a prairie fire, I can tell you that."

I rolled my eyes and leaned against the wall. "Then what do you want this time?"

He rocked on his toes as a smile stretched across his lips. "There's a game going on tonight. The boys were wondering if you'd join us. Poker's more fun when you're there to throw in your two cents. C'mon, Cheyenne! The stakes are the same as always. Each player is given twenty rocks, and once those are bet, we can throw in some goods if we want."

I glanced over my shoulder at the door and crossed my arms. "I don't know. Jet already jumped down my throat for being out so late."

Chad narrowed his eyes and pursed his lips. "Since when did you listen to an adult? C'mon, Cheyenne, don't spoil the fun. It'll just be for a few hours, you know how it goes. 'Sides, it's a school night. Most of the boys want to get home before their parents wake up."

"Well…" I glanced over my shoulder again. The house was quiet, and I felt a desire to rebel against Jet as I smirked maliciously. "I guess a few hours won't hurt anybody."

"Great!" Chad exclaimed. "C'mon, the game is hot!"

I chuckled giddily and opened the window wide enough for me to jump through before I followed Chad down the alley to a secluded area in a canyon a half mile or so from town. A few of the more rambunctious children found the place to hide from their parents, and especially Sheriff Hodgkinson. When Chad and I got there, three other boys were milling around a makeshift table where a deck of cards was stacked.

"About time," a boy about thirteen answered, his lips forming into a tight line. "You deal, Jerry. I told my sister I'd be back at midnight, and it's already eleven-thirty."

"There's your first mistake, Lavin," a boy named Al harrumphed. "Telling a witness where you've gone and what you're doing."

"Ah, she won't tell. I gave her three licorice sticks, and I told her I'd give her the lickin' of her life if she told Ma."

I rolled my eyes and sat on the dirt in front of the table. "Maybe the

157

thought of physical pain doesn't frighten her."

Jerry dealt out the cards and raised his hand to his face. "Not everyone is as stupid as you, Cheyenne."

I bristled at his words. "I ain't stupid. I choose to have my own way, and no amount of pain is gonna stop me from having fun."

Chad rolled his eyes and pushed a rock into the center of the table. "I bet a thousand," he pretended. "Let's not argue about whose being stupid or not. C'mon and bet! I need to get home before my pa beats my hide."

"I'll call your thousand," I replied, sliding my own rock to join the pile, "and I'll raise you another."

The game continued for a solid three hours or so without much conversation to keep the boys awake. After a while, a few of the boys began to yawn and nod, their eyelids drooping with each card they played, yet the game continued. At last, Lavin slammed his cards on the table and yawned noisily.

"I'm gonna get," he said sleepily. "It's nigh unto three o'clock in the morning, and I'm well past my deadline. If my pa ever catches me..." He drew a line across his throat with his thumb nail and rose to his feet.

"Don't be overly dramatic," Chad growled. "Sit back down. The game will end shortly, and you'll get home without a scratch."

"But Ma thought I was in bed, and if she finds out I ain't home she'll question me until her lips are blue. Besides, Susie already knows what I've been doing."

"I need to go, too," Al said as he rose to his feet.

Chad rolled his eyes and threw his cards on the table. "I'm surrounded by a bunch of worthless ninnies. Does anyone want to stay and finish this game, or should we walk y'all home and hold your hand?"

Lavin curled his lip in disgust. "I can exit the game whenever I want to. I'm pulling out."

Jerry repositioned on the ground and stretched his back. "I'm staying to finish the game. I got a good hand, and I ain't 'bout to let that go easily. You ladies can go home if you want, I'm finishing the game."

"My ma will—"

Chad exhaled sharply as he reached into his pocket and brought out a beautiful watch that looked to have cost a fortune. It was made of gold and shimmered in the moonlight. When he opened it up, diamonds sparkled where the numbers should have been.

"I'll make the game more interesting, then," he snapped as he plopped the watch on the table among the rocks. "It's my grandfather's watch. It was given to me on my last birthday, and I have no use for it. I'd be glad to be rid of it."

My jaw dropped as I stared at the beautiful timepiece. "I don't have anything to match that, Chad!"

"Me neither!" Jerry exclaimed. His eyes were large with greed.

"Hold it, people," Chad assured as he lifted his hands over his head. "I'll say it's worth two thousand, but I ain't gonna bet it if y'all leave me." He turned his eyes on the two other boys and raised an eyebrow. "Reckon your folks can wait?"

Al wet his lips with the tip of his tongue, but Lavin shook his head firmly and began backing up. "It's a school night, and my pa will be up in a few hours. I gotta go. I'm out."

Chad waved a hand in the air and picked up his cards. "Never mind school. Just play hooky. Are we gonna bet, or are we gonna whine?"

I pushed two of my rocks toward the pile. "I call."

Al threw himself on his knees and did the same thing. As we continued the game, Lavin shook his head and left the canyon without saying another word. I figured that if he had said something it would have gone unnoticed by the rest of the poker players. I peeked at my cards and smiled.

Three jacks, two aces. This game was looking good.

~TEN~

The ground began to lighten by the time I wandered back in town. I opened my new prize and found that it was nearly six o'clock in the morning. Stifling a yawn, I quickened my pace in hopes of climbing in bed for a few minutes before Jet would come knocking on my door and demand that I get up to help Levi in the stables. I tip-toed around awakening stores and dodged down the alley that led to the back of my house. Slipping through the window, I dropped the gold pocket watch in the drawer of my nightstand and turned to flop on my bed when I noticed the door was opened. Frowning slightly, I thought back to the night before and realized I had closed it before sneaking out of the window.

Exhaling softly, I hooked a strand of hair behind my ear and cautiously crept down the hallway to the living room. Jet wasn't reading the newspaper or preparing breakfast, and my frown deepened. A thudding sound caused me to jump, and I stared down the hall at the room our parents once shared many years ago. A shadow passed by the doorway, and I wondered if Jet would be livid if I stepped into his room. *He will be if I decide to run.* Squaring my shoulders, I closed the distance between me and his door, and peeked my head inside.

Jet sat on the edge of the bed with his back to me as he pulled on his boots. I bit my lip and stepped into the room. "Good morning," I greeted, clasping my hands behind my back.

Jet glanced over his shoulder, then bent to pull on his other boot. "When did you go to bed last night?"

I swallowed hard and rocked on my toes. "Oh, when you sent me to bed.

'Bout eleven, I think it was."

Jet rose to his feet and turned to aim a finger at my nose. "Don't you dare lie to me, young lady! You disobeyed me. Where did you go after I sent you to your room?"

"W-Well…" I glanced down the hallway and wondered how far I could run before Jet caught me. About to the kitchen. I cleared my throat and returned my gaze to my uncle. "What makes you think I went somewhere?"

"Because when I went into your room to wake you up a few minutes ago, your quilt was untouched, and your window was wide open. Don't try to fool me, Cheyenne. Answer me, where did you go?"

"G-go? Um… well…" I backed up until my back hit the wall and bit my bottom lip. "I, uh, I heard a noise, and I went to investigate. I just lost track of time."

He studied me out of the corner of his eye. "I will punish you for disobeying me, but if you keep lying the punishment will be worse," he warned, his jaw firm with a sense of sternness that unnerved me.

I avoided his gaze as I began to rock on my toes. "I didn't intend to stay out all night, I swear it. We were just gonna be gone for an hour or two, honest."

"'We'?" he asked. I cringed. "Who's 'we', Cheyenne?"

I scuffed my feet on the floor and remained silent.

Jet stiffened his back as he motioned to his side. "Come here."

My head shot up as my jaw dropped. "I didn't lie, Jet!"

"You didn't say anything, and I take that for lying. I asked where you were, and I was hoping you'd trust me enough to tell me the truth. Since you won't tell me, I guess I have to teach you to tell the truth."

My eyes burned with heat as I glared at my uncle. "Why are you so concerned if I stayed in bed or not? It doesn't matter. Last night wasn't the first night I've stayed out until the early hours of the morning. Nothing happened last night, so why don't you just calm down!"

Jet placed a hand on his hip and shifted his weight to one leg. "There's a lot of riffraff late at night that I don't want you to get mixed up in. I only want to protect you, and I don't want you out that late again, especially when you have work to do the next day."

I folded my arms over my chest and glanced at the window behind him. "All I did was play an innocent game of poker with a couple of friends. There, I told you."

"What kind of friends?" Jet asked in a stern voice, but I remained silent. "One of them doesn't happen to be this Chad I hear about, does it?"

I bit my lip and hung my head so he wouldn't see my expression.

"I don't like that boy, Cheyenne. He's a bad influence on you, and I don't want you to hang around him anymore."

"Chad is my only friend," I snarled back, staring at my toes. "Without him I'd have no one. You can't tell me who I can or can't be with. I won't let you." I spun on my heel and walked as fast as I dared into the living room, but I whirled around when I heard Jet following me. "You can't just butt in on my life and tell me what to do," I shouted, feeling my temper rising. "You think you can, but you just can't!"

"I tell you these things so you can become better than you are," Jet defended when he entered the room. "People in this town are calling you a tyrant and a brat, but I know you're better than that. I'm trying to help you, Cheyenne, not harm you."

"Help me?" I scoffed and shook my head. "Every time you help me something bad happens. Stop wasting your time on me. It's not worth it!"

"I disagree, Cheyenne," he argued. "I don't think anything concerning you is worthless. That's why I'm trying to help you."

"You wanna help me?" I snapped. "Show me why I should trust you, then maybe you can help me." I turned toward the door and opened it to let the early morning air hit my face. "I'm late to help Levi."

Without saying a word, I slammed the door behind me and stormed down the street toward the stables. The morning was starting out beautifully, with a pinkish-orange glow on the street and store fronts. If I wasn't already tired and upset, I might have enjoyed the short walk to the stables. Instead, I wished I had a shotgun to kill all those cheerful birds, and that I could bring clouds to block out the extraordinary sunrise.

Levi was standing by the corrals when I showed up, and he smiled a greeting when I entered hearing range. "You're here early," he said cheerfully. "I told Mr. Douglas that you didn't need to be here until seven." He brought out his pocket watch and snapped it open. "It's six-thirty."

I curled my lip in disgust and marched past him. "I couldn't stay in that house for another second," I snarled as I barreled through the barn doors.

Levi frowned and followed me. "What's got you off on the wrong side of the bed this morning?"

I spun around in the middle of the aisle and crossed my arms. "Jet. He got all mad because he found out I played poker last night after he tried to force me to go to bed. It was a harmless game, and nothing happened. He's just itching for power over my life, and I hate him for it!"

Levi nodded his head and smiled weakly as he picked up a pitchfork. "I see."

"No, you don't. That man who calls himself my uncle wants nothing more than to bind me in chains and demand I lose all control over my life. I won't let him do that!"

He tossed the pitchfork to me and motioned to the first stall. "You can start with this one." He leaned against the wall as he folded his arms over his chest. "Don't you think you're being too hard on your uncle? All he's trying to do is help you."

"That's what he keeps saying, but I don't believe him. Ryleigh had been working as an adult for three years by the time she was my age. I'm as full grown as I'm ever gonna get, and I don't need Jet!"

"Everybody needs somebody." Levi took hold of a broom and began sweeping the hay in the aisle. "You may not believe me, but I think Mr. Douglas needs you more than you think he does."

I harrumphed as I dumped a forkful into a waiting wheelbarrow. "Why would Jet need me? I've tried to get him to leave. He ought to hate my guts and disown me like—"

"Like everyone else has?" Levi finished for me.

"Honestly, yeah." I straightened to my full height and stared at him. "Speaking of which, of all people you should hate me the most. I've pulled more stunts on you than anybody should."

Levi shrugged as he continued sweeping. "I don't hate you. I'm sometimes disappointed in you. I think the only reason a person would vandalize other people's property or get into as much trouble as you have is because you're searching for attention. You're lonely."

I laughed humorlessly. "You think you've got me all figured out, don't you?"

"No, I never claimed that. It's just what I see in you. So many people have turned their backs on you, and all that built up tension has got to find a way out. I have been praying for you, though."

I rolled my eyes as I shoveled more horse dung. "Don't waste your breath, Levi. God ain't given me or Ryleigh a second thought in a long time, and he ain't gonna change that now."

"Oh, I don't know. God always surprises me with what He can do."

I frowned and continued shoveling manure.

Several minutes went by with not a word from the stable boy, but the silence didn't bother me much. It gave me time to think about Jet's argument that morning, and what Levi mentioned. He had stated that Jet needed me, but I couldn't understand how Jet needed me if he was hardly more than a stranger. The oddest thing was that I wanted someone to care about me, but how could I trust Jet? There was no proof that he would stay once he thought we were no longer in trouble. The frown deepened. Did I want him to stay?

"Ease down a mite," Levi called from the other side of the barn. "You'll hurt yourself if you keep working that hard."

I threw the fork load in the wheelbarrow and sighed. "Maybe Jet would like it if I hurt myself."

"Alright, now quit," Levi said as he leaned his broom against the wall. "Mr. Douglas' anger this morning was a form of concern for your well-being. It scared him to think you were out late, that's all. He wouldn't want you to blow out your back while cleaning out stalls."

"He's a fool," I mumbled under my breath.

"Not when you think about it. You get concerned when your sister gets in trouble, don't you?" He waited until I nodded slightly, then lifted his shoulders in a shrug. "That's how Mr. Douglas feels. You feel concern over something only because you care about it. I think you're being too hard on your uncle."

I averted my eyes and scooped up more manure onto the blades of the fork.

"I told you to take it easy," Levi mentioned as he watched me work. "You'll blow out your back, and then your uncle will be mad at me. You wouldn't want me to get in trouble, now, would you?"

I licked my lips and shrugged. "I guess not."

"Now quit hating your uncle and choose to be happy," he demanded with a teasing smile on his lips.

Despite my attempts to sulk, I found myself smiling back. "Yes, sir."

His smile widened as he playfully punched my shoulder with his knuckles. "See, you ain't so bad. Now c'mon, I got a lot of work planned for you, so you best get to muckin'." He raised a hand when I turned to obey him. "But gently."

My smile grew slightly as I ducked my head. "Alright."

We worked contentedly and silently for at least two hours, each involved in our own thoughts as the town gradually became alive with the buzz of activity. Through the cracks of the barn, I saw the children mill around the school in the distance and found my mouth turning downward in a frown. Penelope pranced about, acting as if she was the head chicken in the coop. The thought made me smile. She sure was mean enough to be a roasting hen.

I had just begun mucking out the second stall when Levi exited the barn to tend to a customer. I didn't pay much attention to him, until I heard the familiar voice of Sheriff Hodgkinson. Leaning the pitchfork against the wall, I tip-toed to the door and held my breath as I listened.

"How are you this morning, sheriff?" Levi greeted as he took the reins from the man.

"I've had better starts to a day." Sheriff Hodgkinson leaned against the fence. "My horse threw a shoe, and I've got a lot to do this morning. Mr. Wilkes over at the mercantile said he was missing his most expensive watch when he opened this morning. I've got me an overnight thief to catch."

"Well, what does this watch look like? I might could keep an eye open for it."

"Well, it's worth fifty dollars. Alford said it was solid gold, with diamonds here and there. A right pretty piece from what I hear."

I gasped and scurried away from the door, causing the pitchfork to fall in my haste. I should've known better than to think that watch Chad bet was his grandfather's, and now the blasted thing was in my possession. A cold sweat popped out on my forehead, and I wiped the perspiration away with my sleeve when I realized what my friend had done.

Levi's head poked in as he studied me with a frown. "You okay, Cheyenne?"

The sheriff entered the barn behind the stable boy, and I bent to pick up the pitchfork. "Yeah. I just saw a mouse and it startled me, that's all."

Sheriff Hodgkinson hooked his thumbs in his belt loops. "I didn't know you had Cheyenne working for you, Hendershot."

"Oh, she ain't working for me. Her uncle asked me to keep her busy until he got off work, is all."

"Shouldn't you be in school, young lady?"

I didn't like the way the sheriff looked at me, and I felt my insides die. "I got suspended yesterday," I explained quickly, studying his expression carefully.

Levi didn't notice the tension in the air. "I'll have a shoe on your horse in no time, sheriff," he said as he led the horse to the other end of the barn. I followed him with my eyes, then tried to ignore the sheriff's gaze as I bent to shovel more manure.

"You sleep well last night?"

I jumped at his question and lifted my gaze to meet his. "Huh?"

"I asked if you slept well. You have dark circles under your eyes."

"Uh…" I felt my mouth go dry, and I averted my eyes. "It was a rough night, but we all get some of those. Bed wasn't much comfortable."

"You didn't go anywhere?"

I bristled at his suspicion but shook my head and kept shoveling.

"I hope to High Heaven you're telling me the truth."

My head bounced up, but I kept my face emotionless. "Of course, I am. Just ask my uncle."

He narrowed his eyes in an unnerving stare. "I intend to."

My heart skipped a beat, but I didn't say another word to persuade him differently. What did I care if he spoke to Jet? Trouble seemed to be a good friend to me, and I used to love treading on that thin line between right and wrong. But no matter how hard I tried to convince myself that I didn't care, I felt a twinge of guilt at what Jet would think. I tried to convince myself that I wanted Jet to be angry at my disobedience, but I couldn't deny that I wanted him to think better of me. Unwanted tears burned the back of my eyes at the thought of disappointing Jet again.

"I'll kill you, Chad," I whispered under my breath as I turned my back to the sheriff.

"What did you say?"

I cringed and swallowed past the tears as I continued shoveling at a steady pace. "Nothing. I was just thinking aloud. I do that often."

"Sure." His voice sounded even more suspicious.

"Here's your horse," Levi interrupted unknowingly. I let out a deep breath and leaned against the wooden handle of the pitchfork.

Sheriff Hodgkinson finally tore his eyes off me and took the reins from Levi's hands. "Thank you, son." He reached into his pocket and brought out a few coins.

I glanced between the two men but found myself staring at the toes of my boots. Relief filled my chest when I heard the sheriff mount his horse and ride down the street. Levi threw me a curious stare, but I ignored him as I finished the rest of my job. The morning ticked by slowly, and I found my body gradually growing weaker with fatigue. When the noon hour arrived, I nearly collapsed in exhaustion as I cleaned up the tools I was using. I would have around an hour of free time before I had to endure a few more moments with Levi, and before Jet demanded more of my physical strength.

As I put the last tool away, I saw a shadow stretch across the floor. "I'm going home, Levi," I said, not bothering to turn around. "I'll be back, of course, but a few moments alone will be…" My voice faded when I glanced over my shoulder. Jet stood in the doorway, his hair sticking out at strange angles, and dirt smudged on his face. I swallowed the lump in my throat and shuffled my foot on the floor. "I, uh… I didn't know it was you."

Jet ran his fingers through his hair, causing it to stick out in more places. "I was hoping to share my lunch with you."

I studied him to see if he hated me, but I couldn't read his stoic expression. I slowly nodded my head as I pushed myself to my feet.

"Are you okay?" he asked when I came closer to him.

"I'm fine." I stuffed my hands into my pockets and lifted my shoulders in a shrug. "I didn't bring food with me this morning. I was kinda in a hurry."

He nodded. "There's some sandwich makings at the house."

Jet's calm behavior unnerved me, especially after the visit with the sheriff that morning. I couldn't tell if Jet knew about the stolen watch, and my heart began to pound in my ears. I swallowed hard and shuffled my feet as I followed Jet down the few blocks it took to get to our house. If he had a lecture on his mind, I would know of it soon enough. Licking my lips nervously, I lowered my head and decided to forget the whole watch ordeal for the moment.

We filed into the house quietly and took turns washing our hands in the basin by the sink before the grime from work could be spread on bread. Jet ambled into the kitchen and began rustling up the sandwich makings.

"How was your morning?" he asked as he handed me an apple.

"Fine."

He lowered himself into the nearest chair. "You don't look good. Are you feeling okay?"

I glanced at him and swallowed hard as I fingered the apple. "I'm fine. Just a little tired, I guess."

"You're sure?" Jet asked again, studying me with his piercing eyes. It felt like he could read my thoughts.

I nodded. "Yes, sir. I'm just hungry."

Jet finally looked away as he finished making the sandwiches. Silence dragged on for what seemed hours. I finished the simple lunch Jet had gathered and found it strangely interesting to stare at my boots. I kept waiting for the question I knew he wanted to ask, but it never came. Maybe the sheriff hadn't talked to him yet about last night. I drew my eyebrows together in a frown. Why was I so concerned over something I was completely innocent in? I wasn't with Chad when he took the watch, and I had no idea that the item was stolen when I gambled for it. I should be angry at Chad for his fool plan, but instead I was afraid for myself.

"Cheyenne?"

My head shot up, and I felt like I had been caught cheating on a test. "Hmm?"

Jet leaned back in his chair and crossed an ankle over his knee, his gaze soft and gentle. "I want to apologize for losing my temper this morning," he said slowly. "I shouldn't have yelled at you like I did."

I studied him for several long seconds, my tongue suddenly glued to the roof of my mouth. I didn't know how to answer him, so I drew circles on the floor with the toe of my shoe and shrugged. "Don't matter."

"Yes it does. I was a fool." He leaned against the table and exhaled. "I was concerned for your safety, and I'm afraid I scared you more than I should have."

"I know. Levi explained it to me."

Jet seemed to relax and leaned a hand on the table. "Well, I'm glad you understand. I was afraid I turned you against me."

I remained silent as I struggled to respond. I listened to the clock tick for several seconds, then pushed myself away from the counter. "I should get back to the livery."

Jet caught my arm as I attempted to skirt around him. "Cheyenne..." His voice faded while he looked into my eyes. With a sigh, he let my arm drop and nodded. "I'll see you later."

My bottom lip twitched, and I bit it in hopes to hide my nervousness. Ducking my head, I hid my fists into my hip pockets and strolled out of the door. The wind had picked up a bit since I had last been outside, but I barely noticed it as it whipped my hair into my face. I stared at the designs in the dirt on the street, but my mind was occupied with the slight conversation with Jet. He was unpredictable, and I wasn't sure how to handle him.

I ran into a man's chest and jumped.

"You better watch where you're going before you get run over by a wagon."

I raised my eyes to find Levi smiling down at me with a gentle smirk. "I, uh, I'm sorry. My mind was occupied, I guess."

Levi took a step back to look into my face easier. "You finish your lunch already? How did it go?"

Filling my lungs with air, I lifted a shoulder in a shrug and shuffled my foot in the dirt. "Fine, I guess. We didn't talk much."

"Well, that's better than arguing."

"I suppose."

Levi stared at me for a few seconds longer, then inhaled deeply. "Well, I have to run an errand for Mr. Shepherd. You go on ahead and clean the barn if you want. I shouldn't be too long."

I nodded and continued trudging down the boardwalk, intent on making eye contact with no one. When I stepped into the barn, I scanned the area and folded my arms over my chest. Levi did his job too well as the place was nearly spotless. Rolling my eyes, I plopped down on a bale of hay and propped my chin in my palm. Well, if there was nothing for me to do, I'd just sit and wait for Levi.

Something thumped on the floorboards of the hay loft, and I flinched. A cat yowled, and hay drifted from the loft onto the ground below. Curiosity furrowed my brow, and I slowly rose to my feet to climb the ladder and see what all the commotion was about. I placed my foot on the bottom rung of the ladder and pulled myself to the top until I could cautiously peek over the floorboards and study the hay piles. Nothing out of the ordinary came to view, and the thumping had come to a standstill. Frowning slightly, I narrowed my eyes as I stepped onto the floor of the loft and placed my hands on my hips.

"There's nothing up here," I muttered to myself, leaning around a pile of hay to find more floorboards. "It was probably just some stupid cat chasing a mouse or something."

I shook my head and turned to go back down the ladder when I heard another yowl. Raising an eyebrow, I followed the noise to the window toward the edge of the loft, keeping my distance in case the cat decided to pounce with claws extended. Scrunching my nose, I kicked the hay with my boot. The cat hissed and bounded out from its hiding place, which startled me when it leapt toward my feet.

I took a hurried step backwards and tumbled when my heel snagged against a crack between boards. Instead of feeling the wooden planks underneath me, I felt nothing but air as I tipped over the edge of the loft and fell ten feet toward the floor below. My breath caught in my throat as a gasp and a loud clatter reached my ears before I landed on my right arm with a heavy crash. Pain shot like an explosion from my wrist to my shoulder, and I ground my teeth together to keep from shouting my agony.

Holding my arm close to my chest, I rose into a sitting position and groaned. "Miserable... cats!" I snarled as my eyes filled with water.

I sat still for several seconds, but then the door shook open as somebody entered the barn. I glanced up to see Levi's frightened face. "Cheyenne!"

Levi began running toward me and I quickly brushed the tears out of the corner of my eyes. "Don't get your trousers in a bunch," I muttered through clenched teeth. "I just tripped. That's all."

Levi knelt beside me and reached for my arm, but I shoved him away. "What in the world happened?" he asked with concern filling his voice.

"Nothing. I fell, that's all." I ignored his hands and struggled to my feet but cringed when I tried put weight on my right arm.

"What's wrong with your arm?"

"Nothing!" I turned frightened eyes on him and hid my arm with my left hand. "Just back off and give me some space!"

Levi pursed his lips as he extended his hand. "Can I please see your arm?"

"There's nothing wrong with it," I muttered, trying to ignore the aching throb I felt. "I just tripped and landed on it wrong."

His eyes were soft with worry as he tried to reach for me again, but I shrugged out of his grasp. The sudden movement sent a jolt of white-hot pain shooting through my arm, and I cried out involuntarily. Levi jumped and spun on his heel. "Don't move, I'm getting Doc Harding!"

"No, wait!" I reached out to grab him, but he eluded my hand and ran out of the barn at a high rate of speed. Blinking the tears out of my eyes, I attempted to stand so that I could hide, but my right knee throbbed with the slightest amount of weight. I whimpered and held my arm close. I hated doctors. All the needles and examinations made me shudder, and I did my best to avoid all contact with them.

I reached out with my left hand and used the nearest stall to pull myself to my feet. Maybe if I used the wall for support, I could make it outside and disappear before Levi returned with the doctor. It was a slim hope, but I didn't want that doctor to touch a hair on my body. I had hopped about three feet when I heard Levi's voice and rapid footsteps. I bit my lip and searched for a place to hide, but there was none.

The two men entered the barn and pinned me with their eyes. The doctor was a tall man, not quite as tall as my uncle, but he seemed to tower above Levi. As he came closer to me, the doctor sized me up with his piercing green eyes.

"What happened?" he asked as he reached for me.

I dodged his hands but lost my balance as I collapsed to the ground in a heap. "Don't touch me!" I shrieked, a lump of tears forming in my throat.

Doc Harding quickly knelt beside me. "Don't move," he said in an authoritative voice. "You'll only make it worse."

I swatted his hands away and shook my head. "I said get away from me!"

Levi spun on his heel as he ran from the barn again, though I wasn't quite sure where he was going. Doc Harding grabbed my shoulders and gently pushed me back against the hay. "Lay still, Cheyenne," he said above my cries of fright. "Let me look you over!"

I stopped trying to fight him as I caught my breath. "I'm fine! Like I told Levi, nothing happened. I was just clumsy!"

The doc ignored my explanation as he gently took hold of my right arm and massaged the muscle from my shoulder down. When his fingers touched the swollen skin around my wrist, I cringed and tried to pull away. He glanced at me but didn't say a word as he continued moving down to my hand and fingers. When he had reached the end of each finger, he gently laid my arm across my belly and reached for his black bag.

Levi returned, with Jet right on his heels. "What happened?" Jet demanded when he met my gaze.

"I-I fell," I whimpered, guarding my arm with my left hand. "I'm fine, just call this doctor off me!"

"She strained her wrist," Doc Harding interrupted, causing my heart to skip a beat. "It's not broken from what I can tell, but it wouldn't hurt for her to wear a splint for a few days."

My lips parted as my face drained its color. "A splint?"

"She was favoring her right leg, too," Levi added, worry lines etched on his brow.

"I know. I was just getting to that." Doc Harding moved to my legs and looked the right one over in the same way as my arm.

I met Jet's worried gaze and felt my insides fade away. Fear settled in my stomach as I watched my uncle's eyes. His lips were firm and seemed to refuse to move, but his eyes held a glint of worry that sank me lower in the pit of confusion. The doctor touched my knee, causing pain to rip me out of the puzzle of my uncle's actions, and I yelped as I turned a glare on the back of his head.

"Get away from me!" I screeched as I tried to roll away from the doctor.

Jet knelt beside me and laid a hand on my shoulder. "Take it easy, Cheyenne. Doc is just trying to help you."

I looked up at my uncle, and I couldn't hide the fear in my voice as I spoke. "Please don't leave me!"

Jet smoothed some hair out of my face as he lowered his voice. "Shh, it's okay. I'm not leaving you. Calm down so the doc can help you. It's going to be okay."

My breath began to even out as I listened to Jet's voice. In my mind, I could see Ryleigh bent over me as she cleaned the blood from a cut on my knee. I wasn't very old and had skinned my knee while racing down a hill, but Ryleigh never left my side and even sang some of Mama's hymns to try to calm me down. As I looked into Jet's gaze, I was reminded of the love Ryleigh showed to me all the years I was growing up. I wanted to believe that he was genuinely concerned for me, and I wanted to trust him. I closed my eyes as he continued to smooth my hair and took several deep breaths as Doc Harding began to construct a splint around my wrist.

~ELEVEN~

The sun felt warm on my face as I sat on the porch, begrudgingly watching the town hurry about its business. If only I could join them in the excitement of the hubbub. I glanced at the cast keeping my wrist from moving and sank lower in my seat. I hated cats. The next time I saw a feline I was sure I would skirt around it to make sure it wouldn't harm me.

The front door opened, and I glanced over my shoulder to see Jet step on the porch with a chunk of ice and a rag in his hand. My lip curled, and I felt myself slink even lower in the chair. Without saying a word, he set the ice on my right knee, which was elevated on a stool. I hated being waited on hand and foot. What did that puny doctor know, telling me to stay off my feet for a day or two? It was just a bruise. The most painful, dreadful bruise I'd ever had in my life, but it was just a bruise that would heal with little problem.

"Daggum cats," I muttered, hiding my eyes with my hand.

Jet chuckled mildly as he leaned against a support beam. "I take it you're not feeling well."

"You're darn right I'm not," I mumbled.

"Eh, don't get let it get to you. It was an accident. You'll be better in a couple of days or so."

I raised my head to look at my uncle. "I could still do things if you'd just let me walk," I complained in a low voice.

Jet raised an eyebrow and cocked his head to the side. "Doc Harding said to stay off that knee until the swelling goes down, and that's just what you're gonna do. Chin up, there's worse things that can happen to you."

I scoffed as I glared at my injuries. "Yeah, like what?"

"You could've broken something, for one. You fell a long way, and you're lucky that you just have a few bruises and a sprain." Jet lowered himself to sit next to me and inhaled deeply. "It's a beautiful day. I'm surprised you're not happier. You don't have to go to school, and now you get time off from work."

I averted my gaze and stared straight ahead at the street. "But I can't do anything. I feel weak."

"I don't think you're weak," Jet assured as he followed my eyes. "You don't have to be embarrassed around me, either. I would have been scared, too."

I cleared my throat as I scooted further away from him. "I wasn't scared," I lied. "I just don't like doctors. I didn't want him to touch me."

"But you're fine now," Jet encouraged in a cheerful voice. "Personally, I'm glad you're not hurt worse than you are. Just keep off your leg for a bit and let your body heal. Is there something you like to do?"

I glanced up at Jet but didn't answer.

"Do you like to sew?" Jet asked as if to encourage me to respond. "I could teach you to whittle a wooden figurine. Or you could read a book."

"I don't like to read," I replied in a monotone.

Jet leaned against the side of the house and remained silent for a moment. "You don't have to be upset," he said at last. "You can choose to be happy."

My eyes forked a fat man strolling down the boardwalk, and hate filled my chest. Clyde Overhaul passed a woman with her arm hooked through her husband's and turned to admire her figure before smiling greedily to himself and continuing his way. My lip curled as my body itched to throw something at him.

"I don't see a reason to be happy," I mumbled, "when I've seen all that I have." Ignoring the ice on my knee, I pushed myself to my feet and hopped on my left foot with the full intention of leaving my uncle, but he grabbed my arm and eased me back into the chair.

"Take it easy," he said as he knelt in front of me, his eyes calm. "You'll hurt your knee if you try to leave."

I sighed harshly and covered my mouth with my left hand as the hard lines on my brow faded. My eyebrows tilted downward, and I found myself looking at the street through watery eyes. I followed Overhaul with my gaze until he disappeared in the bank, and I shook my head slightly as I swallowed hard. I felt so helpless against that man. I glanced at Jet to find his soft eyes watching me. Blinking the tears away, I shifted in the chair and cleared my throat.

"The wind... it blew some dust in my eyes." I glanced out of the corner of my eye to see if he believed my story. "I, uh... don't you have something to do?"

Jet's shoulders slumped in mild disappointment. "Cheyenne, something's not right, and you ain't fooling me. Do you want to talk about it?"

My bottom lip twitched again, and I shook my head. "There's nothing to talk about. I'm just a little sore from the fall."

"You don't have to keep pushing me away," Jet continued, ignoring my hint to drop the subject. "I wish you wouldn't. There's more to life than digging a hole and burying yourself in it, like you have been doing these last few years."

I leveled both of my eyes on him and swallowed the lump in my throat before I tried talking, but my voice still cracked against my will. "That's because for over a decade people have ignored our cries for help. Ryleigh... " I cleared my throat and breathed a shaky sigh. "Ryleigh buried herself into work, and I tried to raise myself. Maybe I'm digging a hole to crawl into because there's nothing worth facing on ground level, did you ever think of that?" A tear trailed over my cheekbone and dripped off my chin as I sniffed to keep my nose from dripping. "Maybe I'm burying myself because there's nobody to pull me out. Or maybe I find more warmth in that cold pit than I ever did above it."

Jet's gaze never left mine, and when he didn't respond, I ground my teeth and sighed in frustration. He never listened. He said he wanted to understand, but he never tried. What was the point of causing wounds to bleed if all he did was stare and forget what I would say an hour later? At last Jet looked away and rose to his full height.

177

"I'm gonna make me a snack. Do you want one?"

His casual question seemed to plunge a knife deeper in my chest. "No."

A look of reluctance crossed his eyes as he turned and entered the front door. Once he was gone, I slammed a fist into my left leg and covered my mouth with my hand. Why had I collapsed in a moment of weakness? It was better if Jet knew nothing about me, or Ryleigh, or what we had been through. I gasped a sob and pushed myself to my feet again, this time snatching a stick to use as a cane. Putting most of my weight on my left side, I crossed the street and stepped onto the boardwalk. Maybe a walk would relax my nerves and set my mind straight.

As I passed the bank, the door almost slammed into my face as Clyde bulled his way through as if he were the only one with important things to do. A small gasp of surprise flew through my parted lips before the fat man recognized who I was, and a deep frown settled on his mouth when he recognized me.

"How is it that every time I see you, I'm reminded of a mangy coyote?" he snarled with venom in his voice.

I cringed at his insult and wiped the last of the tears away with my wrist. "And how is it that you remind me of a pig?"

"Why, you…!" His voice faded before he chuckled calmly and waved a finger in my face. "Oh, no. You ain't gonna anger me today. I don't know why that sheriff doesn't send you away, to a boarding school or something, so you won't be a nuisance to good, upright citizens like myself."

His boastful statement made the hair on the back of my neck tremble as I scoffed. "You? Upright and good? You overwork those people working for you, including Wil and that new bartender, Bob. You gorge yourself off the money they make for you, and I wouldn't be surprised if you spent your share of nights in those women's beds for free. A good, upright citizen wouldn't force girls to sell their souls for money and men, and you wouldn't threaten a sick woman and her children. If you had an ounce of decency in your fat body, you'd lend a hand to help the widows and orphans! You wouldn't own a saloon where all sorts of indecency brews. You're a filthy animal, and none of that's gonna—"

During the middle of my rant, Overhaul's face turned a deep shade of red, and his hand shot out so that his knuckles rasped my jaw in a painful blow. "Your manners haven't changed since the day I first laid eyes on you, caterwauling like you are and insulting me without a hesitation. Where is that naïve uncle of yours? Does he know you're out here disrespecting your elders?"

I fingered my throbbing jaw and scrunched my nose. "You're worse than I thought, hitting a girl. Especially one who can't defend herself!"

"If you don't answer me, I'll do it again," he snarled, his finger acting like an arrow as it aimed at my nose.

"Is this how you treat Ryleigh?" I snapped instead. "I've seen her bruises. You're worse than a pig to beat a woman! Much less a helpless one who thinks she has no other place to turn! She still thinks you're a blessing in her life, and I don't understand how. You beat her black and blue until she bows at your command!"

Overhaul's hand snapped my head backwards, but anger burned over the pain I felt. "You have lost what little brains you had left in that pea-sized head of yours!" he growled as he glared at me. "Your uncle will hear from me, young lady! Someone ought to take a switch to your backside and beat some respect into you," he finished with a snarl.

My eyes narrowed as my nose wrinkled in a scowl. "That would be impossible."

Overhaul leaned back on his heels and folded his hands over his ample chest. "And why would that be?"

I leaned in close, crinkling my nose at his stench. "Because manners are as foreign to me as the church pew to you. No amount of beating will ever put a smidgen of manners into my thick skull, and you ought to know that."

He raised his hand again, but I ducked as it whizzed over my head. When I straightened my spine, he grabbed the front of my shirt and curled his fist in the material. "When I see your uncle again, I will tell him about this afternoon. If he doesn't bend you over his knee and take his belt to you, I will!"

I twitched when my knee throbbed, but I narrowed my eyes menacingly.

"You don't scare me, Overhaul. If you beat me until I can't move, I'll still hate you for what you've done. You can do *nothing* to gain my respect, just like I can do nothing to gain yours. If you tell Jet and he gives me a lecture, or tries to punish me as he sees fit, I'll still hate you. Nothing you do can change that."

With a frustrated groan, Overhaul shoved me backwards with a mighty thrust of his hand. I stumbled over my feet and fell in a heap after wobbling on unstable legs. Muttering what he thought of me under his breath, Overhaul spun on his heel and waddled down the boardwalk, disappearing into another store. I rubbed my jaw, where his knuckles had split the skin along my bone, causing blood to slowly bubble to the surface. Cringing against the aching pain in the right half of my body, I struggled to my feet and leaned against the wall of the bank as I waited for the throbbing to subside.

"There you are!"

I rolled my eyes to the back of my head when I heard Jet's firm voice across the street. I let out a sigh as I turned to watch him march across the street in long strides. I could tell by the way his fists swung by his sides and his hat pulled low on his head that he was upset. I leaned toward the left so that my weight was lifted from my right knee and wiped my face with my shirt sleeve.

Jet stepped onto the boardwalk and glanced at the people walking around us. "What were you thinking?" he demanded in a low voice. "Your knee will worsen the more you walk on it, I've already told you that. What are you doing all the way out here?"

"I wanted to go for a walk," I answered truthfully. "I ain't no cripple. I don't want you to wait on me like I'm not able to take care of myself." I brushed out of his hold and picked at the wrappings on the cast. "I've been on my own for a long time, Jet."

Jet guided me out of a passerby's way, then glanced down at me with his hands on his hips. "I don't care what you're used to doing. I told you to stay on that porch, and when…" His voice faded, and I chanced a glance at him only to cringe. He wrapped his hand around my chin and turned my face to expose the cut on my jaw. "What did you do here?" he asked as he cleaned some of the blood with his thumb.

"I fell," I lied, rolling my eyes. "It's no big deal, honest it ain't. I just tripped, that's all."

"This wouldn't have happened if you had stayed in that chair like I told you to," Jet scolded mildly

as he reached to lift me off the ground.

I shoved his hands away and lifted a hand to stop any protests. "Fine, I'll go back to that dreaded porch," I gave in, "but I will not be carried like a baby. Just get over here on my bad side and let me lean on you. I will *walk* to that chair, Jet."

Without much of a protest, Jet wrapped an arm around my shoulders and held me close as I hobbled back across the street toward the porch. Jet helped me onto the wooden floor and eased me into the chair he had positioned in the corner of the porch. I set my leg on the stool in front of me and folded my arms over my chest as I watched him set the piece of ice on my knee.

"You relax while I find something to put on that cut," he said as he headed back in the house.

I rolled my eyes and turned my head to stare down the street toward the Bull's Head. Overhaul would someday pay for all he had done, and I would gladly watch him get stripped away from all he had built up for himself, just like he had done with Ryleigh and myself. Anger burned at the thought of him hitting me in the middle of the street. If Jet knew what kind of man Overhaul was, he wouldn't be so quick to scold me. Curling my lip, I slipped lower in the chair and wished for the umpteenth time that I did not exist.

Jet returned a short time later with a rag and a bottle of some type of medicine in his hand. He sat beside me and dabbed a little of the bottle's contents onto a corner of the rag. Placing a hand on the side of my temple, he leaned my head onto my shoulder and touched the rag on the scratch. I flinched when sharp pain seemed to shove a needle deeper into my skin, but I growled my discomfort and sat as still as I could. Jet finished cleaning the measly wound Overhaul created with his knuckles and leaned back as he studied the side of my face.

"What did you run into when you fell?" he asked as he corked the bottle.

"The hard floor of the barn," I snarled.

"No, when you fell across the street."

I remained silent as my mind raced for a believable answer. Clearing my throat, I shrugged and shifted under his gaze. "I tripped in the street, and my chin hit the corner of the boardwalk. Those boards are sharper than I thought."

Jet raised an eyebrow as he leaned against the side of the house. "I don't like to be lied to, Cheyenne. I asked you an honest question, and I want an honest answer."

I shifted in my seat and scratched the base of my neck. "I ain't lying."

"Yes, you are. I'm not stupid, Cheyenne. You won't make eye contact, and you keep shifting. I was a kid once, and that's what I did when I didn't want my pa to know what I'd been up to. Now, I don't believe you could've gotten into a lot of trouble in the few minutes I was in the house, so what is it that you're trying to hide from me?"

"Nothing." I looked at him from the corner of my eye. "I ain't hiding nothing, Jet."

Jet sighed and rested his arms on his knees. "Knowing your reputation in this town, I'll find out sooner or later if you've been up to something, but I'd rather hear it from you. I know something happened while I was inside, and I wish you would tell me."

"Nothing happened, Jet, and I wish you'd just drop the subject."

Jet sighed as he rose to his feet. "Have it your way, Cheyenne. I wasn't going to be mad at you for what happened. I just wanted you to trust me." He stuck his thumbs in his pockets and shrugged. "I'm going to get some supplies so we can have supper tonight. Can I trust you to stay put?"

I sank lower under his gaze and studied my cast. "I ain't going nowhere."

"I hope not."

I watched him step onto the street and head toward the mercantile. My frustration melted, and my heart grew heavy. If only I could trust him enough to know he wouldn't leave me to fend for myself.

"I'm sorry," I whispered to my uncle as I watched him disappear into the mercantile.

The next several minutes blended as I drifted into a light nap. The sun felt warm on my face and arms, and I allowed myself to dream of innocent times. I dreamt of when I was the happiest with Ryleigh and was comforted with thoughts of innocence and honesty. It wasn't until the sound of boots thumping on the wooden porch in front of me that I realized I had drifted into a fantasy.

I jumped and ran my gaze upward to look into Jet's slight frown. "Get inside," he said as he helped me to my feet. "I want to talk to you."

My stomach was attacked by bumblebees as I allowed him to help me inside to the kitchen. Once he had helped me into a chair at the table, he folded his arms over his chest and gave me a stern look. "I ran into Mr. Overhaul on my way back," he said matter-of-factly.

I ducked my head and swallowed hard. "Of course, you did."

"He bit my ear off for a solid ten minutes, telling me how disrespectful you were to him. He mentioned some of the things you said. I'm disappointed in you, Cheyenne. Extremely disappointed. Why didn't you tell me when I asked you?"

I cringed at the defeat in his voice. "I didn't think you'd understand."

Jet's shoulders slumped as he sighed. "You're right, I don't. I know you think you hate him because Ryleigh's working for him, but that's no cause to say the things that you did. Just because you don't like a man doesn't mean you have a right to insult him, especially when he is your elder." Jet shook his head as he looked away. "He said you accused him of sleeping with his employees. What do you have to say for yourself?"

I hunched lower in my seat as guilt brought tears to my eyes again. "I'm sorry, Jet." I took a deep breath. "He called me a coyote, and I got angry. I know I said things you wouldn't approve of, but you don't know him like I do. I didn't mean to talk with him. I really was just going for a short walk."

Jet sat in front of me and ran his fingers through his hair. "Why did you say those things?"

"He's not a good man." I motioned to the cut on my jaw. "You saw what he did to me."

Jet stiffened, and when he spoke his voice blasted through the house. "You mean to say he hit you?"

I cringed at his tone and hung my head to avoid looking at him. "It's just what he does. He beats Ryleigh and the other girls in his saloon. I even saw him beat Mama when she was too sick to go to work. This wasn't the first time he's hit me, either."

Jet hooked a finger under my chin and lifted my face to meet his gaze. "Why would he hit you?" he asked in a softer tone.

I shrugged and struggled to speak past tears. "I'm alive. He likes to use people for his benefit, and I don't let him. This is his house, you know. He let Mama rent it when Pa left, and he takes the rent money out of Ryleigh's paycheck so that I can live here. I'm sure he's happy that you're fixing this house up for free. What does it matter if he hits me?"

"It matters because you're my niece, and just a child yet. He has no right to lay a hand on you."

I averted his gaze. "Sheriff Hodgkinson has taken a belt to me before, and Overhaul's hit me when I make him mad enough. Mr. Hyndman has taken my punishment in his hands several times. Why should it bother you?"

Jet looked at me with soft eyes. "A teacher has a right to discipline his pupils when they misbehave in the classroom, and a sheriff has a right to tan the hide of a mischievous orphan. But a man like Mr. Overhaul shouldn't hit you, especially if you're in your current condition. If he wanted you to learn from your mistake, he'd have told me without touching you. You're my responsibility. If you angered him, he should've just told me and let me decide how to deal with your behavior. You are my child, and I get to decide how I'm going to raise you, not him."

I studied him with my brows furrowed together. "What did you say?"

"I said a man like Clyde Overhaul shouldn't lay his hands—"

"No, no, after that," I interrupted. "What you said just now."

Jet frowned and studied me from under the brim of his black hat. "You're my niece, and I get to decide how I'm gonna raise you."

I shook my head and lowered my gaze before he could see the expression in my eyes. "No, you said I was your child."

Jet cleared his throat as an awkward silence settled on us like a thick blanket. "Well, we've got the same blood running in our veins, it's just that you were born in my brother's household," Jet responded at last. "I'm sorry if I offended you."

I shook my head. "No. You didn't offend me, Jet. It's just that, well, you're more of a father to me than Pa ever was." I lifted my head to look into his face. "I'm not used to it."

Jet stared at me with his piercing blue eyes, which held a gentle glow. I noticed again how his eyes contrasted with the black beard on his masculine jawline, but he did not appear near as frightening as he had when I first saw him in the saloon. "No matter whose kid you are, that man shouldn't have hit you, and I'm sorry for coming off so strongly. I should've asked for your side of the story before I accused you."

I glanced away and shrugged. "It don't matter."

"Yes, it does. I should trust you to tell me things like that instead of believing something I hear from people I don't know very well." He wrapped an arm around my shoulders and the other under my knees as he lifted me out of the chair. "You've had enough excitement for one day, and you should rest easy," he said as he carried me into my bedroom.

Without a word, Jet set me on the bed and turned to leave. I watched him head toward the door and bit my lip as I glanced toward my nightstand. "Jet?"

He turned around in the doorway, and his gaze met mine. "Yeah?"

I swallowed hard as I opened the drawer to my nightstand and pulled out the golden watch that I had won in the poker game the previous night. I fingered it in my hands before extending it to him. "I figure you know what to do with this?"

Jet took the watch from my palm and studied it. "Where did you get this?"

"Chad brought it to the poker game last night," I explained. "It was really late, and we all wanted to go home before we got caught. He said he had his grandfather's watch that he didn't want anymore, but he'd only bet it if we stayed a little longer." I lifted a shoulder in a shrug and stared at my lap. "I had the winning hand. I suppose the sheriff spoke with you this morning?"

"He did."

I chanced a glance at my uncle and felt my shoulders slump as I watched him trace the engraving on the lid of the watch. "I didn't know it was stolen, Jet. I wouldn't have played for it if I had. Honest."

Jet finally looked up from the watch and nodded. "I believe you."

"Are you gonna punish me?" I asked cautiously.

He shook his head. "No, I don't believe I will. I'll return it to the sheriff and forget about it." He turned to leave but met my gaze again and cocked his head to the side. "There is one thing I want you to do, and that's stay away from Chad. He only seems to get you in trouble, and I don't think you should be around him."

I swallowed hard as I lowered my head. "Jet?"

"Hmm?"

"I'm sorry."

Jet's lips lifted upward as he smiled softly. "Thank you, Cheyenne. Now lay back and relax."

~TWELVE~

The afternoon activity in the saloon was slow, which was to be expected. Bob played the piano softly, his fingers finding the right notes to a beautiful, melancholy song Ryleigh didn't recognize. Mr. Overhaul was running his daily errands and gaining his two hours-worth of exercise for the afternoon, while Wil worked to restock the bottles and wash the glasses. Most of the other girls were lying in bed in their rooms as they caught up on some slumber that they had missed the previous night. Ryleigh had decided to stay downstairs to help Violet in case a weary cowboy drifted in for a refreshing drink.

Ryleigh lifted the glass of whiskey to her nose and studied the bronze liquid before pressing the edge of the glass to her lips to take a sip. The liquor burned a hole all the way down to her gut, and she sighed when she felt the beginning of a buzz. This wasn't the first day she felt sick, but she couldn't figure out exactly what it was that discomforted her. Her stomach was irritated, and the thought of the food Wil cooked up made her want to vomit. She was exhausted, too. More than usual. Her legs were weak, and all she wanted to do was sleep.

Violet slid in a chair beside Ryleigh and poured herself a glass. "I don't know whether to enjoy the lack of business, or hate it," she drawled as she brought the whiskey to her lips and downed it in one swallow. She shoved a piece of delicate blond hair out of her eyes and hiccupped. "I think I hate it."

Ryleigh attempted to smile and laid her head in the crook of her elbow. "I think I love it," she moaned as she held an arm over her stomach. "It means

I don't have to act excited to see anyone."

Violet poured another glass and studied her young friend. "You've been acting sluggish for the last few weeks. You okay?"

"I'm fine," Ryleigh assured as she raised her head and cleared her throat. "I'm just worn to a nubbin'."

Violet pursed her lips and shrugged. "This ain't the first time I've seen you lookin' like that this week. I think you should see Doc Harding."

Shaking her head, Ryleigh spun the bottle in front of her and scratched her bare shoulder. "No. Mr. Overhaul would have a fit if he paid that doctor only to learn I'm just tired. I'm fine, Violet. I just need these few hours before the evening rush."

"Well, why don't you go on to bed, honey? I can handle things down here until Clyde gets back."

"No, I can rest in this chair, it's no big deal."

"I think it's a big deal." Violet pushed herself to her feet and downed her second glass. "You know how he hates sick entertainers. As soon as he gets back, I'll ask him to fetch Doc Harding over here to look at you."

The back door slammed, and both women jumped as they turned around to see their robust boss waddle into the room. "Get Doc to look at who?" he demanded as he headed toward his office.

Violet straightened her back as she smoothed her skirts. "Ryleigh's feeling a little bit woozy. I thought it best for Doc Harding to look at her."

Overhaul glanced at Ryleigh before he waved his hand in the air as he ambled toward his office. "Tell her to ease back on the whiskey. I need her sober tonight."

Violet chortled a laugh, and Ryleigh laid her forehead on her arm. If only her dear friend would accept the fact that all Ryleigh needed was twenty minutes to take a small nap. "That's not what I'm meaning," Violet continued. "She just had her first drink in four days, and she's been getting weaker by the day. She might be catching a fever of some kind. You just never know."

Mr. Overhaul pinned Ryleigh under his beady gaze, and she lifted her head in hopes he would notice she was well indeed. His eyelids drooped the longer he studied her, and at last he raised a hand over his head in defeat.

"Fine, go get the doctor. But if nothing's wrong with her, his bill is coming out of your pocket," he threatened with a finger aimed like a dagger at Violet's tender heart.

Violet nodded as she planted her hands on her hips. "Understood. Now help Ryleigh to her room while I get the doctor."

Mr. Overhaul curled his lip in disgust, but yanked Ryleigh to her feet and shoved her up the steps and into the room she occupied. When he slammed the door behind him, Ryleigh staggered to the bed and flopped down on the mattress. She felt her body melt on the feathers beneath her, and it just felt good to lay on her aching back and relax. All she needed was a nap. She would be bouncing on her feet come the evening rush if she just took an hour or two of rest.

Her door opened a few minutes later as Violet led the tall doctor to Ryleigh's bedside. "How long did you say she's been sick?" he asked as he knelt beside Ryleigh.

Violet lifted a shoulder in a shrug. "I first noticed it a couple of weeks ago. It's not always bad, though."

Doc Harding rolled up his sleeves before rummaging in his doctor's bag. "Could you give us some privacy please?"

Violet nodded and headed for the door. "I'll just be in the hall if you need me."

The doctor nodded and plugged his ears with his stethoscope. Ryleigh answered his many questions and did as he asked until he seemed to conclude what ailment she had. Ryleigh studied his features as he cleaned up his mess. A worried frown etched lines on his brow, and he refused to look at her. Maybe there was more than sleep that Ryleigh needed.

"What's wrong?" she asked when he never said a word.

He finally met her gaze and threw a thumb over his shoulder. "She's listening. Can she be trusted?"

Ryleigh frowned and nodded slowly. "Yeah. She took me in five years ago when I started entertaining. I've told Violet many things, and she hasn't repeated them to anyone."

Doc Harding rose to his feet and yanked the door open to reveal Violet with her ear pressed against the wood. She bounced to her full five feet, six inches and frowned at the doctor. "You know, there's such a thing as a warning to help prepare a body before trying to trip them by yanking the only support out from under them!"

The doctor ignored her protest and pulled her inside by the arm before locking the door behind her. Violet's gaze turned ashen as she noticed his precautions. "What's wrong?" she whispered in a husky voice that had seen too many cigars in her lifetime.

Doc Harding placed a hand on his hip as he ran the other hand over his mustache. "I'm not sure what to do," he admitted in a low voice. "Normally I would be proud to make such an announcement."

"What is it?" Ryleigh demanded, fear settling in her chest.

The doctor raised his green eyes to meet her gaze and sighed. "You're pregnant."

Ryleigh's heart bounced on the floor as she sprang to her feet. "I'm *what?*" She hugged her stomach and glanced between the two faces. "I *can't* be pregnant! Do you know what Mr. Overhaul will do once he finds out?" she hissed in a whisper.

Doc Harding showed Ryleigh the palms of his hands to keep her from panicking. "Take it easy, he doesn't have to know yet. You can hide it until we figure something out."

"*Hide it?* How can you hide a pregnancy? And what are you gonna do? As soon as Mr. Overhaul hears the news, he'll schedule an appointment with you to get rid of the baby. If you refuse, he'll take me to another doctor, and if that don't work, he'll take care of the baby his own self! I've seen him do it to another girl before." Ryleigh ran her fingers through her hair. "Pregnant? What am I gonna do?"

Doc Harding took hold of Ryleigh's shoulders and looked firmly into her eyes. "I can tell you what you're not gonna do. You're not gonna panic, and you're not gonna hurt that child."

"But—"

"Don't argue with him," Violet interrupted as she rushed to her friend's side. "Listen to me, honey. You can get by Clyde for a few weeks, and he won't know the difference. He'll listen to whatever Doc Harding has to say and he'll just think you're resting up. I'll cover for you, I don't mind. And he's fixing to leave for Phoenix to get more supplies, anyway. A week or two should be long enough for us to think of something, even if that means you packing up that sister of yours and disappearing until that baby gets born."

Ryleigh covered her eyes with the palm of her hand and whimpered. "Cheyenne! I can't let her see me like this! What will she think of me if I show up pregnant? I don't even know who the father is!" She gasped as tears sprung to her eyes. "What will Mr. Douglas think?"

Doc Harding gently eased her on the edge of her bed and aimed a finger at her nose. "You worry about them later. Right now, I want you to close your eyes and try to get some sleep. Don't let Overhaul get to you, you understand me?"

Ryleigh began to sob as she laid on the pillow. "I'm such a fool!" She peeked at the doctor around the crook of her elbow and forced her lips to form words. "How far along...?"

"My best guess is maybe two months."

Ryleigh let out a moan and rolled over with a little too much force. Doc Harding turned to Violet as he picked up his black bag. "Comfort her. Make sure she relaxes and gets some sleep. I've got a story to make up."

Violet nodded as she rushed to Ryleigh's bedside.

Doc Harding opened the door and stepped into the hallway. When the door latched soundly behind him, he glanced over his shoulder and felt his insides die. Ryleigh was but a little girl herself. She shouldn't be worried about whether she was losing or having a baby. She shouldn't be searching her mind to find the father, either. She should be at home, stitching up a new dress as she went to church socials and laughed at the boys as they tried to impress her. Shaking his head, he squared his jaw and marched downstairs to find Clyde Overhaul.

The fat man sat at one of the tables, guzzling a bottle he had taken from the shelf behind the counter. When Doc Harding stepped off the last stair,

Overhaul pushed himself to his feet and ambled toward the doctor.

"Well? How is she?"

Doc Harding turned a glare on the man and set his bag on the counter as he unrolled his sleeves.

"She's overworked, Clyde. She worked herself sick, and I told her to stay in bed for a few days to a week. She doesn't need to be working during that time, is that understood?"

"A week?" Overhaul exclaimed, his voice booming off the rafters.

"That's what I said. Four days at the least."

"But I'm leaving the day after tomorrow to get supplies. I need Ryleigh to entertain my customers while I'm gone!"

Doc Harding narrowed his eyes as he poked the saloon owner in the chest. "Ryleigh needs her rest more than you need your money. It would look awfully suspicious if she were to kill herself working for you. Unless you want the law riding on your rump, you'll do as I say."

Overhaul curled his lip as he backed up a step and leaned against the bar. "Alright, she can rest. But I'm not going to pay to have you come over here to check up on her, and nobody else will be here to see to her needs."

"I gave instructions to Violet. She should be able to carry out my orders by herself, so you don't have to lift a finger to assist." He picked up his black bag and turned toward the door. "I'll send my bill over once I calculate the cost. Good day."

Quickening his step, Doc Harding hurried out the door and he felt his anger rise in his chest at the fear that Overhaul set in the minds of those helpless girls, especially Ryleigh. As he made his way back to his office, he vowed to do everything in his power to watch over the young woman. Even more so now that there was another life mixed into the situation.

* * *

Saturday morning rolled by with the sun shining warmly, the wind at a whisper, and the people smiling happily toward their neighbors as they went about their business. Two days had passed since I had fallen from the loft in the livery barn, but my body ached as though it had happened within the last hour. Although Jet allowed me to walk on my leg, he warned me not to go too far or stress my knee too much, but on that afternoon, I was too bored to sit inside the house.

Jet was working an extra shift at the feed mill to fill out a large order and should be home any minute, but I didn't want to wait for him to walk with me. Picking up a rock, I tossed it a few feet away and breathed in the late summer air. August still gloated of the hot atmosphere, but at night it also held a hint of the climate change that was soon to follow. I always thought it was a bittersweet time of year since I never had been fond of the colder months, but there was nothing I could do to keep the sweltering heat from leaving. Instead, I made a daily vow to spend as much time out of doors as I could and had succeeded for the most part.

Setting my gaze on the ground to watch where I planted my feet, I strolled down the boardwalk in hopes to stretch my aching muscles and keep from growing into an immovable plant. After Jet clocked out of the feed mill, he would want to start on the house again, and this time I planned to assist him.

"*Psst!*"

I frowned as I slowed my step and looked around to see who had tried to gain my attention.

"Cheyenne!"

My lip curled when I heard the familiar youth's voice, and I spun on my heel with the desire to rearrange Chad's nose on his face. "What do you think you're doing?" I snarled as I disappeared into the alley where he hid.

Chad raised his hands by his head. "I swear, I don't know what you're talking about!"

My fist clenched at my side as I advanced on the boy. "Oh, you don't, huh? You just conveniently forgot that the watch I won in the poker game was stolen, right?" I grabbed the front of his collar as I shoved him against the side of the mercantile. "I oughta knock that head off your shoulders! You set me up!"

"Hey, hey, whoa!" he exclaimed when he saw the fiery glint in my eye. "I was wrong, okay? I admit it, just don't hurt me!"

I studied him, then shoved him aside as I let go of his shirt collar. "Why shouldn't I hurt you, you twit? Give me one good reason!"

Chad straightened the front of his shirt as he crooked a finger for me to lean in close. Reluctantly, I obeyed his request. "I got something I wanna show you. I got it from Pa's tin when he wasn't looking. C'mon, it'll only take a second, and you won't even get in trouble!" He grinned and hooked his thumbs through his belt loops. "Besides, I know I got you curious now, and you won't say no."

I curled my lip in a growl as I placed my forearm in his chest and pushed him against the wall again. "If I get into trouble again, I'm gonna tear you in half and feed you to the buzzards!"

Chad matched my growl as he lifted his hands in surrender. "Okay, okay, I swear. You won't get in trouble. Now back off so I can breathe!"

I hesitated for a moment, then lowered my arm and backed up a step as he reached into his shirt pocket. He flashed a mischievous grin and pulled out a brown stick about six inches long. When I realized it was a cigar, I rolled my eyes and turned to leave, but Chad grabbed my arm to stop me.

"Don't leave now, you'll tell on me!" he snarled in a hushed tone.

"What do you aim to do with that thing?" I questioned, motioning to the cigar in his hand.

"What do you think I'm gonna do with it? I'm gonna smoke it! C'mon, Cheyenne. Smokin' is what adults do. You want to be an adult, don't you?"

"Well, yes, but them things are strong. You'll get sick if you ain't careful."

Chad frowned as he dug his fingers into his pocket and brought out a match. "Ah, you worry too much, Cheyenne. Cigars are good for ya! Haven't you ever wanted to try one?"

"No," I snapped as I folded my arms over my chest. "It's suffocating in the saloon, so I never desired to try one."

Chad rolled his eyes and extended the match toward me. "Fine, then you light it while I smoke it."

I glanced at the match and shook my head. "I need to go before Jet gets home. He'll want to get started on the house."

"Stop worrying about your daggum uncle!" Chad screeched as he shoved the match in my hand. "It won't take that long, and you don't even have to try it. C'mon, Cheyenne. You used to be fun, and now you're a boring wimp."

"I'm not a wimp!" I argued as I tightened my hold on the match. "Bite off the end and I'll light it, but don't expect me to stand around while you smoke it!"

Chad grinned as he quickly bit off the end of the cigar and held it in his teeth. Curling my lip with dread, I struck the red tip of the match against the mercantile and cupped my hand around the cigar as I held the flame to the other end. After several seconds, smoke began to burn at the makings inside of the cigar, and I pulled the match away as I studied Chad. He inhaled deeply, then yanked the cigar out of his mouth as he began to cough.

"Whoa, that's good!" he assured in between fits of coughing.

I frowned, but my irritation was replaced by curiosity. "Are you sure? It doesn't sound like it's good."

Chad gulped a breath of clean oxygen and extended the cigar toward me. "Just try it. You'll see it ain't so bad."

"Chad, I–ouch!"

I had forgotten that I still held the burning match in my hand, and the flame reached my fingertips. A shiver raced up to my shoulder as I instinctively dropped the match, and my eyes widened when it landed in a clump of dead grass beside the mercantile. Flame instantly choked out the grass and began to lick at the boards of the mercantile. We both jumped backward when the heat of the fire grew.

"Now look what you've done!" Chad shouted as he turned to glare at me.

"ME?" I yelped. "You're the one who wanted me to light the blasted cigar in the first place! What are you gonna do now?"

Chad narrowed his eyes as he grabbed my left wrist and ran into the street. "Fire! Fire! Somebody, help! There's a fire!"

Several men heard Chad's cries and ran for the nearest horse trough, filling buckets with water before they raced to the mercantile. Before too long, a line of men formed as they worked hard and fast to throw buckets of water onto the angry flames. I bit my lip as I saw the fire fight back, hissing and smoking with each drop that touched it. Two men hurried to soak gunny sacks with water and began to flail at the fire. Several minutes dragged by before the fire was tamed to a small whimper. The only evidence of the disaster was the darkened boards on the mercantile and black grass in the alley.

I swallowed hard when the shouts to "hurry up" died and all eyes swung to me and Chad. I found Jet's gaze among the crowd of men and felt my insides dissolve when he narrowed his eyes suspiciously.

"What happened here?" Jet demanded in a loud voice.

I glanced around the crowd and noticed they were all scrutinizing us with their own skepticism. "We... we were smoking," I explained slowly. My knees began to shake with each word I spoke.

Several men grumbled their anger as they turned to complain to each other, but my gaze never wavered from Jet's eyes. Without saying a word, Jet stepped through the crowd as he twisted Chad's and my ears in each hand and led us down the boardwalk out of hearing range of the townsfolk.

Pulling us in front of him, he finally let go of our ears and jammed his hands on his hips. Silence settled over us as Jet glared between Chad and me as he contemplated what to say. At last, he inhaled deeply and leveled his icy blue eyes on me.

"What on earth were you thinking?" he demanded in a shaky voice. I could hear the rage that he tried to hold back.

Chad glanced at me and pointed a finger in my direction. "Uh, it was all her idea, sir!"

Jet glared at the boy with narrowed eyes. "I'll get to you later." He turned back to me, and I found it hard to look him in the eye. "Answer me, Cheyenne."

I studied the toe of my boot as I gently kicked some dust. "I-I... we..." I hid my arms behind my back as I licked my lips. "Chad wanted to smoke a cigar, and I struck the match to light it. I... must have dropped the match... accidentally." I raised my head to look at my uncle and wished I hadn't. "I'm sorry, Jet. It won't happen again!"

The muscles in Jet's jaw tightened as he turned back to Chad. "You," he muttered in a gravelly voice. "You're always getting my niece into trouble. Don't come around her again, do you hear me?"

Chad swallowed hard as he nodded vigorously. "Yes, sir! I won't come back, I swear!"

Jet grabbed Chad's arm when he tried to dodge around him. "If I hear that you influence my niece badly again, I'll make sure to have a nice long talk with your pa. You gotta learn that there are consequences for your actions."

"Yes, sir," Chad answered again. "I know that, and it won't happen again!"

"Now go home!" Jet commanded as he let go of the boy.

Chad stumbled backwards as he rubbed his arm where Jet had touched him. He glanced at me, frowned, then spun on his heel to disappear down the street. I watched him leave and felt rage flood my chest as I glared at his retreating figure. *So much for your promise, Chad. The next time I see you I should turn you into buzzard bait!*

Jet moved to block my view of Chad, and I cautiously raised my gaze to his face. His blue eyes seemed to burn underneath his black eyebrows, and his arms were crossed over his chest. My heart quickened its pace as I backed up against the store behind me.

"Now, Jet, please—"

"You almost burned down a building," he interrupted in a voice that set my nerves on edge. "You could've hurt someone, maybe even got someone killed!"

"But nothing happened!" I defended. I began backing toward our house at the end of the street. "It was Chad's fault. He's the one who wanted to smoke the cigar. I didn't do anything!"

"I told you to stay away from that boy," he continued, "and you didn't listen to me. You should've known better than to play with matches and cigars. I don't care whose idea it was. You are just as guilty as Chad."

"Jet, please," I begged as I took another step backwards. "It won't happen again. I promise it won't! I'm sorry!"

He took a step toward me and raised an eyebrow. "You disobeyed me, Cheyenne. I can't ignore what you did."

"Jet, I…" I realized that he wouldn't listen to any other explanation and whirled on my heel in hopes that he wouldn't follow me. I ran down the street, up the porch steps, and slammed the front door behind me, but Jet caught it before it latched and followed me into the living room. I spun to face him and tried to ignore the bumblebees in the pit of my stomach. "Jet, please! Let me explain before you punish me!"

"What more is there to explain?" he asked sternly. "You've already told me what happened."

I hung my head as I backed away from him. "I tried to stop him. I promise I did, but he wouldn't listen. I know I shouldn't have let him smoke the cigar, and I'm sorry."

"You could've been hurt," Jet answered, but his voice wasn't as stern as it had been in the street. "I told you to stay away from that boy."

"I know you did. I just couldn't tell him no." I looked up at my uncle with pleading eyes. "Please understand, Jet. He's my only friend."

"Cheyenne, I can't ignore that every time you're with him you get into trouble. I don't want something bad to happen to you. What if you kids start another fire and nobody would be around to stop it in time?"

I lowered my head again. "It won't happen again," I whispered in a quivering voice. I blinked back tears that were beginning to well in my eyes and shook my head. "I swear it won't."

"Don't swear."

I tried to back away from him, but he took hold of my shoulder and guided me to a chair at the dining table. "Why won't you let me go?" I asked in a small voice.

"Because I don't want you to run from me." Jet finally let go of me and sat beside me. "I don't want you to feel you have to take care of yourself."

I brushed a tear away and fingered my cast. "I can't trust you."

"Why not?" Jet asked quietly.

"I just can't! Every time I let someone come close, they take something from me and leave me alone. You'll do the same. You'll get tired of trying to fix us, Jet, and you'll leave. You'll leave and not come back, just like Pa did!"

Jet shook his head slightly. "You've been hurt, and I can see that. You're scared you won't have someone to be there for you. I know you like to get in trouble because then people will pay attention to you." He cleared his throat and took his hat off his head, placing it on the table in front of him. "Your grandfather was a gambling man, just like your pa was, and he was barely around for your father and me. I was a lot like you when I was your age. I got into a lot of trouble, like busting up stores in the dead of night, or entering saloons to try and sneak a drink. As I got older, I found myself getting deeper into trouble. My pa would tan my hide a lot more than I ever want to do to you, but I never listened. I got involved with three other boys that were as good for me as Chad is for you. I rode off with them, living the dream of a young man barely out of his teens, and doing whatever I wanted when I wanted it."

He looked away from me and frowned slightly as he recalled his youthful years. "I spent more than my share of nights in a saloon much like the Bull's Head, and I played rough and hard. I was turning into a gambling man, and I enjoyed the taste of freedom that my father would speak about. And then one night, my friends had an idea to rob a bank. The plan was bullet proof, except for one thing, and that was the fact that two U. S. Marshals were in town after bringing in some outlaws. I was supposed to hold the horses while the others ran in and took as much money as they could hold, but while they ran inside, the banker came out of his living quarters in the back of the building. One of the boys shot him. The bullet pierced his lung and buried itself in his heart, and the blast from the gun alerted the marshals. They were on us like a pack of wolves, and they took us to prison."

I studied my uncle with unwavering eyes. "Why are you telling me this?"

Jet met my gaze again and leaned against the table. "Because you need to hear this. I sat in a prison cell for eleven years, thinking about what I had done in my youth and wishing I had the ability to turn back the clock. When I found your father, I had just gotten out on parole for good behavior." He sighed and twitched his eyebrows. "I don't want you to do the same thing I did, Cheyenne. That's why I care, and that's why I'm not leaving. I never had a steady father figure in my life, and I walked away from my mother's teachings. I don't want my past to be your future. That's why I'm so stubborn."

I studied him for a long time, ignoring the last of my tears that clung to my eye lashes. I couldn't think of anything to say, and at last I broke my gaze and studied the wood grains in the table. Jet watched me in silence for several moments before he shifted in his chair and cleared his throat.

"You don't have to like me," he said glumly. "I just want you to know that I understand what you're feeling, and I'm not leaving. I've already left my family once. I'm not going to do it again."

My chin quivered as my eyes filled with water again. I swallowed hard and closed my eyes. "I'm tired of being alone," I told him in a weak voice.

"You're not alone."

I covered my eyes with my left hand and tried to take a shaky breath without gasping a sob. I wanted to bury my face in his shoulder and let him comfort me, but I still couldn't make myself trust him. The story he had told me reminded me of myself in many ways, and the thought bothered me. I felt myself longing to tame down and become a respectable person, but the fear of being torn apart by the townspeople soon pulled that ridiculous notion from my mind. People were like wolves, and I would be like an elk calf if I were to back down. Shaking my head, I convinced myself to remain strong and sat in silence while I waited to see what Jet would do next.

Jet tried to look me in the eye, but when I didn't acknowledge him, he let out a soft sigh and studied his hands that were resting on his knees. "Please don't run away from me anymore," he said in a soft voice. "I want the best for you, but you've got to trust me."

I finally looked up and blinked a lone tear off my eyelash. "I can't trust anybody."

Jet's eyes dimmed in disappointment as he searched my gaze, and eventually he rose to his feet and patted my shoulder. "I'll be outside if you need me," he said as he stepped onto the porch.

I watched him close the door and wiped my eyes with the tips of my fingers. I was a blasted fool. Closing my eyes, I wondered what I should believe. Jet's confession finally allowed me to understand his persistence, and it was tempting to want to trust him. Why was I still so scared of him? Confusion was an uncomfortable emotion to feel, and I despised it. I shook my head and covered my eyes in the crook of my elbow. Why couldn't everything be so simple?

I stared at the table for a moment before I rose to my feet and wandered onto the front porch. Jet wasn't in sight, so I walked to the porch railing and sat on it. I heard a voice around the corner and glanced over my shoulder toward the alley to see Jet leaning against the house with his head in his hands. His lips were moving, and I strained my ears to hear what he was saying.

"I don't know what to do," he mumbled in a broken voice. "Please, God, show me what to do. I can't get through to her and I care about her so much. What am I supposed to do?"

I frowned as I slid from the railing and tiptoed closer to him. Was he praying? I hadn't heard anyone pray to God as if they were having a normal conversation. And did Jet really say he cared about me? I leaned my shoulder against the house and watched him as he continued to pray. I felt the desire to go to him but fear still held me back.

"Lord, please heal my niece. I don't know what she's been through, but I can see what kind of person she is. Help her to trust again."

Tears blurred my vision, and I hurried back inside the house before Jet realized I heard him. I didn't know how to explain the emotion I felt. I had given up on God, but Jet prayed to him like they were good friends. I couldn't understand why Jet would waste his breath on a prayer for me but knowing that he was praying for me made me feel warm inside. I felt like I had been living in an iceberg my whole life and Jet had brought the torch to melt my prison.

~THIRTEEN~

I stared at the church steps where several families filed inside the building with warm smiles and handshakes. I thought back a week ago and remembered the whiskey I had dumped on Penelope's dress. Swallowing hard, I spun on my heel with the intention of hiding in my bedroom until the service was over.

"Whoa, where are you going?" Jet asked as he took hold of my shoulders and turned me to face the church again.

"Uh, I suddenly remembered something I forgot," I answered quickly, digging my heels into the ground.

"Like what?" Jet asked, folding his arms over his chest.

"Uh…" I bit my lip and whirled to run, but my uncle grabbed my wrist and pulled me back. "Jet, please! I can't go in there, not after what I did last week. I'm not welcomed in there. Please don't make me sit in a pew!"

"Cheyenne, last Sunday is in the past, and I want you to listen to the sermon with me." He offered me a small smile. "You don't have to be afraid. I'm not going to leave you to fend for yourself."

I halfheartedly pulled against my uncle as he led me up the church steps. He stopped in front of the Reverend and extended his hand.

"Good morning," Jet said cheerily as the Reverend accepted his hand.

The parson smiled warmly as he glanced between Jet and me. "I'm glad y'all could make it this morning. I was praying that you would."

"Hmph," I snorted as I rolled my eyes. Jet heard me and nudged me with his elbow as a silent hint to behave myself.

"We're glad to be here," Jet assured as he ushered me inside.

Almost instantly, my eyes pinpointed Mrs. Wilkes, whose gaze narrowed when we walked through the doors. I felt the urge to hang my head and dodge out of the building as fast as my legs could move, but Jet nudged me forward in front of him with a hand on my shoulder. I stared at a spot on the floor in front of the alter and didn't dare glance away from it as I hurriedly ducked into the pew closest to the back. Jet lowered himself beside me and nodded toward Levi Hendershot before he faced the pulpit.

I glanced at the stable boy, who smiled warmly and nodded in our direction as he stepped into a pew next to Mr. Shepherd. Biting my lower lip, I looked at my uncle with pleading eyes in hopes he would change his mind and let me hide until the service was over. He didn't seem to notice me.

The Reverend walked down the aisle and folded his hands in front of him as he turned to face his small congregation. Offering a smile, he lifted his arms as a motion for us to rise and began to sing a hymn I barely knew. After struggling with the lyrics, I pursed my lips and sang a bar song I'd heard Ryleigh sing. Jet heard the words I was singing and stared down at me in shock. At last, he collected himself enough to nudge me with his elbow.

I jumped when I felt his nudge and glanced up at him, but he raised an eyebrow and faced the front as he continued to sing the hymn in his rich baritone. I curled my lip and flopped on the bench in exasperation. Church was a place I had avoided for a long time. I didn't want to feel the judgment I knew was cast my way, and I didn't like the feeling of being caught off guard. Church was a good place to raise a family, unless your family happened to be full of sinners. Then you were expected to get drunk Saturday night and sleep through a hangover on Sunday morning, or wander into a saloon and participate in its activities. I wanted no part of the congregation, not if showing up for a sermon full of meaningless words was what they figured fit and pleasing to God.

Jet turned his head and noticed that I was no longer standing beside him. Giving me a warning look, he snapped his fingers and pointed upward. I narrowed my eyes and shook my head. I wasn't going to stand through the hymn if I couldn't sing the lyrics I knew. I also felt that his silent reprimands were inappropriate since he was the one to drag me to a place I didn't want to go. Exhaling softly, he took hold of my arm and helped me stand on my feet, and he didn't let go until the hymn was over.

As the Reverend made his way to the pulpit, the congregation sat almost in unison, and the sounds of the floorboards creaking and ladies' skirts rustling filled the room. I rolled my eyes and slouched in my seat as the parson opened his Bible and leaned forward dramatically. The instant the Reverend opened his mouth to begin his sermon, I raised my left hand and proceeded to make my fingers talk as if hinting that the man of God used too many words. Jet lowered my hand and pointed toward the front of the church as if to command that I listen to the sermon.

I sighed and laid my arm on my belly next to my cast. This was going to be a long morning. Shifting in my seat, I glanced out of the window. It sure was beautiful outside. Much too gorgeous to be stuck inside a small church and listening to some drawn out sermon about something nobody would put in action. Growling my protests, I slid further down the hard bench and studied the back of a man's head in front of me.

Jet nudged my foot with his boot, but I ignored his hint to sit up. When I didn't move to obey him, he reached over and pinched the soft skin under my left arm, sending a jolt of pain shooting up my neck. I tossed him a glare and scooted as far away from him as I could without falling out of my seat. He frowned at me and pointed towards the ceiling with his thumb as if to silently ask that I sit up. I shook my head as I crossed my arms over my chest.

Leaning toward me, he pressed his lips to my ear to whisper. "Please sit up, Cheyenne. I want you to pay attention to the sermon."

My eyes rolled to the back of my head, but I dug my heels into the floor and scooted back until I sat rigidly next to him. Jet could make me sit upright, but he couldn't make me listen, and that was a fact.

The sermon lasted much too long for my liking, but at last it was over, and the congregation rose for the final prayer and hymn. I didn't try to sing as I listened to the lyrics of Amazing Grace. Suddenly, my mind flew back to a time when a woman once sang those words over a feverish, weak me. She was a bird of a lady, one who looked like Ryleigh, but her face held the beautiful angles of a mature woman. The voice that echoed through my head was comforting, and I found myself longing to hear it once more in person.

"Mama," I whispered, staring straight ahead as I saw her face in my mind. As the last note of the hymn rang out, I spun on my heel and tripped over Jet's boot in my haste to leave the church. I ran down the aisle as the Reverend spoke the final prayer and disappeared out the front door. I hoped to find a place to hide, but my feet stopped at the bottom of the steps.

A few moments later, the people began to file out of the building, stepping past me without giving me a second look. I hung my head as I stepped out of their way, but when a bundle of skirts stopped beside me, I raised my gaze to find Penelope sneering down at me.

"You don't belong here. You belong in a pile of dung." She grinned maliciously and took in my attire of worn shirt and trousers with holes in the knees. "You look like a horse biscuit, and you smell like one, too. I'll bet you'll end up being a brood mare, just like your sister."

Without another word, Penelope lifted her nose in the air and stalked away, her hips sashaying with each step she took. I clenched my jaw in irritation and glanced up to see Jet standing at the top of the stairs. I closed my eyes and hung my head as I waited for him to say something.

His boots thumped lightly on the wooden steps and stopped when he reached me. "I heard what she said."

I snorted and turned my back to him as I walked down the street. "Good. Now you know what the whole town's thinking."

Jet latched onto my elbow to stop me. "Let's go for a walk, Cheyenne. I'd like to talk to you."

I pulled my arm out of his grip and stuffed my hands in my pockets. "I'm not really in the mood to hear one of your lectures, Jet. I'd rather just go home."

"I don't want to give you a lecture," he said slowly. "I just want to talk to you like a normal person."

"Normal people don't talk to me nicely, Jet."

Jet stopped walking and took hold of my elbow again. "Then can I talk to you as your uncle?"

I lifted a shoulder in a shrug and allowed him to lead me down the path to the creek. The short walk was silent, but I didn't mind. When we reached the water, I lowered myself onto the sandy earth and began to play with a rock. Jet sat down beside me and watched the water move in the wind before he spoke.

"There's a lot of people who love to hear themselves talk," Jet finally said as he sent a rock skipping across the surface of the water, "but most of the time it's just gossip that's not true."

I rolled my eyes and shifted on the ground. "Penelope's words didn't offend me, if that's what you're thinking."

Jet glanced over his shoulder and lifted an eyebrow. "They didn't, did they?"

I shook my head firmly and glanced at my cast. "No. People can say what they want 'bout me. I don't give a brass nickel about that. It's when people speak their mind about Ryleigh."

"I don't think that's it."

"Of course that's it," I argued half-heartedly as I dodged his eyes.

Jet studied my side profile for a few moments before he skipped another rock. "I think you've listened to what people have been saying about you for a long time," he said as he watched me run my fingers through the sand. "Those words have become a part of who you are, and you can't outrun them. It seems to me that you've begun to believe that you're all those things that are being said about you, and your sister Ryleigh, and once you believe them, it's hard to accept anything else."

I scoffed as I shook my head. "I don't want to talk about this, Jet."

"I think you do."

"No, I don't!" I spat, finally building enough courage to look him in the eye. "I don't care what people say 'bout me! It's when they compare Ryleigh to a brood mare or a breeding cow. She's not an animal, and they're pigs to say such things about her! And what do you care what I believe about myself?"

Jet's gaze remained gentle and unwavering as he spoke. "Because I know you should love yourself. God created you, too, Cheyenne. He doesn't like when you tear yourself apart."

I rolled my eyes when I felt my irritation rise in my throat. "God don't care two cents what happens to me, and besides, love is a worthless feeling. I've tried to love, Jet, but it's awfully hard when it gets torn apart and thrown back in my face. I've had about all I can stand of that lousy four-letter word."

"Cheyenne, I don't—"

I shook my head and chuckled. "You always do that. You always point out I'm wrong and scold me about it. I told you I don't want to talk about this, Jet."

Jet cocked his head to the side. "Why are you so defensive?"

"Why?" I hugged my middle as I shook my head and turned away from him. "Because I know my mama loved me once. She sang to me that song, Amazing Grace, when I was sick. I barely remember her face, but I knew she loved me. I don't think Pa ever loved me, and as a dumb child I thought that Mama could never hate me. When she took sick, she hid inside her shell, and when she was weak and lying on her death bed, she told me she didn't want me. It was our fault, she said, that Pa left us." I straightened my spine and ground my teeth as I watched the water ripple in the breeze. "Ryleigh has done the same thing. If you want to help, get her to come back before she slips through my fingers."

Silence settled like a heavy blanket over my head as Jet watched me, and I turned to study the water. Jet leaned his elbows on his knees, and at last uttered a sigh. "Cheyenne, I've told you all the words I can. It's up to you to believe what I say. I know you have a hard time taking in something gentle but understand that I'm willing to be here for you if only you'll just come to me."

Shaking my head, I snorted a humorless laugh. "That's just it, Jet. Them's just words."

Jet stood and laid a hand on my shoulder, which I shrugged off. "Let's go find something to eat," he whispered gently, taking hold of my elbow as he helped me to my feet and started down the path.

Hanging my head low, I followed him reluctantly. *I will never come to you,* I thought to myself as we walked in the sand. *You will abandon us soon.*

* * *

Ryleigh exited the saloon, deciding she needed fresh air more than the smokey atmosphere she breathed daily. Her stomach rolled, and she placed a hand on its surface as if the pressure would stop the queasiness. Mr. Overhaul had been gone for a glorious day and a half, but even without the threat of her boss she felt the fear rise in her throat. Maybe she should take care of the baby, then Overhaul would never know, and she wouldn't have to face the embarrassment of carrying a stranger's child. Tears stung her eyes as she glanced at her belly. Somehow, she didn't have the heart to rid herself of the new burden on her shoulders. The baby needed her, and she couldn't make herself harm the innocent being in such a harsh way. Taking a deep breath, she realized she would have to think of something else. The baby would be born, and would live a full life without any worries, she'd see to that.

"Afternoon."

Ryleigh jumped at the greeting and turned to face the stable boy. What was his name? She shook her head slightly and offered a small smile. "Good afternoon."

He held his hat in his hands and appeared nervous. "I, uh, I was wondering if you would care to join me over at the diner? I mean, I know it's the middle of the afternoon, but I have a hankering for a cup of coffee." He bit his lip and lifted a shoulder in a shrug. "I understand if you're busy. Work takes place over pleasure, and I'd understand if you wouldn't want to join me. I can be smelly at times, and I don't have the best of manners." He cringed and lifted pitiful eyes to her. "I'm sorry, ma'am. It was foolish for me to ask, and I apologize."

He turned to leave, but Ryleigh found herself reaching out a hand to stop him. "You don't have to go," she said quickly, wondering why she found him amusing. A smile stretched across her lips as a small chuckle rumbled in her throat. "I'm feeling kinda parched, myself. This afternoon is kind of slow right now, so I don't have much to occupy my restless mind."

A look of shock passed over his features. "Really?"

Ryleigh giggled and stepped onto the street. "Of course! It's been ages since I've had a good cup of coffee. Wil only knows how to mix drinks… " Her voice faded, and she mentally kicked herself for mentioning her profession in an innocent conversation. She expected him to turn hard and insist he go to the diner alone, but the comment didn't seem to bother him. Frowning slightly, she fell into step beside him.

The two entered the diner and sat at a table in the corner of the room. After ordering their coffee, Ryleigh tugged her shawl tighter across her shoulders when she suddenly realized what kind of dress she wore. She lifted her chin and studied her companion out of the corner of her eye before she cleared her throat to stop his fidgeting.

"So, you work over at the stables?" she asked to stir up conversation.

"Yes, ma'am."

"Do you like working with animals?"

"Yes, ma'am."

She huffed and leaned back in her chair. Keeping a conversation rolling was going to be harder than she first thought. Glancing around the room, she finally looked down at her hands and sighed, her mind coming up empty on a topic.

The lad cleared his throat and leaned back in his chair. "Your sister was in church this morning," he said at last. "Her arm don't seem to bother her that bad. I'm surprised, to be honest. She had a pretty hard fall."

Ryleigh's brows drew together in confusion. "Her arm?" Dread settled in her stomach with the realization that her sister might have been hurt badly. "Is she okay?"

He studied her and nodded slowly. "Yeah. The doc said she could take off her cast in a few days. She's lucky. She fell from the loft at the stables and landed mighty hard on her side. I thought she might have crippled her leg, too, but she just had what the doc called a bone bruise. Her wrist took the worse of the landing." He narrowed his eyes and cocked his head to the side. "You didn't know she got hurt?"

Heat crept up her neck and flooded her face. Shaking her head slowly, she lowered her gaze and scolded herself for not being there to help Cheyenne. "But she's okay?"

"Yes. Mr. Douglas has taken fine care of her since the fall." He ducked his head to look in her gaze, but she averted her eyes and glanced toward the kitchen in hopes the waitress was coming with their coffee. "Well, he has his hands full," the stable boy continued. "Cheyenne's one of the most stubborn kids I've ever met. She got suspended from school, that's why she was helping me in the barn. She started a fire yesterday, too."

Ryleigh's blush darkened. "I hadn't realized... I-I mean, she has always been a tad ornery."

"I'd say more than a tad," he corrected, a smirk on his lips. "But I like her. She has guts, and when you ain't on her bad side, she can be nice."

"H-how are her... her grades?" Ryleigh asked cautiously, anchoring a strand of hair behind her ear.

"I wouldn't know. She don't tell me stuff like that. My guess, though, is she don't care what they are. Mr. Douglas will think otherwise when he reads her report card. It seems to me she has no desire to learn. She acts as if she's wasting her time behind a desk."

Ryleigh traced her upper lip, which was beginning to sweat with nervousness. "I'm sorry, Mister...?"

He jumped and offered a smile. "Oh, just call me Levi. Mr. Hendershot sounds too old for me."

"I'm sorry, Mr. Hendershot," she continued, ignoring his comment. "I really don't feel well, and I think I ought to get back to the sal... to my room."

Levi's brow wrinkled with concern. "I'm sorry, ma'am. I didn't mean to upset you. Cheyenne's—"

"It's not that," Ryleigh interrupted, feeling her heart pick up its pace. "I should've put her in an orphanage years ago. I'm a horrible sister, and I did a terrible job at raising her. I-I'm sorry."

She stood to leave, but Levi landed a hand on hers to stop her. "Please," he insisted, his kind eyes making her melt. "I can't drink two cups of coffee by myself. And besides, I don't think you're a horrible sister."

Ryleigh swallowed hard and returned to her chair. "How so? She doesn't go to school, she doesn't mind her manners, and she's running around rampant. How have I not been a horrible sister?"

Levi shrugged, but didn't let go of her hand. "How can a child raise a child?" he asked softly, but his question didn't upset her like she thought it would. "I think you did the best you could. You made sure she was loved and cared for."

"I left her in the care of a stranger," she moaned, covering her face with her hands. "She didn't know Mr. Douglas. I barely know him myself since I was four the last time I saw him. She must hate me."

Levi shook his head and pulled one of her hands away. "Look at me," he said softly, waiting until she raised her gaze. "She doesn't hate you, just like you don't hate her. I'm going over to Mr. Douglas's tonight. We're just going to visit and maybe play some card games. You're more than welcome to come."

The desire to see her sister and know she was being well cared for tugged at the corner of Ryleigh's heart, but shame filled her chest as she shook her head. "I can't, Mr. Hendershot. Not looking like… this," she said, motioning to the knee-length satin dress she wore.

Levi lifted his shoulder in a shrug. "After we finish our coffee, I'd like you to come with me to my quarters. I want to show you something. It's two o'clock right now, so we'll have time."

Ryleigh glanced at the kitchen, where the waitress exited with two steaming cups. "Sorry for the wait," she apologized as she set the cups in front of them. "We had to make a fresh pot."

Levi gave the waitress a smile and turned back to Ryleigh as he waited for her answer.

She shook her head. "What if they don't want to see me? What if it'll be a mistake to go with you?"

He shrugged. "You'll never know unless you try."

Ryleigh curled her fingers around the warm mug and lifted it to her lips. She longed to see her sister's face, yet she was afraid of what Cheyenne thought of her. The more she mulled over the idea, the louder the warning bell rang in her mind, but she found herself wanting to spend time with the quiet man beside her, and to have an excuse to stay out of the saloon a little longer. Violet was tired of finding stuff for her to do, anyway. And maybe Levi was right. Maybe things would turn out better than she thought.

Lowering her mug, she cleared her throat and shrugged. "I guess I don't have anything else to do," she admitted, offering a shy smile.

Levi grinned back and took a swallow of his dark liquid. "Good! Once we finish our coffee, I would like you to see the surprise I bought you."

Ryleigh choked on her drink and wiped the drops from her lips with the back of her hand. "What? No, you shouldn't have spent your money on me! I can pay you back. I-I got... money..."

"Nonsense!" Levi rose to his feet and extended his hand. "C'mon. You'll like what I got you."

"But—"

The stable boy grabbed her arm and pulled her to her feet enthusiastically. "No 'buts'. C'mon, enjoy yourself! Surely you haven't forgotten how to do that."

"But—"

Levi dropped some cash on the table for the coffees, then dragged her along behind him as they exited the diner. Ryleigh caught several people staring at her as she reluctantly followed the boy her age into the street, and a dark pink colored her cheeks. What must they be thinking? Levi Hendershot was a well-behaved young man who worked hard to earn honest wages, but she was a lowly character to sell her talents in a saloon where men gorged themselves on female companions and liquor. Yet, Mr. Hendershot didn't seem bothered by her profession.

Ryleigh stepped off the boardwalk and into the dusty street as she slowed her pace. Several people were already scowling at her appearance, and it made her heart quicken its pace. Ryleigh laid a hand on her stomach in hopes to calm the squirrelly feeling that bounced off her ribs. Something in the back of her mind told her to whirl on her heel and run, to vanish into the saloon where she belonged, but her feet were glued to the sandy earth underneath her.

When Levi realized she stopped following him, he ambled back to her with his hands hid comfortably in his pockets. "You okay?"

Ryleigh fingered the lacy edge of her shawl. "Are you sure this is a good idea? Maybe I should just go back to my room."

Levi shook his head firmly. "I don't think so. How long has it been since you've gotten out? You need an outing. Life ain't all 'bout work, you know. Are you comin'?"

Ryleigh had to stand on her toes to peek over his shoulder at the livery. "Well... I-I guess."

Forcing her legs to move, she followed the stable boy to the end of the street and caught a horrid look from Mrs. Wilkes, who had just exited the mercantile with her husband. Ryleigh's heart began to feel heavy as it sank lower in her chest. The fact that she was seen with Levi had already tainted his reputation, and that knowledge pained her. She hung her head at the realization that Levi hadn't even considered what her presence would do to his good, saintly name. Turning her back on the woman, she concentrated on placing one foot in front of the other.

Levi opened the door to his sleeping quarters and motioned for Ryleigh to walk ahead of him. The room was small. It barely had enough space for the cot and trunk that consisted of Levi's furniture. The stable boy moved passed her when she didn't move and opened the lid to his trunk as he motioned for her to come inside with him. She clasped her hands tightly by her chest as she shook her head. She did not want to enter his room and have the townspeople think he wanted her entertainment outside of business hours.

"You can come here," Levi assured with a soft smile on his lips. "I won't hurt you."

Ryleigh shook her head as she backed further from the door. "No, I... I don't want people to get the wrong idea."

Levi's smile dipped a little, but he nodded and turned back to the trunk. He shoved a few objects aside before he pulled out a ball of beautiful turquoise material. When he stood to bring the material to her, she realized it was a dress. Ryleigh reached out to caress the long sleeve of the simple checkered dress and gasped quietly when she recognized the dress she admired in the mercantile. The design reminded her of the breeze of summer when she was younger. It brought her mind back to her earlier days on the earth, when Cheyenne and herself would go on lazy walks down to the creek and capture their supper from its waters.

"It's so beautiful," she responded in a whisper.

Levi grinned and nodded. "That's what I thought when I saw it. I thought it would be perfect for you."

Ryleigh raised her eyes so she could probe Levi's kind gaze. "Why did you buy a dress for me? I hardly know you."

A vibrant shade of pink crept up Levi's neck and flooded his face. "Well, I… I thought that a lady like yourself should have a dress that you can feel confident in." He ducked his head to avoid looking her in the eye.

Ryleigh let a smile stretch across her lips as she laid a hand on his shoulder. "Thank you. That was very thoughtful of you." She glanced at the dress and fingered the collar. "This dress must have cost you a fortune. I don't have the money now, but I will pay you back. You have my word."

Levi's lips twitched into a shy smile as he shrugged. "You don't owe me a thing, ma'am. I wanted to buy this dress. It's a gift, and I was hoping you would take it." He clasped the back of his neck with his hand as another blush colored his face. "Besides, there's not much use for me having a dress."

Ryleigh giggled as she folded the garment over her arm. "No, I suppose not."

Levi exited his room and closed the door behind him. "I can, uh, walk you down to your room so you can change. We could go for a walk before we have to be at Mr. Douglas's house."

Ryleigh bit her lip and nodded. Levi extended his arm toward her, and she cautiously laid her fingertips in the crook of his elbow. His muscles tensed at her touch, but then relaxed. She refused to look at him as they began walking to the saloon, and she felt her own neck and cheeks filling with color. Ryleigh focused on the saloon ahead of them and tried to steady her breath as her heart began to pound against her ribcage. She hadn't met a man who didn't treat her like an object, and the change was scary and intriguing all mashed together in one emotion.

They had almost reached the saloon when Mr. and Mrs. Wilkes rounded the corner of the neighboring building. Mrs. Wilkes narrowed her eyes when she saw Ryleigh and glanced toward Levi with the same judgmental glare.

"Young man," Mrs. Wilkes commanded in a shrill voice. "What are you doing in the presence of *that?*"

Ryleigh felt Levi stiffen by her side, but he kept his voice soft when he spoke. "*She* has a name, ma'am, and I'm just escorting her back to her home."

Mrs. Wilkes wrinkled her nose as she lifted her chin in the air. "I have always admired a gentleman, but you needn't be a fool. She'll just trap you in her snare." She leaned forward as she dropped her voice to a whisper. "Innocent men have been led astray by such wiles. Why do you reckon she wears such an outrageous outfit?"

Ryleigh lowered her head to study the dress she wore. It was a bright red dress made from satin material, and faux feathers decorated the neckline that dipped to reveal too much of her chest. The dress was held up by two small straps on her shoulders and came to just above her knee. Black pantyhose covered her legs, and her high-heeled boots made her a few inches taller. She licked her lips and refused to look at Levi for fear of what she would see in his face.

"Ma'am, I see nothing wrong with making sure a lady gets home safely," Levi answered, his voice steady.

Mrs. Wilkes harrumphed as she glanced at her husband. "A lady? My goodness, I hope you break free before she tears you apart!"

The mayor nodded his head as he and his wife stepped aside to continue their walk. "Just remember the Lord's teaching, son," he warned as they passed.

Ryleigh glanced over her shoulder at the duo, then turned back to face the saloon. She felt her insides dim. "I'm sorry, Mr. Hendershot. I should have warned you what could happen if you accompanied me."

Levi glanced at her before he resumed walking. "I don't believe what they say." He motioned to the dress tucked under her arm. "They won't be thinking bad of you if they saw you in that dress. C'mon, you go change. If you're not feeling up for a walk, I can come by to pick you up later."

She nodded and let her hand slip from his elbow when they reached the double doors of the saloon. "Thank you. I can be ready by this evening."

Levi tipped his hat toward her and turned to leave. She watched him until he disappeared into the livery. She couldn't quite understand why he was different, and part of her was cautious. He was a good man, and she did not want to taint his reputation any more than she already had. Sighing softly to herself, she gazed at the dress in her arms as she walked through the doors into the saloon. It would feel great to have a sense of normalcy back in her life.

Violet saw her enter the saloon and set a tray of soiled glasses on the bar as she strode to her friend. "You should be in bed resting," Violet reprimanded softly as she motioned to Wil with her eyes. "The doc said you need to rest for four days. C'mon, honey, let's get you upstairs."

Ryleigh glanced over her shoulder at Wil, but he wasn't paying them much attention as he began to wipe down the glasses that Violet left for him. Once in the confinement of her room, Violet let out a sigh of exasperation.

"Don't do that to me again!" Violet scolded, a glare on her lips. "I've never been more scared in my life! Overhaul ain't here, honey, but that don't mean his men are any less observant."

Ryleigh tossed her new dress on the bed as she sighed. "I'm sorry, Vi. I just wanted some fresh air."

Violet glanced at the dress and frowned. "Where did you get that?"

A blush crept up Ryleigh's neck again as she avoided looking Violet in the eye. "Uh, it was a gift."

"A gift from who? Your uncle?"

Ryleigh shook her head. "No, it was... a young man called Levi Hendershot."

Violet grinned as she folded her arms over her bosom. "Ah, so he fancies you."

"No, it's not like that," Ryleigh defended as she reached for the dress. "He told me he was going to visit with Mr. Douglas and Cheyenne, and he invited me to go along. There's nothing more than that."

Violet sashayed to the bed and held up the dress in front of Ryleigh. "And he gave you this dress? My, and it does match your blue eyes. He sure does have taste."

Ryleigh took the dress from her friend and threw it over a chair. "It's nothing, Vi. He just thought I would like this style of dress, and I do. It's not like he's going to come calling. What gentleman in their right mind would want to call on a saloon girl?"

"Either a decent fella, or a naïve one." Violet glanced at the dress with a hint of a smile still on her lips. "I'll just tell Wil that I let you borrow that dress from me, and that you have to see Doc Harding." She raised her eyes to study Ryleigh. "Just, in the future, let me know when you're leaving the saloon so I can give them an excuse for you. Just until we can figure something out," she finished as she motioned to Ryleigh's stomach.

Ryleigh's blush appeared again as she ducked her head. "Thank you."

~FOURTEEN~

I listened to the clock tick in the other room as I stared at the ceiling from my bed. Jet had left me alone for most of the afternoon after our conversation at the creek, but I was grateful for the solitude so that I didn't have to speak to my uncle. I kept pondering Penelope's words, and Jet's understanding of how I felt. I didn't like that he knew what I was feeling. After trying hard to hide my emotions, Jet still read through me like an open book. A wave of defeat hovered over me like a heavy cloak, and I covered my eyes with the crook of my elbow. Jet might understand the deeper part of me, but the rest of the people in Sunset still saw the outer crust of our family. At times it felt like my family was being ripped apart by vultures.

Exhaling a sigh, I pushed myself into a sitting position and stared at my reflection in the small mirror to my right. I saw a young girl looking back at me with a somber expression as black curls fell into her face. The dark brown eyes appeared almost black with depression, and she looked exhausted. The reflection began to blur with tears when a horribly comforting thought appeared in my mind. It wasn't the first time I had contemplated eliminating myself, but now it felt more realistic. Ryleigh confessed to me that she no longer wanted me, and I was tired of trying to defend the insults cast her way. Perhaps I could finally rest if the memories of Sunset and my family were gone.

A knock sounded on my door, and I jumped as I hurriedly wiped the wetness from my eyes. When I didn't answer, Jet slowly opened the door to peek his head inside. I glanced at him and folded my arms over my chest.

"Go away," I attempted to snarl, but I could still hear the hint of tears in my voice.

Jet entered the room and studied me with a soft expression. "Levi will be here in a few minutes. I was just checking on you to see how you were doing."

I lowered my gaze and turned so that he could not see me wipe my eyes with my sleeve. "I'm fine. I was just thinking." I shrugged as I began to toy with a piece of material that was starting to tear away from the quilt underneath me. "I don't even know why Levi is coming."

"He's a good friend, and I thought it might be fun to play a few games this evening." Jet walked further into the room and stopped at the foot of my bed. "I thought maybe it would cheer you up to have him over."

I brought my knees to my chest and set my chin between them. "I said I was fine."

"You've been in your room all afternoon," Jet pointed out cautiously. "I thought for sure you would want to go outside today. It's been beautiful."

"I'm just resting. It's my day off." I pushed off the bed and walked toward the mirror where I grabbed an old hairbrush. "I just took a nap."

Jet watched me as I tried to comb the tangles out of my hair mercilessly, then took the brush from my hands. "Is there something bothering you?" he asked gently.

"No, I'm fine!" I snapped as I glanced over my shoulder at him. "I just don't understand why Levi wants to come here. There are other things to do in this stupid little town. I don't feel up to having company."

"Levi is our friend, and I'm sure he wants to visit because he enjoys our company," Jet answered in a soft tone. "Cheyenne, are you still thinking about what Penelope said to you at church?"

I bit my tongue and whirled away from him before he could see the water in my eyes. "No," I replied when I could control my tears. "It's not the first time I've heard that, Jet. You grow calloused after a while."

"That doesn't mean it doesn't still hurt." Jet laid a hand on my shoulder and nudged me slightly to turn. I slowly obeyed and met his gaze. "You and Ryleigh are not animals. I still care about you girls."

219

I scoffed. "Yeah, you're one against a million, Jet. It's hard to believe the one when so many others are telling you something different."

Jet opened his mouth to reply, but at that time we heard a knock on the front door. He glanced over his shoulder, then back down at me. "That must be Levi. Why don't you come into the living room with me?"

I lowered my gaze and lifted a shoulder in a shrug. "I suppose I don't have a choice. I can't even be alone in my own house anymore."

Jet studied me for a moment before he turned and strode into the other room. I hooked a strand of hair behind my ear and followed my uncle as he requested. I stopped at the end of the hallway and watched as Jet opened the door. He froze as soon as he saw who was standing on the porch, but from my angle I could only see Jet's frame.

"I brought someone along," Levi said from outside. "I hope you don't mind."

Frowning slightly, I ventured further into the living room so I could see who was with Levi. At first, all I saw was the skirt of a blue dress touching the floorboards, but when I raised my eyes to see who the dress belonged to, the blood drained from my face.

Jet stammered for a moment before he cleared his throat. "Uh, no. Not at all. Please, come in."

Ryleigh offered a shy smile and folded her hands nervously in front of her. "I-I hope I'm not intruding," she said in an almost whisper.

She hadn't seen me yet, and I couldn't help but wonder what she was doing standing on the doorstep she chose to leave. Why had she come back into the home of the girl she loathed? Maybe she wished to talk to Jet, or maybe she wanted to throw salt on a wound in my heart. Either way, I felt a surge of anger and betrayal that threatened to bring back my tears.

At last, Jet found his manners and stepped out of the way to allow the two to enter. "No, you're not intruding at all. Why, we'd be happy to have you here! Won't we, Cheyenne?"

Jet glanced over his shoulder toward me, but I couldn't look at him or Ryleigh. "I, uh, remembered something I need to do," I mumbled. I spun on my heel and ran out of the back door before anyone could answer.

I hadn't gotten far when the door slammed against the house, followed by Jet's voice. "Cheyenne, come back!"

I ducked my head to ignore him and continued running toward the creek. I had almost reached the outskirts of town before he latched onto my arm to stop me.

"Cheyenne—"

"Why is she here?" I interrupted, tears coating my voice. "Why is she here after what she said to me, and why didn't you tell me she was coming?"

"I didn't know she was coming," he answered softly. "I don't know why she's here now. Maybe she regrets what she said. But no matter her reason, she's here, and she's welcome in her own house." He studied me with his head cocked to the side. "I thought you wanted her out of the saloon?"

"Well, yeah, but…" I groaned and covered my eyes with my palm. "Her words hurt, Jet. She chose Overhaul over me, and now she's standing in my living room. You don't understand how I feel. She didn't want me, and now she's here like nothing happened?"

"She's here, and she's your sister," Jet reminded gently. "You can't run out on her like you just did. I don't know why she's not working in the saloon tonight, but she's here and that's a start."

"She'll go back to the saloon when she leaves," I mumbled. "She'll probably go to sleep next to a stranger tonight."

Jet frowned and knelt on one knee so he could look into my eyes. "Hey, now, where did that come from? I thought you were always defensive when people passed judgments toward your sister?"

"Maybe I said it because it's true," I answered, trying to keep a straight face as I spoke. "The truth is she's working twice as much at the saloon now, and she won't quit for a night. The truth is that she left me, and she wouldn't come home for a night to check on me."

"That may have been the truth a few days ago, but she came tonight. She wouldn't have come unless she wanted to talk to you. Please come back to the house with me. It may be a good evening."

"I don't know how much I'll enjoy it."

Jet hooked a finger under my chin and lifted my face. "If she came here for a specific reason, she'll tell us sooner or later. You've wanted a chance to see her again, and now you've got it." He rose to his feet as he guided me back home with a hand on my shoulder.

I swallowed hard and allowed him to walk beside me as I trudged back down the dusty path to the house. When we filed through the back door, Levi rose from his seat on the wooden bench in the living room and offered me a smile. "That chore didn't take long," he observed lightly.

I glanced at Ryleigh, who tried to smile, but I turned away from her and entered the kitchen where Jet had created several ham sandwiches. I set them on the dining table and turned to face the men. Jet dragged the bench to the table and motioned for Ryleigh to sit.

"I reckon a light supper wouldn't hurt right now. It ain't much, but it'll put some meat on your bones," he explained as my sister cautiously walked to the table.

She gingerly sat on the edge of the bench, and I sat in the chair opposite from her in hopes of keeping my distance from her. Jet sat in the second chair and smiled at Ryleigh. "I'm glad you could join us. Uh, Levi, would you say the blessing?"

I rolled my eyes and lowered my head as Levi spoke a simple prayer over the food. When he said the final word, awkward silence hovered over us as we passed the sandwiches from one person to the other. Ryleigh stared at her plate, then lifted her head until her eyes leveled on me.

"I... I see your arm's not giving you too much trouble," she mumbled in a soft, timid voice. "What happened?"

"I stepped where I shouldn't have," I snapped, cutting my eyes toward her. "And it's been more bothersome than I care to admit."

She ducked her head and pushed a piece of ham around with her finger.

Jet cleared his throat and cast a glance to me before turning to my sister. "So, do you have the night off?"

Ryleigh's face turned bright pink, but she nodded. "I wasn't feeling good the other day, and Mr. Overhaul gave me a few days to regain my strength. There was nothing to do at the saloon, so I agreed to come with Mr. Hendershot when he asked me."

Jet offered her a kind smile. "I'm glad you came. Gives me time to get to know my other niece."

Ryleigh's lips tipped upward, but she didn't say a word as she took a tiny nibble of her food. Jet

studied her as if hoping she would carry on the conversation, but when she remained silent, he glanced at me. I avoided his gaze as I watched my fingers twitch in my lap. Nothing met our ears except the normal sounds of eating. The clock in the living room announced the seven o'clock hour, but it sounded more like a gong than a chime.

Levi cleared his throat as he glanced around the table. "How are things going at the feed mill?" he asked Jet, trying to stir up a topic of discussion.

"Well, busy enough to pad my wallet," Jet answered. "Not much is happening. It's getting to that time of year when farmers are trying to figure their pocketbooks to see what kind of grain they can buy for their animals. We're making good progress on the house, too."

You mean you are making good progress, I thought to myself as I recounted the days Jet had worked on the house by himself. Biting my lip, I slid lower in my chair and studied the full plate in front of me. I would've rather gone to school than be sitting at the table, but I was afraid Jet would do something if I decided to leave.

Ryleigh glanced at our uncle and clasped her hands in her lap. "I suppose things will pick up before the winter months."

Jet nodded as he brought a sandwich to his mouth. "Most likely."

Ryleigh bit her lip and turned to me. "Mr. Hendershot tells me Mr. Douglas has been getting you to go to school. How is that going?"

My eyes burned with anger, but I didn't meet her gaze or move my lips to reply. Jet watched me, but when I refused to speak, he nudged my foot under the table and cleared his throat. I narrowed my eyes and turned to my sister.

"What's it to you?" I growled in a low voice.

"Cheyenne!" Jet exclaimed under his breath, but I ignored him.

"Surely you remember how much I hate that confining schoolroom. Maybe you've even forgotten that I burned all my homework when you were under this roof. Why the sudden interest in what grades I'm making?" My lip twitched with anger, but I refused to stop talking. "I thought you told me you don't want to talk to me. Why are you here when it's plain you don't want me?"

"Cheyenne, I think—" Levi started, but Ryleigh spoke above him.

"Well, did it ever occur to you that I was busy?" she snapped. "Maybe you were just getting underfoot that day, and I was just overwhelmed. Did you ever think of that?"

Levi exchanged looks with Jet, but I ignored the men as I centered a glare on my sister. "Maybe I wouldn't have been underfoot if you hadn't started working double for that pig of a man! Maybe there are more important things in life than earning your keep in a bed with a different person each night!"

Her face turned bright red, but her eyes narrowed in anger. "You have no right to talk to me that way, Cheyenne. I gave you food to eat, and clothes to wear! I raised you!"

I scoffed as I leaned back in the chair and threw my hand in the air. "Yeah, and what a good job you did! Did you know I stole a bottle from your boss's saloon and got drunk a week ago? If you don't believe me, ask Jet. He's the one who found me. I started a fire and had a stolen watch, just to mention a few other things I've done. Do you honestly think what you did for me was for the *best?*" I snorted my condemnation as I crossed my arms over my chest. "I loved you. You were the only one I had, and then you threw me aside like I was nothing more than a piece of trash. Now you think you can come into this house and pretend nothing's wrong? You're stupid if you think you can waltz back into my life!"

Ryleigh's shoulders tightened as she furrowed her brow. "I never waltzed out of your life to begin with! Do you honestly believe I *wanted* to be doing this, Cheyenne? I never wanted to work in that saloon, but I did it because you needed me. I had to provide for you somehow!"

"And now that Jet's in town you think I don't need you, is that it?" I snapped. "Whatever happened to forever and always, Ryleigh? What about that stuff you promised me when we were kids? You said we would never be separated. You separated yourself! You threw me away! No, you don't care anything about me, and that question about my schooling was like throwing salt on an open wound. Or should I say whiskey? Maybe you'll understand alcoholic terms better."

Ryleigh's bottom lip quivered as she slammed a napkin on the table. "Maybe it was a mistake in coming here," she whispered in a weak voice.

"There's no maybe about it!" I shouted, leaning against the table as I aimed a finger at her chest. "Everyone's right. You're no better than a brood mare, and I don't want you to bring your filth in this house again. You're not welcomed here, and you're *not* my sister."

Ryleigh blinked her large eyes, then ducked her head as she jumped to her feet. "Excuse me," she mumbled as she fled from the table and disappeared out of the front door.

Levi caught Jet's eye as he rose from the table. "I think I should go, too. I'm sorry I couldn't stay longer." Slapping his hat on his head, he hurried from the table and ran after Ryleigh.

When the house settled down to a quiet lull, Jet glanced at me out of the corner of his eye, but I shook my head and stood. "Don't say it," I hissed as my brow furrowed with hate. "Don't say a daggum thing! I said the truth, and don't you dare get onto me!"

I whirled to leave, but Jet grabbed my arm and pulled me back to the table. "Cheyenne, please don't fight me," he said firmly.

"No!" I shouted. "Let go of me. I don't want to listen to any lecture you've got to say about what I said. Let go!"

Jet tightened his hold on my wrist to keep me from fleeing. "You didn't mean all those things that you told Ryleigh. I know you didn't. You were mad because you thought she did you wrong. You had no right to talk to her in that tone. I don't believe you wanted to hurt your sister."

"She's not my sister, and of course I intended to hurt her! She hurt me. I wanted to give her a piece of what she gave me. I wanted to watch her hurt as bad as I have!"

Jet shook his head. "Stop lying, Cheyenne."

"I'm not lying!" I shouted, anger burning in my veins.

"Don't raise your voice to me," he warned as he cocked an eyebrow, "and yes, you are. You ought to be ashamed of yourself. Ryleigh apparently came here because she regretted what she told you. Everybody saw that except for you. You only saw what she has done in the past, and you wanted to judge her for it. I'm disappointed in you, Cheyenne. I know you could've acted better."

I growled in anger when Jet still wouldn't let go of me. Tears began to course down my face, and shame almost choked me. I couldn't hide my pain from my uncle, and I refused to acknowledge him. I hated showing the weakness of tears, and I felt cornered when I couldn't run. At last, I collapsed back in my chair and lowered my head.

"I'm sorry!" I shouted in a gasp between sobs.

Jet finally let go of my arm and remained silent for a moment. "I know," he said sympathetically when my sobs quieted slightly. "I know you didn't mean what you said, but you don't have to apologize to me. Ryleigh needs to know that you don't hate her."

I shook my head, still refusing to look at him. "No, she won't want to hear a word from me."

Jet reached into his back pocket and handed me his handkerchief. "Yes, she will. She still loves you, Cheyenne."

I accepted the handkerchief and blew my nose. "How do you know? Ryleigh has never lied to me."

"I know she loves you because she came here tonight. She didn't have to, but she did. I think she's just as hurt as you are."

I swallowed hard as I played with Jet's handkerchief. "Are you going to punish me?"

"Do you think I should?"

I shrugged and wiped the last of my tears from my eyelashes. "I don't know. I don't know anything anymore. I'm all messed up, and I don't understand anything. Maybe I should be sent to a boarding school."

Jet hooked his finger under my chin and raised my head so he could look into my eyes. "You don't need to go to a boarding school. I know you're confused, but I want to help you. You just have to let me."

226

I shook my head firmly as I swallowed the urge to cry. "No one can help me. It's too late, Jet. And I've just blowed up what chance I had at bringing my sister back."

Jet shook his head as he studied me with kind eyes. "It's not too late. I know a lot of people have given up on you girls, but I'm too stubborn to know what quitting feels like," he finished with a soft smile.

"I don't want to be a girl," I grumbled under my breath. "If I had been born a boy, none of this would've ever happened. I could be working somewhere, maybe even the feed mill, and I could have provided for Ryleigh so that she wouldn't have to be in the saloon. It's all my fault that my family is messed up."

Jet laid his hands on my shoulders and shook his head. "This is not your fault, Cheyenne. I don't want you to blame yourself. God made you as you are for a reason, and you should never want to change that. He has a plan for you."

I rolled my eyes before lowering my head again. "God hates me, Jet. Just like everyone else."

"God doesn't hate you. You are loved, Cheyenne. You're loved by God, Ryleigh, and me."

I swallowed hard. I wanted to believe what he said, but there was no evidence proving that his words were true. I shrugged his hands away and rose from my chair.

"Where are you going?" he asked as he rose to his feet.

"I'm going for a walk."

"I'll go with you," he said as he moved to follow me.

"Jet, please," I objected, turning sad eyes on him. "I need to be alone."

Jet looked skeptical, but at last he nodded his head as he hid his hands in his pockets. "Alright but be back before dark." I rolled my eyes and turned toward the door, but Jet's voice stopped me. "Promise me, Cheyenne."

Sighing, I turned to face him and lifted my shoulders in a shrug. "Yes, sir. I'll be back."

* * *

The lunch pail was slung over my arm, which was now cast free after

Jet spoke to Doc Harding, and the slate with a short piece of chalk was clutched in my hand. Like usual, the children chased each other around the school yard, waiting for Mr. Hyndman to ready the morning's lessons. I sighed past my lack of motivation and stepped on the tacked down grass in front of the school. Almost instantly, Penelope met my gaze, and my eyes narrowed as I turned my back to her. I was anxious to stay away from her sharp tongue and ill temper.

Setting my things in the shade of the nearest corner, I patted my belly and turned to face the crowd of children. Nobody acted as if they had seen me yet, which didn't bother me in the least. Hooking my heel on the bottom rung of the staircase, I leaned against the railing and watched a group of boys amble up to the school in over-exaggerated long strides as they tried to mimic their fathers. I rolled my eyes at their awkward impersonations and turned my head to find Penelope standing in my space. Wrinkling my nose, I stepped away from her and returned my attention to the late comers.

"Nice of you to join us. Finally," she cut in a rude tone.

I glanced at her out of the corner of my eye and lifted my shoulders in a shrug as I leaned against the stair rail. "Trust me, it ain't your polite manner I missed."

She smiled with an insolent sneer as she chuckled stiffly. "You know, I'm beginning to enjoy having you come to school. It's been fun to see how much trouble you get into, and what kind of punishments Mr. Hyndman gives you. I hope you never leave completely. You've been quite entertaining."

"Why don't you just shut it, miss?" I snapped, refusing to meet her gaze.

Penelope raised an eyebrow in mock surprise. "Miss? Well, your manners are improving. Before we know it, you'll start wearing a dress and looking like a natural woman. Perhaps even your tongue will have a lock on it for once."

I scoffed as I attempted to ignore her closeness. "Obviously, your lock is broken."

Penelope reared back in shock and placed a hand over her chest. "My goodness! I *will* tell Mr. Hyndman of the insults you aim at me, and then we'll see if you address me in such an impolite tone!"

Rolling my eyes, I turned to face her and shook my head. "Mr. Hyndman wouldn't harm me. Not after the things I tell him about you."

"And who would he believe?" she snapped. "His smartest pupil who has never gotten in trouble yet, or the one he just suspended?"

I didn't reply as I turned to watch Steven Butte make his way toward us.

Penelope snorted and bounced on her toes when she followed my gaze. "My mama always says that you'll turn out just like Ryleigh." She leaned in close so that her mouth was just inches away from my ear. "And here comes your first customer."

My jaw dropped when I registered what she had said, and I spun around to face her fully. Without so much as a warning, I swung my fist around and slammed it into her jaw. Her head flew backwards as she stumbled to the ground, and her skirts flew in many directions as her body fell limply. When the sound of my fist hitting her rang against the school walls, every child stopped playing to face me. I glanced at my curled knuckles, which had turned red upon impact, and slowly opened my hand.

Penelope sat upright with tears streaming down her face. "You hit me!" she exclaimed, sobs wracking her shoulders. "You hit me for no absolute reason!"

My face grew warm when I noticed some of the adults nearby turn their heads in my direction. Instinct told me to whirl on my heel and run, but my feet stayed glued to the dirt below. When I saw Mrs. Wilkes rushing toward the yard, my insides quivered, and I wanted to hang my head despite my attempts to remain confident that I was in the right.

The mayor's wife bustled onto the school property and bent over her wailing daughter who would barely have a bruise to serve as a reminder of her harsh words. After crooning over her daughter, Mrs. Wilkes bounced to her full height and leveled a hard glare at me.

"You delight in harassing my child, don't you?" she demanded in a voice that grated on my nerves.

"Well, I—"

She slapped me across the cheek and placed both fists on her hips. "How do you like that?" she

demanded. "I'll treat you like you treat my daughter! I'll hit you while you're in the middle of a friendly conversation, just like you do with my Penny!"

Mr. Hyndman appeared in the doorway, his eyes quickly landing on Mrs. Wilkes. "Ma'am? What's going on?"

Mrs. Wilkes shook her finger at the young teacher as she narrowed her eyes. "You had better keep a sharper eye on your pupils, young man. That ruffian just hit my precious baby for no reason whatsoever! The next time something of the sort happens, I'll make sure you are replaced!"

Mr. Hyndman glanced at me. I lowered my head when I saw his disapproving gaze and wished I could run. "I can assure you that I'm doing the best I can with the children, but it would be impossible for me to keep every stray thought and action concealed. I will promise you that I'll talk with Mr. Douglas, and I'll make sure Cheyenne knows her boundaries."

"I should hope the animal is punished!" the sensitive woman snorted, lifting her nose high in the air. "If that *brat* hits my baby one more time, or lashes her tongue out, I'll make sure you are fired, and someone who can offer more discipline will take your place." Mrs. Wilkes helped her daughter to her feet and smoothed Penelope's bodice with her palm. "Penelope will be late for school. I'm taking her to Dr. Harding to make sure her jaw is fine." As she turned to leave, her dark eyes leveled on me and narrowed. "Rest assured, Mr. Hyndman, I will watch how you control your class from here on out."

Penelope sobbed behind her mother as the duo marched down the street clumsily. I watched them until they disappeared in a crowd, then turned to avoid meeting my teacher's eyes. "Cheyenne, I'd like to talk to you before school starts," Mr. Hyndman said to stop me.

I cringed at the sternness in his voice and slowly turned on my heel as I followed our teacher inside the building. He walked down the aisle and sat behind his desk before he turned to give me one of his famous stares. I shuffled my feet in front of him with my hands buried deep in my pockets.

"I didn't see what happened," he began, his voice surprisingly calm and even. "I heard some of what was said through an open window. But Cheyenne, you can't go around fighting my students every chance you get. I've lost count how many fights you've had this year. You have to learn to behave yourself, and I'm afraid that I have to let your uncle know about today's fight as well. I think you're a bright student, but you've got to stop all this fighting. Do I make myself clear?"

I nodded solemnly as I clasped my hands behind my back. "Yes, sir."

He nodded and motioned to the pews in the middle of the room. "Go ahead and have a seat while I call in the other students."

I watched him walk to the front of the school and sighed. "Another day," I mumbled as I did as I was told. Another day to sit through lectures. Another day to endure people's judgments.

A clutter of students clambered into the room like a herd of buffalo, and I sank lower in my seat. Perhaps the day at school wouldn't be too big of a deal and I would be home before I knew it. I glanced out of the corner of my eye to see Penelope's empty chair. No doubt I wouldn't make it through half the day before Penelope came up with more vile insults to tell me. I stifled a groan as I sat stiffly and listened to Mr. Hyndman's Bible reading before he began a lecture over arithmetic.

Steven Butte glanced over his shoulder toward me, but I ignored his gaze as I copied the math problems on my slate. My insides began to crawl the more I remembered Penelope's words about me and the boy, and I felt the desire to hide. Not only was she insulting me, but she also insulted a boy who tried to be nice to me. The filth of her comment made me sick. And Jet would find out. I closed my eyes and tried to come up with a good excuse for the fight that wouldn't make Jet upset, but nothing came to mind.

"Cheyenne?"

I jumped so hard that the pew where I sat scooted backwards from the sudden movement. Several students snickered behind their hands when I looked up from my slate toward our teacher. "Yes, sir?"

Mr. Hyndman motioned to the chalkboard behind him. "I asked if you could solve the third problem for us."

A blush crept up my neck, and I ducked my head as I walked down the aisle to the chalkboard behind the pulpit. Two other students were already working on their problems when I picked up the stick of white chalk. Tiny beads of sweat dotted my upper lip as I stared at the numbers in front of me.

"I bet she can't even count," a student whispered behind me.

A second student snorted as she tried to conceal her laughter. "I bet you're right. She's just dumb. Look at the way she's dressed. She doesn't care what she looks like."

The white numbers began to look blurry, and I rubbed my eyes in hopes to clear my vision. *Concentrate,* I told myself as I reached up to write underneath the problem. *Seven hundred and sixteen times one hundred and seventy-five.* I licked my lips, but my mind was blank with an answer. *I bet she can't even count... She's just dumb... doesn't care what she looks like... She'll end up just like a brood mare... She's a predator... No boy is safe with her around.* A tear fell onto my cheekbone as I slammed the chalk down and raced for the front door.

"Cheyenne!" Mr. Hyndman called, but I ignored him as I bounded down the stairs and into the street.

No matter how fast my legs moved, I couldn't outrun the thoughts in my head.

~FIFTEEN~

The door slammed against the side of the house when I pulled it open, and I cringed when glass shattered in the living room window. I ignored the shards as I raced through the house and jumped on my bed. The words I had heard in the classroom were burning in the back of my head, and I threw a pillow over my face in hopes that it would muffle their echoes. I found it difficult to breath with the pillow pressed so tightly against my nose, and I wondered what would happen if I held it even tighter. Perhaps it would feel like falling asleep.

"Cheyenne?"

I lifted the pillow high enough to peek into the hallway and saw Jet hurrying inside. My stomach filled with dread as I let the pillow fall back on my face. "Go away, Jet."

"Is everything okay? I saw you running from the school and I was afraid something must have happened."

I cringed as I pushed the pillow to the side. Jet's eyes were filled with worry when I met his gaze.

"Please don't make me go back to school," I whispered pleadingly.

Jet sat on the edge of my bed and frowned. "What's wrong? Did something happen? Are you okay?" He quickly scanned my arm for an injury. "Did you hurt yourself?"

I shook my head as I pushed myself into a sitting position. "I'm fine. I don't really want to talk about it, Jet."

Jet looked more confused as he studied me. "There's something bothering you. You can tell me,

Cheyenne."

I tried to think of a story that sounded believable, but I shook my head and decided to be honest with him for once. "I got into another fight at school," I answered quickly before I became too afraid.

Jet's gaze turned downcast as his shoulders slumped. "You were in a fight again? Cheyenne, I thought we've been over this." He shook his head as he sighed. "What happened?"

"It was Penelope Wilkes. She said something that made me mad, and I punched her before I knew it." I looked away from him as I hugged my knees to my chest. "I know what I did was wrong. Mr. Hyndman was going to talk to you about it. I'm not sure what you plan to do to me, but I probably deserve it." I inhaled deeply. "Just, please, don't send me back."

Jet looked away as he listened to my explanation, but then he finally turned back to me and spoke with a patient tone. "What did she say to you?"

"What does it matter what she said? I punched her and she didn't fight back, what more do you need to know?"

"Well, it will help me decide if I need to discipline you."

I lowered my gaze so that my hair could hide my face. "She... she said something filthy, and it made me upset."

"What did she say?"

I hesitated for a moment as I pondered if I should lie, but since I had started to tell the truth, I decided to continue. "She was taunting me like usual, but I can stand most of what she has to say about my appearance or intelligence." I licked my lips and stared at the patch quilt under me. "There's this boy named Steven. He's the one who gave me the black eye, but ever since the fight he's been nice to me. He even gave me one of his sandwiches when mine fell in the dirt the other day. Steven was walking toward us when Penelope told me that I was gonna be like Ryleigh, and that Steven would be the first boy I'd hunt down as a customer."

Jet's expression darkened when I finished my explanation, which made his clear blue eyes seem to spark with live fire. I was afraid that he was

234

going to shout at me for fighting with Penelope, so I continued.

"I know I shouldn't have gotten upset, but I couldn't help myself," I resumed in a rush. "I didn't want her to taint Steven's reputation, and she was on the ground before I realized what I was doing. Please don't be too upset with me, Jet. I promise I'll stop fighting from here on out."

"I'm not mad at you," Jet answered firmly as he pushed himself to his feet. "I'm tired of that Mrs. Wilkes talking about you girls like she is. She's even trained her daughter to do the same."

"It's not just the Wilkes', Jet," I defended. "I... Mr. Hyndman called me to the front to solve an arithmetic problem, and I couldn't. I heard two students say things about me, and I ran. The whole town's been saying stuff like this about me and Ryleigh for years."

"That doesn't make it right. I'm going to have a talk with Mrs. Wilkes," he said as he headed toward the door. "While I'm gone, I want you to go back to school. I know you don't want to, but you need an education."

Without another word, he marched out of my room and through the front door. I stared after him for a few seconds, then slid from my bed as I hurried after him. I stepped onto the porch and found Jet's back with my eyes as he marched down the street. I knew I should obey him and go back to school, but curiosity tempted me to go after him. Biting my lip, I decided to follow Jet at a distance and couldn't help wondering how Mrs. Wilkes would react to Jet's conversation.

I followed Jet to the mercantile and waited until he bounded up the boardwalk stairs and opened the door. The bell above the door seemed to shout his angry entrance, and I ran to an open window and raised on my toes to see what was happening inside. Jet was standing behind a young woman who was purchasing a few supplies from Mrs. Wilkes. Mayor Wilkes was also assisting a customer who was asking about oil lanterns. Jet waited impatiently until the young woman picked up her things and bid Mrs. Wilkes farewell.

As soon as the woman left, Mrs. Wilkes turned to face Jet, and her smile faded a little. "Well, Mr. Douglas. How can I help you?"

"I came to talk to you and your husband," Jet answered flatly. It was obvious he was trying to control his fury.

"Oh? Well, I bet you want to apologize for what your youngest savage did to my Penny," Mrs. Wilkes assumed as she placed a hand on her hip. "If you even know what happened, that is. That Cheyenne is about as wild as—"

"I'm fully aware what happened this morning," Jet interrupted, and I cringed at his tone.

Mrs. Wilkes sensed his frustration and looked at him as if he were a cockroach under her foot. "Yes, of course. Well, as you must understand, Cheyenne had no right to punch my poor Penny."

Jet's spine stiffened. "Ma'am," he replied in a low voice, "I don't condone fighting, but I find it hard to blame Cheyenne for what happened once she told me what Penelope said."

Mayor Wilkes, having sensed the drama about to unfold at the front desk, ushered the last customer outside before he took his place at his wife's side. "Mr. Douglas, I'm sure there's a perfectly reasonable—"

"Your daughter accused Cheyenne of becoming a prostitute," Jet said bluntly, and both Wilkes' cringed at the word.

Mayor Wilkes cleared his throat. "Now, I'm sure there must be some misunderstanding. You know how children's fights are."

"I can understand children getting angry and hitting each other," Jet agreed as he tried to keep his voice even, "but what your daughter said does not come from a child."

Mrs. Wilkes squared her shoulders as she glared at Jet. "She may have overheard her father and I discussing the matter, but what difference does it make? Surely, you're not blind to what the oldest is doing! It's just a matter of time before Cheyenne will follow in her sister's footsteps. Why would you want to be proud of that kind of living? A *prostitute*, as you put it."

Jet placed his hands on the counter as he leaned toward the couple. "I am not proud of the *living* Ryleigh has chosen, but I am proud of my nieces. I am trying to help them, but people like you are making my job harder than it should be."

Mayor Wilkes opened his mouth to reply, but his wife slapped the back of her hand on his chest as she huffed angrily. "Your nieces are savage pieces of trash! Their father never kept his mouth shut, just like that Cheyenne of yours, and their mother was a despicable woman. Even the names of your nieces are horrid! They obviously wanted a boy when they had Ryleigh, and Cheyenne acts just like the Indians she's named after. Those girls will never change. We've put up with their despicable lives all these years, and they keep getting worse and worse."

"Margaret," Mayor Wilkes whispered in a voice barely audible, but she didn't seem to hear him.

Jet leaned back, but I could see his jaw muscles working as he kept his anger at bay. "I can't control what rumors you spread, whether they are true or lies to slam my girls in the ground, but it would make my job a lot easier if you didn't stick your noses in my business. You raise your children like you want to, but please allow me the same privilege. That's all I ask." Jet turned to exit their store, then stopped and glanced over his shoulder. "I will protect my nieces from any sort of bullying, and if I hear that your daughter attacks Cheyenne again, I will be back." Without waiting for a reply, he marched out of the store and onto the boardwalk.

I tried to duck out of his sight, but Jet caught the movement out of the corner of his eye and leveled his gaze on me. I swallowed my fear as I straightened to my full height. "Hi," I greeted as I lifted a hand to wave at him.

Jet's shoulders slumped as he sighed. "When will you ever learn to listen to me?" he asked in a soft voice, but I could hear the hint of amusement in his tone.

I shrugged as I stepped onto the boardwalk beside him. "I'm sure I've showed you I'm too stubborn to pay anybody mind."

Jet gave me a small smile. "And I'm sure I've shown you I'm more stubborn that you are. I've got to get back to work. Go to school like I asked you to, and I'll see you in the afternoon."

I groaned loudly as I glanced toward the schoolhouse. "Do I have to go back? Can I just have the rest of the day off?

"No. You've skipped enough school lately."

I studied Jet and hoped that I could reason with him, but he gave me a look that silently conveyed he didn't want to hear another word on the subject. Hanging my head, I begrudgingly headed toward the schoolhouse as he instructed. I glanced over my shoulder to see that Jet was already walking back to the feed mill, and I found myself replaying the conversation between him and the Wilkes' in my mind. I couldn't recall a time when Jet was more upset, and it felt nice to have someone defend Ryleigh and me.

I didn't remember hearing rumors about us until after Mama died and Ryleigh put me in school. Several people began to treat me differently. Some of them looked at me as if I were an invalid, while others looked at me as though I was contagious with disease. Rumors were spread that Mama got sick in the saloon, and half of the town was afraid to touch us girls in case we had the same illness. I remembered that several people from the church tried to give us things, but Ryleigh refused their charity and they eventually stopped trying. As we grew older, I lost track of the good people willing to help us and noticed that more and more citizens of Sunset looked down their noses at us.

When I mentioned it to Ryleigh, she told me not to pay them any mind. She said that people were often too quick to judge a situation than offer a helping hand, and she explained that we would have to care for ourselves if we wanted anything out of life. Ryleigh also taught me that people can tear someone apart just so they could feel better about themselves. Ryleigh's advice held true for most of the people I met.

As I continued to walk down the familiar path to the schoolhouse, I realized how much Ryleigh poured into me while we were kids. She had answered all my questions with honesty, even if her opinions might have been incorrect at the time. Guilt washed over me when I remembered how I treated her the previous night. She had chosen to spend her night off with her family, and I shouted at her. I shook my head at my own stupidity and wished I could start over with Ryleigh.

Suddenly, my feet stopped moving as I came to full attention. Ryleigh had mentioned that she had a few days off work. Since when did Overhaul

238

give his employees time off, especially more than one day? He never closed his doors for Independence Day or Christmas, and I would bet his saloon would be open on his mother's funeral. The selfish pig wanted money more than the loyalty of his employees, so why had he given Ryleigh a few days off? The cold fingers of fear gripped my throat. What if something was wrong? Forgetting what Jet had asked me to do, I spun on my heel and ran as fast as I could toward the Bull's Head saloon.

Horrible piano music rang out from an open window, and I cringed. Two men cut in front of me to go into the saloon, almost plowing me over in their haste for an alcoholic beverage. I glanced over my shoulder in hopes nobody I knew would see me go in, and after seeing the empty street, I slithered through the double doors and entered the foggy staleness of the place.

A drunk was singing at the top of his lungs, his voice clashing with the already out-of-tune music, and several of the tables were already surrounded by gamblers and feel-lucky cowboys. Half a dozen inappropriately dressed women bounced from one man to the other, but none of them were Ryleigh. Out of the corner of my eye, I noticed one of Overhaul's bouncers, Ray, and ducked behind the nearest man. If I were seen by one of the pig's men I would be tossed into the street without warning, but I had to know if Ryleigh was all right.

I ducked my head as I skirted around each table toward the staircase at the back of the room. I hesitated slightly at the thought that Ryleigh might already be occupied in her room and shivered with disgust. A loud snort sent a jolt of fright running down my spine, and I glanced to my left to see a man fast asleep in his chair with his hat pulled low on his brow. If I could hide my face long enough to inspect the building for Ryleigh, maybe nobody would know I had been in the saloon. With a surge of courage, I reached out to grab the brim of the hat, but the gent snored loudly and rolled his head out of my reach.

Grounding my teeth in determination, I inched closer and tried again. He moved once more, but this time his head moved quickly toward my hand so that my fingernail gouged his ear. With a yelp, he became awake

239

with fists flying. I ducked to avoid being hit and watched in horror as his fist landed with a loud *smack* on the jaw of a large poker player at the next table. The poker player stood up abruptly and swung a fist into the poor drunk's nose. I heard a loud crack of cartilage before the drunk toppled backward onto a table, which broke under his weight. Poker chips went flying in the air, and I covered my head with my arms as they pelted around me.

Just as if someone had dropped a match in lantern oil, a fight broke loose with men leaping on top of each other. I crawled under a table to wait out the explosion in safety, but Ray tossed a spindly man against the table above me, and it fell away to expose my hiding place. Ray saw my curly head, and his eyes instantly lit with rage.

"Hey!" he shouted as he leapt for me.

A drunk slammed his fist into Ray's jaw, temporarily distracting the large man as he threw the staggering gent through the window. Since his eyes were off myself, I jumped at the chance to disappear again. I raced to the bar, dodging bodies and fists as I flew. Once I reached the bar, I whirled around to observe the fight and gasped in shock when a pint glass full of whiskey splashed onto the front of my shirt and face. Some of the whiskey went into my eyes, which began to sting almost immediately. I cried out in surprise, but I could barely hear my own voice over the commotion in the room.

"You? What in tarnation are you doing in here?"

With my eyes still watering, I turned to see Wil glaring at me and offered a tiny smile. "Quite the fight, ain't it?"

His jaw dropped as if to say something, but he narrowed his eyes and reached across the bar for my hand. I saw the fury in his gaze and decided I didn't want to give him a chance to catch me. Grabbing a nearby bottle by the neck, I smashed it over his scalp as hard as I could. A pained expression deepened the wrinkles on his brow as he fell to the floor in a limp heap. Squaring my shoulders, I turned back to the fight before me and scanned the crowd to see if Ryleigh was among them.

A cowboy backed into me and he whirled to grab the front of my shirt as he pulled back his fist. His eyes widened when he realized who he was holding onto and dropped his arm slightly. I glared at him before slamming my heel into his foot, then darted around him when he screamed and backed away.

"Grab that kid!" he shouted at the top of his lungs, his voice booming over the racket of breaking glass and snapping wood.

A few of the nearby men heard the cowboy's cry and made a lunge for me. I managed to dodge most of their attempts until I was almost out of the door. A man not much taller than myself latched onto my arm and wouldn't let go. Grinding my teeth in frustration, I spun around to face him and lifted my knee as quickly and strongly as I could until it sank below his stomach. He blew a breath of stingy air in my face as he grunted his pain, but his grip loosened enough for me to escape through the saloon's doors.

I jumped into the street and stood to my full height as I calmly straightened my shirt. Suddenly, the doors slammed against the side of the building as three men tripped over themselves to exit the saloon at the same time. I yelped out of shock at the sudden noise and felt a shiver of fear race down my spine as I ran toward the schoolhouse. The men shouted angrily behind me, drawing more attention from the town's bystanders than if we were just running. A woman squealed when I raced around her skirts in hopes of slowing down the angry cowboys who seemed focused on ripping me apart.

A man came out of the mercantile with a woman dressed in a plain blue checker dress, his arms full of packages. I didn't see them coming in time to dodge them, and I plowed into the poor gent. We both fell to the ground and I fought against his packages as I struggled to my feet, but I froze when I made eye contact with him.

A blush crept up my neck when I recognized Levi Hendershot staring back at me in shock, and when I looked up, I saw Ryleigh with a hand covering her mouth. I opened my mouth as my mind raced to explain, but one of the cowboys came ripping around the corner and I decided an explanation would be better with Jet present.

Jumping off Levi's belly, I disappeared down the alley, hoping to lose the troublesome men, but as I came out on the other end, one of them latched onto my belt loop and pulled me to a stop. "Let go of me!" I growled as I fought against him.

The cowboy pushed my hands away and wrapped his arm around my midsection as he lifted my feet off the ground. "You're goin' to the sheriff!" he snarled as he carried my squirming self across the street to the jail.

"I didn't do anything!" I shouted. "Set me down!"

The cowboy opened the door to the sheriff's office with ease, even though I tried to block our entrance by latching onto the doorjamb. Unfortunately, one swift tug from my captor left me with splinters under my fingernails as he stumbled inside.

"I brought you mischief, Sheriff," the cowboy snarled, finally setting my feet on the ground. I attempted to run, but he yanked me back and pulled my hair as he twisted my ear.

Sheriff Hodgkinson leveled his gaze on me and chewed on his bottom lip as he slowly set his pencil down. "What happened?"

"This little imp," the cowboy snarled, "started a fight at the saloon. I saw the whole thing."

The sheriff sighed as he pushed himself to his feet. "I'll take it from here."

The cowboy waited until the sheriff took hold of my arm before he stormed out of the office.

Ashamed of being caught, I refused to look up at Sheriff Hodgkinson even though I knew he was staring at me. "Don't you ever get a little tired of coming in here like this, Cheyenne?" he asked sternly.

I didn't answer.

"You do know I'll have to lock you up until that uncle of yours comes to get you."

I swallowed hard but remained quiet as I stared at the toe of my boot.

"I'm gonna have to do something with you if your uncle doesn't come get you by nightfall. I've got a drunk in the cell, and I don't want you to spend a night with him."

I cringed when he tightened his hold painfully on my arm and dragged me to the cells in the back. I knew that he could get away with just about anything with me. Ryleigh used to watch him whip me with a leather strap when we were younger. I knew I could take anything the sheriff decided to give me, but I felt a twinge of fear despite that knowledge. Before the sheriff lead me through the bars of the cell, the front door opened to reveal two silhouettes. I glanced over my shoulder and cringed with dread when I recognized Jet and Levi.

Sheriff Hodgkinson turned to face the two and perched a hand on his hip. "Somebody didn't show up for their babysittin' duty this afternoon," he greeted condemningly.

Jet tossed the sheriff an irritated glare, then glanced at me. I suddenly found it interesting to count the termite holes in the wooden floor. "I'm scared to ask," Jet muttered in a low voice.

"She was found in the saloon," the sheriff answered irritably. "The rest is predictable. Now, I realize you're workin' hard over at the feed mill, Mr. Douglas, but need I remind you that I ain't gonna keep wasting my time chasin' your niece every time you turn your back. I've got a town to run. My days of keepin' up with Cheyenne are over, and I've had it with her. Whatever fantasy you have about straightenin' her path should be thrown out of your head. Do you know how many switches I've broken over her backside? How many nights she's stayed in my cell? How hard she's worked in this office until she earned enough money to pay for her damages? I've done all I could think of to tame her, short of sending her to an orphanage or boarding school, and I believe that's just what she needs."

Jet's jaw tightened, but he kept his voice even when he spoke. "Sheriff, I'm doing the best that I can, and I can guarantee that she'll be punished for her mischief. I'll pay any damages she caused."

The sheriff looked at Jet from under his hat brim. "I'll give you a month to straighten out this kid. If she gets hauled into my office one last time because you ain't watching her, I'm packin' her on a stage and sending her East to a boarding school, do I make myself clear? If you argue, let me remind you that I'm also the Justice of the Peace around these parts, and I do have the right to bring a child out of an irresponsible family."

Jet stared into the sheriff's eyes for a moment before giving his head a stiff nod. "I understand."

Sheriff Hodgkinson finally let go of my arm and hooked his thumbs into his pockets. "One month," he warned as a reminder.

Jet hid his eyes with his hat as he herded me out of the office, and Levi shut the door behind us. The walk to the house was silent and stressful. I ran my gaze up Jet's figure until I found his face, but he refused to look at me.

When the three of us filed into the living room, I found Ryleigh sitting at the table with her hands clasped tightly in her lap. Jet pulled a chair from the dining table and pointed to it as a silent command to sit. I glanced into his irritated gaze, then cautiously obeyed his request.

"What on earth were you doing in the saloon?" Jet asked sternly. "I thought I told you to go back to school. Imagine my surprise when Levi comes running up to me and says you were in trouble."

I glanced at Jet with fearful eyes. "I-I can explain."

"Well, I'd love to hear your explanation."

I cringed at his harsh tone and glanced toward Levi. "I..." I glanced toward Ryleigh and wondered if my suspicions were wrong. Even if something were wrong, I couldn't bring myself to put Ryleigh on the spot in case it would get her in trouble. "I know I shouldn't have been in the saloon, but I was curious. The fight broke out, and I didn't know what to do."

"Why were you in the saloon?"

I looked up at Jet with pleading eyes and hoped that he wouldn't be angry for the lie I was about

to tell him. "I didn't want to go back to school. I didn't want to face Penelope again, so I..." My voice faded when I saw the suspicion in his gaze.

"Cheyenne, please don't lie to me. I want to know the truth."

"That is the truth, Jet," I argued as I avoided his gaze.

"Is it, Cheyenne?" Jet asked, and I lowered my head with guilt. "Why do you smell like whiskey?"

"Some whiskey spilled on me during the fight. I wasn't trying to steal some again, I promise."

Jet sighed as he placed his hands on his hips. After a few moments of silence, he spoke in a calmer tone. "I want you to go to your room, Cheyenne. I'll be in there shortly."

I nodded slowly as I obeyed Jet's request. When I entered my room, I could hear three voices conversating quietly, and I tiptoed to the door so that I could hear what was being said.

"What are you gonna do?" Ryleigh asked in a shy tone.

"I don't know. I can't seem to get through to her no matter what I do," Jet answered, and his voice sounded defeated.

Levi cleared his throat. "Maybe I misjudged what I saw. I mean, I only saw those cowboys chasing her. Maybe she didn't mean any harm."

"I asked her to go back to school," Jet said with a sigh. "I want to believe that she didn't mean to cause havoc in the saloon, but she went the opposite direction of the schoolhouse. I know Cheyenne had a reason for going to the saloon that she's not telling me."

"I agree that she's hiding something," Levi admitted, "but I don't think discipline will help in this case. She looked terrified."

"What are you suggesting I do then, Levi?" Jet was beginning to sound desperate. "As lousy of a sheriff as Hodgkinson is, I know he means his word when he said he'd take Cheyenne away. I need to get her to understand that I'm trying to help her. I don't want her to be sent away."

"Maybe a boarding school is what she needs," Ryleigh suggested. "I couldn't get her to understand, either. Maybe the strict rules in a boarding school are what it'll take to straighten her out."

"There's nothing in a boarding school that will help her in any way," Jet disagreed. "All they do is teach routines and rules. What Cheyenne needs is consistency. Nobody has been consistent enough for her in anything. She feels abandoned by the people she loves, and she lashes out to get attention."

There was a moment of silence before Ryleigh sniffled softly. "It's not our fault for what our parents did, Mr. Douglas. I tried to do right by Cheyenne, but I'm influencing her badly and it's for her own good that she's not around me."

"Ryleigh, I know that you think you're doing the right thing, but you need

245

Cheyenne as much as she needs you. Cheyenne was hurt deeply when you started to distance yourself from her, but she still loves you."

Ryleigh's voice began to crack with emotion when she spoke. "How can anyone love me after what I've done?"

"You've made some mistakes, but you are not unwanted," Jet answered in the same compassionate tone I had heard several times. "Ryleigh, you aren't all those things that people say. I can see the goodness in you, and I know you want to do the right thing. Please don't push your family away."

Ryleigh tried to hide a sob, but I heard the squeak of tears in her voice. "Don't tell me what I should do. I have to go."

"Please don't leave," Jet said in a pleading tone. "You're welcome here. Please stay and let Cheyenne know how much you care about her. She's confused and needs to know that you still love her."

"Mr. Douglas, please understand. She doesn't need my filth. She doesn't know what I've seen, what I've done. I don't want to taint her with my grime!"

I closed my eyes to block my own tears. Ryleigh hardly allowed herself to cry around me, and I hadn't realized the depth of her pain. I opened my door wide enough for me to enter the hallway and cautiously walked into the living room so that I could see my sister. Her back was to me, but she seemed frailer than she had when I first saw her. Jet and Levi stood on either side of her, but both seemed unsure how to approach her.

"Ryleigh, I don't believe what people say about you," Jet continued. He hadn't noticed me yet. "I know you're worth more than they say."

Ryleigh threw her arms around her middle and seemed to shrink under our uncle's soft gaze. "Then you don't know what I've done," she whispered in a hoarse voice. "I... I can't make a living anywhere else. I'm tainted in the eyes of this town, and I can't... I can't get past what I've done."

"Ryleigh—"

"Why didn't you tell me?" I asked my sister as I hid my hands in my pockets. Jet glanced at me,

then at Ryleigh, but she refused to meet my gaze. I took a few steps toward her and stopped for fear she would push me away again. "Why didn't you tell me what you were thinking?"

Ryleigh wiped the blackness of her makeup off her face before she straightened her back and turned to face me. "I had to stay strong for you," Ryleigh defended, and there were no tears in her voice when she spoke. "I couldn't let you see my worries because then you would lose strength."

"Lose strength?" I asked as a frown formed on my lips. "I thought you hated me."

Ryleigh's eyes began to water, but she swallowed hard as she lifted her head higher. "I never hated you. I just want you to be better than me, and I don't want you around to see me."

"I'm not a child, Ryleigh," I argued mildly. "I know you don't talk about it, but I know what happens in a saloon. I know what you did for me when we were kids. I've always looked up to you."

"See, that's what I don't want you to do," Ryleigh interrupted sternly. A mild anger was beginning to light a fire in her eyes. "I don't want you to be anything like me. That's why I must distance us, Cheyenne."

My heart felt heavy with pain, and a hard knot formed in my throat that made it hard to talk. I swallowed past the ball of tears. "Please don't do this."

Ryleigh finally broke her gaze from me as she stared at the wood floor. "I have to, Cheyenne. I can't do anything for you. You must listen to Mr. Douglas from here out."

Before I could try to persuade her, Ryleigh marched through the front door and into the street. Levi glanced at us as he cleared his throat. "I reckon I should get back to work," he said flatly before hurrying out of the door.

Jet glanced down at me when we were alone, and I didn't bother to hide the tear that tumbled down my face. I glanced up at him and sighed shakily. "What did I do to her?"

Jet's shoulders relaxed as he wrapped an arm around my shoulders in an embrace. "You didn't do anything," he comforted as he laid a hand on the back of my head. "Ryleigh has been hurt, too."

I closed my eyes as more tears began to fall. "I want to help her."

"I know you do. I want to help her, too, just like I want to help you."

I pulled out of his embrace as I wiped my nose with my shirt sleeve. "I'm sorry for what I did," I mumbled without looking at Jet. "I know I shouldn't have disobeyed you, but I was scared."

Jet laid a hand on my shoulder. "Why were you scared?"

I remained quiet for several minutes as I battled with my thoughts. Jet had shown me consistently that he wasn't trying to harm us, but I still found it difficult to trust him. I kept thinking that he would eventually leave just when I'd start to care for him, and I was afraid of the hurt that I had felt multiple times. Swallowing hard, I remembered the compassion that Jet showed to Ryleigh and bolstered enough courage to look him in the eye.

"I was afraid something happened to Ryleigh," I answered quickly. "I was heading to the school, and I remembered what she had said last night about having the night off. I've never known Overhaul to let anyone have time off, and I was afraid something happened."

"Is that why you went into the saloon?"

I nodded. "Yes, sir. I was stupid. I wanted to talk to Ryleigh and make sure she was okay, but I accidentally woke up a drunk. The fight broke out and I didn't know what to do. Someone threw a glass of whiskey, and it spilled all over my face and shirt. Then Wil saw me, and I was afraid of what he'd do to me, so I broke a bottle over his head."

Jet listened to my explanation patiently. "I see."

I cringed as I lowered my head again. "Are you upset?"

"I am disappointed. I understand your concern for Ryleigh, but you should have waited for me before you went into the saloon."

I hid my hands behind my back. "I know. Are you gonna punish me?"

"No. I don't want to punish you for the concern you have over your sister, but I do think you owe Wil an apology for hitting him with a bottle."

"Do I have to apologize?" I asked as I looked at Jet with pleading eyes.

"Do you think you were in the wrong?" Jet questioned with his eyebrows slightly raised.

Dread settled on my shoulders like a heavy blanket, and I slowly nodded my head.

"Then let's go. When you're done with the apology, I want you to go back to school for the rest of the day."

"Yes, sir," I mumbled as I turned toward the front door.

Jet followed me as we trudged down the boardwalk toward the saloon. I began to rehearse the apology in my mind as we approached the double doors, and I felt a sense of relief that Jet would be with me in case Wil tried to hurt me. All too soon, I pushed one of the doors aside as I entered the dimly lit bar room and scanned the disarray of broken chairs and poker chips on the floor.

Bob was sweeping the mess when we entered, and when his eyes landed on me, his lip curled with disgust. "Hey, Wil!" he called without turning his back to us. "We got company."

Wil ambled out from the back with a white bandage wrapped around his head. His already cold expression turned to ice, and he aimed a finger at Jet's nose before my uncle could even utter an explanatory word. "You don't even have to ask, I'll tell you. That girl you have in your hand is an outright tyrant, and a nuisance! It might not have been her fist that started the whole thing, but it was because of her that the whole fiasco began. And when I tried to throw her out, she broke a bottle over my skull! You get her outta here before something else happens!"

I felt Jet stiffen beside me, but he remained calm when he spoke. "Cheyenne came to apologize."

"An apology doesn't pay for the damages," Wil snarled as he folded his arms over his chest. "Somebody's got to pay for this mess."

"Cheyenne didn't start the fight," Jet defended stiffly. "She was looking for her sister when she came in here."

"Yeah? Well, I got a different story. If it weren't for that miserable wretch you're trying to tame, we wouldn't have to deal with an angry poker mob that lost their money, or these tables to repair."

"I didn't touch a single poker chip," I defended, but felt my insides die when Wil turned his glare toward me.

"That ain't how Overhaul's gonna hear it." Wil curled his upper lip in disgust. "You started that fight, and somebody's gotta pay."

Jet sighed almost inaudibly. "Fine. I'll pay for the broken tables, but I'm not responsible for the poker game."

Wil glowered at Jet. "Alright, you pay for the tables." He growled the price to Jet. "I will go ahead and tell you," Wil said as he watched Jet count out the bills, "that the next time your niece breaks something in here, or hurts any of our employees, we won't wait for you or let the sheriff take care of it. If she does something like this again, it's personal, and I'll take matters into my own hands until Mr. Overhaul comes back."

Jet paused before handing the cash to Wil. "I'll make sure there won't be a next time."

Wil raised an eyebrow. "If I know that brat, there will be a next time. I just don't know when."

Jet stiffened again but didn't reply as he glanced down at me. I raised my head to look Wil in the eye and took a deep breath. "I'm sorry for hitting you with a whiskey bottle," I said in a rush. At his angry glare, I swept my arm toward the mess as I added, "And for the damages."

Wil narrowed his eyes menacingly. "I think you should leave before I tell you what's on my mind."

Jet nodded as he laid a hand on my shoulder to guide me out of the saloon. Once outside, I breathed a sigh of relief and glanced up at my uncle.

"I guess I should go to school," I acknowledged as I turned to head to the white building at the edge of town.

"Cheyenne?"

I stopped and turned to face Jet. "Yes, sir?"

Jet slipped his hands into his pockets. "I know you heard our conversation earlier," he began quietly. "I just want you to know I meant what I said. I don't want you to be sent to some boarding school."

I studied him for a moment before I nodded. "I'll try to stay out of trouble."

Jet smiled kindly as he patted me on the back. "Go on to school. We'll work on the house more this afternoon."

~SIXTEEN~

The saloon downstairs was pulsating with activity, more than usual for a Thursday afternoon. The sounds of laughter and drunken singing turned her stomach, and she wondered how she had worked in the environment for so long. Filling her lungs with air, Ryleigh stepped in front of her full-length mirror to judge her appearance. A silky red dress hugged her waist, and the neckline dipped to reveal forced cleavage that she wished to hide. She had yet to decorate her face with the paint, and her youthful features looked unnatural with the shameful dress. She longed to embrace the dark freckles that were sprinkled on her nose and cheekbones, but she had been taught to conceal every part of her that made her unique. She was just an object, something that men used to satisfy themselves.

The image in the mirror began to blur when she turned to the side. She could notice that the flatness of her stomach was beginning to round slightly, which served as a constant reminder of the baby inside. Ryleigh had already fallen in love with the child she may never meet, and her heart felt heavy with depression. When she was a little girl, she dreamed about the joy she would feel when the doctor told her she was with child, but now she felt crowded with fear. Unless a miracle happened, she would lose her baby before she could discover the child's personality.

What life can I offer a child? Ryleigh closed her eyes when the tears threatened to trail down her face. She lived in a saloon. Even though her unborn baby was innocent, people would cast unfair judgments and treat the child as though he or she lived a life of filth. Ryleigh couldn't find a solution to her problem no matter the outcome. If Overhaul forced her to be rid of the baby, she would grief and may give in to her depression, but she couldn't offer a proper life if she kept the child.

A rapid knock on her door brought Ryleigh out of her state of worry, and she glanced over her shoulder as Violet spilled inside. Her chest was heaving as she gasped for air, and when she noticed Ryleigh, she hurried to her side.

"Honey, you got to get out of this dress!"

Ryleigh frowned as concern for her friend filled her chest. "Vi, what's wrong?"

Violet smiled widely as she placed a hand on her chest. "I think I've figured out how to help you with the baby."

Ryleigh felt the blood drain from her face as she studied Violet. "What?"

Violet bustled to the wardrobe and pulled out the blue checkered dress. "I was in the mercantile, gathering food for Wil, when I heard that preacher's wife. She's starting a Bible study today for the women, and I just knew you had to go."

Ryleigh's jaw dropped as she slowly sank on the mattress behind her. "I can't go to a Bible study, Violet!"

Violet threw the dress on the bed and placed her hands on her slender hips. "Of course, you can! Listen to me, honey. You ain't gonna get a lick of help while you're in this saloon. It'll be a matter of time before you really start showing, and you know Clyde'll fix you up if you don't have a way to fight back."

"But a *Bible* study, Vi? I haven't stepped foot in a church in years, and I'm sure I'll be unwanted if I tried."

Violet gripped Ryleigh's hands and pulled her to her feet. "Honey, who are the first people to reach out to someone in need? Christians. If anything, you can leave the baby in the church after it's born and let them raise it."

Ryleigh narrowed her eyes as she pulled away. "Violet, stop it! The people who go to church are the first ones to judge. That's what they did to me and Cheyenne."

Violet folded her arms over her chest and frowned. "There could be at

252

least one person who ain't all snotty, but you'll never know unless you try."

"These people already despise me. What do you think they'll do when they find out I'm *pregnant*? I can't face them!"

"This ain't just about you anymore, honey," Violet argued in a low voice. "You wanna keep that baby, don't you?"

Ryleigh hesitated, then slowly nodded.

"Then please try. Do it for your child. I'll tell Wil that you're feeling sick and that I'll cover you this afternoon. You can slip out the back door and be at the church in no time."

Ryleigh glanced at the blue dress and felt her insides melt away like an abandoned bowl of ice cream. "What if I'm not welcome?"

Violet gripped Ryleigh's shoulders in her hands and offered an encouraging smile. "You'll never know unless you try. Please, honey? Maybe the church can help you keep this baby alive. Maybe they'll know something that we don't."

Ryleigh glanced down at her stomach and exhaled a shaky breath. "I'm terrified, Violet."

Violet enveloped her into a tight hug. "I know, honey. I am, too, but I don't know what else to do. At least try the church, and if it doesn't work out, we'll think of something else."

Ryleigh closed her eyes and nodded slowly. "Okay. At the very least, a walk may help clear my mind."

"Thank you," Violet whispered as she pulled away. She wiped a tear from the corner of her eye with her thumb before she smiled at Ryleigh. "You change. I'll go down and tell Wil that you won't be able to work today. Don't be scared, honey."

Violet cupped Ryleigh's cheek in her palm before she hurried from the room and down the stairs. Ryleigh felt a knot tighten in her throat and inhaled deeply to calm her racing heart. She felt numb as she fumbled with the silk buttons in the back of her dress. She let the immodest material fall to the floor around her ankles as she slowly stepped into the more comfortable clothing. As she pulled the dress to her neck, she glanced in the mirror once more. The blue material was plain, but plain was a good thing. Her natural face seemed to match the modesty better than the red satin dress she wore for a living, and she tried to convince herself that she was an innocent woman.

A loud crash downstairs reminded her that she stood in an upstairs room of a saloon and she felt her knees quake as she finished buttoning the blue dress. No matter how innocent she looked on the outside, her inside was black with filth. Ryleigh stared at her reflection for several minutes as she tried to persuade her feet to move. Violet was right that Ryleigh needed to think of her child, but fear held her in place. *Could I even find help in the church, or would I just be exposing myself to judgments?*

"A walk wouldn't hurt," Ryleigh mumbled to herself as she ran her shaking hands down her bodice.

She turned toward the door and slowly opened it to stare into the hallway. Someone guffawed a laugh that sent a shiver down her spine. The regular activity of the saloon disgusted her, and she abhorred her occupation passionately. She laid a hand on her stomach when she remembered that the saloon had stolen her innocence and complicated her life, but no matter how much she hated the barroom lifestyle, she was terrified to walk to the white building on the edge of town. She knew of the judgments people murmured behind her back, and she could only imagine what kind of rumors they would spread once they found out she was pregnant.

Ryleigh stepped into the hallway and began to descend the stairs with a numb mind. She tried to tell herself that she really wasn't going to the church but would just walk around town until she felt better. Once she reached the last step, she glanced into the barroom to see if she could slip out unnoticed. Violet was already hanging onto an arm of a drunken cowboy, who was dropping a few coins down the front of her dress. Ryleigh's lip quivered as she watched her friend accept a slobbery kiss from the drunkard before she settled on his lap to toy with his hat. She knew Violet despised her job as much as Ryleigh, and it hurt to see Violet work twice as hard to protect her friend.

Ryleigh finally tore her eyes away from the scene and slipped out the back door unnoticed. The sun was angling toward the western horizon as it announced the late afternoon hour, and the air smelled refreshing after she had inhaled the cigar smoke inside the saloon. Ryleigh wrapped her arms around her middle as she cautiously walked down the boardwalk. There weren't very many people milling around outside, and she couldn't blame them. The heat of the afternoon caused tiny beads of sweat to form along her upper lip and hairline, but she barely noticed her perspiration when she saw the white church at the end of the street.

You are a tart, she thought to herself as she slowed her pace. *You will be eaten alive if you walk inside those doors. What are you even going to say? Most of these women know what you do. Are you just going to waltz inside and say, "Good afternoon, may I join y'all?" They will scoff at you and snarl at you. You'll be exposed...*

Ryleigh's thoughts halted when she found herself standing on the trampled grass in front of the church. She ran her gaze over the white paint and realized how pure the building looked. A golden bell hung above the door, and the windows looked clean and perfect. Ryleigh suddenly felt as though her neckline dipped low, and her skirt exposed her knees. Her hand flew to her collar to make sure she still wore the blue dress Levi had given her. *You're a fool to come here.*

She turned to leave when she looked up to see a pleasant woman standing a few feet away. Ryleigh recognized her as the Reverend's wife, and her heart sank lower in her chest. Mrs. Atkins had a smile on her lips, but Ryleigh figured she was greeting someone behind her. Surely no one would smile at a pregnant saloon girl like herself, but as she lowered her gaze and took a step to leave, the woman's voice stopped her.

"Are you coming inside?" she asked, her voice flowing with kindness.

Ryleigh's chest filled with sadness and envy for the woman's innocence. "I don't think so."

Mrs. Atkins closed the distance between them and took hold of Ryleigh's arm. "Oh, please don't go. It would be wonderful if you came. You could sit by me. Please?"

Ryleigh glanced toward the church again. "Well..."

"Great! C'mon, or we'll be late!"

"Well…"

Ryleigh's words were cut off as Mrs. Atkins hurried up the stairs into the church with Ryleigh in tow behind her. Almost every head turned to see what the loud commotion was all about, and a blush crept up Ryleigh's neck as she noticed several judgmental glares. Well, the chance to run had vanished. Everyone had seen her, so she might as well stay to keep them from gossiping behind her back. Like her presence would stop them, anyway. Most of the time it seemed that the people in the small town of Sunset talked about her and Cheyenne no matter if they were standing in front of them.

Ryleigh carefully entered the room and lowered herself in a seat next to Mrs. Atkins, who had chosen the farthest pew from the door. An awkward silence settled over the crowd of ladies as Ryleigh studied her hands clasped in her lap. When no one made a move to speak, Ryleigh wet her lips with the tip of her tongue and wiped her sweaty palms on her skirt.

"I, uh…" She glanced up to find Mrs. Wilkes' narrowed eyes centered on her. "There's something I just remembered that I need to do."

She scooted to the edge of her seat as she attempted to stand, but Mrs. Atkins grasped her hand before Ryleigh could make a getaway. "Please stay. It's gonna be a lovely afternoon."

Ryleigh ran her gaze over the circle of women and swallowed hard. "Alright."

The Reverend's wife lifted the corners of her lips into a smile. "Good. Well, since this is our first meeting, and I don't believe I know everyone here, why don't we introduce ourselves? I'll start. I'm Mrs. Atkins, but my friends call me Adele."

The young woman sitting across the aisle breathed a sigh. She appeared almost as nervous as Ryleigh. "I'm Dinah Gray. My husband and I just moved in the area. We came from Kansas with some cattle, and my husband plans to build a ranch south of town."

"That sounds like a respectable occupation," Mrs. Wilkes muttered loudly. Ryleigh felt the reprimand as if the woman had laid a horsewhip across her back, and she hung her head to avoid the gazes of the other women.

Mrs. Atkins cleared her throat and gently asked for the circle to continue, though Ryleigh didn't bother to listen to the other women's responses. As the other women introduced themselves, Ryleigh found it hard to concentrate on what they were saying. Guilt slowly pushed its way up her throat until she could barely breathe. She began to calculate the distance between her pew and the nearest exit, wondering if she could rush out during the opening prayer. *If they ever get to the opening prayer,* she mumbled in her mind.

"Let's move onto announcements," Adele continued, that ever-present smile set firmly on her lips. "We are having a picnic for just us women this Saturday. I would love to see every one of y'all there. Just bring a side and a smile, and we'll have fun."

"Of course," Mrs. Wilkes threw in, "it is a Saturday. Most decent folks close down on the weekend, but for others it's a busy day, so we would understand if you wouldn't be able to make it, Ryleigh."

Heat rose up Ryleigh's neck as her spine stiffened.

Adele stared at Mrs. Wilkes as if she couldn't believe what had come out of the woman's mouth.

Ryleigh swallowed hard and focused on keeping her voice even. "Perhaps I shouldn't go," she whispered softly, but when she noticed Mrs. Wilkes' smug expression, her jaw tightened. "Actually, I'm free that day. I'll even bring some fruit."

Adele's smile returned. "Great! Now that that's settled, let's pray and begin our study."

Ryleigh bowed her head for the prayer and couldn't help but smile as she replayed the disappointment in Mrs. Wilkes' face. Perhaps a picnic would be enjoyable after all, and it felt good to make the gossiping woman just as uncomfortable as she made Ryleigh. Ryleigh glance toward Adele Atkins as she finished the prayer and wondered if Violet had been right. Could the church help her child? Of all the women attending, perhaps Adele could eventually offer legitimate advice. Ryleigh folded her arms over her midsection as she listened to the lesson Adele had prepared, and she mentally prayed for the safety of her baby.

* * *

I dropped the paint brush into the bucket and felt irritation swell inside of me when thick, white liquid splashed onto my clothes. My back, neck, and shoulders ached from painting, and I began to doubt Jet's expectation of finishing this side of the house before nightfall. With a sigh of exhaustion, I collapsed on the porch and groaned.

Jet glanced down at me. His face was speckled with the white paint as well. "You alright, Cheyenne?"

I sighed as I began to massage my neck. "I just need to take a break."

"Well, don't take too long. I want to get this done by supper."

"Do you think we even can?" I muttered begrudgingly as I looked at the gray wood that was still unpainted. "We're not even halfway done, and it's close to evening."

Jet dipped his brush into the paint and began to spread it over the wood. "We can't stop now. The sooner we get it done, the longer we'll have to enjoy it."

I curled my lip as I pushed myself to my feet again. "I don't think I'll enjoy it. All it'll take is a good sandstorm and we'll have to repaint what's been chipped off."

Jet chuckled calmly. "Painting the house makes it look better. We've already done quite a bit to it in the last two weeks."

I scanned the house and mentally agreed with Jet. The porch had new boards, and the shingles on the roof didn't beat against the house in the wind. Jet had also replaced the windows with new glass the day prior, and the house seemed to have less of a draft because of it. Even the white paint helped the house look newer and more welcoming, but I was tired of working.

"It's getting hard to pay attention in school," I muttered as I picked up my brush again. "You're working me so hard that I'm barely awake for Mr. Hyndman."

"I think you're doing fine," Jet said as he reached to paint a spot close to the roof. "You've gotten better at your homework this week."

"I don't even remember what I've done." I frowned when more paint splattered on my nose, and I wiped it away with the back of my hand. "I'm so tired when I do my homework in the evenings that I don't remember what I studied the next morning."

"You'll be fine," Jet encouraged as he turned to face me. "A little hard work never did anybody harm."

I curled my lip in frustration. "This ain't a little, Jet. You've been pushing me so hard that I don't have time to myself anymore."

Jet glanced down at me but didn't say anything as he continued to paint. I shook my head in frustration as I continued to paint beside him. I knew he pushed me to work hard so that I wouldn't give Sheriff Hodgkinson any reason to send me away, but that didn't make painting any more enjoyable.

"If we finish, I'll help you with your homework," Jet said at last.

"I don't need your help," I muttered.

"Suite yourself," Jet answered with a shrug.

I watched him work for several more seconds before picking up the bucket of paint and walking to a ladder that was propped on the unpainted portion of the house. When I had reached the top of the ladder, I balanced the bucket on the rung in front of me and began to spread the whiteness on the gray wood again.

"How much more do you want to do to this house?" I asked as I reached around the bucket.

"Well, a bit more I reckon. The outside is pretty much done, but I noticed the cabinets could use some new boards. It wouldn't hurt to fix some of the furniture, either."

I wrapped my arm around the ladder as I reached as far as I could without falling. "How much more do I have to work for you to pay off the saddle?"

Jet glanced at me out of the corner of his eye but continued his work. "Don't worry about the saddle."

"What do you mean?" I asked as I dipped my brush in the paint. "I've lost count how much I've made. I want to know how much longer it'll be before I pay you back."

Jet stopped painting and looked up at me. "I've decided to forgive that debt. I've seen how hard you work, and I think you've learned your lesson."

My eyes widened, but instead of gratitude I felt my frustration build. "Forgive the debt?" I snapped. "You mean I've been working for you for nothing? I've been working hard these last few days thinking I was paying off that stupid saddle, and now you're telling me this was all for nothing?"

Jet frowned as he watched me drop my brush in the bucket. "I thought you would be glad that you don't owe for the saddle anymore. I'll hold to my word and pay you the seventy-five cents a day." He resumed painting. "Besides, this was not all for nothing. I think we've gotten to know each other better."

"Is that supposed to ease my mind?" I growled as I reached for the brush. "I should stop helping you with this house and go fishing like I did before you came to town!"

"Don't raise your voice to me," Jet scolded. "I can forgive a debt if I want to, and I think you've earned it. You don't have to get upset at me."

"I don't have to get upset?" I barked as I swept the brush quickly against the boards in front of me. "How would you feel if—"

In my frustration, I had forgotten about the bucket of paint that was balancing on the ladder. When I moved my arm rapidly, I hit the bucket and it tipped on its side as it fell to the ground. My eyes widened when I saw a waterfall of white cascade on top of Jet's head. Jet hadn't seen the paint coming, and a yelp of surprise emerged from his throat as I saw his dark mustache and beard turn a bright shade of white. I quickly climbed down the ladder and froze when I noticed the hard glare that he was aiming at me.

I backed up a step as my own anger was replaced by nervousness. "Jet, I..."

Jet took a step toward me, but I didn't give him time to grab me. Spinning on my heel, I raced around the house and into the street. Jet wasn't far behind me, but his presence prompted me to run faster than I had in a long time. As I dodged around several people, I heard snickers that grew into guffaws at the spectacle we made. I glanced over my shoulder to see my uncle plowing through the small crowd of amused onlookers as he dripped white paint with each step he took. I bit my lip and turned back to face the front, in time for me to run into the chest of Sheriff Hodgkinson.

I ran my gaze up his long legs to his face and I found an amused glitter in his eyes a split second before he reached out to grab me. Dodging his hands, I skirted around him and continued running toward the livery stables. I hoped that Jet wouldn't punish me too harshly if Levi were around.

When I bulled through the barn door, Levi straightened to his full height in the stall he was cleaning out and cast me a worried look as he hurried to the aisle. "Cheyenne, what's the matter?"

"He's gonna kill me!" I exclaimed, hiding behind his back just as Jet entered the building.

Levi's eyes widened when he saw Jet's appearance, and I noticed he had to bite his lower lip to keep from smiling. Jet noticed it, too, and aimed an arrow of a finger at the young man. "You make one little noise and I'll tear into you, Levi Hendershot!"

Levi smiled, then pretended he had an itch on his upper lip to hide it. "I'm sorry, Mr. Douglas. I just wasn't expecting this."

"You take that smile off your face!" Jet snarled. "I've been through enough humiliation as it is. Now would you please give us some privacy so I can talk to my niece?"

"Don't do it, Mr. Hendershot!" I exclaimed. "He'll kill me! I know he will. Don't leave me alone with him!" I grabbed Levi's shirt and peeked at Jet from under the stable boy's arm.

"That's enough, Cheyenne!" Jet barked as he moved to grab me.

Levi blocked him. "Mr. Douglas, don't you reckon you ought to calm down before you talk with Cheyenne?"

Jet narrowed his eyes. "You stay out of it, Hendershot. She threw a bucket of paint on me in anger, and I'm not about to let her get away with that kind of attitude."

"Well, I recall a gentleman telling me that when you discipline a child, it's best when you ain't so upset."

"Don't be putting words in my mouth, son!"

Levi shrugged and leaned against his pitchfork. "I didn't. You said 'em. Why don't you clean yourself up in the horse trough? I needed to refill it, anyway. I'll make sure Cheyenne's here when you're done."

Jet glanced at me, then returned his gaze to Levi. "She better be here when I get back," he answered stiffly before turning on his heel and marching outside to the horse trough.

I sighed with relief and stepped out from behind Levi. "Thanks," I said before turning toward the back door.

"Where are you going?"

"I'm gonna disappear."

Levi shook his head and pointed to the empty spot at his side. "No, you ain't. Come back here."

I whimpered and slumped my shoulders in defeat. "Levi, you saved me from what Jet had in mind. Please let me go."

Levi raised his eyebrows as he shrugged. "Well, I promised your uncle you'd be here, and I'm a man of my word. C'mon, why don't you tell me what happened?"

I sighed and followed him to a bale of hay in the corner of the barn. "It was just an accident, Levi. Jet shouldn't have gotten so upset about it."

Levi chuckled as he leaned the pitchfork against the wall and sat on the hay. "I imagine he was kind of embarrassed to be covered in paint."

I rolled my eyes as I lowered myself next to him on the hay. "He didn't have to chase me."

"Well, why did you pour paint on him?" Levi asked as he leaned his elbows on his knees. I could still hear a bit of amusement in his voice.

I shrugged as I mimicked him. "I didn't mean to. Jet told me he wasn't going to make me pay for his saddle anymore, and I got upset. I didn't think it was fair for him to make me work so much and then change his mind. I bumped the bucket and it tipped over before I could stop it."

Levi's lips twitched into a smile, which he tried to hide. "I'm sure he wasn't expecting that."

"Stop it, Levi," I moaned as I covered my face in my hands. "It's not funny. He thought I did it on purpose."

Levi cleared his throat and wiped the perspiration off his upper lip as he stopped smiling. "I'm sorry. Why did you get upset when he told you he wasn't going to make you pay for the saddle?"

"I don't know," I mumbled through my fingers. "I know I shouldn't have, but I felt like he was taking advantage of me. I don't know how long ago he decided to forgive the debt, and I felt like he was just making me busy so he could keep an eye on me this whole time."

Levi was silent as he studied the dirt floor. "Tell me," he said at last. "What would you do if Mr. Douglas wasn't around?"

I sighed lightly as I leaned back on my hands. "Probably what I used to do. I'd try to find Chad and fish with him. Maybe we'd even go on an adventure."

Levi chuckled. "By having an adventure, do you mean using fresh horse manure as a rug in Mayor Wilkes' house?"

I grinned and nodded as I recalled the memory that Levi mentioned. "Yeah, that and poker games. We'd have our dares, too. We pranked Doc Harding a few years back. Told him there was a sick old man five miles out of town, and while he was gone, we switched the labels on all his medicine bottles. Boy, Sheriff Hodgkinson gave me the tanning of my life when they found out what happened, but it sure was fun! My favorites are when we target Overhaul. We've had our share of fun in the saloon."

"Like stealing?" Levi asked seriously.

My head snapped around, and my smile vanished. "Stealing? We only borrowed things from places."

"What about those whiskey bottles you and Chad used to get drunk?"

Heat crept up my neck, and I looked away from him. "That wasn't my idea."

Levi played with a piece of straw and lifted a shoulder. "But you drank it, anyway, didn't you?"

"Well, yeah, but it was just two bottles. Jet paid him back for it, so it ended up not being that big of a deal."

"What about the pocketknife? Or the gold watch?"

I cringed and hung my head. "You heard about the watch?"

Levi nodded as he broke off a piece of the straw. "Do you remember what the sheriff said a few days ago?"

"About sending me to a boarding school?"

Levi nodded again and turned his head to look me in the eye. "Mr. Douglas is fond of you, Cheyenne, and I think you know that. I'm sure he didn't tell you about forgiving the debt because he was afraid that you'd go back to what you were doing before he came. It makes it easier to understand why he got upset when you dumped the paint on him."

"I still don't think he had a right to get upset."

"How come?"

I studied Levi and swallowed hard before looking away as my mind raced for an explanation. "Well, it was just an accident, like I told you. If he's as patient as he's been trying to show me, he would have given me a chance to explain."

"Nobody is perfect," Levi explained. "Mr. Douglas has been concerned about keeping you safe so that Sheriff Hodgkinson won't take you away from him. When a person is worried, sometimes they act irrationally." He glanced at me from the corner of his eye. "I'm sure you can understand that."

"Yes, sir," I admitted. "You think I'm wrong, don't you?"

"No," Levi said as he straightened his back, "I think you're still trying to figure everything out. I know you're not used to having that consistent figure, and I think you're trying to understand it all."

I hesitated, then nodded slowly.

"Give your uncle a chance," Levi continued. "He's still trying to figure out how to be a parent, and he deserves your grace."

"If he's worried about Sheriff Hodgkinson like you're saying, why doesn't he just trust me enough to tell me? Maybe I'd listen better if he were just honest with me."

Levi smiled softly. "You need to trust him as much as you want him to trust you."

"I can't trust him."

"Why not?"

I stared at my feet. "Well, he doesn't know what I've been through. What if..." I closed my eyes and shook my head. "What if he leaves?"

"You don't have to be afraid."

My back stiffened. "I ain't afraid of Jet!"

Levi chuckled knowingly as he shook his head. "It's alright to be afraid, Cheyenne. I know you try to act tough, but I think it scares you when someone like Mr. Douglas reaches out to you with love and kindness."

I shook my head and gave a nervous chuckle. "Jet don't love me."

Levi shrugged as he rose to his feet. "I can't convince you if that's what you want to believe. I'll tell you, though, that Mr. Douglas wouldn't be doing any of this if he didn't love you."

I studied his eyes for several seconds, then slowly lowered my head.

Levi watched me, then picked up the pitchfork. "I've got to get back to work. Just keep in mind what I told you." He glanced at me and leaned against the stall door. "Why don't you find your uncle and see if you can explain what happened to him?"

I looked up at the young man, then rose from the hay without saying a word. I paused before disappearing out of the door to glance over my shoulder. Levi offered a gentle smile and nodded. Biting my lip, I hung my head and trudged outside.

Jet was sitting on the edge of the trough with his elbows on his knees and his head hanging low. His eyes were closed, but his lips moved as he spoke inaudible words. I hid my hands behind my back, afraid to come too close in case he decided to grab me.

"I thought we had a house to paint," I spoke, waiting until Jet raised his head before continuing. "I mean, you wanted to get that side done by this evening, so I guess we better get to work."

Jet frowned and ran his fingers through his hair, which still had a few streaks of white paint. "Are you alright, Cheyenne?"

I nodded as I cautiously approached him. "Sure. I, uh... I'm sorry I got upset at you. I talked to Levi about what happened, and he sorta helped me understand what you meant. I didn't mean to drop the paint on you."

Jet studied me, and I noticed that his eyes softened. "I shouldn't have gotten so angry with you," he said at last. "I'm sorry, too."

I swallowed hard as I began to rock on my toes. "I guess we should go back to the house."

Jet nodded and rose to his feet as we began walking back home.

When we passed the Bull's Head Saloon, a lady cackled from inside. I couldn't help looking up at the horrid noise, and I imagined Ryleigh standing by the bar through the double doors. She would be wearing a red satin dress that exposed the lower half of her legs as she carried glass after glass of alcohol to each customer. Her face would be painted with the vibrant black and red to cover her fatigue. I stopped walking and studied the inside of the saloon. I suddenly felt the desire to grab my sister by her arm and run until the town was a distant memory.

"Cheyenne?"

I glanced at Jet from the corner of my eye, then hung my head and shuffled my feet. "I'm coming."

Jet followed my gaze to the saloon but didn't say anything as he turned to walk me back to the house. We both kept silent until Jet stepped onto the porch and picked up the paintbrush he had discarded before he chased me. He cast a glance at me but continued to remain silent. I met his gaze with a blank one of my own.

"What are you thinking?" I mumbled.

He shook his head and picked up the paint bucket. "Are you okay, Cheyenne?"

I shrugged and shuffled my feet. "I am."

"You just seem awfully quiet."

"Well…" I lowered my gaze and sighed. "I was just thinking about my talk with Levi."

Jet leaned against the railing and folded his arms over his chest. "I'm glad Levi talked with you. I was afraid I was losing you, and I didn't know what to say to bring you back."

I bit my lower lip as I listened to his confession. "How come you don't give up if you think you're losing me?" I asked stiffly as I picked up my paint brush.

Jet lifted a shoulder in a shrug. "I know it doesn't make sense to you. I can't really explain it except that I believe God wants me here." He paused to study my expression, but when I looked away, he continued. "I want to be here, too. I've only been here a few weeks, and in that short time you girls have become everything I care about. I wouldn't be much of a man to run away from my responsibility, especially when you need me the most." He watched me paint for a while, then cupped the back of his neck with his hand. "I hope you can forgive me for losing my temper, Cheyenne."

I refused to meet his gaze as I continued to spread some of the white paint on the house. Jet's admission of his fears scared me, and I wasn't sure I wanted him to admit his weakness. He had always shown me his stubborn strength, and now that I knew he struggled with fear, I feared the day when he became too worn from worry and leave. *Mr. Douglas wouldn't be doing any of this if he didn't love you.* Levi's words ricocheted in my mind, but I wasn't ready to admit that he spoke the truth. The people who claimed to love me all left when I needed them the most. I cleared my throat and shifted my weight to one leg.

"There's nothing to forgive," I answered finally. "You had every right to be angry with me." I chanced a glance at him, but I couldn't hold my gaze on his. "I need to visit the outhouse. I'll be back."

Before he could answer, I stepped off the porch as I ran to the little building behind our house and slammed the door a little too hard once I was inside. I fingered my shirt collar and sat on the little bench behind me. I stared straight ahead and thought back to the stories I'd heard of Pa. I couldn't remember him personally, but what I heard from Ryleigh, he didn't make much time to listen to her childish stories or spend time with her like a father should. Ryleigh told me he was always too busy trying to win money for his family that his children often got in his way.

"It was best if we gave him his space," she once told me when I got a little older and began to question why he wasn't home.

Ryleigh said that Mama was a lot gentler with the way she handled us until Pa left. She worked for Overhaul about three or four years before she became sick. I remembered that she lost a lot of weight almost overnight and was very pale from whatever sickness she had contracted. She acted sterner than I had ever seen her, and during her last few months she pushed Ryleigh to grow up too fast and treated me like I was a nuisance. I remembered wandering into her room when she was dying, and she told me to leave her alone. She called me a brat and said if she was feeling better, she'd see that I understood my place.

Ryleigh had taken over Mama's job at the saloon when she died, and she saw to it to take care of me. She did her best, but she felt just as abandoned as I did. Maybe even more so. There was a time during our childhood when we were inseparable, and if she didn't have that stupid job in the saloon, I was sure we would still be close.

I leaned my head against the wall of the outhouse and bit my lip. Jet offered what our parents hardly ever gave us, and it was tempting to say I believed that he loved us. But words were just words, and like everyone else, he would eventually forget he said them and leave. If I allowed myself to trust him like I did Pa and Mama, even Ryleigh, his departure would hurt worse than any other. I couldn't afford to trust him. I didn't think I could stand to be left alone all over again.

Rubbing my nose on the back of my hand, I scowled and pushed myself to my feet. I wouldn't trust him. I couldn't allow him to come closer. If Jet left the next day, I would have to fend for myself, and it'd be best if I didn't get out of the habit.

~SEVENTEEN~

Saturday peeked through my curtains with the bright yellow rays of morning. I glared through my eyelashes, moaned, and flipped my arm over my eyes. Birds chirped in the town's trees, and people were alive with the hubbub of shopping and the usual day to day business. The smell of coffee intertwined with my nostrils, but the thought of getting up was most upsetting. With a guttural groan, I flipped on my belly, pulled a pillow over my head, and positioned my arm comfortably on the goose feathers beneath me. Perhaps Jet would take a hint and let a poor girl rest on this fine weekend, but just as that thought crossed my mind, a gentle knock sounded on the other side of my bedroom door.

"Cheyenne, are you up?"

I growled and shifted deeper into the pillow.

To my dismay, the door opened to allow my uncle access into the room. "The sun is up, and breakfast is almost ready."

"Go away," I mumbled into the mattress.

Jet playfully shook my foot until I jerked it away. "Cheyenne, there's a lot of work to be done, and if we get finish soon enough, I'll let you go fishing this afternoon."

I threw the pillow aside as I rolled over to face him. "Jet, I'm tired. I've worked hard this week, and I was hoping to sleep in a little."

I tried to flop back on my belly, but Jet stopped me with a hand on my shoulder. "C'mon, Cheyenne. Today is a beautiful day, and you better enjoy it before winter sets in here in a few months."

"There are plenty of good days left," I mumbled as I covered my eyes in

269

the crook of my elbow.

"You'll only have one shot at today, so get up."

I moaned and finally swung my feet over the edge of the bed. "That was the most ridiculous statement I've heard in a long time."

Jet chuckled as he hid his fingers in his pockets. "At least you're up now. You might want to try to tame that mane before a bird builds a nest in it."

I wrinkled my nose and slowly raised my gaze to meet his. "Really, Jet?"

He grinned and playfully punched my shoulder with his knuckles. "I've got bacon with your name on it in the other room. You hurry up that get-along. We've got a lot of work to do today."

Gushing a reluctant sigh from my lungs, I pushed myself to my feet and followed my uncle into the other room. We ate our breakfast in silence, and then Jet glanced at me once his plate was empty. "I have to run down to the store to pick up some more paint. Could you clean up breakfast while I'm gone? I won't be long."

I watched him leave, then stared at the pitiful pile of dirty dishes and curled my lip. Cleaning was never my favorite chore. Grumbling my discontent, I stacked the plates on top of each other and marched to the kitchen sink. I had just started pumping the water when I heard three stiff knocks on the front door. A frown pulled on the corner of my mouth. Hardly anybody came calling on the Douglas house, and if we did have callers, it turned out to be bad news. Pushing hair out of my face, I cautiously walked into the living room and opened the door.

"Chad!" I exclaimed when I saw the red-headed boy standing on our porch. "What are you doing here?"

"I needed to talk to you," he growled, folding his arms over his chest. "Don't you know you've missed three poker games in the last week? And you've missed the most exciting dare yet. What happened to you?"

I stepped on the porch and closed the door behind me. "I don't know what you mean."

Chad rolled his eyes. "Yes, you do. You used to be fun, Cheyenne. You used to be at every poker game, and you were a good partner. Now that you've ditched me, I've lost more money than I've ever had in my lifetime!"

I swallowed hard when I noticed the temper that was rising in his voice. "I'm sorry, Chad. You know Jet. I can't get away from him. He's been working me long and hard, and I'm exhausted by the end of the day. I have no time—"

"No time for your friends, I get it. You would rather waste your life away under the thumb of that man than have fun with people who actually care about you. Some friend you turned out to be. You turned your back on me."

My frown deepened as I listened to Chad's complaints. "I'm still your friend, Chad. Jet's just been making me work on this house, but if I can get off work early today, I can meet with you in the canyon like we used to."

"I'll believe that when pigs fly," he snarled as he spun on his heel to leave.

I pursed my lips and grabbed his shoulder seam before he stepped off the porch. "Now, just wait one blasted minute, Chad!"

He wrenched out of my grasp and shoved me backwards until I fell on the porch. "No, you wait one blasted minute! What kind of friend abandons their pack to help an unwanted stranger?"

Anger boiled in my veins as I pushed myself to my feet, shoving Chad back with a hand in his shoulder. "I have not abandoned you, and I would appreciate it if you would stop talking like that!"

"I won't lie, if that's what you want," Chad growled as he pushed me aside.

I ground my teeth together as I swung my fist toward him. He was prepared for me to fight and ducked before I touched him. Chad stood to his full height as he retaliated, and I wasn't prepared for his hand. My head snapped back when his knuckles collided with my mouth, and I could taste the metallic bitterness of my own blood. I glared at him menacingly as I sprang on top of him, and we both fell down the porch stairs into the street. Chad managed to slither out from under me and grabbed my shoulders as he threw me toward the support beam with all his might. Excruciating pain exploded in my face when my nose smashed into the wood before I could catch myself.

Chad's eyes widened when he saw the blood gushing from my nose and glanced over his shoulder to see if anybody had witnessed the fight.

Without saying a word, Chad ran as if he had just been caught stealing, and I watched him disappear in an alley as my vision began to blur with involuntary tears. I wiped my nose with the back of my hand and saw a streak of red from my fingertip to my wrist. My face pounded with each beat of my heart, and I was sure my nose had fallen off in the tussle. I carefully rose to my feet as I smeared my hand on my trousers and climbed up the porch steps.

Once inside, I glanced at the table with the small pile of dirty dishes and wished I had ignored the knock at the door. I blinked until my vision cleared, then brought the dishes to the sink and pumped some water to clean them. I was almost done with the chore when I heard the front door open and Jet's boots on the wooden floor. The urge to flee entered my mind, but I knew it would be too late for a quick runaway and cleanup, so I kept my back to him.

"You're still washing the dishes?" he asked as he entered the kitchen. "I figured you would be done by now."

I sniffed my nose, which was still bleeding, and lifted a shoulder in a shrug. "I had a little trouble at first. I found a mouse and tried to kill it, but I'm done with the washing. The plates can air dry, so I'll just get ready and be with you in a minute."

Without turning to face him, I tried to hurry to my room, but Jet placed a hand on my shoulder to stop me. He cupped a hand under my chin and lifted my face so that I could look into his eyes. A look of horror flashed across his features. "What did you do, Cheyenne?" he exclaimed as he reached in his pocket for a handkerchief. He placed the material around my nose and tilted my head back.

"I-I told you. I tried to kill a mouse."

He threw a skeptical look at me as he raised an eyebrow. "And did what? Run into the counter?"

"Actually, that's exactly what happened."

"Cheyenne, your nose is bleeding, and you have the makings of two black eyes. Please tell me you weren't in a fight while I was gone."

I shrugged and avoided his gaze. "Okay. I wasn't in a fight while you were gone."

He gave me a disapproving look. "Now is not the time for a joke, Cheyenne." He gently pulled the handkerchief away from my nose and frowned. "It looks like your nose might be broken."

"It's fine," I lied as I took a step back. "It really doesn't hurt, honest. Once it stops bleeding, you'll see that it ain't that bad."

"I know what a broken nose looks like. What were you thinking?" He looked into my eyes as he waited for an answer. I didn't oblige him. "Cheyenne, just because I leave you alone for a few minutes doesn't mean you have to fight someone!"

I shrugged again. "I don't see what the big deal is, Jet. It was just a little scuffle." I cringed when I noticed his disappointed expression. "Are you mad at me?"

Jet hid his fingers in his pockets as he sighed. "You should know better than to fight. It's not proper for a young woman to go around slugging people. I'm more worried about your nose than I'm mad at you for fighting, and I'm gonna take you to Doc Harding."

My eyes widened, and I inched away from him. "Can't you fix it yourself? You said you know what a broken nose looks like."

"I know what it looks like, yes, but I've never had to fix a broken nose myself. I don't want to make it worse, and Doc is trained to handle injuries like this."

"Well, what if Doc Harding is busy? I mean, it's just a broken nose. I bet he has more important injuries to mend."

Jet studied me for several moments. "Are you afraid of Doc Harding?"

I chuckled nervously. "No. Of course not. What gave you that idea?"

"You're acting nervous. Doc Harding has never hurt you. You know that."

"He hasn't hurt me yet, but I don't want to give him the chance in case he changes his mind."

Jet frowned as he folded his arms over his chest. "Doctors are here to help people, so why are you so afraid of one?"

"That ain't none of your business," I grumbled under my breath. "Why I'm afraid of doctors or not isn't something I like to talk about, especially with you."

"Are you still afraid of me?" Jet asked quietly. "You know I won't hurt you. I thought you knew by now that I care for you."

"A person can't control their feelings," I answered quickly as I backed up to the counter. "I just don't want to go to Doc Harding."

"Cheyenne, you've seen Doc when he helped you after you fell from the loft. You know he's not going to hurt you, so why are you so scared of him?"

"He wouldn't do anything for Mama," I mumbled softly. Jet's eyes softened as he waited for me to

continue. "Mama was dying, and he wouldn't help her. That's why I'm scare of him, Jet. I never wanted to see a doctor for anything if I could help it. I know he could've saved Mama, but he watched her die like the rest of this town."

Jet studied me compassionately for a few moments before he spoke in a low voice. "Cheyenne, I'm sorry about all that happened in the past, but you need to let it go. Your mother didn't want to live. Even if Doc Harding treated her the best he could, she still would've died. The patient has got to have the want-to to live, and if they ain't got it, there's nothing anybody else can do."

"I know I shouldn't be afraid, but I can't help it. I keep thinking he'll decide to hurt me on purpose."

"He won't do that," Jet disagreed gently. "He helped you when you passed out from starvation, and he helped you when you hurt your wrist. He hasn't given you reason to distrust him."

I swallowed hard as I nodded slowly. "I know you're right, but I'm still scared."

"I know you are, but I won't leave you. I'll be there when he's fixing your nose, and you'll see that there's no reason to be afraid."

I sighed as I stepped closer to my uncle. "You'll stop him if he tries to hurt me?"

Jet chuckled quietly as he motioned for me to come to his side. "I don't think he'll hurt you on purpose, but if he does, I'll stop him."

I swallowed past my nervousness as I allowed him to lead me outside and down the street to a small building toward the outskirts of town. My heartbeat quickened as we ascended the steps of the boardwalk to the door of Doc Harding's place, and a shiver raced down my back when we entered the small room. A grandfather clock sat in the corner to our right with a desk beside it. Piles of papers were stacked neatly on one edge of the desk, while a cabinet filled with drugs and other medications rested against the wall. A single, nine-pane window allowed for a glimpse of the outdoors where children enjoyed their day off from school, and men continued their work. I swallowed hard and pressed my back against the wall as Jet gently closed the door behind us.

A black curtain leading to the back room parted, and Doc Harding walked into view when he heard us enter. He glanced at Jet over the rim of his glasses, then pushed them up the bridge of his nose as his eyes assessed the bloody handkerchief I held on my nose.

"What happened?" he asked as he headed toward his desk to lay a book next to the stack of papers.

"Cheyenne got into a fight this morning," Jet answered as he silently encouraged me to leave the wall. "I'm afraid she might have broken her nose."

Doc Harding glanced at me and raised an eyebrow. "Another fight, huh? Seems you've been getting into several of those lately."

I remained quiet as I avoided his gaze.

"Well, why don't you and your niece come on back so I can take a better look?"

Jet nudged me to follow the doctor, though my feet were nailed to the floorboards underneath. After a slight wrestling match, my uncle succeeded in getting me into the back room. Doc Harding motioned to the table in the center of the room, and I cautiously raised myself on top of it. The doc gently removed the handkerchief so he could see my nose.

"You must have hit something mighty hard," he mused aloud as he laced his fingers together and placed the heels of his palms around my nose. "You'll feel a bit of a sting, and your nose may bleed some more, but it won't last long." I saw his shoulders flinch as he quickly straightened the bent cartilage in my nose, and I cried out in pain.

"Ow, you daggum medicine man!" I exclaimed as I blinked past the sudden tears.

"Believe it or not, I've been called worse things," the doctor acknowledged as he wiped some of the blood from my upper lip. "What were you trying to do?"

I lifted a shoulder in a shrug as I watched him grab a bottle from a shelf on the wall. "I had to straighten out some kid."

Doc Harding glanced at me from over the top of his glasses as he muttered a suspicious, "Mm-hmm."

I dodged his gaze again and watched as he dropped some sort of ointment onto a piece of cloth. He turned back to me and dabbed the medicine on my swollen lip, which stung worse than when it busted open. The rest of my scrapes and bruises were miniscule, and I began to relax. I scanned the room and felt my lip curl in disgust when I noticed a medical poster of a skeleton with muscle attached to the bones. How anyone could be interested in the human body, I would never know.

Doc Harding glanced at me before he turned to Jet. "She may feel a little sore, but she'll heal fine now."

I pursed my lips as I glared mildly at the doctor. "I feel like a pullet hen ready to start pecking at them grasshoppers again."

Doc Harding leveled those calm eyes on me. "I do believe it was your pecking that got you in trouble to begin with." He turned back to Jet as he told him the price for the visit.

Jet nodded and pulled out his wallet as he counted out some money.

Doc Harding turned to put away his medicine, but he spun on his heel as if he had forgotten something. "Did Ryleigh tell you anything lately?" he asked Jet in a matter-of-fact tone.

Jet's eyes widened a little as he cautiously shook his head. "No. She ain't told me much of anything in the last few days. Is something wrong?"

The doctor glanced at me, then shook his head. "Nothing. She's as healthy as any young woman should be, but I would like to speak with you.

Privately."

Both men glanced at me, and I felt my heart quickening.

"Go outside, Cheyenne," Jet ordered gently. "I'll be out there shortly."

I glanced between the two men, then slipped from the table and forced my stiff legs to move as I exited the building. As I stood on the porch steps, part of me wanted to sneak back inside and hear what the doctor had to say, but another part of me wanted to wait and pretend nothing was wrong. Yet, I couldn't help but feel frightened. Was there something physically wrong with Ryleigh? Was the conversation pointed toward me? Was there something entirely different that the doctor needed to discuss with Jet? The same feeling of helplessness that I felt when Mama died and when Ryleigh drew back filled my chest.

As my mind contemplated several horrible outcomes, I spotted Ryleigh walking across the street with a woven basket slung over her arm. She wore the plain blue checkered dress that she always seemed to wear whenever she wasn't in the saloon. Her brown hair was pulled back into a neat braid, and her face seemed youthful. There was a glow in her expression that normally wasn't there, and she appeared to be happy. Watching my sister disappear in the normal street clutter of people set my mind at ease. Whatever the doctor had to tell Jet surely didn't have anything to do with Ryleigh. With that consolation, I slipped into a sitting position and waited for my uncle to join me on the boardwalk.

* * *

Ryleigh tried to control the excitement and joy she felt bubbling up inside of her. It had been ages since she went on a picnic, and the thought of spending the afternoon with women sent a thrill through her veins. She glanced inside her basket at the fruit she would bring. Her feet faltered as a small frown tugged on her lips and slight disappointment settled in her chest. Perhaps she was letting herself get too excited. Although Adele Atkins seemed pleased that Ryleigh was going to attend the picnic, she felt a small twinge of worry for what Mrs. Wilkes would say. She placed a hand on her small, rounded belly. She wanted to be brave for her little one so that she could give her child a chance to live a respectable life.

277

Straightening her skirt, she turned on her heel and glanced down the street. There wasn't much to do in the small town of Sunset, but she would find something to occupy her mind until it was time to meet. Anything was better than going back to the saloon. Violet even convinced Wil to let Ryleigh run a few errands, even though Violet had already finished the tasks she sent Ryleigh to do. Dropping the handle of the basket into the palm of her hand, Ryleigh waltzed down the street with her head held high. She felt good, better than she had in years. She even smiled and waved at a few townspeople, who only frowned at her gestures and gave her plenty of room to walk, but even the regular judgment didn't stop her joy.

Casting a glance at both ends of the street, Ryleigh bounced toward the stables and entered the barn. The smell of horses and hay met her nose, and she inhaled deeply. She set her basket on a hay bale and approached the nearest horse, which was a black paint with blue eyes. The beauty of the horse took her breath away, and she couldn't resist running her hand down its nose.

"Oh, I, uh, didn't see you there."

Ryleigh jumped at the sound of a man's voice, and she glanced over her shoulder to see Levi Hendershot standing in the doorway with his hair messed up. Without thinking, Ryleigh giggled at his appearance. His hat, now bent in several different folds, was held in his hand, the knee in his jeans was ripped, and his shirt was untucked. A smudge of dirt stretched from his nose to his ear, and he looked exhausted.

The longer she stared at him, the harder she laughed, and she tried to cover her mouth to stop the giggles. "I'm sorry," she apologized when she could breathe again. "I'm not normally this rude."

Levi watched her laugh for several moments, then a smile stretched across his face. "I suppose I do look a sight."

Ryleigh stepped away from the horse and held her stomach as she chuckled behind her fingers. "I'll say. What happened?"

Levi shrugged as he looked at his pathetic hat. "Mr. Shepherd had a horse he wanted me to break. He's a *caballo diablo* if you know what I mean. I thought I had him broke until I took him for a ride. The devil waited until

278

we were five miles out of town and threw me. When I came back, he was grazing outside of the corral."

Ryleigh smiled. "Sounds like you've had an adventurous morning."

Levi snorted as he lowered himself on a bale. "Well, I've got my exercise, that's for sure." He sighed and leveled dark brown eyes on her. "What are you doing here?"

She shrugged and motioned to the basket beside him. "I was invited to go to a picnic with some other ladies this afternoon, and I guess I'm in too good of a mood to stay at home. I've always loved the stable, so I thought I would visit some horses. Unless you mind, then I'll leave."

Levi wagged his head back and forth quickly. "Oh, no. I don't mind. You can stay as long as you like. I need a break to rest, anyway."

Ryleigh smiled shyly and glanced back at the black paint. "Whose horse is this one?"

"Mine. Mr. Shepherd gave him to me when I started the job. Well, 'gave' isn't really the right word. I use some of my pay to buy him each week. But Mr. Shepherd don't mind me using him until I get him bought. I call him Sioux."

"Sue?" Ryleigh giggled again. "That's unusual name for a male horse."

A blush crept up Levi's neck as he tried to smile. "No, I mean like Sioux Indian."

"Ah, well that makes more sense." Ryleigh scratched the gelding's jaw and smiled when he closed his eyes. "He's beautiful."

"Thank you. Maybe we could go riding sometime."

Ryleigh turned back to face the young man. "Oh, I'd like that! I haven't ridden a horse since I was younger than Cheyenne."

Levi smiled that boyish grin that made her heart flutter. "Then we'll take a few horses out soon."

Ryleigh spun on her heel to hide the blush that colored her cheeks at the thought of spending time with the young man, but she didn't run. A small grin played with her lips, but she quickly squelched it as she turned back to face him. "I'm off work tomorrow. We could go in the morning."

Levi shook his head and pushed himself off the bale of hay. "Tomorrow's

Sunday. I'm going to church in the morning."

"Oh." She glanced toward the floor and shrugged. "I suppose the afternoon would work just fine, then."

Levi touched her elbow and made her catch her breath. "I would like for you to come to church with me tomorrow. Your uncle and sister would like to see you, I'll bet."

"I don't know..." Ryleigh's mind raced back to Mrs. Wilkes, and felt her stomach roll over at the thought of invading more of her space. "I don't think that would be a good idea."

Levi leaned against the stall door and looked up at her with those soft eyes of his. "Why not?"

"Well, I'm not sure that my kind is welcome in those doors."

"'Your kind'?" Levi questioned as he straightened his back to his full height. "What do you mean by 'your kind'?"

Ryleigh shrunk back, afraid of the anger she heard in his voice. "Uh, w-well, I'm not... I'm not..."

"You're not what?" he asked, his voice softer.

"I'm not good enough!" she exclaimed. She straightened her back ready to fight in case he tried to argue with her.

Levi cocked his head to the side as he ignored her stiffness. "You're not good enough? And you think the rest of us are?"

Ryleigh planted her hands on her hips and glared up at him. "None of you in that little white church have done what I've done. You ain't allowed things to happen to you that I have. I'm no good in their eyes, and I'll only be judged if I go to church!"

"You've made a mistake, but so have I and everyone else in that church. It's called sin, Ryleigh. Anybody that goes to church isn't perfect, and don't you ever think we are. We are human. Us sinners go to church so that we can learn about God's grace and mercy. Some of us just need a little more prayer than others."

Ryleigh listened to his words, and for some reason felt her anger drift away. "Maybe y'all ain't perfect, but I'm the worst sinner in the bunch."

Levi shrugged and hooked his thumbs in his pockets. "Well, I can't say that or not. I've done some pretty bad things in my lifetime."

She narrowed her eyes. "Like what?"

"Like stealing money from my boss a few years back."

Ryleigh studied him with apprehension. "I still don't know."

"Well, if you won't go to a church full of saints, will you accompany me to one full of sinners?"

"All I have is this dress..."

"That dress is fine. You look beautiful in it."

There was that blush again. Ryleigh suddenly realized how close she was standing to Levi and took a step backwards. "Well..."

"C'mon, Ryleigh. You have no more excuses." He looked at her from under raised eyebrows and crooked a finger under her chin. "Well? What do you say?"

Slowly, a small smile spread across her face despite her efforts to hide one. "Fine, I'll go. There's not much to do in Sunset on a Sunday morning while I wait for you to take me on that ride."

Levi beamed a smile again. "Great! I can pick you up at eight-thirty so we can walk to the church together."

Ryleigh nodded slightly. "Alright," she almost whispered as she studied the way his eyes lit up when he smiled.

He was a handsome young man with soft brown eyes and smooth skin to boast of his youth. He had to be about her same age, and his shoulders were broad from hard labor. Ryleigh didn't have to strain her neck to look at him, and she felt more comfortable around him since he didn't tower over her like most of her customers. His hair was just a few shades lighter than her own and was straight compared to her own uncontrollably wavy hair.

She blushed when she realized where her mind had gone, and she finally broke her gaze from Levi. "I-I'm sorry," she murmured as she tried to hide her face. "I really have been quite rude today."

Levi chuckled. "I don't blame you. Like I said, I probably look a sight, so I guess I'd better get used to a few stares."

Ryleigh offered an apologetic smile before glancing over her shoulder toward the street. "I suppose I should be going. I'm sure some women are already gathering at the creek."

Levi nodded politely as he took a step back to let her pass. "Of course. I'll see you tomorrow, then, Miss Douglas."

"Please," Ryleigh interjected. "Call me Ryleigh."

"Ryleigh," Levi corrected with a grin.

Ryleigh returned his smile as she hurried out of the livery before Levi could see another blush and rushed to the creek just outside of town where the picnic was supposed to take place. Ryleigh couldn't ignore the unusual feeling of delight in the pit of her stomach as she walked down the familiar path, and she smiled to herself when she thought of Violet's reaction when Levi would pick her up on the morrow. Perhaps Violet was correct in stating that Levi fancied her, and the thought excited her.

Adele was already by the lone tree at the creek with a blanket spread on the ground. Ryleigh took a deep breath and hastily walked toward her. "Good morning," Ryleigh called when she was in hearing range.

Adele turned and smiled pleasantly. "Good morning, Ryleigh. I'm glad you could make it. Please, set your basket here," she said as she motioned to the blanket. "The other ladies should be on their way."

Ryleigh glanced over her shoulder down the path and willed the butterflies in her stomach to stop fluttering. "I suppose I was just in a hurry to come. I don't get out often." Her smile faded when she realized what she said, and she hung her head in shame. "I-I mean…"

Adele touched Ryleigh's elbow as she offered a smile. "I know what you mean," she assured sweetly. "It's far too easy for us women to get consumed with our lives that we forget to enjoy ourselves."

"Yes, ma'am," Ryleigh breathed with relief.

Adele turned toward the path and widened her smile. "There they are. We'll socialize and then eat once everyone gets here."

Ryleigh turned and noticed that Mrs. Wilkes was leading the small group of women. Attempting to hide her fear, she clasped her hands in front of her and felt a small flutter in her stomach that was not nerves. She gasped softly when she remembered her condition, and her hand absentmindedly flew to her abdomen. It would only be a matter of time before she began to show, and when she did stick out Clyde would unleash his fury on her. Perhaps she should hurry to find help from the tender Adele Atkins. Ryleigh willed her legs to move as she followed Mrs. Atkins to greet the women, and she pushed her fears aside as she smiled numbly.

"Good morning, Margaret," Adele greeted as she enveloped the woman in a hug. "I trust the business is fine at the mercantile?"

"Oh, yes, fine, fine," Mrs. Wilkes acknowledged with a wave of her hand. "As long as some of these farmers pay their bill. I swear, we lend out more credit than we can handle at times." Mrs. Wilkes glanced at Ryleigh and frowned.

Ryleigh looked away and found Dinah Gray as she laid her own basket next to the picnic blanket. Determined to keep her distance from Mrs. Wilkes, Ryleigh made her way to the young woman and offered a smile.

"Hello."

Dinah glanced over her shoulder and returned the smile. "Hi. I'm sorry, but I don't remember your name."

"That's alright," Ryleigh assured as she extended her hand. "I'm not sure that we've been properly introduced. I'm Ryleigh Douglas."

"Pleased to meet you," Dinah said as she took Ryleigh's hand. "Are you from town?"

Ryleigh nodded and decided it would be best not to mention exactly where she lived in case Dinah's polite demeanor changed. "Yes. I remember you said you live in the country?"

Dinah nodded and motioned toward the south. "It's four miles that way. It's a fairly long walk in this heat," she finished as she fanned her face. "Is it always this hot in Arizona?"

Ryleigh chuckled and she nodded. "I'm afraid it's worse during the height of summer."

Dinah returned the smile but glanced over Ryleigh's shoulder to acknowledge someone else. Ryleigh turned to find herself looking into Mrs. Wilkes judgmental eyes. She scanned Ryleigh from head to toe before she invited herself into the conversation.

"Good to see you, Mrs. Gray," she greeted as she walked past Ryleigh. "Lovely that you could make it."

Dinah nodded. "Thank you. I was just telling Ryleigh that I'm not quite used to the heat here."

"Mm, yes," Mrs. Wilkes murmured as she turned a disgusted look toward Ryleigh. "Have you been around town much, Mrs. Gray?"

"Well, no, not really. Only for supplies and church."

Mrs. Wilkes' eyes seemed to grow hard as stone, but she never wavered from Ryleigh. "Then I must warn you of the company you keep, unless you want to let a wolf into your home."

Dinah's smile dipped as she cocked her head to the side. "I'm afraid I don't know what you mean."

Mrs. Wilkes finally turned to Dinah and huffed a humorless laugh. "Oh, then let me be more straightforward. If you really love your husband, you might want to avoid speaking with Ryleigh. She entertains in the saloon when she's not trying to fake her innocence. I've seen her lure many married men into her room, so I'd be careful around her if I were you."

Ryleigh's cheeks flooded with color as she glanced toward Dinah. "Oh, please don't listen to her. I—"

"You do work in the saloon, don't you?" Mrs. Wilkes interrupted as she folded her arms over her ample chest.

Ryleigh felt her spirits begin to die. "I... well, yes."

Dinah's hand flew to her chest in shock, and she suddenly found it hard to look at Ryleigh. Mrs. Wilkes narrowed her eyes. "It's a good thing I came when I did, Mrs. Gray," she continued. "I would sure hate for Ryleigh to prey on your husband."

"I would never do such a thing!" Ryleigh shouted as she felt her temper rising. "I do not take pleasure in destroying marriages, Mrs. Wilkes."

"Yet you do it all the time," she snapped as she reached for Dinah. "Come on, Mrs. Gray. Go on to the others and I will introduce you to one of your neighbors." She waited until a flustered Dinah was out of hearing range before she turned back to Ryleigh. "I didn't know you had a horse, Ryleigh."

Ryleigh frowned. "I don't."

SEVENTEEN

"Then how come I saw you coming out of the livery earlier this morning?" Mrs. Wilkes questioned as she leveled her unwavering eyes on Ryleigh.

"I don't see how that is any of your business," Ryleigh snapped in a low voice.

"Oh, really? I happen to know that a young, naïve man works there, and I have seen you two together." Mrs. Wilkes leaned in closer as she lowered her voice. "What I said about you destroying marriages is true. I've seen many wives leave their husbands because they were entertained by you in the saloon. With that knowledge in mind, I'll ask you to leave poor Mr. Hendershot alone. He doesn't seem to know what he's getting into with you, and I would hate for his reputation to be ruined by one of your whims to make money."

Ryleigh's jaw dropped in shock, and she felt tears stinging the back of her eyes. "I only have the most honest of intentions with Mr. Hendershot, and I'm shocked that you would suggest such a thing!"

"Are you really?" Mrs. Wilkes huffed with a smirk lifting her lips. "I doubt any one of your intentions is ever honest, Ryleigh. I don't know why you are suddenly coming to church, but you're not welcome to bring your filth near innocent people."

Ryleigh opened her mouth to defend herself, but she realized Mrs. Wilkes wouldn't listen to a word she said. Without another word, Ryleigh spun on her heel and raced back down the path toward the saloon. She was a fool to think she could ever have a chance to give her child an innocent life. Because of her, the baby would be judged unfairly, and Ryleigh could never avoid it.

~EIGHTEEN~

A knock sounded on my door, and I quickly tied a ribbon around the end of my black braid as I turned to face the door. "You can come in, Jet," I called as I straightened my shirt.

Jet opened the door, and I noticed he was carrying a package in his hands. "I guess I probably should have given this to you earlier, but I couldn't find the right timing."

I frowned as I slowly approached him. "What is it?"

Jet laughed at my expression as he handed me the package. "It's not poison, Cheyenne. You don't have to be so cautious."

My frown deepened as I unwrapped the binding. I froze when I saw olive green material. I turned to the bed and set the bindings on top of the mattress as I lifted the dress at arm's length away. It was a fairly simple design, but it looked elegant to me. A soft sigh passed through my lips as I carefully laid it on the bed.

"Do you like it?" Jet asked.

I ran my fingers down the front of the dress. "Yes, I…" I turned to face my uncle with a slight frown. "What is this for?"

"Well, your clothes are a little worn, and I thought that you might enjoy a new dress to wear to church this morning." He motioned to the dress as he hid his fingertips in his pockets. "I hope you don't mind the color."

I shook my head. "Not at all. I like it, Jet. It's just…" I glanced at the dress and sighed. "I've never worn a dress since Mama's funeral."

"Well, it's about time that you had a dress, then," Jet answered joyfully. "You're a young woman now, and you should be able to enjoy such things

286

as a dress." He turned to leave and reached for the door. "Go ahead and change. Once you're ready, we'll head to the church."

I watched Jet close the door, then turned back to the olive dress on the bed. With a new surge of excitement, I quickly changed into the dress and stood in front of the mirror. The faded color of the material seemed to accentuate my dark hair and eyes, and I bit my lip as I spun to see all angles of the dress. I was shocked to see the difference in just a simple change of clothing. The usual shirt and trousers hid my feminine curves, which I hadn't noticed until I put on the dress. Instead of a rough tomboy, I found myself looking at a young lady, and I felt a confidence settle in my chest that I hadn't felt in a long time. I thought back to nearly a week ago when two girls judged my character based off my clothes. They had said I didn't care how I looked, but if they saw me in this dress, they wouldn't even recognize me.

I smiled to myself as I walked into the other room. Jet was waiting at the dining table, and when he saw me, he smiled warmly. "You look very pretty," he complimented as he rose to his feet. "Let's get to church before we're too late."

I nodded as I followed him outside.

The morning was already warm, and I felt a few beads of perspiration pop along my hairline, but I ignored the momentary discomfort as we came closer to the church. When we stepped into the church yard, I felt my heart pound rapidly against my chest. I was nervous for what people would think when they saw me in a dress, and I worried about what they would think.

Jet walked up the eight or nine steps and disappeared inside the church, but I found myself frozen at the base of the stairs. I glanced over my shoulder to see Steven Butte approaching with his parents, and I whirled around in hopes to hide before they noticed me.

"Good morning, Cheyenne," Mr. Butte greeted.

I grimaced and turned to face them. "Morning."

Mr. Butte flashed a kind smile and ushered his wife into the church, but Steven stayed behind. "You look nice today," he muttered with his hands jammed in his pockets.

I opened my mouth to acknowledge his compliment, but Penelope stepped in the circle at that moment and gave me one of her famous sneers. "Well, look who decided to embrace her womanhood." She noticed my bruised eyes and lifted her lip in disgust. "Aren't you a beauty? Just be sure you keep your dress at the proper length. It's not trousers, you know."

Steven frowned at her. "Back off, Penelope. Don't you think you've given her enough of a hard time?"

Penelope's smirk grew as she eyed Steven. "Oh, Cheyenne can handle it. She's so dense that most of what I say goes over her head, anyway." She placed her hands on her hips and sashayed closer to me. "She's trying to act just like her sister. Why, look at how she's dressed! She's gonna try to butter you up so that she can double cross you and steal your reputation." Penelope lifted her nose in the air as she looked at me with disgust. "And we don't want that, now do we?"

Penelope wrapped her fist into the shoulder of my new dress and yanked down as hard as she could. The seams ripped, and the sleeve fell to my wrist. My jaw dropped when I noticed the dangling thread, and anger boiled in my veins. Without a second thought, I reached out and curled my fingers around her puffed, pink sleeve and yanked it with just as much effort.

"Do unto others, Penelope," I snarled as I stuck my nose in her face.

Steven placed his hand on my shoulder as he nudged me toward the church door. "Let's go inside, Cheyenne," he said quickly as concern filled his eyes. "She's not worth it."

I swiveled away from him and closed in on Penelope again. "I don't care. I'm tired of having this pig-nosed prissy harping on me every chance she gets."

"Pig-nosed prissy?" Penelope's jaw dropped, but only for a second before she grabbed the shoulder seam on my other arm and ripped the stitching on that sleeve as well. "You're a self-centered donkey with a ring worm on your rump!"

I muttered an insult under my breath and returned the favor.

Penelope tore my bodice and shoved me until I tripped over a rock and fell on my backside. Steven tried to help me up, but I shoved his hands away and wrestled with my skirt until I rose to my feet.

"Stay out of this, Steven," I snarled. "If Penelope wants a fight, she'll get one." I aimed a finger at the blond. "You just shoved the wrong girl."

I kicked her feet out from under her and was satisfied when she fell in a heap. Unfortunately, her feet wrapped around my ankles to trip me again, and I fell onto the ground beside her. I gritted my teeth and tried to lunge at her, but Steven wrapped an arm around my middle and pulled me away.

"Cheyenne, don't fight her!"

I fought against his hold. "You stay outta this! This is just between her and me!"

"Cheyenne!"

I glanced up toward the church doors when I heard Jet's booming voice and quit fighting against Steven when Jet started marching down the stairs with several other curious churchgoers. Penelope struck up a river of fake tears when she saw her parents rushing her way.

"Oh, Mama, look what that imp did to my dress from Chicago!" Penelope blubbered as she struggled to her feet.

Mrs. Wilkes rushed to her daughter, whom she cried and cooed over, then spun around to me. "I hope you're proud! That dress cost a fortune, and you ruined it!" She puffed out her chest and glared at Jet. "Shouldn't you try to corral that brat before she makes a mess?"

The Reverend fought his way through the crowd and raised his hands for silence. "Hush!" he shouted over the fuss Mrs. Wilkes was making. "This is the Lord's Day! Let's respect that, shall we?" He glanced at me, then Penelope, and planted his hands on his hips. "I'm disappointed in you girls. Apologize to each other and get cleaned up. I've got a humdinger of a sermon to preach."

"I ain't apologizing to *her!*" I exclaimed, aiming a finger toward Penelope.

"Cheyenne," Jet muttered under his breath.

I glanced at my uncle in hopes that he would understand, but he just shook his head and motioned toward the wailing girl in front of me. I hung my head as I muttered, "I'm sorry."

Penelope harrumphed and sobbed into her father's shoulder. "She doesn't mean it, Papa! She beats me up and doesn't even care! Do something!"

The mayor patted his daughter on the shoulder. "There, there, Penelope. It's all gonna be alright." He turned to Jet and motioned to me angrily. "You need to control that tyrant so that she doesn't go around terrorizing innocent people!"

"Tyrant?" I asked, raising an eyebrow. "Penelope's the tyrant! She's the one who bullies me every chance she gets!"

Mrs. Wilkes' jaw dropped in shock as she placed a hand on her chest. "Such disrespect! Mr. Douglas, please control that animal before she destroys something else!"

I felt my bottom lip quiver at her words and ducked my head as I fled from the circle of churchgoers. I had to hold up part of my bodice as I ran, and the familiar path to the house was blurred by tears. I bounded up the steps and raced to my room where I collapsed on my bed. I allowed the tears to create wet stains on my pillow before I sensed Jet's presence.

I glanced up at him and sniffled softly. "It wasn't my fault, Jet."

Jet slid his fingers into his pockets as he leaned against the door jamb. "Steven told me what happened after you left."

"I'm sorry," I muttered as I pushed myself into a sitting position. "I got upset. I shouldn't have ripped her dress, but I was so angry."

Jet nodded but remained silent.

I glanced down at the dress and felt disappointment when I saw the ripped material. "I guess I'm not supposed to have a dress," I croaked as I blinked back more tears. "I'm supposed to be an ugly brat."

"Don't say that," Jet responded, and I could hear the pain in his voice. "I can have someone fix the dress. You can wear it again once it's repaired."

"It's not the dress, Jet. It's what people think of me. I will never change in their eyes, no matter how hard I try to change on the outside."

"It doesn't matter what—"

"Don't say it doesn't matter what people think," I interrupted. "It does, too. I can't move on if they're reminding me of where I came from. I'm filth, Jet! Worthless, disgusting filth. No matter how hard I try, I can't be anything else."

Jet sat on my bed and stared at his lap before he spoke. "You're not filth, Cheyenne. You mean a lot to me, and it pains me to see you hurting. You're worth so much to me."

"You came here too late," I argued as I pushed myself off the mattress. "If you came a few years ago, I would believe that you could change us because I still had hope then. I've given up."

"I can't change you," Jet answered softly. "I can only pray for you and show you that you are loved. You have to give this to God, Cheyenne. He's the only one who can help you."

I scoffed as I crossed my arms over my chest. "I've told you that God doesn't care about me. He never has."

"But He does care, Cheyenne. He cared enough to send me here to love you when you feel unloved. He's kept you safe from harm."

"Has he?" I shouted. Jet cringed at my tone, but I ignored him. "I've lost both of my parents, and I'm losing my sister. Has God really kept me safe from harm, Jet?"

Jet lowered his voice, but his eyes were still compassionate. "I don't understand why God let these things happen to you, but He has a reason. Please don't shut Him out. He loves you."

"Nobody loves me, Jet." I leaned against the wall as I hugged myself. "Not even you."

"That's not true," Jet argued as he stood to make his way to me. "I do love you, Cheyenne, and I want the best for you. God loves you, too."

"God turned his back on me. I'm all alone, and I'm so tired of being alone."

Jet lowered his head in defeat. "Please don't do this, Cheyenne. Don't seclude yourself."

I glanced out the window and swallowed hard. "I know you want me to go to church, but I know I'm not going to get anything out of it." I glanced down at my ripped dress and sighed. "If you give me a minute, I'll change and sit with you, but I won't listen to the sermon."

Jet studied me for a moment, then backed out of the room and closed the door behind him. I blinked the last of my tears away before I changed back into my old attire. I glanced at myself in the mirror again and felt a heavy burden land on my chest. I shuffled to the door and opened it to see Jet standing in the hallway. He didn't say anything as he laid a hand on my shoulder to guide me outside. I shrugged his hand off and walked a few feet away from him until we trudged back toward the church.

When we had reached the church, the congregation was finishing up the last verse of "Shall We Gather at the River," which sounded slightly off-key. We filed through the narrow doorway, and I cautiously looked down the aisle where the Reverend stood by the aged piano with his hands clasped loosely in front of him. On my right, I could see Penelope's family with their noses high in the air as if they were the most important people in that church. To the left was Levi Hendershot with a young woman standing stiffly at his side. Jet removed his hat, then nudged me down the aisle to the closest bench toward the back of the room. I didn't mind being in the back and quickly jumped on the empty seat.

When the last chorus ended, the congregation sat down and turned their attention to the Reverend. I didn't pay much attention to his sermon, and when he bowed his head for the final prayer, I scooted past Jet and exited the building ahead of the parishioners, though I didn't follow my instincts to disappear.

I stood at the base of the stairs and watched as the Reverend positioned himself at the door to shake hands with the people as they exited. Mrs. Wilkes was one of the first to step outside, and when she saw me, she narrowed her eyes and ignored the Reverend's hand as she descended the stairs.

"God does not appreciate such heathens in His House," she snarled as she aimed her nose in my face. "That's why your family is the way that it is. Your family is being punished for your disobedience to God. I can only imagine what punishment God will give you someday."

My bottom lip quivered as unwanted tears sprang into my eyes. I stared into her smug expression, but the longer I studied her eyes, the more mine filled with water. Before I let a tear spill over my eyelashes, I spun on my heel and ran to the back of the church with my head down to hide my weakness.

Blinded by tears, I stumbled up the little hill behind the church where dozens of wooden crosses marked the resting places of the deceased. I slipped through the gate and blinked until my vision cleared. I hadn't been in that little cemetery since they lowered Mama into her grave. Most of it had been well preserved, with the weeds knocked down and flowers decorating the otherwise gloomy place, but one grave looked dark and foreboding. Brushing the tears from my eyes, I walked slowly toward it and parted the tall grass so I could read the name.

Lenora Douglas. Date of birth November 12, 1840. Date of death July 27, 1872. No little message such as "rest in peace" added to the gloomy cross. Not even flowers attempted to bring comfort to the grave. The only bits of color were the white blooms of weeds and the yellow of dandelions that grew naturally in the sandy dirt.

I took in the pathetic view and heaved a quiet sob as I crumpled to the ground with my hands covering my face. In the back of my mind, I heard a voice telling me quite sternly to stop crying, square my shoulders, and face Mrs. Wilkes with an insult on the tip of my tongue, but I couldn't find the energy to carry out the deed. I peeked through my fingers to look at Mama's grave and felt a huge weight of guilt land on my shoulders. She had been forgotten just like this town had wanted her to be, even forgotten by her own children. I couldn't imagine what she thought of us for leaving her alone, and it hurt to dwell on the subject.

The squeaky hinges of the gate moaned behind me, and I jumped as I quickly wiped the tears from my face and forced myself to stop crying. Soft footsteps landed on the ground behind me, until I felt someone's presence beside me. I looked up at Jet, then cleared my throat and brought my knees to my chest.

Jet bent and pulled some of the weeds out of the ground until the cross became visible again, then he straightened it and moved some rocks around to keep it in place. I watched him in silence, not understanding why he had followed me into the cemetery. After cleaning up Mama's grave, he lowered himself onto the ground next to me and wrapped his arms around his knees.

"She was a beautiful woman," he said at last.

I ducked my head as his words entered my ears. I didn't want to hear what he had to say for fear of the return of my tears.

"I met her before they were married, and saw her again after she already had Ryleigh," he continued. "She shared Rod's desire for adventure, and I think that's why they formed an attraction for each other. She used to—"

"Shut up, Jet," I interrupted, my voice cracking with emotion.

Jet stopped talking and turned his head to look at me, but he didn't scold me like I thought he would. I cleared my throat and focused on swallowing the lump that was slowly choking me.

"I don't want to hear about Mama," I mumbled at last. "It just makes me feel guilty."

"Why?"

I closed my eyes and shook my head. "Because you're right. She was beautiful. She just married into the wrong set of troubles, and now her own children refuse to admit they belong to her. I'd always thought Mama had abandoned us, but look at her grave, Jet. Just look at it! No flowers, nothing but daggum weeds. We abandoned her. She's forgotten in this God-forsaken town, and even in her own pathetic family. Mrs. Wilkes was right. Mama was punished for her choices in life. She married a gambling man, and she raised two pathetic girls."

I stopped talking when the tears became thick again, and I expected Jet to speak, but he didn't. After several seconds of silence drifted by, I cleared my throat and attempted to talk around the lump again. "You said Mama wanted adventure. Us girls held her back. There's a reason why she hated us, Jet. We didn't allow her to chase her dreams. Mrs. Wilkes is right. My family is filled with heathens, and I'm being punished for my sins."

"Cheyenne, God isn't punishing you," Jet answered softly.

Anger burned in my veins as my eyebrows knit themselves together. "I don't want to hear what you say about God. You don't know what God feels or thinks about me, and I don't want to hear a bunch of empty words that you don't mean!"

"Cheyenne, I don't mean to make you upset—"

I stood to my feet abruptly and glared down at him through tears in my eyes. "All you've done is make me upset, Jet! You won't believe me whenever I tell you that Ryleigh and I are worthless. Forget us and think about yourself. You've wasted the last several weeks on us and we ain't changed a bit! Start thinking about you, Jet. You don't want to be here for the rest of your life because this town is a prison! Me and Ryleigh are bound to this town, but you ain't. Not yet. Leave while you're still free!" I stopped shouting when my voice cracked, and I looked away as I shook my head. "There's no point in trying anymore."

Jet opened his mouth to reply, but I lowered my head and ran under the fence surrounding the graveyard, ignoring his voice as he called my name. I ran blindly for several minutes until I found myself standing in the bottom of a draw where I dropped to my knees and stared at several blades of dried grass. The wind tussled loose strands of my hair across my face and dried the salty tears on my cheekbones. I glanced at my sleeve and growled a curse as my fingers tore at the cloth. If I was going to be worthless for the rest of my life, I might as look it, too. I wrapped my arms around my belly as I pushed myself to my feet and continued walking forward.

I had reached country that was unfamiliar to me, but the unknown didn't trigger a sense of fear or dread. Glancing upward, I noticed a cliff with a far drop underneath it, and suddenly I felt warmth flood my chest. Maybe I could still find the freedom I'd been searching for all these years. Turning sharply, I began jogging through the grass toward the canyon wall. With quite a bit more energy than I had left, I climbed to the top and looked down below. As I watched the grass wave in the wind, I could hear the voices from the townspeople echo in my mind.

"You're a heathen.... You'll never amount to anything.... You're worthless.... There's only one place for folks like you, and that ain't in the House of God.... God doesn't want you near His House.... Your whole family is being punished for what they've done.... You're next.... You'll be like a brood mare.... Ryleigh doesn't want you.... You're completely alone...."

The words echoed in my mind like a gunshot through a valley. They were

295

right. I had always known they were right, and I had put up with them long enough. I was tired of hearing what they had to say, and I was tired of being corrected for mistakes that I had to make to survive. I was through with being a cockroach for people to squish. If I jumped, I wouldn't have to listen to their opinions any longer, and I wouldn't have to feel as if I were worthless anymore. The thought sounded appealing. I closed my eyes and allowed the wind to blow my hair into my face. All it would take was one little jump....

* * *

Ryleigh closed her eyes and smiled with contentment as she sat in the saddle of Mr. Douglas' horse. It had been too long since she rode on the back of a horse, and the animal underneath her felt majestically powerful. Despite the warning she received from Mrs. Wilkes, she allowed herself to enjoy Levi's pursuit. The church sermon was refreshing. The Reverend spoke about forgiveness, and the subject filled her with hope for her future and her child. She ate a delightful noon meal with a man who treated her like the woman she wanted to be, and she was beginning to enjoy his attention.

Levi shifted in his saddle and sighed happily. "I reckon I ate too much fried chicken," he muttered right before a belch rumbled in his throat. He chanced a glance at Ryleigh and turned a shade of pink under his Stetson hat. "Beggin' your pardon, ma'am."

Ryleigh grinned. "I've been feeling like that myself, honestly."

Levi returned a smile and guided Sioux toward the west. "It's a good day," he remarked as he filled his lungs with air.

Ryleigh closed her eyes again and sighed. "This is my favorite time of year. The heat of summer ain't so scorching, and everything is sort of calm before the winter storms hit. The sun just kinda warms the earth and makes everything feel fresh." She opened her eyes and glanced at the man beside her. "It's like starting over almost."

"I suppose." Levi smiled at her and caused butterflies to flitter against the walls of her belly. If she didn't know better, she would've thought that the little one did a flip, too. "The sunsets this time of year are breathtaking. It's

296

like God has a paintbrush and guides it across the sky each night."

"There's beauty everywhere. You only need to go searching a little for it sometimes."

"Sometimes God just brings the beauty right in your life," Levi replied as he sneaked another look toward Ryleigh.

She blushed and looked away, but her shy smile faded when she noticed something in the far distance. Squinting her eyes against the sun, she frowned and pointed to the southwest. "What's that over there?"

Levi followed her gaze and lifted a shoulder in a shrug. "I don't know. Looks like a weed or something to me."

Ryleigh pulled her horse to a stop and stood up in the stirrups in hopes to get a better view. "It doesn't look like a weed."

"I don't know what else it could be," Levi answered. "Maybe it's just a coyote."

Ryleigh wasn't convinced as she continued staring at the object. "It's too tall for a coyote. Let's ride over there. I'm curious."

Levi shrugged again and pointed Sioux's nose in the same direction. "I'm sure it's nothing, but I suppose it wouldn't hurt to investigate."

They both remained silent with their eyes trained on the dark spot on the horizon, but after they had ridden a couple of yards, Levi frowned and thumbed his hat back. "That kinda looks like Cheyenne, don't it?"

Ryleigh frowned and shaded her eyes with her hand. "It does. I can recognize her hair. What's she doing way out here by herself?"

"I don't know, but let's find out," Levi drawled as he nudged his horse into a canter.

Ryleigh did the same as curiosity swelled in her chest, but when they were still several yards away, Ryleigh sensed that something was wrong. Fear's cold fingers gripped her heart as she shouted above the wind, "Something's not right, Levi!"

Levi slowed Sioux to a jog and cupped a hand around his mouth. "Cheyenne!"

The young girl spun around as if she had been caught stealing, and she stared at the duo with wide, fear-filled eyes. "Go away!" she shouted.

Levi nudged Sioux into a faster pace.

"I said go away!" Cheyenne repeated as she stepped closer to the edge of the cliff. She looked like she was about to jump.

Ryleigh's breath caught in her throat as she pulled her horse to a stop.

Levi kept Sioux going at a fast pace, and when Cheyenne turned to face the drop-off in front of her, he leapt out of the saddle and wrapped an arm around her stomach right as she launched to jump. Cheyenne fought against him as he pulled her away from the edge in a ravenous attempt to break free from his hold.

"Let me go!" she cried, but Levi took hold of her biceps and held her at arm's length away as he looked in her eyes.

"Cheyenne, look at me," he said above her shouts, but she continued to fight him until her knees gave way and she fell to the ground. Levi knelt on one knee but kept a firm hold on her arms as she hung her head and sobbed uncontrollably.

Ryleigh watched her sister with wide eyes. She had never seen Cheyenne act so desperately, and knowing that she would've jumped and hurt herself, maybe even kill herself, scared her more than the news of the little one inside of her. She covered her mouth with her hand when she saw Cheyenne crumple into a ball of tears and frustration.

"Let me go," Cheyenne moaned between sobs. "Let me jump!"

Levi's jaw tightened, but he didn't say a word for a long time as he kept a firm grip on Cheyenne's arms. At last, he cleared his throat and spoke in a soft tone. "I don't know what I'd do if you were to jump."

Cheyenne's eyes turned fiery underneath her tears as she tried to pull away from the young man. "You'd rejoice, is what you'd do!" she growled. "You wouldn't have a heathen in your presence anymore! Leave me alone!"

"I'm not going to leave you alone!" Levi answered sternly. Cheyenne strained against him again, but Levi successfully pulled her to him as he ducked his head to look into her face. She wouldn't look at him, so he cupped her chin with his hand and lifted her head. "You have no idea how many people you'll hurt if you killed yourself."

Cheyenne's jaw tightened, but her attempts to fight him were weakening.

"Nobody would be hurt if I died, and I'm just doing you and the town a favor by ending it all!"

"No, you're not, and get that notion out of your head!"

"You don't understand," Cheyenne whimpered, seeming to melt to the ground through Levi's fingers. "My whole family is a bunch of heathens. I hear that wherever I go! Mama got sick as a punishment for marrying a fool like Pa, and Pa died because of his rambling. Ryleigh is being punished for working in a saloon, and I'm next! I don't want to live through the humiliation of more rumors spread around this God forsaken town! I'm not gonna give them leverage to tear me apart anymore. I want to control what happens in my life!" Sobs shook her shoulders as she lowered her head until her chin touched her chest.

Tears burned in Ryleigh's eyes. She wanted to rush to her sister's side and hold her in her arms, but she felt glued to the saddle. All she could do was shake in the stirrups and blink back her emotion. Guilt flooded her chest at the thought that she had something to do with Cheyenne's actions, and she wished she could turn back the clock to change everything that had happened.

Levi stared down at Cheyenne with sorrowful eyes, seeming at a loss for words. At last, he rose to his feet and pulled Cheyenne up with him. "Let's go to town," he spoke at last, his voice also quaking slightly with emotion.

Cheyenne dug her heels into the ground and plummeted her fist into his arm. "No! No, let me go! I want to stay here! I don't want to see Jet!"

Levi picked her up without another word and carried her squirming body to Sioux. After he set her behind the saddle horn, he swung up behind her, pointed the horse's head to the east, and spurred him into a canter. Swallowing her own tears, Ryleigh gripped the reins with both hands and urged her horse into the same speed as Sioux, but the path in front of her turned blurry as the salty drops of water began tumbling down her face.

Even though the ride into town only lasted a few minutes, it felt like an eternity to Ryleigh as she tried to wrap her mind around what Cheyenne was thinking. Didn't she know Ryleigh would be lost without her? Didn't she know she had so much more in her future? Didn't she know that the opinions of others didn't matter? Didn't she know that Ryleigh adored her and never wanted to hurt her from the start? Ryleigh wiped her eyes on her sleeve when their horses stopped in front of the house they rented from Overhaul. Levi jumped out of the saddle and pulled Cheyenne down with him. Ryleigh swallowed hard and swung her leg over the horse's rump as she placed her feet on the ground to stand on wobbly legs.

Cheyenne attempted to tear away from the stable boy, but Levi kept an arm wrapped around her to keep her by his side. "Please!" Cheyenne yelped. "I don't want to see him!"

Levi ignored her protests and knocked on the door rapidly. It opened almost immediately to reveal Jet. He glanced down at Cheyenne, who crumpled under his gaze, and his eyes filled with worry.

"What happened?" he asked in a rushed breath.

Levi opened his mouth to explain, but Cheyenne interrupted him. "Nothing happened!" she bellowed. "That's the problem!" She wrenched out of Levi's grasp and turned to run, but Jet was able to catch her arm before she could disappear.

Jet took hold of her shoulders and knelt so he could look in her eyes. "Where have you been? I was worried sick when you ran off like that. What were you doing?"

"It doesn't matter what I was doing!" she snapped, then glared toward Levi with a menacing stare. "Levi stopped me!"

Jet's face turned white as he stared at her with wide eyes. "What do you mean?"

Levi looked at Jet with solemn eyes and cleared his throat so that he could speak. "She tried to jump into a ravine," he explained quickly.

Cheyenne let out a growl of frustration as she fought against Jet. She pulled against him so hard that she lost her balance and fell backwards on the porch, but Jet helped her to her feet. "Let me go!" she yelled. "I don't want to be here. Let me be!"

Jet wrapped an arm around her middle as he walked through the threshold without a word. She fought against him until Jet finally brought her inside and closed the door.

The memory of Cheyenne's shouts still pierced Ryleigh's ears, and she covered her mouth as tears gathered in her eyes again. Levi glanced over his shoulder and noticed how Ryleigh gripped the porch beam to keep from falling over. Without saying a word, he gathered her trembling body to his chest and held her tightly as she let go of the hold on her emotion. Ryleigh buried her face against his neck.

"Shh," he whispered in her ear as he held her close. "It's gonna be okay."

"No, it's not!" she cried into his shoulder. "I drove Cheyenne to this. This is all my fault!"

Levi hooked a finger under her chin and gently turned her head up so he could look in her eyes. He used the pads of his thumbs to brush the last of her tears away as he cupped her face in his hands. "It's not your fault."

"Yes, it is! I should've been there!" Ryleigh closed her eyes tightly as more tears spilled over her lashes. "I let my pride get in the way. Cheyenne needs me! She's always needed me, and I pushed her away. It's all my fault!"

Levi's eyes filled with compassion as he planted a soft kiss on her forehead and brought her to his chest again. "It'll be okay."

* * *

I struggled against Jet as he closed the door behind us, but his grip was so tight that his knuckles were turning white. I didn't want to see Jet or hear what he would say, and I wished that Levi had left me alone long enough for me to jump. Even if I hadn't died upon impact, perhaps I would be hurt enough as punishment for the person I had become. Now I wouldn't even get the chance to find my freedom.

"Let me go!" I screamed when I couldn't break his hold.

Jet brought me to the dining table and sat in one of the chairs as he took hold of my arms. I avoided his gaze when I saw his fear and sobbed quietly as I stopped fighting against him. Jet brushed some of my hair out of my face, and when he spoke his voice was thick with emotion.

"Cheyenne," he began, but he lowered his head and rubbed his eyes with his thumb and forefinger.

"I was doing you a favor," I told him stiffly. "I should be punished for what I am, and I wanted to jump so that you and I could be free of a burden."

301

A GIFT OF GRACE

Jet met my gaze and I saw tears for the first time since I'd met him. "Cheyenne, please don't say that. You are not a burden to me."

"I'm a heathen," I argued as I sniffed my nose. "I can't take it, Jet. No matter what I do I'll always be a heathen. I need to be punished."

Jet shook his head as he cupped his hand under my chin. "There's always grace. You don't have to die to be free. You mean so much to me, and I don't want to lose you."

I closed my eyes as I sank into the chair opposite from him. "I want to believe you, but I'm scared." I stared at my hands in my lap and swallowed the ball of tears in my throat. "I've thought about dying many times before, but I didn't do anything because I thought Ryleigh needed me. Ever since she began working more, I started having more of these thoughts."

"Ryleigh still needs you, just like I do. I know you've been hearing a lot of bad things lately, but they are not true."

"How do you know?" I asked as I finally looked at him. "What they're saying is true. Ryleigh does work in a saloon, and my pa was a gambler who left his family. Mama was a bitter woman, and I don't even know what I am."

"People are quick to judge," Jet answered softly. "They don't always look at the big picture. I see what kind of person you are, Cheyenne. Don't let their bitterness consume you. Let God take this from you."

"I don't know how," I whispered as I hung my head again. "I don't know if God would even want me."

Jet leaned his elbows on his knees. "Yes, He does. Everybody sins and we all deserve to be punished, but God gives grace and forgiveness to those who ask Him for it. He wants you to come to Him, just like I want you here."

"Jet, I…" I looked into his eyes and saw the depth of his care. My worries of Jet leaving seemed to fade and I finally understood that he was telling me the truth from the first night I saw him in the saloon. I threw my arms him as I buried my face in his neck. "Please help me," I sobbed into his collar.

Jet wrapped his arms around me and held tightly as he began to pray. "God, please heal Cheyenne. Let her know she is a beautiful young woman

302

made in Your image, and that You have a purpose for her on this earth. Let her know she is loved and that she can be healed by You."

I listened to his voice as I clung to him, and I began to feel a sense of peace lift the burden off my chest. *Please forgive me,* I prayed in my mind. *I'm sorry for the things I've done, and I want to be free. Please forgive me, God.*

Several minutes dragged by as Jet held me, and at last my tears faded. I swallowed hard before I pulled away from Jet and wiped my eyes with the tips of my fingers. "I prayed to God," I told him quietly. "I asked Him to forgive me."

Jet gave me a soft smile. "God never abandoned you. You are safe here, Cheyenne."

"I know," I said slowly as I nodded. "I'm sorry for all I've done to you."

"I forgive you," Jet replied with a smile.

I studied him closely before I took a deep breath. "You're not going to leave, are you?"

Jet shook his head as he looked me in the eye. "No, I'm not. I care too much for you and your sister to leave you alone. Both of you girls need to know you are safe."

"I'm not used to feeling safe," I answered. "We've always been alone, and it felt like I had to protect myself when Ryleigh wasn't around."

"I know, but that's in the past. Right now, you have a God who can give you His forgiveness, and you've got an uncle who is willing to help you."

I was silent for a moment. "Do you think you can help Ryleigh, too?"

Jet frowned slightly as he looked away. "I'm afraid your sister is surrounded by fear. I'm not sure how to reach her, but I've been praying that she will come home. She has some issues that she's dealing with right now."

Worry pulled at the corners of my heart as I studied him. "Jet, is Ryleigh okay?"

Jet didn't look at me as he sighed. "I'm not sure. I know there's something on her mind, but I don't think she wants to tell anyone about it. I don't know how to approach her about it, either."

"Well, knowing Ryleigh, she's too proud to admit she needs help," I said quietly. "If there's something bothering her, she'll keep it to herself unless it becomes public."

"That's what I'm afraid of," Jet mumbled. He looked up at me and smiled, though it never reached his eyes. "All I can do is keep praying for her, like I do for you." He rose to his feet and cupped a hand around my chin. "I keep praying that both my girls know they are loved."

~NINETEEN~

I stared at the picture of Ryleigh and me on the nightstand and squinted against the dark to try to see her youthful features. I couldn't stop thinking about what had happened earlier that day with Jet. I finally accepted him as a part of my family, especially when I allowed myself to trust him completely. I thought back to Ryleigh and wished that she realized she needed family, but I understood her desire to be alone. Still, Jet revived my concern for my sister, and something didn't feel right. The clock chimed twice in the living room, and I rolled over to stare at the ceiling. Perhaps a short walk in the night air would calm my mind enough to allow me to sleep a few hours before school.

Sighing softly, I pushed myself off the mattress and crept toward my door. I opened it enough to poke my head in the hallway and glanced toward Jet's room. His door was closed, and the house was silent. I tiptoed into the living room and slipped out the front door quietly. Once on the porch, I inhaled the night air deeply and glanced up at the stars in the sky. The moon was large, and it cast a silver glow on the land.

I stuffed my hands in my trouser pockets as I stepped into the street. The only sound that penetrated the night came from the saloon as the piano music drifted through the air. The occasional guffaw of male voices also rang out, and I worried where Ryleigh would be at that hour. I absentmindedly strolled down the boardwalk until I reached the livery. Climbing on the corral fence, I watched the stars shimmer above the desert. The orange sand almost looked blue at night, and I found peace in the difference of scenery.

Suddenly, I heard a small noise behind me and glanced over my shoulder to see a lone silhouette slip out of Doc Harding's office door. I frowned as I jumped from the fence and lowered to the ground so as not to be seen. My frown deepened when I recognized the red hair of a boy, and I wondered what Chad was doing inside of the doc's office. Chad scampered in the shadows as he headed toward the north, and I felt the urge to follow him. I kept my distance as I trotted down the road that led to Chad's house a little over a mile out of town. Even from a distance I could see him glancing over his shoulder as if he expected someone to be following him.

After almost half an hour of sneaking, I saw Chad disappear into Mr. Dillon's barn and soon after the orange glow of a lantern shine in one of the windows. I ran silently down a little hill until I reached the barn and pressed my back against the wood as I inched closer to the window to peek inside.

"Are you sure nobody saw you?" a low voice asked. I crouched low to the ground when I reached the window and held my breath.

"Of course, I'm sure!" Chad chided in his voice that still pitched. "I promise you that nobody was even in the street when I came out."

The sound of fabric rubbing against fabric met my ears and I frowned with curiosity. "Well, as long as you're sure," the older boy mused, appearing to have a cautious tone in his voice. "Here's the ten cents I promised. Do you think you can get more before the week is out?"

"Oh, sure! No problem. The doc keeps it in an unlocked drawer at night, and I know how to get in. It won't be hard." Chad cleared his throat and chuckled. "But, uh, I was wondering something."

"What's that?"

"Shouldn't we, y'know, split the stuff? I mean, that way it don't go to waste."

Curiosity fueled me to inch closer to the edge of the window, and I peeked above the sill to see Chad facing a boy who I did not recognize. The older boy held a velvet sack in his hands, and when Chad had begged for whatever was inside of it, he curled his lip in a growl and pulled the drawstring to open the pouch. Chad's hand flew out as the older boy timidly dropped white powder into Chad's palm. I narrowed my eyes and watched as they both dumped a handful into their mouths and swallowed, then hurry back to the pouch for more. When the older boy licked the last of his second handful, he looked up and saw my shadow from the corner of his eye. He almost dropped the pouch in his haste to hide it.

"I thought you said nobody followed you!"

Chad whirled around at the boy's comment, and his eyes grew large. "Cheyenne!"

Noticing that I wasn't welcome, I hurriedly bounced to my feet and turned to run back up the hill, but Chad had exited the barn and wrapped an arm around my neck painfully as he tackled me to the ground. "What are you doing here?" Chad snarled with an elbow in my throat. "And who did you tell? Is your uncle behind you?"

I narrowed my eyes and shoved his arm away. "I never thought you'd slip this low, Chad. Stealing morphine from Doc Harding? Don't you know that stuff is dangerous?"

Chad narrowed his eyes and aimed a shaking finger at my nose. "You stay out of it! This is my business. Mine, and Jared's! We're only taking what we need and doing what we have to. Who knows where you are?"

"Nobody!" I shouted. "I was taking a walk and I saw you. Jet thinks I'm still in bed. Now let me up!"

Jared joined Chad and folded his arms over his chest. "How do we know we can trust her?"

Chad turned to glare at me, and I returned it with my own. Surely Chad remembered the good times we'd shared, and my loyalty to him and his heists. Surely, he wouldn't still be angry with me about my absence. My courage began to fade when his lip curled into a snarl.

"She can't be trusted. She listens to strangers more than she helps her friends."

My jaw dropped as I felt my heart pound. "Chad!"

"Then what do you suggest we do?" Jared questioned as he glared at me menacingly.

Chad narrowed his eyes and stared at me with an angry glare that made my skin crawl. "We'll make sure she don't talk."

He raised his fist and smashed it into my jaw at a high rate of speed, and I saw purple and green stars dance in my eyes. I shook my head to clear the spots and shoved him on his back with my forearm in his chest, but my advantage didn't last long before Jared wrapped his arms around my middle and threw me off Chad as if I was no more than a bundle of weeds. Both boys pounced on top of me and began to sink their knuckles into my stomach. I kicked and yelled as I tried to get up from under them, but they kept shoving my head back against the rocky ground. After what seemed hours, their punches, scratches, and bites lessened until they pulled themselves off me and grinned down at the work they had done to my body.

I glared at them as I coughed and curled my lip in disgust. "I thought we were friends, Chad," I growled when I could breathe.

Chad's grin grew as he folded his arms over his chest. "You're so stupid, Cheyenne. Did you honestly think that after you betrayed me, I would want to save your sorry hide? Ha!"

I pushed myself into a sitting position. "I told you I hadn't betrayed you! Jet just wouldn't let me get out of his sight."

"And yet here you are. Alone." Chad scoffed and shook his head. "You're a horrible liar, too. He probably sent you to find out a way to hang some crime on my head. But I'll tell you what. If you ever mention this morphine to your blasted uncle, I will personally come to your room and beat you until you lose your mind."

I groaned in disgust as I slowly pushed myself to my feet. "If you think I'm scared of you, you're wrong."

Like a snake striking its prey, I snatched the pouch out of Jared's hand and quickly stuffed it into my trousers pocket. Both boys leapt on top of me as they clawed at my pocket to grab the drug, and we all tumbled to the ground. Vile words that I had only heard in the saloon flowed out of Chad's mouth as he succeeded in ripping the pouch out of my pocket. Jared pulled my hair to shove me back as he reached for the morphine. After regaining my footing, I jumped toward Chad in hopes of pulling the pouch away from the boys. Chad dropped the drug during the tug-of-war, and all three of us dove for the pouch. I reached it first and took off running with both boys chasing after me and shouting curses that made my skin crawl. I whirled around the corner of the barn and disappeared into the nearest horse stall. The mare I hid behind snorted nervously as Chad scrambled around the corner like a mad animal. I ducked under the horse's neck, and she reared back on her haunches as a scream rumbled in her throat.

"Get back here, Cheyenne!" Chad shouted as he raced after me.

Jared tried to corner me as I exited the stall, but I ducked around his claw-like hands and raced deeper into the dark barn. I could hear the boys running noisily behind me, but when I ran out of the door I stopped in my tracks and felt the blood drain from my beaten face. Chad was the next to come out, followed by Jared, and both slid to a halt when they came face-to-face with the orange glow of a lantern. Mr. Dillon narrowed his eyes as he inspected each guilty face.

"What's going on here?" he demanded in a voice that made my knees quake.

"We were just trying to take morphine away from Cheyenne, Pa!" Chad explained in a rush. "She started taking it last week, and we were trying to get her to stop!"

My jaw dropped as I whirled around on my heel. "Chad!"

Jared nodded and pointed to the pouch in my hand. "She was taking quite a bit of the stuff when we found her. She won't give it up."

I turned to face Mr. Dillon and squirmed under his suspicious gaze. "That's a lie! I was trying to take it away from Chad! I swear I didn't even know he was stealing Doc's morphine!"

Mr. Dillon extended his hand, palm up. "Give me the pouch." I hesitated, but gently laid the pouch in his hand. He snatched it and jerked his head toward the house. "Everybody get inside."

Chad glared at me but obeyed his pa as we began trudging up the hill to their house. Jared's eyes darted back and forth as if trying to find a direction to run, but Mr. Dillon straightened his back and positioned himself behind us so that neither of us could flee. When we entered the house, Mrs. Dillon was wrapped up in her shawl and was watching us with suspicious curiosity. The door finally closed behind us, and I suddenly wished I had stayed in town rather than running on impulse after a person I thought to be my friend.

Mr. Dillon tossed the pouch on the table and pointed to the chairs. "Sit down. Now." We all obeyed in unison with our heads hung low. Mr. Dillon walked around the table to face us and laid the lantern down. "I'm not sure who to believe, but morphine is an extremely dangerous drug. I suspect all y'all are guilty, and as far as I'm concerned I ought to line y'all up and take my belt to your backsides." His eyes landed on me. "What are you doing here so late?"

I swallowed hard and ducked my head even lower. "I followed Chad."

Mr. Dillon folded his arms over his chest and scowled. "Does your uncle know you're out here?"

I hesitated, then shook my head.

"Why does your neck look bruised?"

I glanced at Chad out of the corner of my eye, and he had a glare pressed deep on his brow. "I fell while I was running," I lied. I didn't want to get Chad into more trouble than he was in already. "I ran into a tree branch when I wasn't looking."

There was a moment of silence, then Mr. Dillon ripped his hat off the peg by the door and shrugged on his jacket. "Chad, you stay here with your mother until I get back. I'm takin' these two kids home to their parents."

Chad growled and crossed his arms over his chest as he watched us follow his father into the front yard. Within a few minutes, Mr. Dillon had his wagon hitched up to two horses and guided them down the two-rut road to town. I sat across from Jared, who stared at me with an angry glare. Awkward silence followed us all the way to the outskirts of town, and by the time we pulled past the livery the sky was beginning to lighten with the morning rays of the sun. Mr. Dillon guided his team to the western edge of town where my house was located and pulled to a stop. I stared at the front of the house with anticipation and bit my lower lip when Mr. Dillon walked up the steps. I cautiously rose to my feet and made my way to the end of the wagon and jumped to the ground right as Mr. Dillon knocked on the door three times. After a few moments of silence, the hinges squeaked their protest as Jet swung the door open.

I cringed when I saw him and tiptoed to the edge of the porch, but Mr. Dillon grabbed my arm and pulled me up beside him. "I'm not sure who's at fault, but I found your niece with my son and the boy in the back of my wagon behind my barn. They had morphine."

Jet's eyes flung to me, and they were filled with an emotion I couldn't read that made my knees quiver. I swallowed hard and ducked my head so he couldn't look in my eyes. Mr. Dillon didn't say another word as he turned and climbed back in his wagon and drove away with Jared in the bed. I swallowed hard as I studied my toes.

"I can explain."

"What were you doing?" Jet snapped in a low voice. He looped his fist around my shoulder seam and pulled me into the house as he closed the door behind us. "I thought you were still in bed, and then I hear you were caught with morphine! What were you thinking?"

"I promise, Jet, this ain't what it looks like."

"Then why won't you look at me, Cheyenne?"

I swallowed hard and cautiously raised my head to look him in the eye.

He studied my face and his frown deepened. "What happened to your neck? And your clothes are filthy."

"I got into a fight... again. I promise, Jet, I didn't mean for this to happen."

"Do you thrive in scaring me half to death? I thought you were past all this, but then I learn that you are out late at night again!"

I lowered my head as I inched away from him. "I'm sorry, Jet. I-I... I couldn't sleep and thought a walk at night would help. That's when I saw Chad with the morphine, and I was trying to take it from him and that other boy before they hurt themselves. They beat me up, and... and I promise I only followed Chad after I saw him leave Doc Harding's office."

Jet crossed his arms over his chest. "You know I don't trust that boy. Why did you follow him?"

"Because..." I shook my head and backed away. "I don't know. I got curious, and I wanted to know what he was doing. I didn't think he would turn on me like he did."

"Did you eat the morphine?"

I frowned as I wrapped my arms around my middle. "No. I may be a lot of things, Jet, but I wouldn't take drugs like morphine without a reason."

Jet walked a few feet away as he ran his fingers through his hair. "Yesterday you wanted to kill yourself, and now I learned that you were around a very dangerous drug. You could have overdosed on it and died before anybody found you."

My bottom lip quivered when I realized the reason for his anger. "I'm sorry, Jet. I'm so... so sorry."

I buried my face in my palms and sank onto the wooden bench in the living room. I could not remember a time that I regretted more than that moment. I expected Jet to continue to scold me, but instead I felt his arms wrap around my shoulders as he brought me into a gentle embrace. I returned his embrace as I clung to his shirt. For several long minutes, Jet held me tightly until I felt his shoulders begin to relax. At last, he pulled me away from him and cupped my face as he looked into my eyes.

"Cheyenne, I'm sorry, too. I love you, and I was afraid you were trying to hurt yourself."

I looked away and exhaled a shaky breath. "I'm in big trouble, ain't I?"

Jet lowered his hands as he sighed. "I don't know."

"I'm gonna be sent away, ain't I?"

Jet's jaw tightened as he ran his fingers through his hair again. "I don't know."

I nodded and glanced over my shoulder to watch the sunrise. Normally, I would have been filled with contentment to watch such a beautiful dawn, but now it made my insides curl in a tight ball. If Chad and Jared both claimed I was guilty of stealing the morphine, I would have no way to prove the truth. The only witnesses were three teenagers with at least two who had a reputation with trouble. I bit the inside of my cheek as I hung my head in shame.

"I don't want to leave," I whispered under my breath.

Jet glanced at me and patted my shoulder. "I know. I just don't think I have much choice in what the sheriff decides."

I closed my eyes and nodded. "This is all my fault."

Jet shook his head as he curled a finger under my chin to lift my head. "No, don't say that. We'll figure this out together, one way or another."

I slowly rose to my feet and cringed when my sore muscles shouted their retort. I walked to the window to watch the town of Sunset wake up for the day. My eyes landed on Mr. Dillon's wagon as he headed back to his ranch. As he passed our house, he cast an ugly glare toward the front door as if to curse it himself. I shuttered and felt my heart sink lower to the floor. Jet came behind me and laid a hand on my shoulder.

"Cheyenne, if you have nothing to be ashamed of, there is no reason for you to be afraid."

I glanced up at my uncle and slowly nodded. "I suppose I should get ready for school. It'll start here in a few hours."

* * *

Walking to the schoolhouse that morning felt more like walking up the stairs to a gallows pole. As I ascended the steps, I glanced around the school yard as the young children played a game of tag and the older students read their books or talked with their friends. I saw Steven next to the flagpole, and he raised his hand in a greeting. I tried to offer a small smile as a response, but quickly hung my head and ducked inside.

Mr. Hyndman was the only one in the school, and he was writing some passages on the chalkboard when I quietly slid in a seat at the back of the room. Mr. Hyndman must have heard me come in, because he turned around to see who might have entered the building. When his eyes landed on me, he raised an eyebrow in surprise.

"Cheyenne. I wasn't expecting you to be here this early."

I bit my lip and lowered my head. "Good morning, Mr. Hyndman."

"You've had a good weekend, I presume?"

I scoffed at his statement and folded my arms over my chest. "I've had better."

"I'm sorry to hear that. At least you are here and ready to learn."

I nodded as I played with a loose string on my trousers. Mr. Hyndman cleared his throat when he realized I wasn't in a talkative mood and walked to the front door to ring the bell. As the students filed in begrudgingly, my eyes caught a few harsh sneers from several of the pupils. Penelope was one of the first students to come into the room, and when she saw me, she wrinkled her nose as if she caught whiff of a scent she did not like. Chad avoided my gaze as he shuffled to his seat, but I knew he had seen me. Part of me was nervous for the morning recess to come for fear of what he would do to me.

Mr. Hyndman walked to the front of his desk and read a Bible verse before he acknowledged his pupils. "Good morning! We're going to start today by reading some passages. I'll call on each student to read what I have written on the board. When I call your name, I want you to stand and read what I ask you."

I watched as Mr. Hyndman called a young boy's name, who rose and began to read from the passage on the chalkboard. Several minutes dragged by, and I began to count the seconds ticking on the clock on the wall rather than listen to the other students. About ten or fifteen minutes passed when I heard the front door open quietly behind me. Curiosity caused me to glance over my shoulder, and my stomach turned to mush when I saw Sheriff Hodgkinson and his deputy enter the schoolhouse. I quickly whirled around to face the front and pretended to be engrossed in the passage another student was reading.

The sheriff stopped beside me and removed his hat as he made eye contact with Mr. Hyndman. "I beg your pardon for interrupting this morning," Sheriff Hodgkinson said in a gruff voice. "I am needing to speak with a few of your pupils, Mr. Hyndman."

Mr. Hyndman glanced at his students as they turned in their seats to look at the sheriff. "Very well. I trust you will be quiet while exiting."

Sheriff Hodgkinson nodded as he placed his hat back on his head. He motioned to the deputy, who quietly walked to the bench where Chad was sitting. The sheriff tapped my shoulder and crooked his finger as a command to follow him. I glanced up at him, then slithered out of my seat in defeat. I kept my head down to try to ignore the curious glances from the students as I followed him outside. Without saying a word, Chad and I followed the lawmen across the street to the jailhouse. My knees began to shake when he opened the door for us to file inside. Chad crossed his arms over his chest when he passed me and seemed to purposely step on my toe. I grimaced but bit my lip to keep from saying something I would regret.

When my eyes adjusted to the dim light, I noticed Doc Harding sitting in the corner of the room, and Jared stood beside him. Sheriff Hodgkinson skirted around us to sit at his desk and slapped his hat on a corner of his chair while his deputy positioned himself behind us to block escape. The sheriff picked up a dark red, velvet pouch that was laying on his desk and toyed with the drawstring. I immediately recognized it as the morphine pouch that Chad had the night before.

"Now," the sheriff began with a no-nonsense tone. "I realize some of you children have been in this room before for many other confrontations, but this is the last straw. Do you recognize this?"

Chad glanced at Jared and shook his head. My eyes narrowed in their direction, but I refused to speak.

When no one answered, Sheriff Hodgkinson motioned to Doc Harding. "This pouch is the property of the Doc, here. He keeps an extremely dangerous medicine in here that I am sure you have heard of before. This medicine is very addicting if used incorrectly, and it should never be in the hands of a few mischievous teenagers. I know at least two of you children are used to telling lies," he stated, glancing between me and Chad, "but we do not have time for deceptions this morning. I want each of you to tell me the truth about what happened last night, and don't you even think about leaving out one little detail."

I glanced between the sheriff, Doc Harding, and the boys standing next to me. I found myself hoping Chad would tell the truth and accept the consequences of his actions, but there was a little sliver in my brain that told me he would be the first to throw me into the fire. Chad snaked a glance in my direction and curled his lip.

Sheriff Hodgkinson exhaled sharply as he leaned his elbows on the desk.

"Look, we can either do this the hard way, or we can do this the easy way. I would appreciate it if you young'uns would take the initiative for once and own up to your mistakes. Do I have to separate y'all to make you talk?"

Chad shifted his weight to one leg as he turned a glare at me. "It's just like I told my Pa last night. Cheyenne first stole morphine about a week ago, and when I found out about it, I tried to take it from her. She was crazy last night for the stuff, and she attacked me and Jared when we tried to take the morphine away from her."

Anger burned in my veins, and I felt my face turning bright red. "That is a bald-faced lie, Chad Dillon! You were doing the dirty work for Jared here. He was paying you to get the morphine for him, I saw you two! I was trying to get the morphine away from you!"

The sheriff raised an eyebrow as he leveled his eyes on me. "Is that so, Cheyenne? When Mr. Dillon came in my office this morning, he told me you had this pouch in your hands when he found you in his barn."

My knees began to shake, but I lifted my chin to keep from showing my fear. "I took the pouch from Chad."

The sheriff nodded unbelievingly as he jabbed his hand toward me. "You have quite the bruise on your neck this morning, and it looks fresh. How did you get that bruise?"

I hated the tone of his voice but ignored the temptation to insult the lawman. "It's because Chad and Jared beat me up after they found out I overheard them. Chad put me in a chokehold and tackled me to the ground. They didn't want me to tell on them that they took the morphine."

Jared shook his head and shoved his hands into his trousers pockets. "No, sir. I never hit women. My pa would take a switch to my backside if'n I ever got the notion to do that."

Sheriff Hodkinson's suspicious eyes landed on the tall boy. "You know, Jared, you are pretty new to our area, and I would hate for you to get mixed into the wrong crowd. I couldn't help but notice you are hiding your knuckles. If you did get in a fight with Cheyenne, your knuckles would have bruises from hitting her. May I see your hands?"

Jared hesitated, but slowly took his hands out of his pockets and approached the sheriff with his palms facing upward. The sheriff took hold of his hands and turned them around so that he could examine the boy's knuckles. The sheriff raised his eyes to scorch Jared with his gaze and cocked his head to the side.

"You were saying about fighting women?"

Jared lowered his eyes to his knuckles. "Well, sir, I may have lied a little bit ago. You see, when Chad tried to take the pouch from Cheyenne, she sorta turned into an animal. Like a badger. She tried to attack him, and I had to keep her from tearing into Chad. She started hitting me, and I hit her back to try to get her to stop."

My jaw dropped. "That is *not* true!" I marched over to Doc Harding and stuck a finger in his chest. "*You* believe me, don't you? Do you think I would steal morphine from you?"

Doc Harding looked at me with sad eyes. "Cheyenne, I saw someone leave my office last night. The person I saw was not as big as Jared, and I know you have been stealing things lately."

My eyes started welling up with tears as I spun around to face the Sheriff Hodgkinson. "You gotta believe me. I went for a walk and saw Chad leave Doc's office. I followed him and I... I..." I could tell halfway through my explanation that the sheriff had already made up his mind. I glanced over my shoulder in time to see Chad hide a sneer.

Sheriff Hodgkinson rose to his feet and nodded at his deputy. "I think I've heard enough explanation. Boys, you may go. Thank you for your honesty."

My lip curled in disgust as I watched the two cheats leave the office. The worst that I feared had come true. My friendship with Chad was only so that he could get things from me, and he was more than willing to sacrifice the truth for his freedom. I couldn't understand how the swine could get so lucky.

When they left, the sheriff motioned for me to come to him. I shook my head and refused to move. "What are you going to do to me?" I demanded.

The sheriff frowned as he marched around his desk and grabbed my arm in a tight grip. "As of right now, you are in my custody. Your uncle has been

317

warned, and this little stunt of yours was the last straw. There is a stage that will be coming to town tomorrow, and you will be on it. I'm sending you to a boarding school where they will make you behave."

My heart sank to the floor. "No, please don't do this! Give Jet a second chance. I want to stay here!"

Sheriff Hodgkinson dragged me to the back of the jailhouse and tossed me into an empty cell. He locked the barred door before I could pick myself off the floor and slipped the key into his pocket. "You are in my custody. I can do whatever I please to you. Besides, a boarding school is just what you need for your behavioral issues. They will teach you how to become a true young woman. You will be much safer in a boarding school than you are with that uncle of yours."

Without waiting for my reply, the sheriff marched back to his desk and left me alone in the cold cell. I glanced around the room and noticed how suffocating it was behind the bars. My heart began to race as panic overtook my anger at being betrayed. I hadn't wanted to believe Jet that Chad was bad for me, but his latest trick proved that I couldn't trust the boy.

I slid down the brick wall until I sat on the dirty cot in the corner of the cell. My destiny was now schedules, lessons, and rules. I buried my face in my hands as tears began to roll down my face. It was strange how life turned out. Just a few weeks ago, I wanted Jet to leave Sunset and be alone. I thought back to the day before when Mrs. Wilkes had uttered those hurtful words to me after church. I wanted to end it all then and be free of the chains that bound me to this town. I had been so upset when Levi interrupted my plan for freedom, but then I realized that Jet was the father figure I never had and always wanted.

I pictured my uncle in my mind and wondered how he would react when he realized what happened. He had shown me that he didn't want me to leave, and I worried about how he would feel knowing my fate was out of his control. I blamed myself for my distrust in Jet and knew that Jet's actions in the last few weeks were only to protect me. He had mentioned to me time and again that he was not in Sunset to hurt me, but I had been too stubborn to listen. I was determined that I would drive him away, and

I had refused his kindness for fear of betrayal.

"I'm a fool," I muttered to myself as I wiped my tears away. "If you had just listened to Jet, you wouldn't have been framed by Chad and be in this daggum cell."

I pushed myself to my feet and walked to the barred window. If I stood on my tip toes, I could see the shack that Jet made into a house. Jet had brought life into our dreary world, and I was a fool to not see it until it was too late. I wrapped my arms around the metal bars and wished I were strong enough to tear them apart. I had spent many hours in this cell, but now I realized how the prison seemed cold and dark. I had thought I was trapped in a prison before, but nothing compared to the desperate feeling I felt in my chest.

I glanced at several of the townspeople as they darted to and from stores, and felt my heart sink a little lower when I picked out Levi in the crowd. I hadn't given much credit to the young stable boy, either. He had always shown me a kindness that I ignored. Even before Jet came to town, Levi never ratted me out for the devious acts I committed against him, and he had always been kind to Ryleigh and me.

Levi looked up from the street and met my gaze. A shiver raced down my spine when I saw the concern in his eyes as he redirected his path to lead to the barred window. I immediately dropped back on the cot and pretended I hadn't seen him, but before too long I heard his voice filter in through the bars.

"Cheyenne? Is that you?"

Stifling a groan, I rose on my toes so that I could look over the windowsill at Levi. "Yeah, it is."

Levi's frown deepened as he searched my gaze. "What did you do to get in there?"

I sighed as I laid my head against the metal bar. "Nothing. I was just at the wrong place at the wrong time."

"What do you mean? Surely the sheriff has a reason to keep you behind bars."

"That's the thing," I scoffed sarcastically. "He thinks I've been stealing

319

morphine from the Doc because of what happened last night, but I swear I never touched the stuff. Now he's keeping me in here until tomorrow when he can send me to a boarding school."

Levi raised his eyebrows as he lowered his gaze. "Why would the sheriff accuse you of something like this?"

I wiped the leftover tears off my cheekbones as I lowered myself on flat feet with my back against the wall. "Because I went out to Chad's place last night, and Chad had the morphine. I tried to take it away from him and got caught holding the drug."

"Does Jet know?" Levi asked on the other side of the wall.

"He knows about last night. I don't think he's heard of the current news yet. But I don't know how much good it would do if he did know. Sheriff Hodgkinson claims that he has custody over me now, and that's why he's sending me to the boarding school."

Levi was silent for a few moments. "Jet deserves to know. I'll go tell him."

"It's not going to do any good," I argued, but did not hear a response from Levi. I peeked over the windowsill again to see Levi trotting across the street toward the feed mill and sighed. "The sheriff ain't gonna release me."

* * *

Levi dodged around a few passersby and hurried to the back of the mill where Jet should be filling sacks with grain. After scanning the small crowd of workers, he spotted Jet in the corner as he was tying one of the sacks. Levi darted around a few of the other men before he stopped beside Jet.

Jet looked up from his sack and frowned with confusion. "What are you doing here, Levi?"

Levi lowered his voice as he threw his thumb over his shoulder. "I just spoke to Cheyenne."

Jet noticed the concern in Levi's voice and straightened to his full height as worry etched a few lines along his brow. "She's supposed to be in school. Did she sneak out of class?"

Levi shook his head firmly. "That's what I thought at first. She's in a cell at the jailhouse. I thought she tried to skip school and got in trouble, but then she told me about getting caught with morphine. I guess the sheriff is the one that got her out of school because Cheyenne told me he was sending her to a boarding school in a few days."

Jet's eyes hardened as he listened to Levi's explanation. His jaw clenched so hard that Levi was certain one of his teeth would break. Instead of saying a word, Jet spun on his heel and marched toward the street. Anger as hot as a boiling river of lava flowed through Jet's veins, and he could feel his face burn with the extra blood. Jet's vision had narrowed to one tunnel as he strode down the street toward the jailhouse. With a powerful surge of energy, Jet leapt up the steps leading into the jail and barged through the wooden door without knocking.

Sheriff Hodgkinson glanced up from a stack of papers on his desk, and when he saw Jet his mouth turned into an upside-down grin. "I figured it would only be a matter of time before I saw your face in my doorway," he snarled without a greeting, "but I had hoped it would be a bit longer yet."

"Where is she?" Jet bellowed, forcing his feet to stay planted on the floor.

"I have to keep an eye on her now. I have put her into my custody." The sheriff rose from his desk as he calmly slid his fingertips into his pockets. "She has a tendency to cause too much trouble, and I, for one, would like to enjoy a few days of peace and quiet."

Jet began to see purples spots in his eyes as he forced himself to breathe calmly. "Locking her in a cell is too much, sheriff," Jet answered in a low voice.

"I need to know where she is at all times," the sheriff argued with his eyes narrowing to slits. "Besides, she was found stealing morphine this time."

"You don't know it was her!" Jet yelled as he advanced a few steps. "What evidence do you have against her?"

"This is none of your concern, Mr. Douglas," the sheriff snapped, his own face beginning to turn a shiny shade of pink.

"I'd say it is! I am her uncle, and I have been taking care of her for the last few weeks. I have a right to know what evidence you have against her!"

"Mr. Douglas, she is none of your concern. I let you have your time of fulfilling a fantasy you promised to a dead man, but I've got a job to do. She has disturbed the peace far too long, and I will not put up with anymore of her nonsense!"

Jet threw a hand in the air. "Just like that, huh? You're gonna turn your back on her just like that? What Cheyenne needs is people who do not bash her character and who do not tell her she won't amount to much! The reason she has been misbehaving is because of ignorant, selfish people such as yourself!"

Sheriff Hodgkinson cocked his head to the side. "I would watch my words very carefully if I were you, Douglas. I won't have you insulting my town like that."

"And I won't have you insulting my niece like you have!" Jet closed the distance between him and the sheriff and leaned over the desk until their noses almost touched. "Show me the evidence that convicts Cheyenne of stealing morphine. I want to know what kind of evidence is keeping her behind bars!"

The sheriff narrowed his eyes as he folded his arms over his chest. "I received word from a very reliable source that she was caught holding the pouch of morphine."

"Did anybody ever see her take the pouch?" Jet defended. "Did anyone ever see her take the morphine?"

"Doc Harding mentioned that he saw the silhouette of an adolescent sneaking around his office last night," the sheriff snarled. "I'm afraid you've lost this battle."

Jet stuck a finger into the sheriff's collar bone. "You said Doc saw an adolescent, not Cheyenne. How does he know he pegged the right adolescent?"

"Douglas, I've had just about enough of your—"

"Sheriff, even the most hideous of criminals deserve a trial. It is their right! At least look into this a little more and see if you have the right person behind those bars!"

"Mr. Douglas!" the sheriff shouted at the top of his lungs. "That's enough! Based off her history, I would not put it past Cheyenne to do something like this, and I will not risk having her do it again by releasing her to you!" He leaned in close so that his nose was just inches away from Jet's face.

"You had your chance, and you messed it up. She is leaving on the next stage to the boarding school, and they will do to Cheyenne what you could not."

Jet ground his teeth together until his jaw muscles ached. Without saying another word, he spun on his heel and marched out of the room. Levi had been standing on the boardwalk just outside of the jailhouse but had raced to stay in stride with Jet when the tall gentleman burst from the office door.

"What are you going to do now?" Levi asked in a quiet voice.

"There's got to be a way to stop such vulgar accusations! I know Cheyenne is innocent, I just can't prove that! Wouldn't even give her a chance to defend herself. How dare he take her away from me?"

Levi stepped in front of Jet to make him stop walking. "Mr. Douglas, anger ain't gonna solve anything. Maybe Sheriff Hodgkinson ain't gonna give Cheyenne a chance, but that doesn't stop us from ordering a town meeting. We can gather the town together and see what they decide. If they think this decision was rash, then we could bring it to the sheriff and see if he will at least delay her departure to the school until we can figure something else out."

Jet forced himself to look Levi in the eye. "And what if they are all like the sheriff?"

Levi lifted a shoulder in a shrug. "Then at least we tried. Mr. Douglas, there's not much else we can do."

Jet ran his fingers through his tangled hair and sighed. "I just can't stand the thought of her going to a boarding school. All they would do there is take away her personality, and that is not what she needs at this time in her life!"

"Then let's give this a try. We'll need to talk to the Reverend to see if we can use the church for the meeting, and then spread the word to everyone."

"Who would come if we told them it was for the welfare of Cheyenne?" Jet argued.

Levi hooked his thumbs in his pockets. "We don't have to tell them what the meeting is about. We could just tell them that there is an important town meeting to discuss the welfare of one of its citizens. Cheyenne is a citizen of Sunset."

Jet sighed as he ran his hand down his face. "Fine. I'll go find the Reverend Atkins, and then we'll start spreading the word."

Levi nodded and turned to head back to the stables.

Jet blinked the grime from his eyes as he headed toward the mercantile. He remembered the first time he had seen Cheyenne. She had stolen a sweet bun from the shelves and tried to get away with the crime. As much as he loved his niece, Jet couldn't help but think the town only remembered the Cheyenne in the past and did not know the true Cheyenne. The people also harbored feelings against his oldest niece. His heart hurt when Doc Harding told him of Ryleigh's unexpected pregnancy, but he couldn't find a solution to help her. He knew he was losing both of his nieces, and he felt helpless. Jet had ridden into the small town of Sunset with the expectation that both girls would welcome his help and would be relieved that they would not have to fend for themselves any longer. Then he realized just what they had to put up with, and he understood their hesitation for help. The only kind of help they received resulted in more pain. Jet would do anything to turn back the clock and to be there for his nieces all those years ago when their mother died, but he could only try to fix the mess they were in now.

Grabbing hold of the door handle, Jet entered the mercantile and was greeted by Adele's sweet smile. "Good morning, Mr. Douglas!" she greeted in a chipper tone. "It is a mighty good pleasure to see you."

Jet slowed his steps as he looked into her kind eyes. "Morning, ma'am. I was wondering if the Reverend might be around?"

Adele noticed the seriousness in Jet's voice, and her smile vanished. "No, but if you wait just a moment, I'll fetch him."

Jet nodded and concentrated on slowing his breathing as she disappeared through the back door. Several minutes later, the Reverend appeared with an ashen look on his face. "Mr. Douglas," he greeted solemnly. "Adele said you wanted to see me?"

Jet nodded and exhaled slowly in hopes that the action would calm his heartrate. "Reverend, I came to ask to use the church for a meeting." Jet quickly filled the Reverend and his wife on the events that had happened in the last few hours.

When Jet had finished his explanation, the Reverend shook his head in sorrow. "That poor girl. Yes, you are more than welcome to use the church. The care for Cheyenne should be in the hands of people who love her. We will use it once school is out this afternoon."

Jet nodded somberly. "Much obliged, Reverend."

~TWENTY~

Ryleigh glanced both ways before she stepped out into the dusty main street. It was near the two o'clock hour, and the town was abuzz with activity. Ryleigh clutched her package of goods as she scurried across the street. She had purchased some soft linen and new sewing needles. She wasn't good at being a seamstress, but she decided that the little one needed a gown whenever it was time for the arrival. The thought of sewing something for the baby warmed her heart, and she was looking forward to creating the simple gown. She might even try to form tiny socks if there was enough material.

Ryleigh dodged a pile of horse dung as she skipped up the boardwalk in front of the saloon. Eventually, she would have to find her own place. An upstairs room in a saloon was no place to raise a child. She pushed the thought aside and nudged her way through the double doors. She hadn't stepped far inside when she smelled the familiar scent of cigar smoke. Ryleigh threw a glance over her shoulder at the poker tables and turned over chairs. No customer sat waiting over there. Shrugging her shoulder, she headed to the stairs when her eyes caught sight of an overbearing man leaning against the bar. Her feet froze in their tracks as her eyes met the beady, rat-like holes of her employer.

When Overhaul saw her enter the building, he pushed away from the bar and adjusted his big belly over his belt buckle. He looked rounder than the last time she had seen him, but his menacing glare and strong jaw still sent shivers down her backbone. Clearing her throat, Ryleigh forced her feet to move again and shot a glance at Violet, who was favoring her jaw with her fingertips. She refused to look at Ryleigh.

Ryleigh returned her gaze to Overhaul and lifted her chin. "I did not realize you were back," she managed to say around a small quiver in her throat.

Overhaul ran his lustful eyes down her figure before returning his gaze to her face. "I got back an hour ago. I was just talking to my girls about how the place ran while I was gone." He took a step toward Ryleigh as he lifted an eyebrow. "Violet, here, has been telling me how she's been working twice as hard since I left. It seems that someone hasn't been pulling her weight around here."

Ryleigh's eyes flicked across the room to Violet again. The young woman ducked her head and moved her hand away from her jaw to reveal a purple and green bruise that was beginning to form. Ryleigh's breath caught in her throat when she realized the intent behind Overhaul's otherwise casual conversation. She clutched the package in her hands as she spun on her heel to exit the saloon, but Overhaul moved surprisingly fast as he blocked her escape. Quicker than a bolt of lightning, his hand shot out and smacked against her jaw. The impact of the blow caused her head to bounce back and neck to pop. Before her eyes quit rolling in her head, Overhaul grabbed a chunk of her hair and jerked the package out of her hands.

"Where have you been?" he bellowed. His voice made her ears ring.

"I had to get material to mend some of my clothes," she lied. Her knees began to quake underneath her, and she hoped that Overhaul would not sense her fear.

Overhaul pulled her head back until her neck hurt as he glared deep into her eyes. "Have you forgotten that you work for me?"

"I have not forgotten!" she snapped. "How can I forget such a foreboding vulture as that?"

Overhaul backhanded her cheekbone as he shoved her toward his office. Her hip smacked against the corner of a table, and she grimaced in pain. "I'll teach you where your loyalty should lie!" Overhaul bellowed as he closed the distance between them.

Ryleigh tried to dodge his hand, but Overhaul pushed her inside the office in front of him with little effort and slammed the door. Ryleigh grabbed the edge of his desk to steady herself and whirled on her heel to face her boss. Overhaul pounced in front of her with claw-like hands. Before she could scream for help, she felt his slobbery mouth encase her lips in a stomach-churning kiss. His hands were controlled by his lust as he grabbed the neckline of her dress and pulled hard. The material bit into her skin as the seams began to pop, and Ryleigh tried to pull away from him. Overhaul pinned her against the wall as he attempted to drown her in his saliva. Ryleigh reeled back her fist as she prepared herself to smash it against his skull or back. When her punches did not seem to faze him, she bit his lower lip until she tasted the iron of blood.

Overhaul yelped and backed away enough for her to skirt around him. Ryleigh had just taken hold of the doorknob when she felt Overhaul's rough fingers bite into her shoulder. She cried out in pain, but soon saw purple stars when Overhaul punched her jaw. Ryleigh flew across the room and bounced her head against the farthest wall. Overhaul acted like a wild dog who had just cornered a baby rabbit as he twisted his fist in her dress again. She cringed when she felt his touch against her chest as he pulled the material from her body.

Ryleigh let out a small gasp of fear when she felt the dress fall to the floor to expose her bloomers and camisole. Overhaul's eyes took on the unhealthy glow of a predator when he saw the smoothness of her neck, and he shoved her against the wall as his fingers curled around the lacey neckline of her camisole. Ryleigh prepared herself to feel the material bite into her skin again and squinted her eyes shut as she anticipated the sound of ripping material. When she noticed his hesitation, she opened her eyes to see that he had stopped his attempt to shame her and was now staring at her swollen belly with large eyes.

Fear settled deep in Ryleigh's chest, and for a moment she thought she could not breathe. She felt the desire to run but could not make her wobbly legs move. She suddenly felt sick to her stomach and wanted nothing more than to protect the little one inside of her. Slowly, Overhaul raised his eyes to meet hers, and an evil, lopsided grin exposed his yellow teeth. Without saying a word, he snaked his hand behind her head and tangled her hair in his fist. He yanked the door of his office nearly off its hinges in his haste to drag her out into the open.

Ryleigh glanced at the bar as Overhaul dragged her by her hair toward the swinging double doors. Violet met her gaze with a mournful expression before she covered her face in her hands. Tears welled in Ryleigh's eyes as she reached behind her head to pry Overhaul's sausages from her hair. A groan escaped Ryleigh's throat when one of the double doors smacked the left side of her temple, but she did not have time to dwell on her pain.

As if she were nothing more than a sack of feed, Overhaul threw Ryleigh into the street. The same pile of dung she had evaded earlier was now creating a stain on her undergarments. Ryleigh slowly raised her head and felt a bright red blush creep up her neck when she noticed several of the townspeople venture out of stores to see what the commotion was all about. She quickly averted her gaze and tried to slink away when Overhaul's voice stopped her in her tracks.

"Come and see this *fine* specimen, folks!" he shouted at the top of his lungs. She could hear the vengeance in his voice and felt her hopes die. "Come see how grand this pathetic creature is. I am gone for a few short days, and when I come back, I find that she's been hiding a pregnancy!" Overhaul slowly began to laugh, and his laughter burned her ears. "She lives a lie even among her own scum."

Ryleigh's eyes began to fill with tears as she listened to the words from her employer. She slowly raised her gaze to see the judgmental faces of a few shop owners, and to hear a few snickers from rude men. She tried to hide her body behind her arms as she listened to Overhaul's boisterous laughter and felt the first tear tumble over her lashes as she glanced down at her growing stomach. She could hear a few scoffs from some of the women nearby. Suddenly, something warm and wet landed on her cheek, and she glanced up to see that Overhaul had just sent a spit wad her way.

A shuffling sound behind her caused her to glance over her shoulder. Levi Hendershot draped a jacket around her shoulders as he knelt to urge her to her feet. Positioning himself between Ryleigh and Overhaul, he ignored a derogatory term Overhaul snarled at the duo. Levi led Ryleigh out of sight of the townspeople behind the stables and stood in front of her.

Ryleigh refused to look at him as she clutched the edges of his jacket in a death grip. When she didn't respond, Levi wrapped his arms around her and pulled her to his chest. For a moment, Ryleigh buried her face in his shoulder and gave into her tears. Levi held her until Ryleigh realized that she had tarnished his reputation enough. Pulling away from his embrace, Ryleigh backed away from him and tried to hide her middle from his view.

"It's true," she snapped in a rush. "I am pregnant, and I don't know whose child I'm carrying. It could be some out-of-town stranger who has already moved on for all I know!"

Levi looked into her eyes softly. "Did he hurt you?"

Ryleigh gasped a sob as she hung her head. "I deserve what he did to me and more. I'm worse than scum!"

Levi reached out to cup her elbow gently. "You are not scum, Ryleigh. Let me take you to Doc Harding. If Overhaul hurt you, I want to make sure you and the baby are okay."

Ryleigh fixed her full gaze on Levi. "It doesn't matter. Overhaul knows about my condition now. I know what he will do."

Levi noticed the quiver in her voice and how she appeared so weak and frail. "I won't let Overhaul hurt you. He may know that you are with child, but he won't lay another finger on you. I'll make sure of it."

Ryleigh pulled the edges of the jacket tighter around her. "You are a good man, Levi, but I insist. If the people in this town see you with me, it would ruin your reputation."

"Never mind my reputation, Ryleigh. I would much rather make sure you are taken care of than in the hands of that monster in the street."

Ryleigh hung her head in shame. "I am no better than 'that monster in the street.' I might even be worse."

Levi curled a finger under her chin as he raised her head so that he could look into her eyes. "I am not upset at you. I care about you too much to let you get hurt."

Ryleigh frowned as a few tears landed on her eyelashes. "Why?"

"Why what?"

"Why do you care about me?" Ryleigh snapped. "I'm unwed and pregnant. If I go out there in the street again, I will be mocked and humiliated!"

Levi shook his head. "Ryleigh don't listen to them. Don't listen to yourself, either. You are not worth any less than those people in the street. By the looks of you, I'd say Overhaul hurt you, and I want to make sure you and the baby are fine. I'm going to take you to Doc Harding, and I don't care what people think."

Ryleigh allowed the last of her tears to fall over her lashes before she hung her head in shame and nodded. An overwhelming surge to protect the small woman in front of him swelled in Levi's chest. It took every ounce of strength for him to keep his anger at bay. No woman should be treated the way Ryleigh had, and he wanted to make sure it would never happen to her again. Wrapping an arm around her shoulders, Levi led her through the shadows to avoid the accusing eyes of the townspeople. Within a few minutes, they appeared at Doc Harding's office, but the door opened before Levi had a chance to knock.

The Doc glanced into the street as he ushered the two in his office. "Take her back here," the doctor instructed as he led the couple to the back room and motioned to the examination table.

Levi made sure Ryleigh was stable, then turned to go back out in the street toward the mercantile. By this time, Levi's anger had resided and was replaced by concern. Ryleigh was a strong woman, and that had been one of the many attributes that attracted him, but even he began to wonder what would happen to her now. Every person had a caving point, and he would hate if something worse would happen to her.

Levi bounded up the stairs of the mercantile and meandered through the aisle of goods until he got to the ladies' dresses. As he looked through the dresses, his ears perked at the sound of Ryleigh's name. He glanced toward the front and saw two women huddled together as they whispered not-so-quietly.

"Such a shameful thing," one woman said rebukingly. "That family had it coming. They never go to church, and God punishes those who refuse to obey him."

"I don't even know if that sow is even sorry that she's pregnant," the second woman responded. "It's such an embarrassment to see such sinful behavior in our very own streets! Why, I'm only glad my children were not around to see such disgrace!"

Levi ground his teeth together as he plucked a simple brown dress from the rack. He brushed past the two women and laid the dress on the counter, ignoring the accusing stares they cast his way as he paid for the piece of clothing. As he turned to exit the store, his eyes locked with the frowning women and he tipped his hat more out of duty than politeness.

"Ladies," he managed to utter before he marched out of the mercantile.

The people in this town did not understand the hurt of the two Douglas girls. They were quick to cast judgments, but never lent a listening ear or a helping hand. Weren't Christians supposed to be the first to offer help to a struggling, hurting lamb? Levi tried to shake the angry thoughts out of his mind as he strode back to Doc Harding's office. Ryleigh was still behind the curtain when he entered the office, but the Doc was leaning against his desk. Without saying a word, the Doc took the dress from Levi's hands and turned to the curtain as he quietly cleared his throat.

"Ryleigh?" the Doc spoke softly. "Here, put this on."

A small, white hand cautiously appeared from behind the curtain as she accepted the dress the doctor handed to her. Levi's eyebrows dipped downward with worry for the young woman. When Doc Harding backed away from the curtain, Levi motioned for the Doc to come closer.

"How is she?" Levi asked, concern filling his voice.

Doc Harding sighed as he shoved his hands in his pockets. "The baby is fine. And physically, she is too. She just has a few bruises and scratches that will heal over time, but I'm afraid she is too damaged in here." The doctor motioned to his heart.

Levi nodded and turned when the curtain parted to reveal Ryleigh. She looked even paler, and several dark bruises were beginning to form on her face. Her hair had been brushed and pulled back into a simple braid, and the brown dress fit her modestly. She refused to look at Levi as she stepped into the room like a wounded kitten.

"Thank you for the dress," she said barely above a whisper. Her eye lashes were still wet from the tears that were shed.

Levi longed to envelope her into an embrace, but he refrained. A broken woman like Ryleigh would need her time to heal, and he did not want to rush her into anything unwanted. "You're welcome," he muttered as he lowered his head.

Ryleigh's bottom lip quivered as she hugged her middle. "How am I going to face Cheyenne?" she whimpered, the sound of tears thick in her voice.

Doc Harding lowered his gaze. "You may not have to."

When Ryleigh's head bounced up, Levi realized she must not have heard about Cheyenne's verdict. "What do you mean?" she asked, worry starting to infiltrate her voice.

The Doc quickly explained Cheyenne's situation, and with each word that was said, Ryleigh's head sank lower and lower. Levi's heart seemed to stretch thin as his mind raced with a solution to help both sisters, but no idea came to fruition.

Ryleigh rubbed her eyes once the doctor finished his explanation. "I can't believe that Cheyenne would do such a thing." She turned those big, blue eyes on the doctor, and the hurt Levi saw in them made him feel like he was nothing more than vermin. "Cheyenne may have caused a lot of trouble in the past, but I don't think she'd ever steal something as dangerous as morphine."

The Doc shrugged as he frowned. "She told me she was innocent this morning, but I don't know what to believe. She's done things in the past that made it seem reasonable that she would take the drug."

Ryleigh inhaled slowly. "But are you sure she is the one you saw?"

Doc Harding's shoulder slumped as he slowly shook his head. "I've asked myself that very same question. I know I didn't see a large person take it, but it was in the dark. I just don't know any more."

"And they are going to take my sister away from me just because of this?"

Levi cringed at her tone. "We're trying to fight it, Ryleigh. Jet and I have organized a town meeting at the church this afternoon once school lets out. Jet tried to talk sense into the sheriff, but he won't listen. We were going to try to convince the townspeople to consider what is best for Cheyenne, and at least delay her departure until we can find out who really stole the morphine."

Ryleigh glanced at the clock on the wall and dropped her hands to her side. "School should be out by now. I want to go to this meeting. Cheyenne is more important than my pride." She glanced toward Levi and extended her hand to him. "Please, come with me."

Levi accepted her hand and tucked it in the crook of his elbow as a silent encouragement. He felt her death grip on his shirt sleeve as they headed for the door, but he laid his hand on hers to calm any fears she felt. Within a few minutes, Levi, Ryleigh, and Doc Harding quietly entered the church. The meeting had already started, and Jet stood at the front of the church with the Reverend by his side.

"All I am asking is that you consider what is best for Cheyenne," Jet pleaded in a strong voice. "I realize this is out of my control, but I ask that you think if your own children. Would you rather send them away to a school where they feel all alone or would you rather a child stays with a family that loves them?"

Sheriff Hodgkinson, who stood with his arms crossed in the corner of the room, scoffed loudly. "Douglas, that tyrant in the jail cell has caused more damage than a tornado."

Jet locked eyes with the sheriff. "Yet when a tornado destroys a town, don't the townspeople unite to clean up the mess and rebuild? I agree that Cheyenne needs help, but I don't think a boarding school is what she needs."

Mr. Shepherd rose to his feet. "Mr. Douglas, I told you that first day you brought the brat into my stable that no man could tame her. You've tried for several weeks, and with no success. I am tired of her destroying my belongings, and I would be glad to be rid of her until she can learn better manners. As far as I'm concerned, there is nothing more to discuss."

Ryleigh began to fidget at Levi's side, and he patted her fingers to reassure her. She glanced up at him, then back to the pulpit where her uncle stood.

Jet locked eyes with Ryleigh, and his gazed softened. "I understand my nieces may have irritated you. When I talked to my brother before he died, he had mentioned they were in trouble. They are my family, and family helps each other in times of need. I am not willing to give up on them, and if I have to, I will take my nieces with me when I leave this town. If you are determined to send Cheyenne away, please let her stay with me and we will leave."

Levi stiffened when Mrs. Wilkes glanced over her shoulder and narrowed her eyes at Ryleigh. A deep red colored Mrs. Wilkes' face as she abruptly rose to her feet and aimed an accusing finger toward Ryleigh. "Mr. Douglas, you may think your nieces are innocent, but have you noticed what has happened to the eldest? She is the most despicable being in this building!"

Mrs. Wilkes stepped into the aisle and stormed to stand inches away from Ryleigh's nose. "Why, this harlot has entertained the vilest of men in the most disgusting of ways, and now she has humiliated the town by carrying some stranger's offspring! I have mentioned before that she is no better than a cow fit for breeding, and she just proved what kind of animal she is. She is the most disgusting piece of trash that I have ever seen, and I would imagine God is set to punish her as she deserves! Why, even the Good Lord would be appalled to have such a wretch in his church!"

Jet took a step down from the pulpit as his face turned a bright red. "Mrs. Wilkes, I am not oblivious to Ryleigh's condition, but I don't judge her for past mistakes! I came here to help both of my nieces, and when I learned of Ryleigh's pregnancy, I became more determined to protect them!"

Mrs. Wilkes whirled around to cast the same glare toward Jet. "Mr. Douglas, your nieces deserve to be punished. And you ought to be ashamed of yourself! You are determined to defile the House of God with a drunken, drug-addicted monster and this lowly scum that belongs in hell!"

Ryleigh bit her lip as she pulled her hand out of Levi's grasp. Levi turned to catch her, but she disappeared through the church doors. Anger boiled in his veins as he spun on his heel to face Mrs. Wilkes.

"How dare you play God!" he scolded, his voice radiating off the church rafters. "It is not up to us to judge a person's heart. And what better place for a broken person to be than in church? I thought Jesus came to save the sinners. How is my sin any different than Ryleigh's?"

Mrs. Wilkes pursed her lips into a snarl. "You came to this town and got a decent job at the livery. You never let your shadow fall on the saloon until that disgusting woman lured you into her trap! I've seen you two together a lot lately. How do we know this baby isn't yours?"

Levi felt his heart rate quicken as he glared into the hateful woman's eyes. His chest heaved as he attempted to calm his anger, and at last he spoke in a low voice. "We are all unworthy of the love and forgiveness God offers freely, and I will *never* turn someone away from the church doors. I can't stop you from spreading rumors that I am the father of Ryleigh's baby, but if judging me makes you back off Ryleigh, I would be glad to be the center of your ridicule."

Mrs. Wilkes' jaw dropped. "Do you mean to say that you admit to being the father of Ryleigh's unborn child?"

Levi glanced at the congregation as they studied him stoically. "'Judge not, that ye be not judged. For with what judgment ye judge, ye shall be judged. And with what measure ye mete, it shall be measured to you again.'"

Levi spun on his heel before anyone else could speak and slammed the door behind him as he raced down the street to catch up with Ryleigh. Her head was hanging low, and even from a distance he could see the tears rolling down her cheeks as she fled from the church. She didn't even stop when he called her name. He reached out to cup her elbow before she could evade him.

Ryleigh whirled around and tried to yank her arm away. "Please, Levi, leave me alone!"

Levi took hold of her other arm and forced her to meet his gaze. "Ryleigh look at me. You are not those things. You're a beautiful woman with a strong spirit, and you are not an animal."

Ryleigh broke free from his grasp and motioned to her stomach. "What kind of woman gets pregnant and doesn't even know who the father is? I *am* an animal. She's right. I am no better than a cow, and I am not beautiful.

How can God ever forgive me for the sins I've committed? I do belong in hell."

Levi lowered his hands as he looked into her helpless face. "Jesus died on the cross for *all* sinners, Ryleigh. All. Not just a select few."

Ryleigh shook her head violently and pointed toward the church. "If God cared about me, why do the Christians in that church tell me otherwise?"

"A church is full of people, and people aren't perfect. People judge and they say horrible things that are not true no matter what building they are in. Please don't let the words of ignorant people chase you away from the love and grace of God."

"How can I face this town now that they know I'm pregnant?" she bellowed. "How am I supposed to raise this child? I work in a saloon. A *saloon!* That's no place for a child to grow up. I don't even know if I'll be able to give birth to this baby before Overhaul is done with me. I can't stay in this town with this humiliation." She turned to leave, but suddenly whirled on her heel and looked Levi square in the eye. "Why are you so kind to me?"

Levi swallowed hard as he removed his hat from his head. "Because I love you. I think I've known for a while. I want to take care of you, and your baby, if you'll let me."

Ryleigh's eyes softened as she took a step back. "I can't give you what you want. I've... I've been with other men. I can't give you what every wife should give her husband."

"Do you really think that bothers me, Ryleigh? I would love you more than the physical. You're a strong, beautiful woman, and I would be honored to have you as my wife."

Ryleigh took another step back. "You don't even know me. If you marry me, I'll tarnish your reputation. This whole town knows what I've done, and they know I'm pregnant out of wedlock. If I marry you, you'll be judged just as harshly, and I couldn't do that to you."

"Ryleigh, for once, don't think about other people." Levi chanced a step toward her and was relieved when she didn't flee. "It doesn't matter what this town thinks of us. Maybe it won't be easy, but it would be worth it.

Tell me what you want."

"Levi…" Ryleigh glanced toward the street, but the town was empty. "More than anything, I want to be close to my sister and raise this child inside of me. In a perfect world, I would. But you saw the people in the church. They've held a grudge on Cheyenne and me, and they are not going to budge. Cheyenne is going away, and I don't even know if I'll ever set eyes on my baby." She turned back to Levi. "I've ruined my life, and Cheyenne's. Please don't ask me to ruin yours, too."

Levi felt his spirits fade in his chest, but he was too stubborn to back down. "Ryleigh, no one is going to ruin my life. I know the weight of my decision, but I still choose you."

Ryleigh managed a small smile, though it never reached her eyes. "You're a kind man, Mr. Hendershot. This world will do good if there were more people like you in it. I…" Ryleigh glanced over her shoulder and cringed when she saw Overhaul standing on the boardwalk in front of the saloon. "I need to get back to the saloon."

Levi felt helpless when he saw the smirk on the saloon owner's face. "Why do you always go back to him? He abuses you."

Ryleigh leveled the two oceans of her eyes on him. "I owe him. You may not know this, but my father was not a good man. He gambled most of the money he earned, and then some. He had the temper that Cheyenne does, and he loved to drink. Mr. Overhaul would give him loans to put food on our table, but my father would gamble with the loan money. Before too long, he was in a tremendous amount of debt, and it was terrifying. One night, he ran out on Mama. Never said a word, nothing. He just left her with all this debt. Mr. Overhaul offered Mama a job so she could pay back what we owed. She… she ended up doing the same job that I am, except she got sick from it and died. I was eleven, and Cheyenne was only six. I didn't know what to do, and Mr. Overhaul offered me a job."

"But surely that debt is paid off now. You've been working in the saloon for eight years."

Ryleigh opened her mouth as if to say more, but her lips soon closed again. Without saying another word, Ryleigh turned and slowly made her way

338

back to the saloon. Levi's skin crawled at the way Overhaul wrapped his arm around her waist before they walked in the saloon together. It pained him to watch her walk inside the building with a man who mistreated her so badly, but he couldn't force her to marry him. Levi hung his head and felt his heart splitting in two as he trudged past the saloon toward the livery. He had wanted to show Ryleigh how much he had come to care for her, and not just for her outward beauty. She longed to be a wife and to raise a family, but her head was so full of lies that she believed that dream was impossible.

Levi glanced over his shoulder when the piano began to play again inside of the saloon. "Please, God. Show her that I love her."

~TWENTY-ONE~

P*link!*

The sound of rain as it hit the bucket in the other room seemed to be a blast from a gun. I gathered my knees to my chest and watched as the shadows of the tree limbs danced on the cold floor. In the other room, Sheriff Hodgkinson was snoring loudly. I glanced at the wall and counted the bricks again. It had been several hours since I was put in the cell, but it felt like an eternity. The sheriff made sure I did not have any visitors, and even the town seemed unusually quiet. With a sigh, I pushed myself to my feet and stared out of the barred window. Sunset had been a home to me, no matter how much I hated it in the past. It did not surprise me that I would be blamed for a crime I didn't commit, but it still hurt.

I watched the rain come down in sheets, but then my eyes found a shadow hurrying down the street. My eyebrows knit together slowly when I realized the shadow was a boy, and when he got closer, I recognized Steven. He saw me peering out of the window and changed his course toward me.

"What are you doing here?" I hissed when he was in hearing range.

"I had to come talk to you," he answered as he peered up at me. "I don't know how much you've heard."

I frowned. "What are you talking about?"

"It's about you and Ryleigh. Your uncle tried to organize a town meeting to put you back in his custody this afternoon. Pa and I went."

I rolled my eyes and sighed. "Let me guess, they decided to send me to the school anyway."

Steven nodded slowly. "Yeah, but that ain't what I had to tell you. Your sister came to the meeting. Did you know she's pregnant?"

"Pregnant?"

The word seemed foreign to me even when I said it. Ryleigh? Pregnant? I shouldn't have been surprised, but the unsettling feeling still weighed heavy in my chest. I glanced over my shoulder in the direction of the saloon, even though all I saw was a brick wall. My self-pity was suddenly replaced with concern for Ryleigh. I recalled only one other time when a girl from the saloon got pregnant. Overhaul had taken her out of town, and when she came back, she looked defeated and miserable. A week later she was found hanging from the neck in her bedroom.

I turned back to Steven. "Where's Ryleigh?"

"I don't know."

"What do you mean, you don't know?" I snarled impatiently. "Where did she go after the meeting?"

Steven bit his lip. "Things sort of got heated between Ryleigh and Mrs. Wilkes. Mrs. Wilkes said some awful things to her, and she left. Levi got mad and tried to defend Ryleigh, but then Mrs. Wilkes accused him of being the father to the baby. He never denied it."

I frowned. "Why wouldn't he defend himself? I know Levi. I've never seen him go into the saloon. He's a respectable man. There's no way he could be the father."

Steven shrugged. "I'm just telling you what I saw. He chased after Ryleigh, but I saw him later at the stable and he wasn't happy. But, Cheyenne, Ryleigh's gone."

I gripped the bars in a death grip. "What do you mean, gone?"

"I stayed in town to help Pa pick up supplies, and I saw Mr. Overhaul hitching a wagon with her sitting in the front seat. She looked pale, and she had several bruises on her face. I couldn't sleep, and I had to let you know."

My heart plummeted to my toes. "Why didn't you tell Jet, or your own pa?"

"My pa told me it was none of my business, and I couldn't find your uncle." He frowned when he noticed my complexion. "Are you okay?"

341

Bile rose in my throat and I felt like vomiting. "No, I'm not okay. I need to get to Ryleigh." I slammed my palm against the brick wall and growled in my throat. "But I can't get out of this prison!"

Steven licked his lips, then glanced over his shoulder at the furious storm. Without saying a word, he darted toward the boardwalk and disappeared from my view. My chest felt heavy with anger when I saw him leave, but a moment later I heard the creak of the front door as it opened. I jumped off the cot and squinted in the darkness toward the office. Lightning lit up the room, and I saw a glimpse of Steven as he tip-toed toward the sleeping sheriff.

"What are you doing?" I hissed in a hushed tone. "You'll wake him up and we'll both be in trouble!"

Steven lifted a finger to his lips to shush me, then reached for the keys that were perched on top of some paperwork on the desk. The papers shuffled, which broke the rhythmic pattern of the sheriff's snores. Steven froze and watched as the sheriff shifted in his chair. A few moments later, the rhythm of the loud snores resumed. Steven exhaled softly and crept to my cell with the keys in his hand.

"You need to get help," he whispered as he stuck the metal into the keyhole and unlocked the cell, "and you can't do anything while you're in here."

I opened the cell door and stared at him. "If the sheriff finds out that you're the one who helped me escape, you'll get your hide tanned for a week."

Steven shrugged. "It's not right how this town is acting, and I think Ryleigh's in danger. If the sheriff knows you're gone, maybe he'll organize a search party to get you back before the stage comes. Maybe by then, you could lead them to Ryleigh."

A small smile spread across my face. "You're brilliant, Steven."

He returned my smile, then shoved me toward the door. "You better get before the sheriff wakes up."

I nodded and crept out of the jail silently.

A loud thunderclap shook the sky when I slipped through the door, and I winced as I saw the streets flood from all the rain. I ground my teeth together with determination and stepped into the mud. Overhaul was a greedy man, and he would not want Ryleigh bearing a child. Men paid for young tarts without baggage, and a baby was baggage in his mind. No doubt Doc Harding would not perform the needed surgery to rid the baby, so Overhaul would be making a trip to Phoenix where a doctor would be willing to perform such a deed for a large sum of money.

My heart pounded loudly in my ears as I ventured to the edge of town. I had never left Sunset before, but I knew which road would lead me toward the city. I brushed some of the rain from my eyes just as more fell in my vision, and I huffed a loud sigh as I started to run down the road. Just the thought of Ryleigh having to endure such a procedure built a wall of emotion in my chest. Tears started to mix in with the rain, and my blurred vision caused me to trip in the mud. I fell to my knees with my hands sinking in the mud in front of me.

"God," I cried, though I could barely hear my voice above the thunderous rain. "What are You doing? Hasn't Ryleigh been hurt enough?"

No one answered my questions, and all I could hear was the roar of rain. I raised my head and saw nothing but streams of water as it created puddles in the mud. Who was I kidding, trying to catch up to Ryleigh on foot in a rainstorm? They were in a wagon and had several hours head start. Even if I did catch them, what would I do? I was still considered a nuisance, especially to Overhaul. Rage burned hot in my veins when I thought of the saloon owner. He enjoyed playing my family like puppets on a string. If my father didn't have a gambling problem, he wouldn't have created such a debt that was left as a burden to the rest of his family.

I pushed myself to my feet again and forced myself to jog through the mud. Throughout time, all the members of the Douglas family let Clyde Overhaul push them around and allowed him to be the puppet master. I suppose the trend had to stop somewhere.

"Please, God," I muttered under my breath. "Please let me reach Ryleigh. Please let this end."

* * *

Shouts from the street jarred Jet out of a fitful slumber. Swinging his boots to the floor, he bounced off the mattress and didn't bother to smooth the wrinkles in the quilt. Within a few strides, he had reached the front door and yanked it open in time to see Sheriff Hodgkinson marching toward the little house. Jet felt his upper lip curl in disgust as he leaned his forearm against the door jamb. He had dealt enough with the law officer, and he was not in the mood to hear more of his squabble. The sheriff sloshed through the mud in the streets until he could clamber up the wooden steps of the porch.

"What in tarnation are you doing, Douglas?" the sheriff snapped in a no-nonsense voice.

Jet let his eyelids close halfway as he sized up the lawman. "I'm getting up to enjoy the nice morning. Things always smell fresh after a good rain."

"That ain't what I mean, and you know it."

Jet raised an eyebrow. "I beg your pardon?"

The sheriff poked Jet in the collar bone as he took a step closer. "Where is she?"

"Who?"

"Don't you be playing smart with me, Douglas!" the sheriff snapped. "I should arrest you for interfering with my authority!"

Jet couldn't help a small smirk that tugged at the corner of his mouth. "Are you saying that Cheyenne escaped?"

Sheriff Hodgkinson's jaw muscles worked so hard that Jet thought for sure a tooth would break. "All I'm saying is that she couldn't have gotten out of that cell without help, and I'm tired of you getting in my way!"

Jet lowered his arm and stepped on the porch, forcing the sheriff to back up a few steps. "As much as I would have loved to take my niece out of your cell, I had nothing to do with her escape plan. I rarely am involved in her mischievous schemes. She's tricky, and you of all people should have known that. After all, didn't you tell me you used to handle her before I came to town?"

The sheriff narrowed his eyes. "Move aside, Douglas. I have to search your home."

"No, you don't," Jet argued as he jabbed a finger in the sheriff's chest. "You would be trespassing if you did, and I would hate for the good people of Sunset to see you charged with such a crime. Cheyenne is not here, and I don't have any idea where she went. Knowing her, she figured it was more important than to wait for the stage to take her to that boarding school of yours."

The sheriff sized up Jet before backing down the steps. "If Cheyenne is not back by noon, I'll charge you with kidnapping."

Without waiting for another response, the sheriff turned his back to Jet and marched through the mud back to his office. The small crowd that followed the sheriff began to disburse slowly, except for one teenage boy who had been hiding in the back. Jet recognized him as Cheyenne's friend, Steven. The boy glanced over both shoulders before he crept closer to Jet.

"Sir?"

"What's the matter, boy?" Jet asked in a soft tone.

"I know where Cheyenne went, and she's going to need help. I told her I'd give her a few hours head start but knowing what she's up against…. She just can't do this alone."

"Slow down, son. What are you talking about?"

Steven bit his lower lip before leaning in even closer to whisper. "I saw Overhaul take Ryleigh away in a wagon, and I was afraid he would do something to her. I helped Cheyenne escape so that she could try to stop them. I was sort of counting on the sheriff organizing a search party for her, but he just seems happy to sit on his rump and wait until he can throw you in jail."

Jet felt his heart sink to his boots as he listened to Steven's explanation. "Where did they go?"

Steven jutted his chin toward the east. "That way. I'm betting they're off to Phoenix to have one of them fancy doctors fix Ryleigh."

Jet jumped into the street and patted the boy on the shoulder before he ran to the mercantile. If Cheyenne went to confront Overhaul, she would be needing more than a hot-tempered uncle. Fifteen minutes later, Jet, along with the Reverend and Doc Harding, hurried to the livery to organize their own posse. Levi was barely mucking out the stalls when they entered the stable and Jet wasted no time in jerking the pitchfork out of his hands.

"Levi, I need you to open up the tack room for us," Jet commanded.

Levi glanced behind Jet at the two gentlemen. "Where are you going in such a rush?"

"I think the girls are in danger, and we're going to find them."

Worry instantly etched itself across Levi's brow, and he glanced over his shoulder toward the office. "I'm coming, too," he answered firmly as he turned to lead his own horse out of the stall.

The small crew of men quickly saddled their steeds and were soon on the road out of town. As they rode in a smooth canter, Jet began to pray that his nieces were in no harm. Both of his girls had their faults, and the last few weeks were not easy, but Jet could not stand to think that either one of them were in physical pain. He had seen that Cheyenne was beginning to heal and trust again, and he hoped that her progress would not be altered during the events of the next few hours.

Jet scanned the land in front of him for tracks, but all he could see was mud and left-over puddles from the rain. "Please let us find them," Jet prayed under his breath as he continued to scan the landscape.

Jet chanced a glance at Levi from the corner of his eye. He had known for a while that the young stable boy had developed feelings for Ryleigh, and he thought it had been good for Ryleigh to see how a gentleman treated a woman. All Ryleigh knew about men was that they used her for their own pleasure and humiliated her in front of the whole town. She had made a mistake in her youth, but she did not deserve to be treated like an unemotional object to be tossed from owner to owner. Levi had shown her that she was still a woman and capable of a good life. Jet admired how Levi tried to protect her and showed her kindness. Kindness was something rarely given to the Douglas girls, and that was part of the reason for their retreat. Ryleigh had built a wall around her that even Jet could not penetrate. Somehow, Levi had been gentle and caring enough to take that wall down brick by brick.

Even Cheyenne had grown during Jet's stay. He believed that she stole and caused havoc to gain attention. For the townspeople, it was easy to ignore two orphan girls, especially when one was spending most of her time working in the saloon. Cheyenne was left by herself, and her young mind decided to cause a ruckus just so people would acknowledge her. She was a bright young woman, even if she used her smarts to get into and out of trouble. After years of fending for herself, she had created a reputation that she was a rough street kid. Jet was bewildered at her behavior when he first arrived in Sunset, but now he understood her desire to be accepted and loved. In his mind, Cheyenne was just as wounded and humiliated as her sister.

Perhaps that was the reason for them to be so close and yet so distant. Cheyenne constantly wanted Ryleigh's approval and was hurt the most when Ryleigh had retreated further in her work. And yet, Cheyenne always eyed the saloon, and her tense shoulders would relax every time she spotted her sister. Even when the sisters were torn apart, Cheyenne would stand up against Clyde Overhaul. She blamed the saloon owner for the toils her family had endured during her lifetime. Her eyes would fill with hatred every time she would see the man walk down the street. Jet understood her frustration with Overhaul, but he was nervous that her bitterness would cause her to do something drastic to save her sister.

Jet refocused his attention to the road ahead and urged his horse to trudge through the mud. *Please don't let it be too late, Lord. Help us find my nieces and put all of this to rest.*

* * *

Ryleigh moaned softly as she crawled to the edge of the wagon to peek outside. Clyde had traveled several miles before he stopped the wagon to wait out the storm. With nothing else to do, he and his men had decided to entertain themselves with her through most of the treacherous storm. Ryleigh pushed a strand of her unruly hair out of her face and ran her hand down to her stomach. Tears burned in her eyes when she felt a small tremor to reassure her that her baby was still alive. For now. A wave of several emotions settled heavily on Ryleigh's chest. She was ashamed to have sinned and become with child, and yet she felt an enormous love for the child whom she had not yet seen. She wanted to protect the little one inside of her from any harm, but grief was almost suffocating her. The reason she was in the wagon, the reason they were heading to Phoenix, was to get rid of the "burden" snuggling close in her midsection.

Several tears fell when Ryleigh once again realized what she was about to do to the innocent child. Her innocent child. How could God forgive her now? She had allowed herself to be soiled and damaged, and now she was going to allow a doctor to take the baby before full term. Ryleigh wiped her eyes as she pushed up the strap of her camisole, which was stained and ripped in several places. Very cautiously, she curled her fingers around her brown dress, which was also torn at the bodice. Her body ached from the trials of the previous night, and she wished she could shut out those memories just as easily as shutting her eyes. She pulled her dress over her head and attempted to tame her wild hair before slowly inching to the edge of the wagon.

Overhaul, Ray, and Wil were sitting around a campfire when Ryleigh slid into the mud. They all glanced her way and grinned lustfully as they sized her up. Ryleigh grimaced and walked a few feet away to a small shrub to relieve herself. She hated the person she had become. She hated that she was soiled. She hated that she was unforgiveable. Ryleigh laid a hand on her stomach again and felt her bottom lip quiver uncontrollably. How could she live if someone so innocent died? She was the one to be put to death. She had committed so many sins and did not deserve to live when someone so small, so blameless had to die. She remembered the story of the only other pregnant saloon girl she knew, and she began to understand the temptation to give up.

Ryleigh sank to her knees and covered her face with her hands as sob after sob shook her shoulders. "Please," she mumbled between cries. "Please let my baby live. I don't care if you take me during childbirth. My baby needs to live. Please, God, if you're still listening to me, please switch our roles. Let me die. I don't deserve to live. But please, let my child survive."

A small rustling sound made Ryleigh's skin crawl, and she glanced over her shoulder to see Overhaul heading her way. She lowered her hand and grabbed a rock by her boot with the intention of beating him away if he had the inclination to her hurt or her child again. Overhaul's narrow eyes slid down her figure when he reached her, and his lips curved upward to reveal his yellow teeth.

"Good morning, darlin'. Hope you slept well last night."

Ryleigh's lip curled in disgust when he laughed at his comment, but she did not respond.

"C'mon, now, honey," Overhaul uttered in a snarl. "Why don't you give me a good morning kiss?"

Ryleigh stood to her full height and held her fists at her side. "I wouldn't dream of kissing you."

Overhaul's grin dipped a little at the corners, and an unhealthy fire lit in his eyes. "Now, honey, you best be nice. I might be the only friend you got, and I'd hate for you to throw that friendship aside. Who else is going to comfort you while you recover from the surgery?"

Ryleigh's lip began to quiver with rage and grief, but she could not find the words to speak.

Overhaul lifted his hand and caressed her bruised cheek with his fingernails. "See? That's better, isn't it? You know good ol' Clyde will always take care of you."

Ryleigh began to shake and tightened her hold on the rock. "I-I don't know how taking care of someone means that you beat them."

Overhaul's fingernails began to bite into her skin as his grin completely vanished. "What kind of talk is that? You know good and well that you wouldn't have a house to live in all those years if it weren't for me! You would still be looking for a job if it weren't for me!" He leaned in close, and Ryleigh could smell the whiskey on his breath. "If it weren't for me, you would be all by yourself with no one to love."

"What do you know of l-love?" Ryleigh stuttered. Her heart pounded in her ears, and she knew that if she continued to talk in such a tone that she would be beaten. "W-who have you ever loved? You sit in your office and gloat over your money. You like having me around because I bring in more money for you."

Before she could duck, Overhaul smacked his knuckles against her jaw. The impact of the blow knocked her to her knees, and she quickly drew her fist behind her head. Without thinking of the consequences, she threw the rock with all her might and was surprised at her own actions when it smacked against Overhaul's chest. Ryleigh scrambled to get her feet underneath her as she tried to run away, but Overhaul's claws bit into her arms painfully. She felt the toe of a boot as it slammed into the back of her knee, and she crumpled to the ground. Overhaul pounced on top of her and pinned her against the earth as he clawed at her dress once again.

Ryleigh began to scream above the laughter of the other two men and tried to fight against Overhaul's hold. Suddenly, a small arm appeared behind Overhaul as it wrapped around his throat. Clyde's eyes widened as he began to choke, and he reared back for Ryleigh to scramble free. Ryleigh spun around to see what had happened, and her heart plummeted when she saw the black mess of hair that belonged to her sister.

Cheyenne tightened her chokehold on Overhaul's throat and wrapped her legs around his middle as tight as she could. After watching the rodeo for a few seconds, Ray wrapped his arm around Cheyenne as he pulled her off his boss. Cheyenne fought against his hold but was unable to free herself. Overhaul spun around and spat an insult toward Cheyenne when he recognized the soaked teen, and air caught in Ryleigh's lungs when Overhaul backhanded Cheyenne across her face. Blood instantly started pouring from her nose.

Ryleigh took hold of Overhaul's forearm before he could hit her sister again. "Please stop!" she screamed at the top of her lungs.

Overhaul flung her aside as if she were nothing more than a burlap sack. "Stay off me, you wench!" he growled in a booming voice.

"Don't talk to my sister like that!" Cheyenne yelled. She fought against Ray to no avail. "Let her go!"

Overhaul grabbed Cheyenne's arm and pulled her away from Ray as he slid his belt through the loops on his jeans. Ryleigh ran toward Overhaul to try to stop him again, but Ray took hold of her arm this time and covered her mouth with his hand. Cheyenne clawed at Overhaul's hand and kicked at him, but he dodged her attempts to harm him. Without bending the belt in half, Overhaul let the leather sail through the air with the buckle end loose. Ryleigh watched in horror as the belt slapped against her sister's body and wrapped around her. Overhaul hit her several more times with the belt, and with each blow Cheyenne's face turned redder and redder. Tears fell from her eyes, but she refused to scream.

Overhaul twisted her ear lobe when he was done beating her and bent to look her in the face as he shouted a word that made Ryleigh cringe. Cheyenne glared at him and spat blood into his face. Overhaul threw her to the ground, causing Cheyenne's face to bounce in the sand. Ray let go of Ryleigh, and she raced to her sister's side as the two men stalked back to the campfire to pack.

Cheyenne picked herself up and wrapped an arm around her ribs as she looked in Ryleigh's eyes. "Ryleigh?"

Ryleigh bit her lip as she tore a piece from her petticoat. Very carefully, she began to clean the blood from her sister's face. "Cheyenne, you shouldn't have come here." Her voice began to crack when more blood oozed from Cheyenne's nose. "You should have stayed in the jail where you were safe."

Cheyenne pushed Ryleigh's hand away as she threw her arms around her neck in an embrace. "I couldn't sit there once I found out. Steven let me out, and I came here as fast as I could. I wanted to make sure you were okay." She pushed away from Ryleigh and glanced at her swollen belly. "I wanted to make sure you both were okay."

Ryleigh held back a sob as she laid a hand on her stomach. "I'm so sorry, Cheyenne. I've made a mess of everything, and I'm so ashamed."

Cheyenne scooted closer and grimaced as she wrapped an arm around her ribcage. "I'm not mad at you, Ryleigh. You're my sister. We're supposed to look out for each other, right?"

Ryleigh lowered her head. When their mother had first passed away, Ryleigh was terrified. She had taken Cheyenne back to their shack and promised her she would let nothing bad happen to Cheyenne. The years before Jet's arrival, the girls had been strong for each other. Ryleigh always searched for Cheyenne through her saloon window at night, and Cheyenne would stop by the saloon to watch out for Ryleigh.

"I've done such a bad job at that," Ryleigh whispered as she lowered her head. "I thought I was providing for you, but I was just making the situation worse. Now look at us. I'm pregnant and don't even know who the father of my child is, and I'm fixing to get rid of my baby. And you're here. You shouldn't be here. Overhaul hates you so much…. You need to leave while you still can."

Cheyenne shook her head violently. "No, I'm not leaving without you! We're family. We need to stick together."

Ryleigh cupped her hand around Cheyenne's face in a loving caress. "But I can't stand to watch Overhaul beat you. You don't deserve his anger."

Cheyenne managed a small smile. "I'm tougher than you think I am. I haven't exactly been the perfect child, either. The way I see it, if Overhaul is beating me, then that's just a few minutes he's not paying attention to you. We'll figure out a way home. You don't have to go through with this."

Ryleigh opened her mouth to argue, but Overhaul reached their circle and yanked Cheyenne to her feet.

"I don't know how you got past the sheriff," Overhaul growled toward Cheyenne, "but your timing is always impeccable."

Ryleigh reached out to lay a hand on Overhaul's arm. "Please, let her go."

Overhaul glanced at Ryleigh, but then leveled his glare back on Cheyenne. "She'll just be a nuisance to me back in Sunset. There's a children's home in Phoenix. I'll just leave her there and then she'll never get in my way again."

Cheyenne glared up at Overhaul with a gaze that could set fire to green grass. "As long as you have my sister in your nasty pig hands, I'll never leave you alone!"

Overhaul clenched his jaw as he slapped Cheyenne. Without saying a word, he spun Cheyenne around and tied her hands behind her back. When he had finished tying the knot, Cheyenne sent a spit wad flying toward his face. Ryleigh's eyes widened when she saw the wad splash against his cheekbone, and Overhaul sent his fist flying toward Cheyenne's head. Cheyenne crumpled upon the impact and collapsed motionless in the sand.

Overhaul wiped the saliva off his face as he motioned to Ray. "Get her loaded up in the wagon. We've got a lot of distance to travel today."

~TWENTY-TWO~

A dizzying pain slowly brought me back to reality, and I cautiously opened my eyes to see Ryleigh with her head buried in her knees. I licked my lips and frowned at the taste of dried blood. I blinked against the bright sun that shown through a hole in the wagon canvas and groaned softly when my muscles ached. My ribcage was sore from where Overhaul's belt buckle slammed into me, and my wrists were burning from the rope tied tightly around them. I glanced at my sister again.

"Ryleigh?"

Ryleigh peeked up from her knees and looked at me with her sorrowful gray eyes, which were red rimmed from crying. She studied me for what felt like a solid minute before she buried her face again.

I scooted closer to her and tried to push myself into a sitting position with my shoulder. After struggling for a few seconds, I relaxed on the floor and concentrated on breathing without hurting my ribs. "Ryleigh, I can't get up. Can you help me?"

"I can't." Her voice was muffled in her skirts. "They tied me up, too."

I noticed that her arms were behind her back as well and sighed. "Are you giving up?"

Ryleigh raised her head again so she could look in my eyes. "What else am I supposed to do? I can't fight Overhaul, or he'll beat you. Maybe even kill you. He'll hunt me down if I run away. He's going to force me to get rid of my baby."

"And you're just going to let him?" I asked sternly. "Why do you always cave into him?"

"We have a debt to him, Cheyenne."

"Do we really?" I snarled. "Pa got into debt when I was just a baby. I'm almost fifteen now. Can you honestly tell me we still owe him?"

Ryleigh hesitated, then slowly shook her head. "No. Violet found his record books, and she showed me that the debt has been paid off."

I frowned. "When did you find this out?"

"Yesterday morning. Violet was cleaning his office, and she found his books in a locked cabinet."

"Then why are you still working for him?"

Ryleigh lowered her knees to expose her growing stomach. "Because I'm good for nothing else. I didn't realize our debt was paid off before Mama died. I don't think she realized it, either. Overhaul wanted me to work for him because he thought I was the prettiest girl in Sunset. He thought he could make a fortune off me, and he did. It was always his intention for me to entertain his male customers, even before Mama died. And I fell right in his trap. The night that I first became soiled... he was the first one to do it. He told me I would be nothing but a harlot and that I better get used to hands touching me. I was so ashamed. I was scared of God and his judgment, and I felt that I couldn't have a better, cleaner life. Everybody would judge a saloon girl, and they wouldn't trust their husbands around me. I would drive away business if I became a clerk or seamstress or anything else."

I bit my lip as I laid my head on the floor of the wagon. "Are you still scared of God?"

"Cheyenne, don't you see who I've become? I've entertained so many customers that I can't even count them. I'm pregnant with a child who will never know their own father." Her voice trembled. "I'm fixing to torture this child. How can God even look at me, much less forgive me? I've sinned too much. He has to hate me."

I swallowed hard. "I used to think God turned His back on us. I thought that was why Pa left us and Mama had to die. Everybody used to tell me that God was punishing our family. I just sort of accepted the fact that we would be punished for the rest of our lives." I glanced up at Ryleigh and tried to inch closer to her. "I don't think that anymore. It took me a while to change my mind. I thought Jet was just part of our curse when he first came, and I hated him for trying to help us. I think now he was an answer to prayer."

Ryleigh frowned as she looked down at me. "What makes you say that?"

I shrugged. "Well, I used to blame God for leaving us alone. I was angry that there was nobody to support us or be proud of us. Even though I hated Jet, he was always there. He stood up to some of the people in town who told him we weren't worth his time, and he was always there to listen to me, even if I told myself different. He was there for you, too. He tried to let you know you were better than scum. And then there's Levi. He loves you, you know. He defended you when people accused him of being your baby's father."

Ryleigh jumped, but I couldn't tell if it was from shock or because the wagon hit a bump in the road. "Levi did that?"

I nodded. "I used to think he was pathetic, but he helped us, too. He was kind with me even though I caused him more trouble than—"

"What does this have to do about God? How do you know you're not twisting something together?"

I glanced up at her and shrugged. "I can't prove it. I've just seen it. I don't think God ever turned His back on us. I think maybe we turned our backs on Him."

The wagon lurched again, and Ryleigh groaned. "I wish I could believe you and that God can forgive me and give me a second chance."

"I think He can." I sighed as I tried to get comfortable with my hands behind my back. "I used to think the same thing, but Jet kept telling me that God wanted to forgive me and loved me. I didn't want to believe him because it was easier to blame God for everything than to come to Him for healing. The day I tried to commit suicide, Jet prayed over me and I let God take my hurt. I still have a long way to go before I'm fully healed, but I have this peace about everything now."

Ryleigh glanced toward the front of the wagon where Overhaul and Ray sat. "I can't let my baby get hurt," she whispered almost inaudibly. She glanced down at me and nodded. "We have to get out of here. Do you think you can bite through my knot?"

I offered a tiny smile. "I can try."

Ryleigh glanced over her shoulder, then turned so her back was toward me. I pushed myself up with my shoulder and worked my teeth around the knot that bound her wrists. The rope was tough, and it tasted like lantern oil and grease. I grimaced at the taste but continued to work the knot with my teeth until it budged. After a few minutes of struggling, her rope became loose enough for her to slip her hands through. She leaned forward and untied a rope that was snug around her ankles before she turned to me and rolled me on my stomach. Once my hands were free, we both glanced toward the front of the wagon to see if we had been noticed. Both men were staring at the land in front of them. Ryleigh nudged my shoulders with her palms as we sneaked to the back of the wagon.

Ryleigh quickly loosened the canvas so we could slide through and motioned for me to go first. I shook my head. "I want to make sure you get down easily, so you don't hurt the baby," I whispered. "I can jump out once you're okay."

Ryleigh hesitated, but then nodded in agreement.

I took hold of her hand as she carefully backed outside. Since the wagon was moving, it was difficult for her to find good footing without making too much noise. She stumbled once, but I held on tightly to make sure she did not fall. When her feet were firmly on the ground, she let go of my hand and looked up to face me. Her eyes grew wide as she motioned for me to come quickly. I glanced over my shoulder and saw that Overhaul had handed the reins over to Ray and was awkwardly trying to get in the wagon bed. I bit my lip and swung my feet over the edge of the wagon. Because of my haste, I tumbled to the ground and rolled a bit until I could get my feet underneath me.

"Stop!" Overhaul shouted when he realized what was happening. "Stop the wagon!"

I ran toward Ryleigh and grabbed her hand as we raced off the road into the Arizona desert. If we could only outrun Overhaul, we would have a chance to double back toward Sunset and get help. Ryleigh tripped over a cactus plant, but with a grimace she hiked up her skirts to run even faster. Ryleigh wasn't as used to running, and she was slowing me down. I had gotten used to racing away from trouble that I had developed good speed over time, but I didn't want to let go of my sister's hand and leave her to fend off Overhaul once more. I tightened my hold on Ryleigh and tried to urge her faster.

"Cheyenne, slow down!" she pleaded. "I can't keep up!"

I glanced over my shoulder and saw Wil galloping toward us on his horse. "We can't slow down!" I shouted. "You gotta keep up!"

Ryleigh wrapped her skirts around her fist and pumped her legs even harder, but the horse was faster. Wil soon passed us and blocked our path with his horse. I slid to a stop in the sand, whirled in the opposite direction, and grabbed Ryleigh's hand as we began to run again. Ryleigh tripped during the rapid change, and she fell into the sand. By this time, Ray and Overhaul had caught up to us and were closing in the gap between us and freedom. I turned back to Ryleigh and pulled on her arm to get her to stand.

"C'mon, Ryleigh!"

"Cheyenne, stop!" Ryleigh argued softly. She looked up at me with pleading eyes. "I twisted my ankle."

My heart sank when I realized her words. I glanced at Overhaul and shuddered at the expression on his face. Part of me itched to run, but I knew I couldn't leave Ryleigh to face Overhaul by herself. All it would take is one hard hit to her stomach for Overhaul to finish her baby. I threw myself to the ground in front of her and watched the three men as they closed in around us. My lip curled when Overhaul advanced on us in those waddle-like strides of his.

"Leave us alone!" I yelled as loud as I could.

Overhaul paid no attention to my warning as he curled his fist around my collar and pulled me to my feet. "You should have never been born!" he hissed in my face. Pieces of his spittle splattered against my eye lashes. "You have been nothing but a cactus in my hide ever since I met you! I should just kill you and be done with it."

"Clyde, please," Ryleigh interrupted. "Just let her go."

"I'll deal with you later!" Overhaul bellowed. He curled his fist in my hair as he turned to march back to the wagon.

I reached behind me to pry his fingers loose, but he was stronger than me. "You're nothing but a pig!" I growled as I struggled to get my feet under me. "You talk a big talk. If you kill me, the law will be after you. You might be able to force someone to work for you, but you can't get away with murder."

Overhaul tightened his grip on me. "It wouldn't be murder. It would be an accident."

My eyes widened at his threat. I didn't like the tone of his voice. When my heart sank with fear, I began to kick his leg and punch at him to break free of his grasp. Overhaul grunted in pain as he pulled me in front of him and finally let go of my hair. The back of his hand seemed to have come out of nowhere as it landed on the side of my head. The impact of the blow caused my body to fly into the sand. Before my eyes stopped spinning, Overhaul placed a knee in my back to pin me down as he began to beat me with a stick. I tried to slither out from under his knee, but he had taken hold of my arm and shoved my fist between my shoulder blades. The harder I fought against him, the harder he hit me in the back of my legs. A harsh scream scratched at my throat when I realized I couldn't get away.

"Clyde, please stop!" Ryleigh pleaded somewhere behind me, but her employer didn't listen.

I felt a tingling sensation on my legs that made them seem numb with pain. I lowered my head in the sand as I gave up fighting him. My shoulder began to throb from his hold on my arm, and my lungs burned with each breath that I took. At long last, Overhaul threw the switch away and grabbed my arm as he yanked me up. I glared up at him through narrowed eyes.

"You think that's supposed to scare me?" I snarled, though my voice quivered with tears.

Overhaul grabbed my weakened wrist in a dreadful hold as he pulled me toward him. "You've always been too stupid to know when to back down.

You've pushed my buttons far too long, and I am enjoying punishing you."

"Is this how you treat Ryleigh?" I asked as I grimaced with pain. "You abuse her, just like you've abused me. You need to be in jail, Overhaul."

Overhaul sneered at me and a low, evil laugh rumbled in his chest. "Do you think that sheriff would put me in his cell? I own the sheriff. He only does what I tell him to, and that includes keeping you out of my way. You're quite the handful savage."

My lip curled in disgust. "You're the vilest pig of a man I've ever met! I will never stop fighting you. As long as you're free, I'll always fight you!"

Overhaul clasped his hand behind my neck as he shoved me against the wagon. I slumped against the wagon wheel and slid into the sand. The strength in my arms and legs left me, and I found it hard to even breathe without pain. Somewhere in the distance, I could hear Ryleigh's voice as she pleaded for Overhaul to stop beating me and to let us go, but I couldn't make out any response. I watched from my sandy bed as Overhaul bent to cover her mouth with his in an awful kiss before he grabbed her arm and forced her to climb in the wagon seat next to him.

I rolled on my side and grabbed onto the wagon wheel to try to pull myself to my feet, but the wheel was soon jerked out of my grasp when Overhaul urged the team into a trot. I watched the wagon ride away until it disappeared. I attempted to push myself to a sitting position, but my ribs burned, and I collapsed in the sand again. Tears blurred my vision, and I felt torn inside. Ryleigh was still with Overhaul. I began to wonder if I had made a mistake by following her alone. I should have brought Jet with me at least. What had I been thinking when I decided to follow her alone? Without a horse? I shut my eyes and covered them in the crook of my arm.

I began to drift in and out of consciousness over the next several hours. The desert was eerily quiet, except for the wind as it snarled through the sage brush and cactus plants. Every time my mind swirled back to consciousness, I noticed an agonizing pain in my ribs, legs, and head. The pain seemed to intensify with each beat of my heart, and my throat constricted with tears. *Help us,* I prayed each time I became aware of my surroundings.

I opened my eyes after fighting through the fogginess of pain and stared at the desert. The sun's orange rays darkened the sand, and long black shadows stretched over the land. *Someone has to know we're missing,* I thought to myself as I recalled Steven's words the previous night. *Wouldn't someone be coming to get us? Please, God... let someone come.*

The wind continued to whisper through the desert and toy with my curls, which blew across my face lazily. I closed my eyes and listened to my heartbeat, which seemed to be growing louder and louder by the second. Frowning slightly, I peeked through my eyelashes and noticed a wavy shadow on the horizon. In fact, the shadow split until four dancing figures came into view. I had convinced myself that dehydration was creating a mirage when I heard the unmistakable whinny of a horse. Fighting against an invisible weight on my chest, I propped myself on my elbows and squinted against the brightness of the evening. Four riders were approaching quickly, and I could recognize the black hat of the man in front.

A new burst of energy flooded my chest as I raised my hand above my head. "Jet! Uncle Jet!"

Jet pulled on his reins when he reached me and jumped from the saddle before the horse had completely stopped moving. He knelt in the sand beside me and gathered me to his chest as he held me tightly. At last, Jet gently pulled me out of the embrace and cupped my face in his hands as he looked into my eyes.

"I sure am glad to see you," he said in a low voice. He noticed the bruises on my face and frowned as he studied the tears in my clothes from Overhaul's beatings. "Are you alright?"

"I'll be fine," I answered in a groggy tone. "I tried to get him to leave Ryleigh alone, and he beat me. I tried to stop him, but I couldn't. I tried to stop him, Jet. He still has Ryleigh. I'm so sorry...." My voice quivered, and I closed my eyes when my vision began to blur.

"Shh, take it easy," he soothed as he hooked one of my curls behind my ear. "You did good, Cheyenne, and I'm proud of you." He glanced over his shoulder at the men he brought and rose to his feet. "Doc, stay here with

Cheyenne. Make sure she's fine and can travel. The rest of us will keep riding to catch up with Ryleigh."

I grabbed Jet's trousers before he could swing back in his saddle. "Please don't leave me here. I want to come with you!"

"Do as I say, Cheyenne. Let the doc look you over. We'll be back before you know it, and then you can ride with me."

Doc Harding dismounted from his horse and dug out his black briefcase from the saddlebags before he walked toward me. I dodged his extended hand and reached out to Jet. "Take me with you, Jet!"

Jet swung back up top his steed. "You'll be fine, Cheyenne. You're in safe hands now."

"I know I am, but Ryleigh is still with that pig. I want to make sure she's safe, too!"

"You'll be of no help to us if you're seriously injured," Jet pointed out before he touched his heels to his horse's haunches. The other two followed Jet and disappeared down the same road as the wagon.

Doc Harding knelt beside me and wrapped an arm around my shoulders as he pulled me into a sitting position. He propped me against a small boulder before he began to rummage through his black bag for some supplies. Doc pulled out a bronze bottle that he dabbed on the corner of a cloth and curled his finger under my chin so he could look at the gashes on my face. He washed some of the dried blood away and gently lifted my eyelids to examine my eyes. As he was looking for other injuries, he began to shake his head.

"I do not understand what possesses a man to beat up a child," he muttered under his breath.

"Overhaul ain't a man," I pointed out. "He's a monster."

Doc Harding placed a hand on my ribcage, and I grimaced. He glanced up at me and grabbed his stethoscope. He listened to my breathing for a moment before pulling out a roll of bandages. "You have a concussion, and few cracked ribs. You'll need to lift your shirt so I can wrap them. Don't try to move too fast or it'll probably hurt like the dickens."

I nodded as I pulled my shirt high enough for him to wrap my ribs. When he noticed the welts from Overhaul's belt, he frowned deeply but did not say a word as he covered them up with the white bandage. Even though I knew I was safe with Doc Harding, I found it hard to relax as I remembered Ryleigh's expression when Overhaul beat me. I was terrified of what he would do to my sister now that I wasn't around to distract him, and an ache more painful than my broken ribs weighed on my heart. I glanced over my shoulder down the road and prayed that Jet would find Ryleigh before it was too late.

* * *

The longer Jet rode, the angrier he became. He couldn't believe how a man could pound on a child so much that she could be almost unrecognizable. *And that man has been in control of your oldest niece,* he thought to himself with disappointment. He should've fought harder to help Ryleigh instead of letting her be near to that monstrous man. In eighteen hours, Overhaul had laid his hands on both of his nieces and Jet had been unable to stop him. If he had listened to Cheyenne more, maybe they wouldn't be in this mess.

Jet shook his head as if to clear his thoughts and studied the wagon tracks in the sand. Several times while riding down the two-rut road, Jet had wondered if they would be able to find his nieces. A gentle voice had continued to prod him further down the road, and when he laid eyes on Cheyenne, he felt relieved to have listened to his conscience. He glanced over his shoulder at young Levi, who had clenched his jaw ever since they found Cheyenne. No doubt the lad was just as angry, but Jet hoped Levi would have the sense enough to keep his emotions at bay. Once they caught up to the wagon, they would need their wits about them. The Reverend on the other side of Jet kept muttering inaudibly to himself, and Jet wondered if he was covering the small posse in prayer. He knew they sure did need it.

Stars had glittered the night sky before the glow of a campfire came into view. Jet reined his horse to a walk and glanced at Levi. "You alright, son?" he asked when he noticed the color drain from Levi's face.

The stable boy met Jet's gaze and gave one nod. "I'll be better knowing Ryleigh is safe."

363

Jet nodded to acknowledge the statement and began to pray for a calm mind so that he didn't immediately strangle Overhaul, but the closer they came to the campground the hotter his blood ran. When they reached the camp, Jet scanned the area to see what they were up against. Two men he had seen in the saloon were mumbling amongst themselves by the fire, but he could not see Overhaul or his niece.

Suddenly, a shrill scream pierced the evening air, and Levi lurched in his saddle. Something crashed inside of the wagon, followed by maniacal laughter that sent shivers racing down Jet's backbone. Another thud sounded, and Levi jumped out of his saddle without reining in his horse. Jet dismounted quickly and strode after Levi, even though his own worry urged him to run faster. The two men by the fire saw the men approaching and raced toward the wagon to apprehend them.

"What do you think you're doing?" the taller of the two demanded.

"You've kidnapped someone," Levi answered with a low, stern voice, "and we've come to get her."

Wil chuckled with amusement. "You mean the tart? Let's just say she's on a business trip with the boss."

"You are holding my niece against her will," Jet snapped as he advanced on the bartender. "That sure sounds like a kidnapping to me!"

The Reverend positioned himself between Jet and Wil. "Let's not start a fight, men. We just want to take Ryleigh home."

Ray snorted heartlessly as he joined the circle of men. "What do you plan to do? You're just a weak, old preacher, and that spindly thing over there is just a boy. The way I see it, there's only one able-bodied man in your group, and that makes you outnumbered."

Jet clenched his jaw until he could hear his teeth grind in his head. Skirting around the Reverend, Jet let his fist sail through the air before it collided with Ray's jaw. The bouncer wasn't expecting a brawl, but he quickly retaliated with his own punch. Jet dodged his knuckles and grabbed Ray's shoulder as he pulled the bouncer downward. Jet's knee collided with the soft tissue of Ray's stomach, and he smashed his fist against the back of Ray's head before the man crumpled to the ground in defeat.

Jet turned his glare on Wil. "Are you wanting to fight, too?"

Wil slowly shook his head and raised his hands in the air.

"Tie him up, Reverend," Jet commanded as he stormed to his horse to grab a rope.

At that moment, another shrill scream pierced the night air. "Let me go!"

Levi raced to the wagon when he recognized Ryleigh's voice and jumped inside without a second thought. When he entered the canvas, he saw Overhaul bent over Ryleigh as if he were a wolf devouring his prey. Ryleigh looked at Levi, and her bottom lip quivered for just a moment before Overhaul's frame hid her from sight. Levi glared up at the man, who had already taken off his shirt in the process of harming Ryleigh.

An evil grin spread across Overhaul's mouth when he saw the intruder. He grabbed Ryleigh's jaw and forced her to look at Levi. "Look who came to your rescue again?" he leered in a drunken voice.

Ryleigh tugged against her captor but had no success. "Levi, please don't leave me!"

"Let her go, Overhaul," Levi growled.

"Or what?" Overhaul snarled, and all sense of his joking ceased. "Ryleigh is my employee, and I am having a conference with her."

Levi reached around Overhaul to grab Ryleigh's hand, but he was soon shoved against the side of the wagon. The fat man waved a finger in Levi's face as if to scold a child. "Uh-uh, she stays with me. I left you some other deposit to grieve over."

Levi narrowed his eyes but ignored Overhaul as he addressed the woman he loved. "Cheyenne is fine. She's with Doc Harding. Your uncle and the Reverend are outside. You'll be safe."

He extended his hand toward Ryleigh, but Overhaul slapped him away. "You stable boy, I said the woman is mine!"

"I heard you!" Levi snarled as he glared into Overhaul's beady eyes. "Ryleigh is not your captive. She can choose where she wants to be!"

"Honey, you best stay with me if you know what's healthy for that stupid sister of yours," Overhaul hissed over his shoulder.

Levi pressed his hands against Overhaul's shoulders and shoved him away from Ryleigh. The momentum of the sudden movement caught him off guard, and Overhaul tumbled backward to the floor. Levi grabbed Ryleigh's hand and lifted her in his arms. He barely felt her weight as he hurried to the back of the wagon, and her whole body was shaking. Levi had just handed her to Jet when he felt someone grab his shoulder. As he was spun around, a fist landed on Levi's jaw and snapped his head back rapidly. A second fist was sailing through the air, but Levi shielded the blow with his forearm before he felt the burst of pain on his person.

Overhaul pounced on the young stable boy, and they both tumbled out of the wagon and onto the ground. Levi managed to stand up even with Overhaul trying to weigh him down. With all his might, Levi sailed a fist through the air and heard a loud crack when it bounced into Overhaul's nose. Blood instantly poured out of both nostrils as he charged Levi and tackled him to the ground again. This time, Levi felt two legs straddle him as Overhaul placed his hands on his windpipe and pressed down. Just as the world was growing black, Jet landed a boot in Overhaul's face and made him double back in a somersault.

Jet pulled back his fist as he bent over Overhaul. "That will be enough!" Jet shouted in an authoritative tone.

Overhaul slumped his shoulders, which just accentuated his pot belly even more, and shot a glare toward Jet. "Now I understand which side of the family Cheyenne gets her traits from," he snarled. "What do you think you're doing, Douglas?"

"My niece will no longer be working for you. We're taking her home."

Overhaul smiled slyly. "You're talking nonsense. Ryleigh owes a debt to me, and she hasn't paid it off yet."

"I do not owe you a dime."

Overhaul's sneer vanished as his eyes landed on Ryleigh. The fire light made the bruises on her face and neck appear darker, and the flames accentuated the tears in her dress, which was starting to look more like rotting material. She held her head high and set her shoulders back confidently.

"You know full well the debt has been paid off," Ryleigh continued in a clear voice. "You just wanted me for yourself. You've always wanted me, haven't you? You weren't just being friendly to Pa when he needed money, even though you knew he had a gambling problem. You wanted him to go into debt so that you could have me. And I fell for your lies." Ryleigh narrowed her eyes and shook her head hard. "I don't want to be yours anymore. I'm tired of you controlling me. I let you in my head and was miserable for years with the guilt and ugliness I felt."

"No, honey," Overhaul urged as desperation crept into his voice. "You can't leave me. Look at all that I've done for you! I gave your family a house to live in—"

"More like a mouse trap!" Ryleigh interrupted. "When we moved in, it felt like we had to compete with a family of rodents! My uncle is the reason that shack looks like a house now. You held me hostage and separated me from Cheyenne. Why didn't I see this before?"

"All that I did was for you," Overhaul growled as he pushed himself to his feet. "Your sister took after your daddy, and I didn't want you to be influenced by low self-control and laziness. Cheyenne is not attractive and does not listen well. She tried to talk you into turning against me. I couldn't stand for that to happen."

Jet frowned as he listened to Overhaul's explanation. "You're worse than I thought, Overhaul. I just thought you were greedy for money."

The Reverend knelt behind Overhaul as he began to tie his hands behind his back. "What do you think you can do?" Overhaul taunted. "The sheriff will just pardon me, and I'll come back for Ryleigh."

"What we're doing is a citizen's arrest," Jet defended when the Reverend had finished tying the knot. "We'll wire for the judge to come, and you can stand trial then."

Jet grabbed Overhaul's arm and led him to Ray and Wil, who were sitting by the fire at the edge of the camp.

Levi turned around to face Ryleigh and extended a hand toward her. "Are you okay?" he asked when he saw her sway on her feet.

Ryleigh laid a hand on her stomach. "I… I don't feel too good."

Levi caught Ryleigh right as she collapsed. "Jet! Jet, we need to get Ryleigh back to Doc!" Levi shouted as he lifted her limp body into his arms. He ran toward his horse and placed Ryleigh in his saddle before he mounted behind her. He didn't wait for a response from his companions as he turned his Sioux's head and spurred him back down the road they had just traveled.

* * *

I stared down the dark road and repositioned on the rock. I had chewed on my bottom lip until it was raw and chapped, and my fingers had worn a new hole in my trousers from fiddling with it so much. I took a deep breath and groaned involuntarily when my ribs protested.

"You ought to be taking it easy," Doc Harding scolded from a fire he had made a few feet away.

"They should've been back by now."

"Well, they ain't back yet, so you need to relax and try to get some sleep."

I glanced at the doctor as I shifted into a slightly more comfortable position. "How can I sleep when Ryleigh is out there with him? At least when he was distracted with me, he wasn't hurting her. I need to be with her."

"I promise you that she's safe with Jet and the others. As a friend and as a doctor, I ask that you come by the fire to warm up. I'm surprised you haven't caught the pneumonia from traveling as far as you did in the rain."

A twig snapped in the distance, and I returned my gaze to the road. "What was that?"

Doc Harding looked up from the fire and squinted into the darkness. "That sounds like a rider."

"Doc!"

I recognized Levi's voice before I saw him, and I jumped from my perch on the boulder much to my body's protest. Levi reined his horse to a stop and pulled Ryleigh out of the saddle on his way down. He brought her to Doc Harding and laid her on the ground.

"She collapsed when we got her. I don't know what's wrong, but I know he beat her."

Doc grabbed his black bag and hurried to examine my sister by the fire. My heart pounded in my ears as I watched him kneel beside her, and I found myself studying her stomach. Ryleigh had additional bruises on her face than the last time I had seen her, and her skin was as pale as a New Year's snow. I inched closer to her and saw that her chest barely rose and fell with a faint breath.

"Where's Jet?" I asked barely above a whisper.

Levi glanced at me and pointed back up the road. "He's behind me with the Reverend and prisoners. I came ahead so Ryleigh could get medical attention."

I glanced back at Ryleigh and felt my lip quiver. She looked close to death, and I couldn't stand to see her so sick. I slowly rose to my feet as I turned toward the road and started walking. Doc and Levi didn't notice as they both worked diligently to make sure Ryleigh was healthy. I wrapped an arm around my midsection for support as I followed the two-rut road. Tears began to flow at both relief and worry. I felt relieved because Ryleigh was back with me, but she was hurt so bad that it frightened me. I found myself wishing I had been a better sister. More persistent. If I had been more persistent in her life, maybe she would have left the saloon ages ago.

A wagon rumbled up ahead, and a chill ran down my spine. Overhaul had done his best to kill me, and I could feel the pain of his wrath with every breath I took. I had no idea how Ryleigh could survive his many "lessons" that he dealt night after night. If he treated her like he did me, she shouldn't be living after eight long years.

A horse and rider came into view, and I realized it was my uncle. When Jet saw me, he dismounted and placed his hands on my shoulders. "Cheyenne? Are you okay?"

I began to nod, but then rocked my head back and forth before I fell against him in exhaustion. Jet wrapped his arms around me in a consoling embrace as I began to cry softly into his shirt. He cupped a hand around my head as he held me tightly. For several long moments, he comforted me without saying a word, and that meant more to me than the sound of his voice. At last, Jet pulled away from me and knelt so he could look into my face.

He wiped my tears away with the pads of his thumbs and exhaled slowly.

"You're safe now. Nothing bad is going to happen to you."

I studied him with tearful eyes before I looked away. "Is Ryleigh going to die?"

Jet didn't respond for several minutes, and when he finally spoke his voice was thick with emotion. "I don't know. All we can do is pray."

I glanced behind Jet at the Reverend, who was driving the wagon with his horse tethered in the back. Reverend Atkins' face was downcast as he watched from the seat, but he drove the team of horses around us and headed toward the soft glow of Doc's campfire. I watched him leave and gasped a sob.

"I'm scared, Jet."

Jet laid a hand on my shoulder. "I know. I am, too." He cleared his throat. "Are you alright, Cheyenne?"

I finally tore my gaze away from the orange campfire in the distance and glanced up at him. "Doc said a few of my ribs are cracked, but I'll mend. It's not me that I'm worried about."

Jet nodded as he motioned to his horse. "Can you walk, or do you want a ride back?"

I shook my head as I began to trudge back to the camp. "I can walk."

Jet fell into step beside me as he led his horse by the reins, and I began to pray with each step that I took. *Please save Ryleigh.*

~TWENTY-THREE~

I stared at my hands, which were clasped in my lap, as I listened to the silence in the room. The only sound that penetrated my ears was the ticking of the clock that hung on the wall. Levi sat in one of the dining chairs with his elbows on his knees as he twirled his hat with impatience. Jet stared blankly out of the window as the townspeople walked down the street, and Reverend Atkins stood by his wife who sat in the second chair.

I glanced at a petite blond sitting on the floor in the corner of the room. Violet's face was covered with purple bruises, and her lip had been cut open and was swollen. She kept fingering the feathers along her neckline, but nobody seemed to notice the dress she wore. When we had ridden into town the night before, she was one of the first people to rush toward us. I soon learned that Overhaul had beaten her as punishment for helping Ryleigh in the saloon, and I felt compassion toward her.

Exhaustion added weight to my eyelids, but I refused to close them in case Doc Harding came out with news about Ryleigh. He hadn't said much, except that she had been beaten badly and he needed to monitor her to make sure she would pull through. I pushed myself off the bench and grunted softly when I felt the sharp ache in my ribcage. Placing a hand around them for support, I shuffled toward Levi and lowered myself onto the floor.

Levi glanced at me and offered a smile, though it didn't reach his eyes. "How are you feeling?"

I lifted a shoulder in a shrug as I leaned my head against the wall. "I've been better."

Levi nodded but didn't speak.

I scanned the room once more before I watched him twirl his hat again. "Can I ask you something?"

"Hmm?" Levi sounded like he was dragged out of deep thought, and he glanced down at me as though he forgot I was there. "Oh. Yeah, sure."

I took a deep breath and flinched when my ribs ached. "Steven Butte helped me get out of the jail, and he mentioned the town meeting y'all held for me. He said everyone knew Ryleigh was pregnant already, and you were accused of being the father." I glanced up to look him in the eye. "Why didn't you defend yourself if you knew you were never with Ryleigh?"

Levi glanced at me and sighed. "It's hard to explain."

"I have time," I assured softly as I glanced toward the hallway. "There's not much to do while we wait."

Levi nodded and stopped twirling his hat. "I guess you should know. I wanted to ask your sister to marry me. I love her, and when I saw Overhaul humiliate her in the street, I wanted to protect her." He shifted uneasily in his chair as he cleared his throat. "I thought she loved me and would want to marry me, so I wanted to take some of the judgment off her. I want to raise her baby as my own."

"If Ryleigh loses the baby," I continued slowly, "would you still want to marry her?"

Levi returned his gaze to me and studied me before he slowly nodded again. "Yes."

Violet looked up from where she sat, and her eyes glimmered with tears. "You really are a kind man," she murmured. "I told Ryleigh that only a decent man, or a naïve one, would want to pursue a lady of the evening."

Levi studied her, then turned his attention back to his hat as he began to twirl it again. "I may still be naïve," he argued. "I don't know if she would want another man to care for her after this."

"Give her time, son," Mrs. Atkins encouraged with a soft smile. "Once she heals, she may be able to think about that more clearly."

I watched Levi as he spun his hat at a faster pace and reached out to stop his hands from moving. "She'll come around," I assured as I looked him in the eye again. "I couldn't think of a nicer man to provide for her."

The door to Jet's room opened as Doc Harding stepped into the hallway, and every eye swung around to him as he walked into the living room. He glanced around the circle of people concerned for Ryleigh and inhaled deeply.

"The baby is fine," he answered at last. "Ryleigh did a good job of protecting the child."

"How is she?" Levi asked as he rose to his feet.

Doc glanced at him with a somber expression. "She has been abused. Her outward wounds will heal fine, and she should regain her physical strength after she rests in bed for a while." Doc lowered his gaze as he began to wipe his spectacles with the end of his shirt. "It will take more time for her to heal on the inside."

Jet listened to the doctor, and I could see his jaw muscles constricting as he tried to keep his anger under control. He turned away from us as he headed toward the front door without a word.

I struggled to my feet and tried to catch up to my uncle. "Jet!" I called when he was still faster than me. "Where are you going?"

Jet glanced over his shoulder and hid his frustration when he saw me. "Stay here, Cheyenne. I need to send a telegram to the judge in Phoenix."

I watched him leave and felt the dread grow inside of me. I knew Jet wanted to bring a case to the judge to show that Overhaul abused his power over my sister, but I couldn't think of any evidence that would prove our claims.

"Can I go see Ryleigh?" Levi asked behind me.

"Only for a few minutes," Doc allowed as he stepped out of the hallway. "She needs her rest."

I listened as Levi stood and retreated down the hall, but I continued to watch Jet as he disappeared out of sight. A gentle hand landed on my shoulder, and I glanced behind me to see Violet.

She offered me a small smile. "Don't be afraid," she said in a low voice. "I know where Clyde keeps his books. I'll make sure to show them to the judge when he comes."

I returned her smile and hoped that what Violet could find would help our case, but there was still a small sliver of dread in the back of my mind. Overhaul had been able to sneak around his other crimes for many years, and it was hard for me to believe that he wouldn't find a way out of this one. I wanted to forget what had happened to my family over the last several years, and I desired for Overhaul to pay for what he did to start all our pain.

"Cheyenne?"

I turned to find that Levi had returned with his hat in his hands. "Yeah?"

"Ryleigh asked to see you," he answered softly.

My feet refused to move. I wasn't sure I wanted to see Ryleigh in her current condition, and I didn't know what to say to her if I went. Violet must have sensed my hesitation because she nudged my elbow gently.

"Go on," she encouraged. "It'll be okay."

I glanced at her before slowly approaching Jet's bedroom at the end of the hallway. The walls seemed to stretch for miles as I cautiously walked to the door and knocked. When a feeble voice told me to enter, I opened the door wide enough for me to slip through and glanced toward the bed. The curtains were drawn to make the room darker, and a lone candle was the only source of light on the nightstand. Ryleigh looked pale as she opened her eyes to see me enter. I hid my hands behind my back as I studied her from the doorway.

Ryleigh lifted a hand and motioned me toward her. "Come here, Cheyenne."

I reluctantly left my position at the door and sat on the edge of the bed. As I studied her face, I couldn't help but notice all the bruises and cuts created by Overhaul. My stomach lurched as I tried to imagine the pain she must be feeling.

"I'm not dying," she said with a smile when she noticed my discomfort.

I looked into her eyes and inhaled slowly to loosen the tightness in my chest. "I know. Doc said you'll heal fine."

"See? I'm tougher than I look," she teased as she reached up to hook a strand of my hair behind my ear. "How are you?"

"I'm fine. I'm just a little sore, but nothing too serious."

Ryleigh's smile faded as she laid her arm over her stomach. "I'm sorry I dragged you into this. I never meant for you to get hurt."

I shrugged as I glanced toward the flame of the candle. "It's not your fault. I couldn't stand the thought of you alone with Overhaul."

"I shouldn't have worked in the saloon," she continued as she watched my expression. "I shouldn't have been so proud. I knew there were people who wanted to help us, but I was too stubborn trying to prove that we didn't have a problem."

"Don't blame yourself," I argued in a low voice. "You didn't know any better."

Ryleigh smiled to herself as she closed her eyes. "I think I did, but I was too prideful. I'm sorry I put you through all of this."

I lifted a shoulder in a shrug. "It doesn't matter now. It's all in the past."

Ryleigh reached out to take hold of my hand. "I just wanted you to know that I did what I thought was best for you. I've always loved you, Cheyenne, even if it didn't seem like it at times."

My vision blurred, but I blinked rapidly to keep the tears from falling. "I love you, too, Ryleigh."

"Come here," she invited as she opened her arms toward me.

I buried my face in her neck and held her tightly for several minutes. I finally pushed away from her and planted a soft kiss on her forehead. "You should rest," I instructed as I rose from her bed. "We'll have plenty of time to talk after you regain your strength."

* * *

Nearly three weeks passed since the accident with Overhaul, and Jet allowed me to go back to school after getting the okay from Doc Harding. I adjusted the lunch pail on my arm and straightened the skirt of the olive-green dress Jet had given me what seemed ages ago. Adele Atkins had graciously offered to mend the dress, and I appreciated her kindness. Several of the younger children were tossing a ball back and forth, and I smiled at their joy as I passed them.

Steven saw me approach and lifted a hand in greeting. "Good morning, Cheyenne!" he called with excitement in his voice. "I'm glad to see you out and about."

I waved back as I stopped a few feet from him. "It's good to be out. I've run out of things to do back home."

"How is everyone?"

I lifted a shoulder in a shrug. "Fine for the most part. Levi comes over in the afternoons to keep Ryleigh company, but she hasn't left the house yet. Doc says she should be able to, but I get the feeling that she's scared."

"What about the judge from Phoenix?" Steven asked as he lowered his voice.

"As far as I know, he's supposed to come on tomorrow's stage. I know Ryleigh is supposed to testify, but I'm afraid she'll be too weak to face Overhaul again."

Steven glanced behind me and stiffened. "C'mon, let's go to the tree."

"Why?" I questioned as I turned to look behind me to see what caused Steven's demeanor to change. Penelope Wilkes had a permanent glare fixed on her face as she sashayed through the yard toward us, but I didn't feel annoyed at her presence. "It's alright, Steven. I can handle her."

Penelope stopped in front of me and frowned distastefully. "What are you doing here?"

A grin lightened my features as I snorted a laugh. "Usually if kids go to school it's so they can get an education," I answered wittily as Steven chuckled behind me.

Penelope narrowed her eyes at our laughter. "I thought you were leaving. I've heard Sheriff Hodgkinson is still wanting to send you to a school. Perhaps you'll finally learn how to be a woman if you're forced to abandon your whims."

My smile faded a little at the mention of the sheriff. I had been hoping to avoid Sheriff Hodgkinson in case he still had a notion to carry out his threat, and I had evaded him so far. Jet hadn't mentioned what he wanted to do about the sheriff since Ryleigh had been ill, and I didn't have the heart to bring it up. My happiness slowly melted away at the thought that I might not be around to see Ryleigh's baby or to enjoy a whole family again.

"I haven't talked to the sheriff lately," I answered flatly.

Penelope chortled a laugh as she lifted her nose in the air. "Well, I suppose it'll just be a matter of time, won't it? You better enjoy your last few days of bullying people." She skirted around us as she began to ascend the stairs. "I doubt you'll be around for much longer."

Steven watched her disappear inside before he turned to face me. "Is she telling the truth?"

I lowered my gaze as I lifted a shoulder in a shrug. "I guess so. Sheriff Hodgkinson hasn't come calling, but maybe he's just waiting until I'm healed enough to travel."

"That's not fair!" Steven exclaimed as his brows furrowed in anger. "After all you've been through, surely he won't send you away."

"He still thinks I'm the one who took the morphine," I pointed out.

"Well, maybe there's proof that we can find. I could try to talk to Chad and see if he'll admit to taking it."

I began to follow Penelope up the stairs. "Thanks for the thought, Steven, but Chad'll never admit he was wrong. I know how he is."

Steven didn't reply as he followed me into the schoolhouse, and I was grateful for his silence. Once in the school, I set my lunch pail on the floor by the door and carried my slate to a pew as I sank in the seat. Mr. Hyndman was looking through a book at his desk, and he glanced up when he saw us enter. He nodded a greeting toward Steven before he turned toward me. I could see the kindness in his eyes and wondered if he always tried to show me compassion that I ignored.

"It's good to see you, Cheyenne," he welcomed. "How are you feeling?"

I returned his smile and pretended to rearrange my slate in my lap so that I wouldn't have to look him in the eye. "I'm fine. Doc said I could come if I took it easy. I couldn't stand to stay inside another day."

"Well, I'm glad you could make it this morning," Mr. Hyndman assured kindly before he turned to greet another student.

Restlessness settled in the pit of my stomach as I listened to the lessons, and I found it hard to focus on Mr. Hyndman's teachings. My mind was filled with thoughts of the upcoming trial and my future, and the joy I felt when I climbed out of bed that morning diminished to the size of a snowflake by the time school was dismissed later that afternoon.

Our house seemed to shrink as I trudged across the sandy road, and I remembered the days I helped Jet rebuild it. I treasured the memories of working beside Jet, even if I hadn't realized his true intention at the time. Jet had invested his time in me during the last month and a half, and I dreaded the thought of leaving him behind. My chest felt heavy with depression as I climbed the steps onto the porch and slipped inside the living room.

Violet was bent over the dining table when I entered, and she glanced over her shoulder. Her bruises had faded now, and I noticed that her angelic face was not covered in the usual makeup the girls at the saloon wore. In fact, she was also wearing a modest brown dress that almost touched the floor. When she smiled at me, I saw a spark of hope in her azure blue eyes that ignited the bumblebees in the pit of my stomach.

"Hello," I greeted flatly as I set my lunch pail and slate beside the books she had sprawled on the table. "What are those?"

"These are Overhaul's records," Violet explained as she pointed to one of the books. "I was able to find them all the way back to when your ma started working for him. This proves his fraud, don't you see?"

I glanced at the list of names and numbers. "Are you sure?"

Violet nodded enthusiastically as she flipped to a page toward the beginning of a book. "He kept a list of who borrowed money from him. He was always greedy, so he wanted to make sure he got his money back." She glanced up at me and lifted a finger in the air. "With interest, of course."

I glanced at the table and counted nine books. "Are you saying he took advantage of more people than just my family?"

Violet nodded as she picked up a book and thumbed to a page almost halfway through. "Here's the information on me. He lent me money to travel here and buy new clothes." She showed me a list of numbers. "As you can see, he took half of the money I earned and used it to loan to other people, while a quarter went to my actual debt. I didn't realize I was only getting a quarter of my pay. He's done similar things with almost every one of his employees."

I glanced up when Jet entered the room, and I quickly averted my gaze as I pretended to be fascinated by the scribblings in front of me. I couldn't make myself face him in case Penelope was right about Sheriff Hodgkinson.

"Ryleigh will be out in a minute," Jet announced as he leaned his hand on the back of a chair. "She wants to look at them herself."

I could feel Jet's eyes on me, but I ignored him. "I hope this will be enough."

"It should be," Violet guaranteed as she planted her hands on her hips. "I even found various other papers with his handwriting in case he tries to say we fabricated all this evidence."

"I supposed we'll find out soon enough," I mumbled as I turned away from the table. I brought the lunch pail to the kitchen and emptied the contents on the counter.

There was a slight shuffling sound in the hallway, and I glanced over my shoulder to see Ryleigh walk into the room. Like Violet, her bruises had faded, but there were still dark circles under her eyes and her face was pale. I glanced toward her middle and noticed that her stomach was visible under her dress. Ryleigh squared her shoulders as she ambled toward the table to bend over the books.

"Just like I told you," Violet said excitingly as she motioned to her display. "Everything is here."

Ryleigh picked up the book closest to her and cringed. "If only I had known..."

"You couldn't have known," Violet assured as she laid a hand on Ryleigh's shoulder. "He kept his books well hidden, and it was a miracle that I found the one. There was no way you could have known back then."

"You shouldn't blame yourself, Ryleigh," Jet defended from across the room.

Ryleigh glanced at him, and I noticed the sadness in her eyes. "It just feels like all those years were wasted."

The depression in Ryleigh's voice broke my heart, and I turned around quickly before anyone could see the tears that were beginning to pool in my eyes. I grabbed my slate and headed toward the hallway.

"I need to do my homework," I muttered as I disappeared in my bedroom.

I could hear the three as they discussed the evidence, but I tried to ignore their words as I stared blankly at the arithmetic problems I had copied onto the slate. I attempted to solve the first problem, but I couldn't focus. With a sigh of frustration, I threw the slate on the mattress and glanced at the photograph on the nightstand. Ryleigh looked young and carefree in the picture, and I could tell just how degrading Overhaul had been to her for nearly a decade. My skin crawled when I remembered how he desired her when she was just a child, and my resentment almost choked me. I knew that Ryleigh was terrified of facing her former employer, and I couldn't blame her. She needed her family around her when the time came. The photograph began to swim, and I turned away from it. She would need her family, but I would be sent away.

Why did I have to be so obstinate in the past? I closed my eyes as I recounted all the trouble I had caused and wished that I could undo my mistakes. I should have thought of the consequences if I ever pushed the line too far, and now I had no control over my fate. Ryleigh needed me, and I felt that I had betrayed her. I wouldn't be around when her baby would be born, and I wouldn't be able to form a relationship with my niece or nephew. I sank onto the mattress and cried softly into my hands as my mind raced for a way for me to stay in Sunset.

A gentle knock sounded at my door, and I quickly wiped my eyes as I hurried to grab the slate. "You can come in," I said in a straight voice.

Jet opened the door wide enough for him to peek inside. "Violet left, and Ryleigh is sitting on the porch with Levi. I wanted to see how you were doing with your homework."

I glanced at the slate and felt my shoulders slump in defeat. "Not very well."

Jet walked to my bed and lowered himself on the mattress as he studied me. I still could not make myself look him in the eye. "There's something bothering you, isn't there?" he asked after a few moments of silence.

I set the slate aside and straightened the wrinkles out of my skirt. "I guess I just have a lot on my mind."

"I think we have a chance at the trial," Jet encouraged.

I shook my head and studied my hands in my lap. "It's not just the trial."
"Then what is it?"

My chest heaved when I inhaled shakily. "I'm scared. I talked to Penelope today, and she told me Sheriff Hodgkinson still wants to send me away." I forced myself to look at my uncle and willed my tears to stay back. "I won't be here for Ryleigh or the baby, and I don't want to leave now that I have a family again."

Jet studied me as his expression softened. "It's going to be okay, Cheyenne," he said in a low voice.

"How can it?" I argued. "I was a stupid child, and now that I have to face the consequences, I don't want to pay. I didn't even think about what could happen."

"You have to trust God," Jet encouraged as he cupped my face in his hand. "Just like you did when you went after Ryleigh. God is in control."

"It's hard to trust Him, Jet."

Jet pulled me into an embrace as he smoothed my hair. "I know it is, but we are not in control. He has a plan, and I know it's going to work out."

I closed my eyes as I buried my face in his neck. "I hope so."

* * *

I bit my lip as I twitched in my seat. Several of the townspeople had filed into the pews behind me, but their presence only unnerved me more. Jet sat to my right with his hat in his hands. He was looking straight ahead and seemed almost as nervous as me. Levi and Ryleigh sat on the other side of Jet, and Levi was holding Ryleigh's hand for support. For once in an awfully long time, Ryleigh had no trace of a bruise or cut on her person, and she wore a dress that accentuated her curves in the most modest of ways. She even pulled her hair back into an attractive bun. At a glance, she seemed like a normal woman, except for her growing stomach. But if one really studied her face, they would notice the fatigue and fright in her eyes. She was hesitant to walk in public, and she often twitched when someone reached out to touch her. Levi had patiently stayed by her side as she healed, but she even shied away from him at times.

The door at the front of the church opened as an officer led Clyde

Overhaul to an empty pew across the aisle from us. I glanced at Overhaul, and he shot a glare toward my family that sent shivers of dread racing down my spine. Since Overhaul had been behind bars, he had taken on the appearance of a large rat with what seemed to be a red glow to his gaze. I forced myself to face the front and swallowed hard.

"All rise for the honorable Judge Boyd," the officer called out.

The small gathering of people rose to their feet as a skinny judge wearing a white wig appeared. He frowned at the crowd, then stood behind the pulpit and motioned for us to sit. "This court is now in session," the judge growled in a surprisingly low voice. He turned to the officer and mumbled something I could not hear.

The officer turned to face the audience in a rigid stance. "Calling Mr. Clyde Overhaul to take the stand."

I watched as the fat saloon owner rose to his feet and raised his right hand to be sworn in. Part of me wondered if Overhaul could keep his promise to tell nothing but the truth, and I rolled my eyes as I forced myself to lean back in my seat.

"Mr. Overhaul," the judge barked. "Please state your case."

Overhaul turned a horrid glare in our direction, and I couldn't help but squirm. "Sir, I believe I have been mistreated and blackmailed. I have been forced to sit in a cell while my establishment is left unattended. I have unfinished business with an employee of mine. She owed me a debt, and she was working for me to pay what she owes. In the last few months, she has done nothing but scam me out of what I deserve. Her, along with the rest of her family. I need to run my business, and I need my employee back so that she can finish paying her debt to me."

The judge cast lazy eyes toward my family. "Miss Ryleigh Douglas, could you please rise?"

Ryleigh's face paled even more, but she slowly stood to her full height and clasped her hands in front of her. "Your Honor?"

"Raise your right hand." The judge waited until she rigidly rose her hand before he continued. "Do you solemnly swear to tell the truth, the whole truth, and nothing but the truth so help you God?"

"O-of course."

Judge Boyd motioned to Overhaul, who was glaring at my sister menacingly. "Mr. Overhaul says you've been trying to blackmail him. How do you defend yourself?"

Ryleigh glanced at Overhaul and shuddered softly. "Your Honor, my family did have a tremendous debt to Mr. Overhaul. My father was a gambler, and Mr. Overhaul had loaned us about five thousand dollars. Once my father left us when I was six, my mother worked diligently in the saloon to help pay off the debt we owed." She glanced toward Overhaul, then back at the judge. "She worked double shifts seven days a week for five years. She even repaired the ladies' dresses in the saloon to earn cash for food. Because of her sacrifices, she was able to pay off the debt with a little extra before she passed."

"That is outrageous!" Overhaul bellowed from across the room. "Where have you gotten your numbers?"

Ryleigh swallowed hard but lifted her head higher as she refocused her gaze on the judge. "Your Honor, I have written on a sheet of paper what rates we are given as workers in the saloon. May I?"

Judge Boyd nodded and extended his hand as Ryleigh gave him a piece of paper with numbers sketched in pencil. The judge glanced over her writing, then faced Overhaul.

"Mr. Overhaul, how much do you pay your employees for a ten-hour day?"

Overhaul frowned and threw his hand in the air. "I pay my employees a fair wage!"

"How much, Mr. Overhaul?"

The saloon owner's frown deepened as he tossed a glare toward Ryleigh. "A dollar fifty for a ten-hour shift."

"According to Miss Douglas, she states that her mother worked double shifts. Is that correct?"

"There is no record of—"

"Your Honor," Ryleigh interrupted. "Mr. Overhaul kept a log in his office of how long each of his employees work. That is how he kept track of how much I was bringing in." Ryleigh motioned to Violet, who held the stack of books in her lap. "I had Miss Humphrey look in the records to find my mother's log. It will be under Lenora Douglas. There is also evidence that Mr. Overhaul has written showing how he runs his establishment."

Judge Boyd motioned to the officer to retrieve the books, and he flipped to a marked page in the top book. Overhaul glared toward Ryleigh, and his face began turning a bright shade of red. Dreaded silence filled the one-roomed church as the judge read through the log. After what seemed an eternity, the judge set the paper on the pulpit and eyed Overhaul through narrow slits.

"Mr. Overhaul, these records show that Mrs. Douglas did work double shifts for nearly five years. That makes a little over five thousand dollars that she earned. Miss Douglas stated the debt her father owed was only five thousand."

"Rod owed me more than five thousand!" Overhaul folded his arms over his chest. "I've never seen that book in all my life. Ryleigh could've made it just to blackmail me!"

Judge Boyd motioned to the first book. "Officer Brandy, would you mind showing Mr. Overhaul these pages?"

The officer took the book without saying a word and showed it to Overhaul.

"Tell me, Mr. Overhaul. Is that your handwriting?" the judge asked.

Clyde glanced at the scribblings scratched in ink. "No."

"Your Honor?" Ryleigh interrupted as she clasped her hands in front of her. "If I may, I do have a few bills that Mr. Overhaul signed for when he had Doc Harding run regular examinations on his employees."

Judge Boyd motioned to the officer, who strode to Ryleigh to collect the bills. Ryleigh accepted the papers from Violet and handed them to the officer as he silently prompted. The officer compared the log with the writing on the bills before he nodded stiffly. "The writing looks the same, sir," Officer Brandy announced after reviewing the penmanship.

Judge Boyd glared at Overhaul and aimed a bony finger his direction. "Lying in court is a serious offense, Mr. Overhaul. This does not help your case." The judge turned to Ryleigh. "As far as the amount of debt, is there any record proving the loan?"

"The Douglas family owes me more than five thousand dollars!" Overhaul bellowed. "That despicable miscreant," he snarled, pointing toward me, "has broken many of my belongings and destroyed hundreds of dollars' worth of equipment!"

Ryleigh looked at Overhaul with her calm oceans. "Your Honor, if you need proof, Mr. Overhaul has also gone into detail of the amount of money he loaned in those records. As we have just mentioned a few minutes ago, my mother had paid off the debt before her passing. I worked in the saloon for eight years. Until recently, I only worked one shift a day for seven days a week. If you wish to check my mathematics, that means I was paid roughly four thousand dollars, plus the tips I received as an entertainer. Besides what I brought in daily, Mr. Jethro Douglas also paid for damages my sister has caused over the last month."

Judge Boyd ran his tongue over his teeth. "You may both be seated." The judge stacked the books as he rose to his feet. "This court is on temporary break until I have reached my conclusion."

My heart dropped as I watched him walk out of the church. Officer Brandy positioned himself behind the pulpit with his arms crossed over his chest in order to keep the peace. Several people behind me whispered back and forth. Occasionally, I heard mine and Ryleigh's name spoken and cringed. The townspeople spoke often of us throughout my entire lifetime, and I couldn't help but wonder what they were discussing now that they learned more of our despicable story.

Jet must have noticed my tension. He took hold of my hand and gave it an affirming squeeze. I glanced up at him, and his mustache twitched as he attempted to smile down at me. I nodded and returned my eyes to my lap. *God, please help us,* I prayed silently as I pinched my eyes shut.

After nearly an hour of waiting, the hinges on the door echoed in the church, and Officer Brandy moved to the side. "Please rise for the honorable Judge Boyd."

I rose on wobbly legs as I watched the judge stride back to the pulpit like a head rooster among hens. He picked up his gavel and turned hard eyes on Overhaul. "I have reviewed the records and I have concluded that Mr. Clyde Overhaul is guilty of committing fraud, mental anguish, and perjury. Upon further review, it seems that Mr. Overhaul has been running a fraudulent business for years. Because of the said crimes, I hereby charge Mr. Overhaul to thirty years in the state penitentiary, and due to his fraudulent business, his properties will be foreclosed and auctioned to the highest bidder." Judge Boyd pounded his gavel once on the wooden pulpit. "This court is adjourned."

Overhaul whirled on his heel and reached claw-like hands toward Ryleigh. "You miserable whore, do you think you've won? I'll come back for you, for what's mine! I've wanted you ever since I laid eyes on you. Don't think I won't take you back one day!"

Ryleigh laid a hand on her chest when Overhaul lunged her direction, but Officer Brandy caught him and snapped a pair of handcuffs around both wrists as he directed the fat man out of the church. Overhaul screeched a stream of profanity until the church door closed soundly behind him. Levi laid a hand on Ryleigh's shoulder, and she spun around to bury her face in his shoulder.

"You did fine, Ryleigh," Levi comforted as he embraced her gently. "He can't hurt you anymore."

"Oh, Levi, I was so scared!" Ryleigh gasped against his shirt. "I thought for sure he would find a way to hurt us again."

I glanced over my shoulder at the people of Sunset. Some had left, while others still milled about the room, eyeing my family as if we were the new circus in town. My eyes pinpointed Sheriff Hodgkinson and felt my heart drop in dread. Seeing him reminded me of my conversation with Penelope, and any joy I felt about our victory suddenly vanished. I studied Jet out of the corner of my eye, and his spine stiffened when he saw the sheriff amble our direction.

"Douglas," the sheriff greeted when he stopped in front of us.

Jet laid a hand on my shoulder and nodded slightly. "Sheriff."

Sheriff Hodgkinson glanced down at me before leveling his lazy eyes back on my uncle. "I wanted to talk to you."

"Look, Sheriff, I don't think now is the time to discuss—"

"Hear me out, Douglas. Pains me to say it but seems like you were right. I caught young Chad Dillon and Jared with morphine a few days ago and had a stern conversation with them. They both eventually admitted Cheyenne's innocence, and I wanted to offer my apology." He glanced down at me and hooked his thumbs in his pockets. "Reckon I rode too hard on you, Cheyenne."

I bit my lip and lowered my gaze.

"This town needs a sheriff who takes the time to do his job right," Sheriff Hodgkinson continued, "and I reckon I've abused this badge long enough." He slowly unhooked the silver badge from his chest before handing it to Jet. "As part of my last duty as acting sheriff, I want to appoint you as the new sheriff of Sunset, Douglas."

Jet frowned. "I don't think I understand, Hodgkinson. Why me?"

"Well, son, you showed gumption by coming here and helping those two girls. This town turned their backs to them, especially me. I was influenced by money, and I let my greed get the better of my judgment. A good sheriff won't let people influence him. Now raise your right hand."

Stunned, Jet glanced down at me before he slowly raised his hand beside his head.

"Do you swear to protect the people of Sunset," Hodgkinson began in a low voice, "and treat them fairly with good judgment?"

"I swear," Jet answered confidently.

"Then I appoint you as actin' sheriff." Hodgkinson pinned the badge on the left side of Jet's shirt before touching the tip of his hat in a farewell. "Good luck, Sheriff Douglas."

Jet watched Hodgkinson exit the church before glancing down at me with a grin. "I reckon you'll be staying in Sunset permanent now."

A joy that I had not felt in a long time exploded in my chest as I threw my arms around my uncle. "Oh, Jet! I can stay!" I pulled away from him and grinned widely. "You'll make a great sheriff."

Ryleigh rejoined our circle and glanced at me. Tears of relief still clung to her eyelashes, but the color had begun to glow in her cheeks again. "Cheyenne?"

I flung my arms around her neck and hugged her tight. "We did it, Ryleigh! You're a free woman! I love you so much."

Ryleigh wrapped her arms around me. "I love you, too," she whispered into my hair, and her voice was thick with emotion. She gently pulled away after a few seconds and hooked a strand of my wild black mane behind my ear. "We're a family again."

Levi cleared his throat and looked softly into Ryleigh's gaze. "Could I talk to you for a minute?"

Ryleigh wiped the tears from her eyes and turned to face him fully. "Of course."

Levi chanced a glance toward our uncle before he gulped air down to his lungs. "I know you have been through a lot, and you've shown your strength through it all." He clasped a hand around his neck as he shuffled awkwardly in front of her. "I, uh, I know I ain't much and I don't have much, and I know I've asked you before, but..." Levi cleared his throat again as he gently took hold of Ryleigh's hands. "Ryleigh Douglas, will you marry me?"

A deep red rushed up into Ryleigh's face, but instead of ducking her head, a bright smile sent a sparkle to her eyes. She gazed into his face and seemed unable to speak for several moments, but then she sighed softly with a quiver in her voice. "Yes, Levi," she whispered at last. "Yes, I will marry you."

Levi grinned from ear to ear as he threw his arms around her and spun her in the air. "Ya-hoo!" he shouted, causing the stragglers from the trial to turn around in surprise.

I laughed at his excitement and turned to Jet, who was beaming with pride. Several times in my youth I had questioned God, even blamed Him, for what happened to my family. A happiness that I couldn't explain filled my chest as I glanced between the happy faces of the people who I loved. God had shown us His forgiveness and mended our brokenness, and I rejoiced in His grace.

Epilogue

November's cool breeze blew sand into my eyes, but I rapidly blinked it away as I gazed at the outside of the church with anticipation. Despite the chill of fall, it was a beautiful day for a wedding, and I could not be more excited to witness the joining of Levi and Ryleigh in marriage. I glanced down at my olive-green dress and smoothed an imaginary wrinkle as I tightened my hold on the golden band in my palm. I glanced over my shoulder at Violet, who stood behind me with an equally excited expression.

Shortly after Overhaul's trial, the judge auctioned the saloon and the house as he had concluded. The bank was able to purchase the saloon and hired Violet, with a little persuasion from Jet, to transform the saloon into a restaurant and hotel establishment. Violet employed most of the remaining women in the saloon to work for her as housekeepers and cooks, and the new business seemed to be thriving. Jet was also able to get a loan to purchase the home he had rebuilt and appointed Levi as his deputy. Because of the raised income, Levi was able to rent a small house for himself and his bride-to-be, and I was grateful that they would not be far from me. Ray took over Levi's job at the livery, while Wil found employment at the gunsmith, and Bob decided to try his luck in another town. Chad still attempted to cause mischief, but his heists were becoming few and far between due to Jet's persistence. The Wilkes' still turned up their noses if we walked by, but the bullying finally stopped.

The musical tune of Mendelssohn's Wedding March erupted from the church piano, and I held my breath as I ascended the stairs into the church. Levi stood at the front next to Reverend Atkins, and he seemed nervous as he watched me and Violet walk down the aisle as Ryleigh's bridesmaids. Mrs. Atkins glanced over her shoulder from her seat at the piano and smiled warmly at us when we stopped at the altar. I scanned the small crowd seated in the pews to witness the wedding. Doc Harding sat toward the front of the church, and Mr. and Mrs. Butte were behind him with Steven in the pew at the back. Dinah Gray and her husband sat on the opposite side of the church, and she smiled at me kindly.

The doors of the church opened again, and I glanced toward the entrance in time to see Jet enter with Ryleigh holding onto the crook of his elbow.

"Please rise for the entrance of the bride," Reverend Atkins announced as he motioned to small congregation.

The people stood and turned to look at Ryleigh. She was beautiful as she smiled toward Levi. Mrs. Atkins had helped Ryleigh sew a new dress with light blue material for the wedding, and the color pronounced her clear blue eyes. Ryleigh's long brown hair was also braided in what looked like a halo around her head, and her face was clear of the gaudy makeup. The dark brown freckles on her nose and cheekbones accentuated her beauty, and her face shone with joy. Her stomach was visible as she walked alongside Jet, but her pregnancy did not hide her natural curves.

I glanced at Levi and felt my chest swell with happiness. He gazed at my sister as if she were the most beautiful woman on earth, and I saw the trace of a tear in the corner of his eye as he watched her. As Jet and Ryleigh reached the altar, Mrs. Atkins ended the chorus and turned on the bench to watch the ceremony.

"Who gives this woman to be married?" Reverend Atkins began.

Jet glanced down at Ryleigh and offered her a proud smile. "I do," he said as he took her hand and placed it in Levi's elbow.

Levi beamed toward Ryleigh before they both faced the Reverend as the rest of the congregation sat.

"Dearly beloved, we are gathered here this day, in the presence of God, to witness the joining together of Levi and Ryleigh in holy matrimony."

I watched Ryleigh as the Reverend continued in the ceremony. Occasionally, she would sneak a glance at her soon-to-be husband and the grin on her lips reminded me of the joy she held as a child. I respected Levi for bringing a little bit of happiness back in her life, and I knew he would take

390

care of my sister in the years to come.

"May I have the ring please?" Reverend Atkins asked as he turned to me. I quickly handed him the golden band, which he gave to Levi. "This ring that you give to Ryleigh is a symbol of your unending love for her. It will signify your marriage and covenant to God to care for each other." He waited until Levi slipped the band on Ryleigh's left finger before continuing. "It's time for the vows. Do you, Levi Hendershot, take Ryleigh to be thy lawfully wedded wife, to have and to hold from this day forth, for better, for worse, for richer, for poorer, in sickness and in health, to love and to cherish, for as long as ye both shall live?"

Levi glanced at Ryleigh and smiled lovingly. "I do."

"And do you, Ryleigh Douglas, take Levi to be thy lawfully wedded husband, to have and to hold from this day forth, for better, for worse, for richer, for poorer, in sickness and in health, to love and to cherish, for as long as ye both shall live?"

Ryleigh met Levi's gaze and nodded vigorously. "I do."

"By the power of God vested in me, I now pronounce you man and wife," the Reverend finished as he closed the Bible in his hand. "You may kiss your bride, Levi."

Levi turned to face Ryleigh and caressed her face lovingly as he bent to kiss her lips. A deep shade of red traveled up Ryleigh's neck until it glowed in her cheeks as she kissed him back. When they parted, Reverend Atkins lifted his arm toward the congregation as he proudly declared, "I now introduce to you for the first time Mr. and Mrs. Levi Hendershot!"

Everyone in the church clapped enthusiastically as Levi and Ryleigh turned to face them, and my chest swelled with pride. I knew since childhood that Ryleigh's dream was to become a wife and mother, and she thought she would never have a chance to accomplish that dream after her employment at the saloon. I found myself rejoicing that God had given her a second chance and redeemed her from her bondage.

The next several months were filled with anticipation as we began counting down the days until a new little citizen of Sunset would make an appearance. Our excitement for the new baby especially grew one warm day in mid-March. Jet and I had just sat down to eat our evening meal on a Wednesday evening when someone pounded a heavy fist at our door. Jet frowned as he pushed himself away from the table and opened the door to reveal a very pale-faced Levi.

"It's Ryleigh," Levi answered before any question could be asked. "The Doc is with her right now, and I think it's time."

Jet offered a small smile under his mustache. "She's a tough woman, Levi. She's in good hands, and I'm sure you'll be a proud papa before the night is over!"

Levi ran his fingers through his hair as he glanced over his shoulder. "Jet, I'm so nervous...."

Jet grabbed his hat off the peg on the wall as he clapped Levi on the back. "C'mon, I'll walk with you to get the nerves out. You'll be no use to Ryleigh if you're all jittered up."

I sprang out of my chair as I raced toward the two men. "Can I come, too? I want to be there to welcome my new niece or nephew."

Jet smiled down at me as he wrapped an arm around my shoulders. "Perhaps a walk would do us all some good."

I followed the men outside and closed the door behind me. Levi kept twisting his fingers in knots and running his hands through his hair until we made it back to his home behind the jailhouse. Levi lowered himself on the porch rail as he stared with a blank expression toward the door. It was almost as if he were too scared to enter his own house. I sat on the steps leading up to the front door and cupped my chin in my hands. The evening light turned from orange to red to dark blue, and still nothing sounded on the other side of the door. Jet leaned against the support beam and stared out into the street. I grinned to myself when I noticed my uncle's nervousness. *So much for being strong for Levi.*

Suddenly, the door opened to reveal Doc Harding in the pale moonlight. His piercing eyes scanned the small crowd on the porch before they landed on Levi. The Doc grinned from ear to ear. "Your wife would like to see you now."

Levi swallowed hard as he bounced to his feet and ran inside as if the house were on fire. The Doc chuckled to himself as he stepped out on the porch and inhaled deeply. "I'll never get used to seeing new life," he mentioned almost to himself. "It's the most beautiful experience I could have as a doctor." He glanced toward Jet. "You should be proud of your niece. She'll make a great mama."

With a smile still lifting the corners of his mouth, Doc Harding stepped into the street and strode to his office.

I glanced up at Jet. "Are you proud of her?"

Jet smiled softly as he cupped a hand around my face. "I'm proud of both my girls."

"So, you don't regret coming here?" I asked. "We didn't necessarily make it easy for you."

"Cheyenne, if I could turn back time I would do it all over again. You girls have come a long way, and I believe it was by the grace of God that all these things took place."

The door opened again, but this time Levi stood in the orange glow of a lantern, and he was holding a small bundle of blankets. He glanced between the two of us with an eternal grin spread across his mouth. Tears glimmered in his eyes as he lowered the bundle to reveal the soft, pink skin of a tiny baby's face.

"Meet Grace Mae Hendershot," Levi announced softly as he gazed at his daughter with pride. "Our beautiful gift of Grace."

About the Author

Cindy R. Escobar resides in the Texas Panhandle with her husband of two years. She grew up in the Texas Panhandle, and it was her love of western movies and the imagery on her father's ranch that inspired her love for creative writing.

You can connect with me on:

f https://www.facebook.com/cindyrescobar1998

Made in the USA
Coppell, TX
02 May 2021

54820175R00231